THE DARKENING SEA

Mariner's Library Fiction Classics

STERLING HAYDEN
Voyage: A Novel of 1896

BJORN LARSSON
The Celtic Ring

SAM LLEWELLYN
The Shadow in the Sands

RICHARD WOODMAN
The Darkening Sea
Endangered Species
Wager
The Nathaniel Drinkwater Novels:
The Bomb Vessel
The Corvette
1805
Baltic Mission
In Distant Waters
A Private Revenge
Under False Colours
The Flying Squadron
Beneath the Aurora
The Shadow of the Eagle
Ebb Tide

THE DARKENING SEA

Richard Woodman

SHERIDAN HOUSE

First U.S. edition published 2000
by Sheridan House Inc.
145 Palisade Street
Dobbs Ferry, New York 10522

Copyright © 1990 by Richard Woodman

First published in Great Britain 1991
by Macdonald & Co (Publishers) Ltd
London & Sydney

Library of Congress Cataloging-in-Publication Data

Woodman, Richard, 1944-
    The darkening sea / Richard Woodman.—1st U.S. ed.
        p. cm.
    ISBN 1-57409-075-5 (alk. paper)
        1. Great Britain—History, Naval—20 th century—Fiction.
        2.Family—Great Britain—Fiction. I. Title.

PR6073.O618 D37 2000
823'.914—dc21

                                                            00-021881

Printed in the United States of America

ISBN 1-57409-075-5

For
Andrew Stephen Banyard
(1945-1989)

Contents

Part One – Blood

1916-1924

'If blood be the price of Admiralty, Lord God, we have paid in full.'

Rudyard Kipling

CHAPTER ONE

Jutland

Above the surface of the sea hung a dense pall of drifting smoke. As he struggled in the water he dragged the sickly sweet smell of it into his gasping lungs. Floundering, he retched salt water, then fought for his breath, staring uncomprehendingly up at the filthy yellow swirl. Only half conscious, he saw it was full of the writhings of ghosts.

'Well, my boy,' Vice Admiral Thomas Martin said abstractedly to his nephew, 'their lordships have appointed you to a ship.' The Admiral flicked at a letter on his desk as James Martin stood in the study before him. 'You're going to join Tom on the *Indefatigable*, James. You know what she is.'

'Yes, sir.'

He and his cousin Tom knew everything there was to be known about most of the ships in the Royal Navy and had done long before they left the domestic comforts of The Reddings for the spartan dormitories of Osborne and the life of naval cadets. James opened his mouth to rattle off the details of her eight twelve-inch guns, her secondary armament, her torpedo capability and defensive armour, but the Admiral's lack of attention intimidated him. Instead he merely added:

'A battle cruiser, attached to the Second Battle Cruiser Squadron under the command of Sir David Beatty.'

'Yes,' the Admiral said, 'Beatty . . .'

He heaved himself to his feet and stood staring out of the French windows that overlooked a terrace and the walled garden behind the house. 'Still a young man for so important a command.'

James heard the bitter sigh and knew it was not the wind-whipped rose bushes that his uncle saw but the fluttering of his own lowered flag, struck ignominiously a year earlier on the express orders of the Admiralty. Watching his uncle gaze out over the storm-ravaged prospect of his beloved garden, James felt sympathy for a man he respected but had never loved, a man who had stood in the place of James's dead father, but a man whose station in the world had always seemed so remote as to be accessible only through cousin Tom, the Admiral's son. But at Dartmouth his fellow cadets had made no distinction as to the subtlety of their relationship. It was enough that James's surname was synonymous with that of a disgraced admiral.

Vice Admiral Martin had been appointed to command a squadron of battleships and cruisers four months after the outbreak of war with Germany. They were elderly ships, pre-dreadnought battleships and armoured cruisers in want of gunnery practice. The Admiral had ordered them out of the Medway. Off the Tongue lightvessel he had met an escort of equally elderly destroyers which fanned out ahead of the heavy ships to protect them from submarines. Passing through the Strait of Dover the squadron ran into a south-westerly gale. In the worsening conditions the destroyers had difficulty in maintaining station and signalled the flagship they were running short of coal. Off Dungeness, thinking himself out of danger and shrouded by darkness, the Admiral dismissed them. His big ships drove to the westwards, pitching into the heavy seas of the open Channel. As the night wore on the Admiral ordered a reduction in speed to reduce the wear and tear on ships and men. A few hours later, south of the Isle of Wight, as the cruisers threw spray masthead high and the capital ships wallowed through the sea silhouetted against the grey light of dawn, the rearmost battleship was struck by a torpedo from a German U-boat. Ten minutes later a second torpedo hit the stricken ship, and shortly afterwards a third. HMS *Tremendous*, already listing heavily, capsized and sank. The heavy seas made it impossible to launch boats and rescue those of *Tremendous*'s company who survived the explosions, and the presence of the U-boat threatened his remaining ships. Admiral Martin signalled his squadron to proceed westwards at their best speed. At Plymouth official obloquy met him in a curt order to haul down his flag and, in the time-honoured phrase, 'proceed on shore'.

It was the Admiralty's euphemism for dismissal.

They are blind, James had written in desperate commiseration to Tom, *to the plain fact that the battleship is as vulnerable to the submarine as she is to the mine. It is a hard fact for us to swallow* . . .

So Cadet Martin had suffered from his uncle's misfortune at the hands of the young wiseacres at Dartmouth. An introverted boy, he had borne the matter with fortitude – more fortitude, it transpired, than the Admiral, whose persistent application for a court martial to clear his name was firmly refused and whose application for any other appointment was ignored.

Perhaps the Admiral, in his bitterness, guessed something of the effect his disgrace had had on his young nephew. The boy faced him unblinking as he turned from the window.

James was dark like his mother, not tall and blond like the Admiral's son Tom. He wished he could talk to Tom and explain what had happened. But Tom, the fruit of a late marriage to a younger wife, was already with the fleet in HMS *Indefatigable*. A sense of foreboding swept over the old man.

Boys like Tom and James had been lost with the *Tremendous*, and with the cruisers *Aboukir*, *Hogue* and *Cressy*, sunk by a single U-boat within sight of the Dutch coast in less than twenty minutes. Others had gone with the light cruiser *Pathfinder* and the hushed-up loss of the battleship *Audacious*. Still more had died with his own dear friend Kit Craddock off Coronel, when von Spee's new ships had out-gunned Sir Christopher's ageing squadron and caught them in black silhouette against a bloody Pacific sunset . . .

It was getting dark now, a grey, late spring dusk that seemed to the Admiral full of the desolation of war. The book-lined study with its two models and the spirited painting of a torpedo-boat destroyer at high speed was filled with an oppressive, preternatural gloom. Shaking off his sense of foreboding, Admiral Martin forced a wan smile.

'I think this will prove to be a young man's war, James.'

'Yes, uncle.'

The Admiral sighed again, aware the stilted phrase was

5

inadequate to convey what he wanted to say, and that this was too complex, too self-revealing and too cruel to enunciate. Moreover, he longed to say it to Tom, not to his own brother William's boy.

'You have all your kit then?' he asked instead.

'I have everything, sir, thank you.' There was a hint of respectful impatience in the boy's voice.

'Your divisional officer at Dartmouth spoke well of you. That would have pleased your father. It is a pity you never knew him, James.'

'Yes, sir.'

James felt awkward at this singular unbending on the part of his uncle.

'Well,' the Admiral said, returning to his desk and bringing the interview to an end, 'I have been able to pull a few strings; their lordships owe me that much. You'll have a friend in Tom; he should save you from the worst excesses of gunroom initiation and you'll learn your business under Sowerby.'

'Yes, thank you.'

James would be glad to see Tom again. They were closer than brothers though he always stood, as he did now, in his cousin's shadow.

'You travel by the night train?'

'Yes, sir. I shall be at Rosyth tomorrow forenoon.'

The Admiral held out his hand. 'Do your duty, my boy . . . and don't upset your mother with the business of farewell.'

'Mother!'

He was numb with cold, fully conscious now, aware that his legs and loins had no feeling in them. He was growing tired with the effort to stay afloat.

'Mother!'

He began to thrash about again, a spasm of reaction against the onset of despair. His flailing arms struck flotsam breaking surface from the wreck far below. There should be other people near him. He began to call names, especially Tom's, but water got in his mouth again and he choked and coughed. No one answered, and overhead the coils of smoke were thinning.

6

He could make one last effort and call for his mother. She always came when he called.

'Mother!'

She was sitting in the stern of the skiff, one hand trailing in the still water of the lake, watching a pair of buzzards circling over the rabbit warrens of Heald Brow. It was the last evening of a brief holiday during the hot and final summer of peace, and James was rowing his mother the length of Coniston Water.

They had rented a house beside the lake. James and his mother, Aunt Anne, the Admiral's vivacious younger wife, Tom and Vera, a distant and orphaned cousin of the boys who was the Admiral's ward. Two maids completed the noisy party, for the moderating influence of the Admiral and, more importantly, Ferris, the Admiral's manservant, had been left behind. Ferris and his wife to mind The Reddings, the Admiral to wait upon the King during the high jinks of the Fleet Review at Spithead and then the mobilisation crisis.

As naval cadets both Tom and James had been at the Review, but although the reservists remained on board their ships while the governments of Europe postured and the diplomats exchanged notes of an increasingly irreversible nature, cadets like Tom and James had been granted leave. Tom was due to return to Dartmouth before joining the fleet, and James was still at Osborne. Both had mixed feelings about coming home.

'If there is a war, Jimmy, and we aren't involved it will be terrible,' Tom had said the night before they came north to the lakes; but nothing had happened, and the first week of August had proved as hot as those of July.

'It won't last,' said Aunt Anne, the serrated shadow of her twirled parasol flickering across her untroubled face as she gazed out over the placid waters of the lake.

'Don't talk like that, Anne,' James's mother had cautioned.

'Oh, Harriet, don't be so silly and superstitious. I'm talking about the weather . . . but as for the other matter Thomas says the Kaiser won't stick to Austria if we stick by the French. It's too ridiculous.'

'Are you sure you want to follow Tom into the Navy, Jimmy?' James's mother asked now, still staring at the soaring buzzards which caught the setting sun while the shadows of the western hills crept across the lake.

Pulling easily on the sculls James had answered her as she feared he would.

'Yes, mother.'

'It seems that war is inevitable; even up here the newspapers are full of it.'

'They are the same papers we have in London, mother.'

She looked at the serious face of her son and smiled sadly. 'Yes. How silly of me to think we could run away from it all.'

'The fleet has not dispersed since the King reviewed it,' he said solemnly.

'No,' said his mother, mourning another departure. He reminded her so much of the husband she had loved for so short a time: the steady brown eyes, the straight nose and square jaw. He was no longer a boy, but a young man; a handsome young man, too handsome for cannon fodder.

She bit her lip and looked up, away from his face, seeking the wheeling buzzards again. James's father had died in China of wounds sustained during the suppression of the Boxer Rebellion. 'For Queen and Country' read the epitaph upon the memorial tablet in their parish church, and while James derived a certain protective mantle from the great and glorious thing that had deprived him of a father, his mother discovered a more traitorous truth.

'You don't *have* to follow Tom, you know,' she said with a sudden asperity that reminded James she was not really the equal she had seemed during the last few, carefree days.

'I know. I'm not *following* him. I just want to join the Navy.'

He pulled a few strokes and then stopped, resting on his oars. In the evening stillness the sound of drips from the oar blades and the chuckle of water at the stem of the skiff could be heard clearly, and with it the faint mew of the distant buzzards. Out on their starboard beam a fish jumped with a plop, the expanding rings of its disappearance marring the smoothness of the lake.

'If I'm following anyone, mother, I'm following father.'

'Then promise me something,' she said with a sudden, stricken urgency. 'You'll not marry; not while there's a war.'

8

'Mother,' he laughed, 'I'm not old enough to marry, I don't know anyone I want to marry, and Tom says the war will be over before either of us has been promoted to sub-lieutenant.'

'I hope to God he's right.'

'Oh, mother . . .' He shipped the sculls and leaned towards her. She sniffed and waved him away.

'It's all right. I'm not going to spoil a perfectly lovely evening. Row round Peel Island and then we'll go back. Only don't pull too fast. We spend so little time on our own, you and I.'

He smiled, an unmanly lump in his throat, and they doubled the island in silence. Only when they were halfway back to the landing stage did she speak again.

'James, I can give you just a little advice about life.'

'Go on.'

'Life is . . .' She shook her head as if speaking with an effort. 'It's beset with difficulties. You mustn't seek happiness; too many people try to do that and it simply doesn't work. But just occasionally you, and perhaps someone else with you, will experience a moment of absolute perfection . . . a moment like this one. Do you understand?'

He had stopped rowing again and nodded dumbly.

'*This* is happiness, James,' she whispered in the numinous stillness, 'at least for me. *This* is the gift of life given to us by God.'

God.

'God help me!'

He floundered again, kicking wildly, his cold legs responding feebly to his abject panic. He began to remember things in their proper sequence now, to separate them chronologically, recalling, too, that he had once heard the whole of one's life passed before you as you drowned.

The moment of panic passed. He no longer feared drowning, for death promised an eternity of warm darkness; if only he could remember what had happened.

Distant and rumbling the rolling concussion of guns came to him over the poppling surface of the sea. He realised he had been aware of them for a long time. They were salvoes of heavy calibre guns . . .

When they fired, the searing heat of their blast and the terrible thunder of their discharge . . .

A wave slopped across his face. He spat frantically, aware of swallowing water. It was getting rougher as the wind rose. He recalled hearing the wind earlier that day . . .

The chilling wind of the battle cruiser's passage, the ship's wind, shrieked in the signal halliards, and the canvas dodger slapped against the stanchions of the top where he crouched with his signalmen: Midshipman James Martin, dogsbody to the Signals Officer of HMS *Indefatigable*.

From time to time he looked down on the gold-leafed cap of Captain Sowerby as he conferred with a knot of officers exposed on the navigating bridge and they all trained their binoculars on the port bow.

Astern, between the massive tripod masts, the ship's three funnels belched sulphurous smoke which spread low over the sea. Through this shimmering haze he could just make out the pyramidal shapes of *Warspite, Valiant, Barham* and *Malaya*, the new 'super-dreadnought' battleships as they sought to keep up with Beatty's coursing battle cruisers.

Beyond them, somewhere over the rim of the world to the north, lay Admiral Jellicoe's Grand Fleet, hurrying south in anticipation of Beatty luring the enemy onto their guns.

As the afternoon wore on, James reflected on his luck. For months these ships had lain at anchor, their crews fighting boredom. The monotony had been relieved by games of football, route marches and, for the officers, golf and gardening in improvised circumstances ashore. There had been the occasional practice shoot in northern waters, and the artificially induced excitement of amateur theatricals combined with endless drills that seemed to be purposeless, except to captains and flag officers fearing their precious capital ships might share the fates of the *Audacious* and *Tremendous*, victims of the U-boat and mine.

But James had no sooner joined Beatty's Battle Cruiser Fleet, no sooner made his number with a smiling and already popular Tom, than he had been caught up in the thrill of this pell-mell chase of the Imperial German High Seas Fleet.

'We were just waiting for you, Jim,' grinned Tom, as the news to raise steam to full pressure spread through the ship;

and James had found the sentiment echoed throughout the *Indefatigable*.

'You must be a lucky 'un, sir,' remarked the Chief Yeoman of Signals in that condescending tone senior petty officers reserved for newly joined snotties.

The Admiralty's order had galvanised the anchored ships of the Second Battle Cruiser and Fifth Battle Squadrons to a frenzy of activity. Signal projectors had winked frenetically, bunting had soared up and down halliards, and picket boats thrashed hurriedly around the fleet. Black clouds of smoke rose from the grey ships' funnels and by evening the Firth of Forth was left to the small fry, the hospital ship *Berbice* and the repair ship HMS *Cyclops*: Beatty's Battle Cruiser Fleet had passed beneath the bridge attended by a cloud of destroyers. The promptitude with which the fleet slipped its moorings was a tribute to Beatty's leadership; the exactitude with which the Admiralty timed their order for departure rested on their possession of the German cipher which revealed to a nicety the departure of the enemy fleet from Wilhelmshaven in the estuary of the Jade.

Simultaneous with Beatty setting course to the east, Jellicoe left Scapa Flow in the Orkneys. Their intention was to intercept the sortie of the Kaiser's ships and annihilate them.

Much earlier that same afternoon of 31 May 1916, the scouting cruiser HMS *Galatea*, investigating the smoke of an innocent neutral steamer, discovered beyond the merchantman a German vedette engaged on the same task. *Galatea* signalled Beatty's flagship, HMS *Lion*, that she had made contact with Admiral von Hipper's advance ships. The news was flashed from ship to ship: enemy in sight. Marine buglers sounded action stations as each fleet swung towards the other. Midshipman Martin, grinning with excitement, ran aloft to huddle behind the dodgers of *Indefatigable*'s forward searchlight platform with his signallers, uncertain, untried, but acutely aware that the men around him, the Captain and officers on the bridge, the gun crews and the magazine parties, the men in the ammunition hoists and at their stations in the sick bays, hose, and damage control stations were eager to be in action.

Looking over the dodger until the ship's wind tore the

11

tears from his reddened eyes, James stared at the might of Britain's Royal Navy: great, smoking dark grey ships slicing white furrows through the deep blue of the sea. Red and white battle ensigns streamed from every masthead, except where St George's cross proclaimed the viceregal presence of an admiral, and the whole puissant mass was screened by the black, dart-like silhouettes of destroyers, leaping and cleaving the seas while the heavy ships barged through them.

James longed to capture the moment in watercolours, trying to commit details to memory, so that later he could illustrate his snotty's journal . . .

'Signal from Flag, sir, alter course . . . form on line of bearing.'

James dutifully passed the instruction by voice-pipe to the bridge, but sharper eyes had anticipated him.

'Execute!' snapped the Yeoman.

'Execute!' repeated James as the imperative flag-hoist was jerked down from *Lion*'s yardarm, but *Indefatigable*'s deck was already canting to the heel induced by her rudder.

'Our Davy-boy's giving it the works!' said one of the signallers, deftly unhooking the Inglefield clips and removing the answering pendant from their own halliards.

The line of the six monstrous battle cruisers opened in echelon.

'Keeps the gun sights clear of the other buggers' smoke, sir,' the Yeoman explained obligingly.

'I know, Yeoman, thank you,' acknowledged James.

The huge barrels of *Indefatigable*'s main, full-calibre armament were elevating as the turrets swung to align the twelve-inch guns on a line of smoke blurring the perfection of the horizon to the south. Manoeuvring round the big ships, the lean, dark hulls of the destroyers tightened their screen, protecting the mighty Goliaths from the sling shots of submerged Davids. James knew their supplementary role was to engage the enemy's screen and deliver their own torpedoes at Hipper's ships. James looked again to port, ten, twenty degrees on the bow.

The smoke smudge was much longer now, with hard-edged shapes visible beneath it. He shuddered with pure excitement. The sight of the two fleets converging at maximum speed, with relays of stokers, their sinews cracking as they shifted ton after ton of coal into the glowing maws of the boilers hidden in the ships' hulls, seemed a sight of sublime majesty. It was, he knew, the moment for which the Royal Navy had patiently waited eighteen months, the moment for which his uncle had lived and been denied, the moment in which these ships would justify their expensive existence and repudiate those sour comments that vilified a service which, it was said, skulked at Scapa and Rosyth while volunteer infantrymen died futilely by the drove in the mud of Flanders.

To the waiting Midshipman Martin it seemed it was his privilege to participate in an epitome of the patriotic endeavour he had been brought up to believe he owed his country as a sacred duty. What mattered death, he recalled the poster reading, if England lived?

It was a great and glorious thing to die for one's country . . .

'Anti-flash 'ood, sir. And yer tin 'at.'

'Oh, yes, thank you.'

The Yeoman, head shrouded in a white balaclava, drew down his own chinstrap and picked up his binoculars again. 'Don't worry, sir; it's the waiting that's the worst.'

'Yes.' James was conscious that his throat *had* gone dry and his heart bumped uncomfortably in his chest. He hoped he showed no trace of fear on his face.

'Won't be long now, mates,' added the signalman who had applauded the Admiral's tactics.

'There . . .'

It seemed the men about him sighed with a strange, tense satisfaction. Far to the south-east tiny yellow pinpricks sparkled along the enemy line.

'They must be all of twenty mile away,' said the Yeoman, amazed. 'There goes the bloody *Lion*!'

James choked off a foolish cheer and raised his binoculars ready to mark the fall of their own shot, but he could not resist a glance at the flagship. She was accounted the best looking ship in the world with her three tall funnels that belched a solid pall of dense, black smoke; very different now from the day in Kronstadt when, her great guns shrouded in awnings, her quarterdeck tricked out with signal flags, she had been the venue for a magnificent ball hosted by Beatty in honour of Tsar Nicholas II of Russia.

13

It had been the same fateful day that a Serb named Princip had put a bullet into the Archduke Ferdinand in the obscure town of Sarajevo.

Suddenly, *Lion*'s eight huge 13.5-inch guns in their four heavily armoured turrets belched fire and armour piercing shell at the enemy. A *frisson* of almost terrifying excitement ran through James. As the delayed concussion swept over *Indefatigable*, his heart leaped again with an ecstatic mixture of fear and joy.

This, he thought as he concentrated on the distant German line waiting for *Indefatigable*'s broadside, was one of those divine moments of which his mother had spoken.

A shocking, drenching spray stung the men on the platform. Tall columns of water reared alongside, were shredded by the wind in a hiss like buckshot, and vanished.

'That was a straddle, by Christ!' the signalman shouted. 'The buggers've got our range already.'

'They can't have,' snapped the Yeoman.

But the significance of this exchange was lost on James as ahead of them *Princess Royal, Tiger, Queen Mary* and *New Zealand* rent the air with their opening salvoes.

'Come on *Indy* . . .'

Then the concussion of their own guns, the searing heat of the blast and the sickly sweet gases of the cordite propellant engulfed them.

'Watch for the fall of shot. Must be all of fifteen bloody miles . . .'

They peered through their glasses, supplementing the spotting officers in the top above their heads, while in the steel hull below them, joining the ceaselessly toiling stokers, other men were sweating in the turrets, ramming home armour piercing shells of lyddite and their cordite charges; moving more ammunition from magazine to handling room, transferring shells and charges into the lifts and up the barbettes to the ready-use positions in the turrets to be next into the breeches of the guns.

Somewhere forward in A turret, cousin Tom was doing his bit. James darted a quick look as the twin barrels of A and B turrets swung in compensation as the battle cruisers followed *Lion*'s alteration of course designed to confuse the German gun-layers.

14

It failed, for the next moment the ship was again surrounded by the tall columns of water marking a second straddle. Then their own guns bellowed again and smoke and spray were whipped away with the heat.

'They've hit *Lion*!'

'Bloody hell!'

Smoke and flames belched from the flagship's amidships turret. She began to sheer to starboard. As the terrible rumble of the explosion aboard *Lion* died away, the thin imperious whistle of the voice-pipe shrieked at James. He bent obediently forward to answer it.

And then he seemed momentarily imbued with divine vision, for he observed, quite distinctly, the meteor strikes of three shells and saw himself, hand outstretched, part bent above the voice-pipe, from outside his corporate form. Light, bright as the sun, flashed beyond the bridge. The heavy, armoured top of A turret cartwheeled slowly across his disembodied line of sight and then he felt himself swept upwards, cocooned in an embracing warmth and lifted high above the sea so that, ever afterwards, he remembered Jutland as a diorama of ships spread below him.

He accepted with a marvellous equanimity that his soul had left his body, for he could hear nothing. And yet there was no silence, but a noise so vast, so terrible, as to be incomprehensible and past human understanding. It was then he knew he was dying.

Mercifully, he never knew the moment he fell in the sea.

Overhead the pall of drifting smoke had thinned, though the sickly taint of it lingered in his gasping, shocked lungs. He fought to keep his head above water, staring up at the filthy yellow swirl as it slowly dissipated against the sky. Gradually, as full terrified consciousness returned, he realised he was all that remained of the great warship.

And he cried out as the smoke left him alone amid the wreckage on the sea.

'Mother!'

Cold permeated his body, anaesthetising him against the latent effects of hitting the water. Shock hit his conscious mind and, after a further flurry of panic, he began to surrender to an overwhelming lassitude. He began to whimper, a last manifestation of spirit before a final loss of will.

He was going to die.

Tom was already dead, blown to pieces as *Indefatigable*'s magazines detonated from the high-explosive flash that had travelled down the unprotected barbette of A turret and into the cordite and lyddite stored below.

He was going to die as had the other one thousand and seventeen men of the ship's company; one tiny, insignificant coin in the price his country paid for command of the sea. Perhaps, he thought, as he relinquished his hold on life, he had to die in this final, isolated manner, to pay a more personal price; a sacrifice called to account for the carelessness of his uncle who had thought his battleships had nothing to fear from U-boats and had widowed whole streets, they said, in Chatham.

'You must be a lucky 'un, sir,' he thought he heard the Yeoman say.

'Then promise me something,' his mother said quite clearly. 'You'll not marry; not while there's a war . . .'

He had never known a woman, not the way some lads of his age had. He had kissed Vera and when his curious hands had reached for the soft and irresistible cones of her breasts she had pushed them away.

'No, Jimmy, not you.'

And he had known then that she loved Tom. Everyone loved Tom, but for Vera the phrase meant something special.

Sea water slopped into his face and he coughed; the reflexive action stirred a last, bitter response of anger. Why should *he* pay for the old Admiral's mistake? Why must *he* die alone when Tom, lucky Tom, had died instantly with the gun crews of A turret? And why should *he* die having known only Vera's plaintive rebuff?

'Martin, you are a cock-virgin, aren't you?' the odious cadet captain at Dartmouth had said to him.

'No, I'm not.'

'Yes, you are. Your charming cousin Tom told me.'

'No! Tom wouldn't . . .'

'Ah, so it's true. Come on, it's nothing to be ashamed of.'

'Get off!'

16

He waved his hands, splashing futilely at the surface of the sea, batting at ghosts. He could no longer feel any sensation in the genitals they had so assiduously boot-blacked, but his hand struck something and out of that half-recalled hatred he found the will to grasp it.

The lashed bundle of buoyant cork life-preservers had torn themselves free of their lashings and risen from the doomed ship. Laboriously he hauled himself onto them and lay inert. For a long time he lay as he had floated, slipping in and out of consciousness with time and memories playing tricks upon him. In the end these ghostly visitations ceased. In the end there was only the long, long corridor of eternal darkness.

He was all that remained of the great ship, for overhead the smoke had drifted away.

CHAPTER TWO
Aftermath

There were, he remembered afterwards, distant voices and clumsy hands and vague, unfamiliar noises, but they were so far away that they might have involved someone else. There had also been a more personal sensation, a vigorous and agonising pummelling administered by a thickset man bent over his naked body. He thought he heard someone say 'that'll kill or bloody cure' before the impression vanished and a blissful warmth enfolded him.

Hours later he woke tucked in a narrow bunk set high against a panelled bulkhead enclosing a small cabin lit by two salt-encrusted portholes. Two beams of sunlight streamed into the cabin at a low angle, and it occurred to him that, if it was dawn, he was a prisoner and heading east; if it was sunset he was heading west and safe. The bunk smelt of another human being, and it trembled slightly as the ship, whatever it was, rolled gently. He shut his eyes, uncaring whether or not he was free or captive and glad only that whoever his rescuers were they had saved his life.

And then he heard the tremendous explosion of the *Indefatigable*, heard it consciously for the first time hours after the event, heard it as a manifestation of hell itself. He sat up screaming, the sweat starting from his pores. 'Tom . . . Tom!'

Breathing heavily he strove to master his fear, staring about the cabin, fastening on its details, the locker, bookshelf, small table and chair and a pair of photographs, one of a woman, the other a girl. A polished oil lamp swung in gimbals and he tried to read the titles on the books, focusing his eyes with difficulty. He could only make out the word *Olsen's*.

He knew then he was aboard a German ship, a small one by the feel of her and the fact that beneath a heavy pilot jacket a uniform reefer's sleeve gleamed with dull and unfamiliar lace. He was a prisoner.

Suddenly the door flew open. They must have heard him screaming. His heart was hammering and in a final paroxysm of fear and shame his bowels voided themselves. The thickset man bent over him again. Pockmarks showed through a dark stubble and brown eyes set in folds of wrinkled flesh peered down at him.

James Martin cringed in the bunk, face to face with the enemy.

'By 'eck, lad, you've shit yerself.' A pudgy nose wrinkled in offence. 'Heard you shouting up in wheelhouse. Reckon you should, shitting in my bunk like this.'

It dawned on James with painful slowness that this was English spoken with a Yorkshire accent.

'I'm terribly sorry,' he managed. 'Where am I?'

'On board the 'Ull trawler *Girl Stella*, lad, or she was a trawler before this bloody war. Admiralty requisitioned we are.' He smiled reassuringly. 'I'm Skipper Bawden, though King's lost his head and given me a bloody commission as a lieutenant RNR, the daft bugger. Only for the duration, like,' he added with a twinkle in his eyes, suggesting the matter would be improper during peace-time.

'Pleased to meet you.'

James held out a hand, incongruously formal as the cabin filled with the fecal stink of his shame. 'I'm awfully sorry . . .' He found himself racked with sobs.

'Easy, lad.' Bawden put a hand on his shoulder. 'Can you manage to tell me who you are?'

'Yes, yes of course. Midshipman James Martin, HMS *Indefatigable*.' He made an effort to control himself. 'I think she blew up.'

'Aye, lad. And she weren't only one.' Bawden patted his shoulder again. 'Now let's get you cleaned up and then you must get some grub inside you.'

'I'm sorry . . .'

'Forget it. Can you stand?'

Shakily he stood swaying beside the bunk while Bawden briskly rolled the fouled bedding up and stuffed it in a bucket.

'The Mate caught sight of you at dawn,' he explained. 'We were out on patrol looking for nonexistent submarines and we'd seen the smoke of the action and heard the guns. All night you could see the gun flashes. We were called up by a TBD, the *Badger*, looking for survivors from your ship and the *Queen Mary*.'

'The *Queen Mary*?' queried James, astounded that another of the great battle cruisers had been lost.

'Aye lad. I think she blew up too. Don't say much for our bloody Navy.'

Bawden relieved James of his soiled clothes, stuck his head outside the cabin door and yelled for hot water.

'No shortage of that on a steam trawler,' he said, smiling reassuringly. 'I'll get you some clean gear.'

He rummaged in a drawer below the bunk.

'The *Queen Mary* . . . she had nine-inch armour.' James shook his head in disbelief.

'Happen she did, but man proposes and God disposes. Nine-inch armour hasn't stopped a deal of widows and orphans being made by yesterday's work.'

The door opened and James glimpsed a curious face. Bawden traded a bucket of boiling water for the one containing the soiled bed linen. 'Put that in a bit of gill net and tow it astern a while. Lumpy . . . Deckie-learner,' he added, for James's benefit, pouring the water into the battered enamel bowl. 'Right, lad; there's hot water, soap, a towel and some clothes. Come up to wheelhouse when th's ready.'

A pint mug of stew and a wad of bread and butter was waiting for him in the wheelhouse supplemented by a thick brew of aciduous tea. The tiny, cramped space overlooked the trawler's foredeck and high, flared whale-backed forecastle. The forepart of the little ship was silhouetted black against a glorious sunset.

'This is the Mate, lad. He's the one to thank. If he hadn't spotted you on that heap of life-preservers, well . . .' Bawden left the sentence unfinished. The Mate was a short, wiry man with thinning hair. He took one fist off the *Girl Stella*'s huge steering wheel to grasp James's hand in an iron clasp. James felt the stumps of two missing fingers.

'I did bugger all but see 'ee, son. Skipper saved 'ee.

Rubbed you down wi' hot towels and two bottles of Haig. You was pretty near dead wi' cold.'

'I owe you a great deal,' James mumbled inadequately, looking round at the faces gathered in the wheelhouse.

'Aw, forget it. All in a day's work.' Bawden's great fist punched him gently on the shoulder. A few days ago, self-consciously aware of his rank, such an uncompromisingly patronising and familiar gesture would have affronted James. But here, crammed in the tiny wheelhouse with these men to whom the dangers of war were but a variation of the dangers they experienced in their peace-time calling, he felt no resentment. He smiled, warming to their hospitable camaraderie.

Watching the young survivor, Bawden saw for the first time since his awakening the light of life in the Midshipman's eyes.

'Hell of a bloody thing to be blowed up,' remarked the Mate, passing the wheel spokes easily through his mutilated hands. 'Reckon it's good enough excuse to shit Skipper's bed, eh?'

James flushed; then joined in the laughter.

James Martin felt secure aboard the cockleshell craft as at dawn she doubled the low sandy spit of Spurn Head with its lonely lighthouse. The equally featureless coast of Lincolnshire lay to the south where, from Donna Nook, it swung north-west, forming the south bank of the River Humber. Catching the first rays of the rising sun, the hydraulic tower of Grimsby rose slender as a minaret above the lock-pits of the port.

Martin took the wheel himself as *Girl Stella* headed up into Hawke Road. Skipper Bawden leaned from a forward window clasping a mug of lethally stewed tea. Clouds of smoke issued from his pipe and filled the air with the aroma of equally murderous shag.

'One pipe a day, at dawn,' he said conversationally, 'and now starboard a bit . . . aye . . . meet her and steady as you go.'

'Steady as we go. Course north fifty west, sir,' said James, spinning off the counter-helm.

'Nor' west a half west'll do here, lad. Different ships have different long splices. You remember that when you're back in Navy; there's too many in Navy who think they know all the right answers.' He blew out a cloud of smoke. 'Till there's a bloody war and the realm needs defending. Then it's all hands to the pumps including Skipper Bawden and the *Girl Stella*.'

'I shan't forget, sir.'

'Call me Skipper,' said Bawden with mock asperity. 'Don't take any notice of this.' He tipped the peak of his naval hat with a thumb and indicated the wavy bullion lace on his sleeve. 'It means bugger all.'

'Aye, aye, Skipper.'

Their eyes met and exchanged smiles of friendship. James found he liked the man, warmed to his direct and simple character.

'There she is.' Bawden raised a set of battered binoculars and Martin craned to see over the high-riding bow. Bawden jangled the engine room telegraph and *Girl Stella*'s bow dropped as her speed fell off. Then James saw the ram bow and the funnels and the enormously tall masts of a protected cruiser.

'*Saint* bloody *George*, flagship of the Admiral of Patrols, Rear Admiral Ballard. My gaffer for the duration.'

Bawden opened the wheelhouse door and shouted orders below. Figures appeared on the forecastle.

'Hard a starboard,' he ordered, and *Girl Stella* swung into the flood tide and dropped neatly alongside the grey sides of HMS *St George*.

'Time for you to leave, lad,' he said. 'Come and see us again if you can find five minutes; we'll be in Hull Fish Dock for a boiler clean.'

Half an hour later a neat, elderly paymaster lieutenant of the Admiral's staff interviewed Midshipman Martin.

'You say you were part of the ship's company of HMS *Indefatigable*?'

'Yes, sir.' It astonished James that the assertion should be doubted.

'And you were steaming in line ahead?'

'We'd opened in echelon, sir, in conformity with the senior officer's motions, sir, as I've already explained . . .'

'But then,' interrupted the incredulous staff officer, 'your ship just exploded?'

'Well, we had opened fire, I think, yes. I think we had just opened fire.' James was confused; the recollection seemed to hurt him.

'You seem a little vague. It's unusual for battle cruisers to simply blow up.' The Paymaster Lieutenant snorted.

Something snapped in James's head. 'This one did! This one went bang! A bloody big bang and I found myself in the water.' He added 'sir' to mollify the astonished officer. He had explained what little he knew of *Indefatigable*'s loss at least four times.

Eventually they led him off and locked him in a cabin. Later a surgeon had come and palpated and auscultated him, chatting cheerfully in an incomprehensible gibberish as he did so.

'Drunk any toasts to *Der Tag*, eh, young fellow? Come a cropper at the old *Entscheidungsschlacht,* eh?' The surgeon peered attentively into his ears.

'I don't understand you.'

'Not a spy left by an *Unterseeboot*?'

'Is that what they think I am?' James sat up indignantly only to be pushed firmly back on the bunk.

'That hurt?'

'Yes. Sore.'

'And that?'

'Yes . . .'

'You say you were blown clear by a big explosion?' James nodded. 'Have you noticed any loss of hearing, any blood in your urine?' James shook his head. 'In your faeces?' He shook his head again. 'Have you passed any solids?' James flushed and nodded. 'Involuntarily?'

'Yes.'

'You're lucky to be alive. I can't discover any aneurism – arterial distortion – though your kidneys, liver and spleen seem bruised and I'm keeping you under observation. Paymaster Lieutenant Courtney said you were rude.'

The doctor stared into James's eyes and ears and ran his hands over James's skull. Fingers dug in the ganglion of intersecting cords at its base, in the nape of his neck.

'Ouch!'

'Hmm. I'll have you transferred to the sick bay. They'll want to interview you again. It's lucky you can remember

23

your name, otherwise they were prepared to convince themselves you were deliberately dumped from a U-boat to be picked up as a survivor and used as a spy.'

'That's ridiculous, I'm a British Midshipman.'

'The Huns are damned clever, especially Huns in U-boats.'

'But my ship just exploded, sir. We were hit by three shells and she blew up, sir.'

The surgeon raised a sceptical eyebrow. 'Tell that to the marines, my lad. The executive branch of His Britannic Majesty's Navy has a perhaps understandable prejudice against believing its battle cruisers explode with more facility than the shells they fire. Scuttlebutt has it that our hits did little damage.' He smiled, patting James's shoulder as a signal that the examination was over. 'So forgive them their reluctance to believe your story. I expect we'll hear the truth in a day or so.'

It took a week before Beatty's Jutland despatch reached the Admiralty and was corrupted by the press to suggest Britain's glorious Navy had had its proud nose bloodied by the parvenu Boche. Indignant senior officers pointed out that the palm of victory belonged to the possessors of the field, and the Kaiser's magnificent High Seas Fleet had bolted for the shelter of the Schillig Roads. But while the loss of the pre-dreadnought battleship *Defence* could be technically justified on the grounds of obsolescence, the same could not be said of the sudden, terrible explosions of the *Indefatigable* and *Invincible*, still less so that of the *Queen Mary*.

'She was one of the "Splendid Cats" wasn't she?' asked Surgeon Lieutenant Wilmott, sitting on James's bunk.

'Yes, sir. A sister ship to *Lion* and *Tiger*.'

'*Lion* nearly went too.'

'Yes . . . I remember. A hit on Q Turret.' James frowned at the memory.

'So it seems; it was the Royal Marine mounting, and only the quick thinking of the major in command saved her. Apparently he ordered the flooding of the magazine below. It was the last thing he did as he'd already lost both his legs. So it seems the BCs suffered magazine explosions caused by flash . . .'

'I don't believe it.'

'Neither did Beatty.'

24

After a week of disbelieving suspense punctuated by the rumour of naval disaster, the confirmation of so Pyrrhic a victory had released a torrent of informed gossip which transmitted itself through the fleet with the spontaneity of a bushfire.

'Anyway, that's the news and I daresay, whatever the obfuscations of their lordships, it'll prove true.'

Wilmott smiled at the Midshipman. He was professionally curious about his patient. To have survived the combined effects of exploding cordite and lyddite in massive quantities followed by a night's exposure was a remarkable feat; yet the slim young man bore no obvious signs of physical toughness and Wilmott worried about the state of his mind, for Martin's introspection seemed morbidly unnatural.

Admiral Ballard's secretary had told him privately that there were over six thousand casualties, far more than the most sanguine estimates of German losses. Wilmott was anxious to avoid young Martin being among the wounded, for wounds of the mind were less easy to heal than those of other parts of the body, and Wilmott knew Midshipman Martin's trauma had scarred him deeply.

'I see you've been drawing,' Wilmott said, picking up a well-executed pencil sketch. A line of battle cruisers belching a cloud of smoke steamed at speed through a lively sea. Ensigns streamed from their mastheads and low destroyers sliced through the sea along their flanks. The guns were foreshortened, elevated aggressively towards the observer. 'It's very good. You have a definite talent.'

James ignored the compliment. 'I lost my watercolours with the ship.'

Wilmott, still holding the drawing, cocked an eye at the young man. It was the first personal remark he had made. 'Is this what it looked like?'

'It's how the enemy must have seen us.'

The Midshipman's detachment worried Wilmott. He sensed he was close to a medical truth; professional intuition and curiosity kept him probing. Clumsily he sought the question that he sensed, in answering, would free his patient.

'Admiral Beatty's despatch said you engaged at a range of eighteen miles. I'm no expert in these matters, but practice firing is usually at ten thousand yards, isn't it?'

'The Germans were very accurate.'

The cryptically flat observation was almost dismissive, except, in an atmosphere of excuses and recriminations that formed the principal aftermath of the battle, it was disarmingly honest; as detached and accurate as the drawing. At a loss Wilmott turned the sketch over.

'Wasn't this paper supplied for you to write home on?'

'The orderly told me a letter would be censored.'

'That's no reason not to let your family know you are alive.'

'I can't write home.'

'Why not?'

'Because I lost a cousin.' James explained about Tom. 'The news will kill the Admiral, coming on top of the loss of the *Tremendous*.'

Wilmott frowned. 'Vice Admiral Martin?' James nodded. 'I expect the Admiralty have already done your dirty work for you – and added your name to the missing. I think it's time you went home and faced up to things.'

'Perhaps,' said James uncertainly, his mind confused.

The following day he was visited by *St George*'s Commander and Admiral Ballard's secretary. Both men asked after his uncle and the Commander brought the news that he would be released next day for survivor's leave.

'Were there *any* others, sir?' James asked.

'I don't think so. You're a lucky fellow. Give my regards to the Admiral. I was his "doggy" on the old *Courageous* and he was a decent old boy. I'm sorry about his son.'

In an ill-fitting outfit of slops, James bade Surgeon Lieutenant Wilmott farewell.

'Keep getting plenty of sleep, my boy, and if you have any ear or headaches, consult a physician.'

'Aye, aye, sir.'

'I'm glad you weren't a Boche spy.'

The tender landed him next morning at Hull. For a moment he stood uncertainly on the quay. A watery June sunshine failed to warm him, for the wind was south-east, strong enough to cut the yeasty surface of the Humber into rank upon rank of vicious little waves. He made up his mind and began walking, asking directions. The small, huddled houses between the docks and the Hessle Road tugged at a childhood memory.

They had gone north with the Admiral whose duty it was to accept a new torpedo-boat destroyer from her Tyneside builders. Mrs Martin had launched the ship and they went as a family, Tom and James keen as mustard to attend, Vera accompanying them because no one wanted to leave her behind.

'She's one of the "Tribals",' the ten-year-old Tom had enthused.

'What d'you mean, a "Tribal"?' asked Vera.

'They're named after native tribes: *Cossack, Viking, Crusader* . . .'

'They're not tribes! Crusaders aren't a native tribe,' said Vera contemptuously.

'Well *Zulu* is, and so is this one. She's *Iroquois*.'

'I thought there were six tribes of Iroquois,' put in James, who had recently made the acquaintance of Fennimore-Cooper.

'Oh, don't you start. You're both infuriatingly pedantic.'

'What's pedantic?' asked Vera.

'Fussy,' explained Tom, seizing the ascendancy again.

'I'm not fussy,' snapped Vera.

'You are a bit,' said James, rallying to Tom.

'Anyway she's got two four-inch guns, two eighteen-inch torpedo tubes and a top speed of thirty-three knots!'

'Phew, that's fast.'

And she had looked small, lean and wicked alongside the fitting-out jetty at Swan Hunter's, just in from her trials and still with the red ensign at her stern and the builder's house flag at her masthead. The two boys, in sailor suits, had stood rigidly to attention like the paraded ship's company. Speeches were made and the red ensign came down to be replaced by the white, and the ranks of sailors gave three short, sharply orchestrated cheers.

But it was not this little ceremony that had engraved itself on his young and impressionable mind as he now recalled, walking the streets of Kingston-upon-Hull, but the sunset view he had had at the close of that day. Looking down on the river from the train he had seen the River Tyne wind into the distance the colour of dull steel. The rising banks were covered by the harsh outlines of cranes, the chimneys of foundries and row upon row of back-to-back houses. Details were lost in mist and smoke, receding gradations of tone, paling towards the horizon. He was still haunted by that view.

'Golly,' Vera had said, 'isn't it dirty?'

'It's where the shipwrights live,' Tom had replied. 'We saw lots of them at the shipyard.'

James still remembered the rows of faces in old coats and dark overalls, flat-capped and collarless to a man, even the apprentice boys, hardly older than himself, stiffly respectful (or so it had then seemed to James) as their lordships took possession of the fruit of their skill and labour.

They were the same small houses he walked past now, though the flat land lent no enchantment to the view, the same rank upon rank of meagre dwellings with which he felt the same sense of kinship he had discovered with the crew of the *Girl Stella*. This, he thought, was what they were fighting for. It seemed little enough.

Beyond the houses lay the fish docks and he found *Girl Stella* alongside in the Albert Dock, her boiler-clean in progress. Within minutes he was with Skipper Bawden.

'Why lad, 'tis good to see you.'

'I came to thank you properly,' James said, shaking the massive paw.

'What were that for, lad?'

'Why, for saving my life!'

'Oh, ay. Right-oh.' Bawden's eyes twinkled even as he played out the charade of being the flinty deep-water skipper. 'You'll be off for your survivor's leave, then?'

'I've no ship . . .'

'They'll find you another one. It's men this war wants, not bloody ships.' Bawden followed James's eye as he stared at the six-pounder gun set just abaft *Girl Stella*'s funnel. 'Not in a hurry to go home?' Bawden asked shrewdly.

James shrugged.

Bawden eyed him closely, considering; then said, 'Would you like to come and have a bite to eat with the missus?'

'Oh, yes please!'

Bawden had not been deceived. 'Right, lad, give me ten minutes with the Chief and I'll be with you.'

28

Bawden, when ashore, lived in a neat villa off the Anlaby Road. His wife was a tall, fine-boned Scot, once one of the girls who came south to the fish quays of Hull, Yarmouth and Lowestoft in an annual migration that followed the silver shoals of herring and were themselves enmeshed in matrimony.

'This is the lad I were telling you about, lass. Midshipman James Martin. Real Andrew, not Wavy Navy like me.'

'Mr Martin, do please come in.'

'I thought he could do wi' a bit of dinner.'

'Yes, of course.' Mrs Bawden wiped herself on her apron and shook James's outstretched hands. 'Please go in the parlour.'

Bawden ushered him in. It was a dark, high-ceilinged room, small by Reddings standards, but comfortably furnished with two winged armchairs either side of the fireplace. An oil painting of a trawler hung over the iron mantelpiece and lace curtains obscured the window in the bay of which an opulent aspidistra overflowed an elaborate Doulton plant pot set on a table.

'You're honoured, lad,' remarked Bawden drily. 'Not everyone gets shown into parlour.'

'I don't want to put your wife out.'

'You won't . . . whisky?'

'Er, yes, yes please.'

Bawden handed him a glass half full of Scotch. 'Never touch ought else,' he said, pouring his own. 'Never one for the ale like some of the lads.'

'I hope you like beef pie?' Mrs Bawden joined them having cast off her apron. 'Do sit down, Mr Martin.'

'Please call me James.'

She accepted a glass of watered whisky from her husband. The tiny act bespoke an intimacy and it was clear that Bawden was a successful fisherman.

'You've had a lucky escape, James,' Mrs Bawden said, sipping her drink. After the rough Hull accents with their curt idiom, her voice was as soothing as the whisky was warming. He shuddered as it hit the pit of his stomach. 'Are you cold? Shall I light the fire?' She rose.

'Don't fuss the lad. Sit you down. Where's Stell'?'

'She'll be here in a minute. She's been helping at the

church hall. There's a great deal of work being done for the comfort of the soldiers, Mr Martin. We'll be able to eat as soon as she arrives.' She smiled at James and it joined the Scotch in making him welcome. 'It must ha'e been dreadful in the battle.'

'Yes, it was.'

'Don't quizz lad, Meg. He needs rest and quiet.'

'I'm all right really. I just don't seem to be able to . . .' He hesitated, the whisky and the attention of these two friendly people emboldening him. 'Able to *feel* anything.'

For a moment a silence fell upon them. Mrs Bawden sought some maternal formula to console the young man while Bawden stared into his whisky. A shadow flitted across the window.

'There's Stella.' Mrs Bawden stood and left the room as a key turned in the front door lock. Bawden winked at James as a whispered conversation took place in the hall.

'You'll like the beef pie,' he said.

Mrs Bawden returned to the parlour. 'This is our daughter Stella.' She gestured. 'Stella, Mr Martin.'

'Please call me James,' he said, only this time it was for the girl. 'How d'you do.'

His first impression as he took her outstretched hand was of her eyes. They were green, an oddly sub-aqueous colour that exactly suited the subdued daylight filtering through the lace curtains. She too was smiling, and he felt suddenly, absurdly happy. Her hand was cool and her grip firm; she had her father's dark hair and her mother's features. James felt his heart hammering foolishly.

'I hear you've been busy with war work,' he said.

'Yes.' She let go of his hand.

'Well, lass,' said Bawden, putting down his empty glass, 'let's get at that beef pie.'

'Dad!' Stella remonstrated.

'Come on,' insisted Bawden, 'James and I are half starved, aren't we, lad?'

They moved into the next room where a table and chairs shared the space with a black-leaded range. The air was filled with the delicious smell of beef pie.

'Is your uncle an admiral?' Mrs Bawden asked as she dished up.

'A vice admiral, actually.'

'Is that different?' asked Stella.

'Not really,' said James, feeling his pedantry might be misunderstood. He sensed the difference in their class was perceived, at least by Stella and her mother, as something reprehensible; meaning that the present moment was unique and could not be repeated. Looking at Stella he desperately wanted to dismiss such thoughts. 'It doesn't matter to me,' he said awkwardly. 'I ought to have been calling Mr Bawden "sir".'

'I hope you'll do no such thing,' expostulated Mrs Bawden, passing her husband a steaming plate and indicating that whatever the conventions in an admiral's household, those in a fisherman's were firmly based on matriarchal principles. And he found himself telling them about the Admiral and Tom, and Vera and his mother, and joining his ship. The feeling of liberation from a great weight grew until he realised he was dominating the conversation and stopped abruptly.

'Oh, I'm sorry, I'm being an awful bore.'

'No, no, lad, you talk it out of yourself,' Bawden said.

It came to him that he had stopped his narrative before those last terrible seconds of the explosion.

'No, it's not . . .' He flushed.

'D'you think fisher-folk haven't spent most of their lives at war, James?' said Mrs Bawden softly, gathering up the plates. 'We know horrors aplenty without the need for a Kaiser.'

'What happened to Tom?' asked Stella and Mrs Bawden paused.

James turned to the girl. 'He was lost when the ship exploded. These three shells hit the ship and' – he swallowed hard, unable to take his eyes off Stella's face, as though looking at her made it easier to remember – 'she just blew up.'

The silence that greeted these words was broken as Mrs Bawden resumed clearing the table.

'It must have been terrible for you,' Stella said, rising to help her mother. James stood too, aware that at The Reddings a maid would have attended to the matter. 'No, please sit down,' Stella said, adding, 'have you told your mother you're all right?'

'No, I haven't.'

'Because of Tom?'

31

'Yes.' His thoughtlessness shamed him from this sudden exposure.

'The lad's had enough on his mind, Stella,' said Bawden. 'Help your mother wi' dishes, lass.'

'No,' said James, 'Stella's quite right . . . but I don't know what news has been released about the battle. They kept me rather in the dark on the guardship.'

'Well, there's some say it's a national scandal and there's talk about a defeat. It seems we lost six thousand men.'

'*Six thousand?*' James drew in his breath; the number was incomprehensible. 'Six thousand! What about the enemy?'

Bawden shrugged. 'Estimates say it can't be much more than two thousand, though don't ask how they know these things.'

The women rejoined them with a steaming pudding. 'It's my husband's favourite, James. Figgy duff.'

'Helps keep cold out,' said Bawden grinning, and dismissing talk of battle casualties from his table.

'I think we should telegram your mother,' said Stella.

'Why don't you take James down to the General Post Office, Stella?'

'And then station?' Bawden cocked an eye at James as he spooned duff off his plate.

'I, er . . . that six-pounder of yours, Mr Bawden, when did your gunners last strip it down? I mean I could take a look at it.'

'Know sommat about six-pounders, do 'ee then?'

'I was captain of one on the training cruiser.'

'How did you make out?'

'Top.'

Bawden nodded and held out his bowl for a second helping of duff. 'Sleep on board then.'

James sighed with relief. The telegram would release him from an immediate obligation to go home and confront the Admiral, and his mother would know that he himself was alive. He stole a glance at Stella and found her watching him.

'If you've finished, I'll take you to the post office.'

'Let the lad have a cup o' tea.'

'No, it's quite all right.' James rose from the table and thanked Mrs Bawden.

'You'll be welcome back for a bite of supper,' she said.

32

'Aye, you'll find ship a bit quiet in harbour.' Bawden reached for his pipe and tobacco jar, clearly enjoying a different routine at home.

When the young couple had gone, he and his wife exchanged looks.

'Don't be silly, woman,' Bawden said, emitting smoke so that the flame of the spill danced up and down, 'they're nobbut children.'

'They weren't looking at each other like children,' Mrs Bawden cautioned as she bustled round the table. 'And we were that age when . . .'

Bawden shook the spill to extinction and replaced it in the pot over the range.

'I don't want *that* happening to Stella,' he growled.

'You didna mind it happening to me.'

'Don't be daft, lass; you didn't have an admiral in the family.'

'No.'

Bawden rounded on his wife. 'Now don't let that give you ideas, Meg. Men like him don't marry girls like our Stell', but they're not beyond gettin 'em into trouble.'

'I thought you liked the lad.'

'I do.'

'This war's going to change a lot of things,' she said curtly. 'Now come and dry the dishes.'

'Was it very terrible?'

They were walking back from the post office where Stella had demonstrated a marvellous practicality in drafting the telegram. Her presence had confused him, for immersion and hospitalisation following the traumatic explosion of the *Indefatigable* had suppressed the unavoidable and omnipresent desire that dominates the thoughts of young men. Stella had reawakened it with a wrench that was almost painfully intense. As she had bent over the yellow form he had studied the down on her cheek and the form of her hand; he had caught the scent of her dark hair and all but reached out to touch the soft curve of her breast as he threw off the last physical effects of his ordeal.

And now the question sought unwittingly to remove the mental scars, for it was prompted by a genuine concern that showed in the strange green eyes regarding him from under the brim of her hat as they walked slowly back towards the Anlaby Road. For Stella's instinctive sympathy asked the question that Surgeon Lieutenant Wilmott's gropingly clumsy professionalism had failed to find; but even if Wilmott had found it, James Martin could not have answered a man as he now did a woman.

'Yes, terrible. When the ship exploded I've no idea what really happened to me. I know I was thrown clear and fell in the sea, but I don't remember it. All I can remember clearly is a feeling that I had lost my soul.' He paused, stopping her, then walking on again. 'No, that isn't right . . . I felt my soul had lost my body. Do you understand? I mean I felt my body and my soul had separated.'

'You felt you were dying?'

He stopped again, his hand catching her so she too stopped and they faced each other. Impulsively he grasped both her shoulders, unaware that his eyes were full of tears.

'No. I felt I *should* have died, can you understand? I *should* have died and not survived.'

'You mean,' she said, frowning but accepting the burden of his confidence without flinching, 'you don't feel lucky escaping with your life?'

'No,' he said with a sudden vehement bitterness, 'I don't feel lucky at all . . . except in meeting you.' He hesitated, torn between the opportunity this unexpected moment of intimacy offered to kiss her or to explain a greater and perplexing emotion. 'Apart from that, I feel damned!'

'Poor James,' she said, touching his cheek lightly with her fingers.

CHAPTER THREE
HMS *Iroquois*

'In transit, sir,' James reported from the after bridge.

'Steady as you go,' ordered the Captain.

'Steady as you go, sir,' replied the man at the wheel.

'Revs for sixteen knots, Sub,' said the Captain, leaning on the canvas covered bridge rail, his unlit pipe curling down from his mouth, his bridge coat collar turned up as the wind and swell met them at the Tyne Piers.

Acting Sublieutenant James Martin kept his professional eye on the two square white towers of the leading lights, while his artist's eye stole a glance at the huge statue of Admiral Lord Collingwood and the ruined arches of Tynemouth Abbey to the north. Astern, the river wound a grey thread into a backcloth of monotones. Then, as the long lean ship trembled slightly to the increase of speed and her three black funnels belched even blacker clouds of smoke, the two squat granite towers of the pier lighthouses swept past and HMS *Iroquois* was at sea.

'Steer north eighty east.' The Captain, a lieutenant commander of the Royal Naval Reserve, having acknowledged the helmsman's acceptance of the order, straightened from the rail and cast his eye over the destroyer's tiny, cramped compass platform.

'Well, Sub, think you can take her? Visibility's not too good, 'bout a mile and a half, but I'll put my hat on a breeze before the evening. Course north eighty east.'

'Very well, sir. North eighty east.'

The Captain lingered a moment, standing at the top of the ladder and staring astern. North and South Shields faded into a misty blur. James Martin knew the Captain had said goodbye to his wife in a cheap hotel only that morning.

'Keep a good lookout, Sub, especially for fishing boats and periscopes.'

'Aye, aye, sir.'

But already the Captain had gone with a squeal of his hands on the steel rails of the steep ladder. He would be back shortly, to doze in a deck chair while the *Iroquois* made a sweep east and south, chasing a reported sighting of a U-boat. Acting Sublieutenant James Martin checked the lookouts, closed the voice-pipe to the engine room and settled down to the routine business of watch-keeping.

There had been something fateful in his appointment to *Iroquois*, the same ship he had witnessed commissioned at his uncle's coat-tails all those years earlier. And yet there was a kind of satisfaction in the matter, a kind of providential sanction that helped ease the guilt of his survival from *Indefatigable*. Even the association with his uncle, coming as it did with the tragedy of the old man's sudden death, seemed almost symbolic, a handing over of the torch of family tradition across the unrecovered corpse of cousin Tom.

As he swept the mistily indistinct horizon with the heavy Barr and Stroud binoculars, his mind's eye conjured up the awful scenes of his eventual homecoming.

Vera had met him, gaunt and no longer girlish, but dry-eyed with grief in a house that seemed to James – nursing the double guilt of survival and love for Stella – to be awash with tears. Aunt Anne's tears and wails filled the summer stillness of the nights as he had lain unsleeping in his bed. The maid's snuffles had filled the days and his mother's tears, compounded by relief at her own son's restoration, had torn from himself sobs of relief and sadness for Tom and their lost boyhood.

Worst had been the Admiral's weeping. Vera had told James the Admiral had hardly said a word since the news came from the Admiralty, but had spent his days uncharacteristically collarless in his rose garden, tended only by Ferris.

'You had better wait in the study while I go and tell him you are home,' Vera had said, leaving James by the French windows, watching Vera's long skirt sway across the lawn until she bent beside the Admiral.

He looked up, caught on one knee, his paring knife

36

reflecting the glare of sunlight, like an ancient knight awaiting investiture. Ferris leaned forward to help him to his feet, then Vera followed, two steps behind, as the Admiral approached the house.

James fell back into the shadows of the study, his heart pounding. He heard the Admiral's steps upon the terrace and then his breathing and saw the bulk of him blocking the open windows.

'James, my boy?' The old man's voice was uncertain, his eyes still adjusting from the brightness outside.

'Here, sir.' He stepped forward.

'Where have you been?' There was reproach in the Admiral's voice, reproach for his tardy return home and reproach for his surviving Tom.

'They kept me on the Humber guardship, sir, the *St George*. They thought I might be a Boche spy.'

He might have added he was medically unfit to travel, but he traded that excuse in his conscience for not mentioning the three days he had lingered as unofficial gunnery expert in HM Trawler *Girl Stella*.

The Admiral sighed and shook his head. He poured himself a drink and, with his back to James, asked, 'How did it happen?'

James told him. About the impetuous hunt of Beatty's ships; about sighting the Germans and the long range fire; about the speed with which the enemy got their range and then the three shells and his brief glimpse of the armoured roof of A turret, Tom's station, spinning in a cartwheel through the air; and then the whole bloody ship going up in a shattering explosion. At the word 'bloody' the old man turned, then poured and held out a drink to his nephew. James had the odd feeling that the word and the gesture admitted him to the company of grown men.

'We heard,' the Admiral said, clearing his throat, 'that a Midshipman Martin had been picked up.'

The tactless implication of the remark stabbed James like a wound. Without saying 'then we found out it was only you,' the Admiral went on:

'I made enquiries. Two other men from *Indefatigable* were picked up.'

'I didn't know, sir.'

37

'They are prisoners in Germany.'

James felt no relief at the news: they might as well be dead. 'He cannot have known anything about it, sir,' he said.

'No.'

That evening James, his mother, aunt and Vera sat down to dine without the Admiral. An oppressive silence hung over the table until the sharp, intrusive crack. They found the old man stretched on the terrace clutching a tattered white ensign. He had shot himself.

Iroquois had proved a welcome haven after the distress of the hurried funeral. Vera had seen him off and he could not stand the reproach he read in her eyes. He was not himself even sure that the Admiralty's acting commission as sublieutenant had been addressed to the right Midshipman Martin RN.

But the *Iroquois*, though she too provided reminders of Tom, was closely linked in his imagination with his own boyhood. Sent north to her builders for repairs after a night action with German destroyers off the Belgian coast, James had found the old ship in dry dock. Streaked with the rust of hard service and the red lead of new plating, she was a mess of dockyard confusion and disordered neglect with two thirds of her crew on leave. Her captain, whose peace-time occupation had been Chief Officer of one of Alfred Holt's Blue Funnel liners, was philosophic about it, but First Lieutenant Ennis, a bright, young 'straight-striper' from the regular Navy like James himself, rushed futilely about the ship, maddened by the stone-walling of the dockyard mateys and the soothing dismissals of the bowler-hatted Geordie foremen.

'Doan you worry, Mister; she'll be arl reet in a day or twa.'

And so she proved, her scars patched and painted, her boilers cleaned and rebricked, with a hundred tons of best Northumbrian steam coal in her bunkers, she sliced eastwards into darkness and the rising wind her captain had predicted.

James lay in his bunk, the fear of the dream still sweating out of him. He reached over and switched on the single, naked electric light that illuminated the tiny cabin. He had rarely slept more than two hours at a stretch since the explosion of the *Indefatigable*. Except, he thought, turning his mind with

38

an effort away from remembered horrors, when he had slept on the *Girl Stella* and dreamed of her skipper's daughter. He tried to concentrate on other things, but Stella's image would prevent him sleeping again. He turned on his side and stared at the small watercolour stuck on the steel bulkhead. It showed HMS *Iroquois* alongside in the Tyne.

He was proud of the little painting, the assiduously laid on washes, pale in the distance, a broken horizon and chimney pots and roof gables and splodges of smoke; gradually gaining tone as the terraces crowded down to the river where, in the foreground, on a slab of water that echoed the slight glow of the sky, the low black hull of the TBD cast its own reflections. He had enjoyed painting it, despite the fact that it had cost a shilling to bribe a foy boatman to pull him across the river. It was a kind of act of homage to that boyhood memory of Tyneside as being an epitome of England, an epitome somehow inimical to the England of The Reddings.

He rolled over, switched off the light and settled down to sleep again. He felt an affinity for the ship too; she was small and human sized, and could scarcely prove more vulnerable than the massive, futile *Indefatigable*. Her long hull trembled as it rose and fell, staggering periodically as the flare of the bow thrust a wave aside. *She* had survived a shell in her boiler room; she was all right. A good ship . . .

He was finally sliding into sleep when the alarms crashed into his consciousness, summoning *Iroquois*'s company to action stations. James thrust his feet into his boots and seconds later felt the midnight chill of the upper deck as he stumbled forward to the forecastle four-inch gun. Pulling the anti-flash hood over his head he counted heads, pale figures gathered round the single-barrelled mounting.

'Gun's crew closed up, sir.' The grey figure loomed up to him.

'Edwards?'

'Who else, sir?'

Edwards's cheekily amusing insolence was typical of the camaraderie of a small ship, a mild rebuke for his own stupidity. Edwards was at action stations with his false teeth removed. The tone of his voice was very different from that of the smart matelot whose impeccable grin set Geordie dance halls a-twinkle.

39

'Forward four-inch closed up, sir,' he shouted into the voice-pipe, and heard the First Lieutenant's cool acknowledgement. Then the Captain's voice buzzed tinnily in his ear. 'Sub?'

'Sir?'

'We've had another report of a periscope, about five miles away. May be nothing, but we're going to investigate. Might need you in a hurry, so load AP and stand by. If I get the chance to ram . . . well, you know what to do.'

'Aye, aye, sir.'

James relayed the gist of the Captain's instruction and the armour piercing shell was thrust into the gun's breech. The block closed with a sharp clang.

'If we go in to ram . . .'

'We'll run like hell, sir, don't worry.'

'It's probably a bloody whale spouting; those Merchant jacks get jittery every time a seagull shits in the sea.'

'What would you know about it, Tosher? Or does falling out of the liberty boat make you a submarine expert?'

A low laugh ran round the gun mounting. Tosher Hughes, a whiningly abrasive man in his forties, had been on First Lieutenant's report, not for the drunkenness that had caused his loss of balance but 'for acting in an unseamanlike manner', a far greater crime in the eyes of the Captain. It would have been very different in a battle cruiser, and James felt himself warm again to the little ship as they settled to wait. He felt so much more at home here than in the impersonal bulk of the *Indefatigable*, less under the influence of Tom's ghost.

James craned round the gun shield to stare at the horizon. Already the summer dawn lit the sky and the horizon showed sharp, its regularity broken by the jagged silhouettes of four fishing vessels. He thought briefly of Bawden and then, inevitably of Stella, and was caught in a sudden burst of spray as the ship increased speed and leapt with great bounds from wave crest to wave crest.

'Bugger'll be gone now. Heard us coming and scarpered,' remarked Edwards with the fatalistic resignation of long-service experience.

'Must be doing thirty-three knots,' James replied, dodging back behind the gun shield.

40

'Think of the poor bleedin' stokers, sir, when you're up there ringing on the revs.'

James grinned. 'Unlike you to worry about the black gang.'

'I could murder a cup of kye.'

The thought of hot, sweet cocoa was unbelievably seductive as they waited at their stations. James listened to the idle chatter of the ratings.

'I was dreamin' about that bit of fluff you was with, Dusty, back in Shields.'

'You cheeky sod.'

'She was all over me. Said she didn't really fancy you.'

'Ha! *You* was only dreamin'.'

'She said 'er old man 'ad 'eard about you and was comin' ter get you.'

'Thank Gawd you was only dreamin'.'

Rank upon rank of wave crests ran down towards them as the easterly wind came, in the North Seaman's expression, 'up with the sun'. *Iroquois*'s sharp bow rose, then dipped slicing through them. The fishing boats were on the beam now and *Iroquois* leaned under helm as her commander took her round to the south-eastwards in a long curve. The sun, distorted by refraction, rose redly, dragging itself clear of the horizon with an elongation of its lower limb.

'See anyfink, sir?' asked Ordinary Seaman Goodrich, a sharp-mouthed, thin Cockney lad with a curious upturned nose which had earned him the soubriquet Pinocchio.

'Only an awful lot of sea, Goodrich,' replied James, ducking another shower of stinging spray. From behind the gun shield they could see the drifters falling astern. Ahead the sea lay like a grey waste. For a further half an hour they stood south-east at speed, then the Captain ordered the revs cut. *Iroquois* slowed, swinging northwards on a half-hearted search that everyone now knew was fruitless.

'Fucking U-boats,' said Edwards succinctly.

Then they heard the lookout's cry and the staccato command in the open voice-pipe's bell-mouth:

'Train right twenty, maximum depression!'

With racing heart James relayed the order. The relaxed attitudes of the gun crew disappeared in an instant. The training handles were manned and with a jerk the mounting

41

slewed on its axis, the breech rose as the barrel dropped and the men crouched expectantly.

'Check! Check! Check!'

The tense figures relaxed with a deflating exhalation of held breath and whispered swearing.

'Sub?'

'Sir?' James bent to the voice-pipe and the Captain's voice.

'We thought we'd seen a conning tower. It's two boats of survivors. Leave your gun crew closed up and take some torpedo men amidships. Get a couple of nets over the side.'

'Aye, aye, sir.'

The two boats came into view under the flare of *Iroquois*'s bow as James leaned over the starboard side and made sure the nets hung clear. Their contents were a pitiful sight, men shivering in the cold despite the season, in singlets and drawers, men ejected from their bunks in the last hours of the night.

'How long since you saw the U-boat?' asked the Captain through a megaphone as the boats crabbed under the bridge.

'Disappeared to the east on the surface a couple of hours back,' a figure at the helm of the second boat shouted back. He was a grey-haired man with a blue gaberdine raincoat over maroon and white striped pyjamas. The next twenty minutes were occupied in assisting the survivors up the ship's side. As the empty lifeboats drifted astern and *Iroquois* turned under increased engine revolutions, the man in the sodden striped pyjamas introduced himself.

'Captain Millar, Master of the *Jedburgh Abbey* of Newcastle.'

'Come and meet the Captain, sir.'

'Glad to see you, Captain,' Millar said.

'Glad to see *you*, Captain Millar. Last time we met –'

'The Jockey Club, Shanghai.'

'Three places lower than you,' said Lieutenant Commander Young, shaking the offered hand. 'Now what about this U-boat?'

'He'll be thirty miles away by now. He surfaced and shelled us; shelled us while we took to the boats, then put a torpedo into the old girl.' Millar suddenly became pensive, mourning his ship. 'I'd been in her since she was built, on the Wear.'

'I'm sorry.'

Millar came to himself. 'I'm forgetting. I've got a couple of men injured, splinters. Have you a doctor on board?'

'I've something that calls himself a surgeon probationer.'

'He'll do. I'll go and find him.'

'Then find my steward, Captain. He'll give you something to wear. We can't have Abbey Line masters improperly dressed aboard here.'

The two men grinned, the easy informality of the Merchant Marine a support to them, for *Iroquois* had failed in her hunt and the enemy had sunk a ship. To the watching James it seemed an odd way to cope with defeat.

For eighteen months *Iroquois* beat about the North Sea in so fruitless a manner as to insinuate the doubt that the Royal Navy was not pulling its weight. Casualties in Flanders mounted steadily and the U-boats struck with impunity, despite the top secret 'mystery ships' that were rumoured to have provided the counter-stroke to the submarine. Judging by food shortages and whispered merchant ship losses, there were either insufficient numbers of them or they were overrated.

Not that *Iroquois* was idle, far from it. In a confused night action with an unknown number of enemy destroyers off the Weser estuary, James learned the unfortunate fact that the hellishly evocative stink of cordite made him sick; he also learned that Zeppelins were difficult to shoot down and they had more luck with a lone *Albatros* biplane which was jointly claimed by *Iroquois* and the next ship astern in the flotilla of destroyers the aeroplane was casually reconnoitring. At midsummer, supposedly synchronous to some mighty offensive to the south, they escorted four monitors in a bombardment of enemy positions inland, beyond the low, grey line of the Flemish coast. The shoal draft hulls of the monitors wallowed like half-tide rocks, their incongruous guns in enormous turrets mounted on tall barbettes better suited to battleships. The offensive earned the allies two hundred yards of shell-churned earth and an extra three hundred thousand names for the roll of the glorious dead.

By the early autumn of 1917 *Iroquois* was in dock, blown down for a boiler clean and a bottom scrape, a routine that took her not to the Tyne, nor to Hull as James secretly prayed, but to Chatham and the Royal Naval Dockyard that was even less caring about ageing TBDs than Geordie shipyards.

'As you're too young for women,' Geoffrey Ennis, the First Lieutenant announced to James, 'this is a jolly good chance for you to see what a dockyard can do.'

'I didn't think you approved of dockyards, sir,' James replied.

'I don't; that's why I'm taking a spot of leave.'

'I might develop a taste for women, sir.'

'You might develop something else if you knock about with some of those hereabouts. Isn't that right, Oakley?'

The Gunnery Officer looked up. 'If you say so, Number One. I wouldn't know.'

Ennis made a face at the gunner, smiled at James and went to pack. James followed him from the wardroom, sat in his cabin and wrote to Stella.

Their correspondence had been fitful and stilted, but it had withstood the separation and had lost an early, groping sterility. It offered James a lifeline that he clung to desperately. The harsh regimen of sleepless sorties and somnolent harbour 'rest' periods that formed the routine of the destroyer patrols had gradually cured him of his insomnia. The bad dreams faded, and only the smell of cordite had the power to unman him. He was unable to throw this off, but his men were roughly kind to him, for he was a survivor of the *Indefatigable* and looked on as a good-luck charm. He did not appreciate this, for it was the antithesis to his own view of himself.

Although he had saved his meagre pay and made plans to go north to see Stella, he was glad enough of the excuse of duty to avoid going home to The Reddings. Since the death of the Admiral normal life there had ceased. Aunt Anne, distraught at the loss of Tom, had become unhinged upon the suicide of her husband. James's mother was having a wretched time, while Vera had retreated into herself. There was talk of having to sell the house, talk of having to commit Aunt Anne to an institution and talk of 'reduced circumstances'. A waspishly recriminating letter from Vera had persuaded James he was better off where he was, so he accepted Lieutenant Ennis's order with equanimity.

At the end of a week, out of dock and lying alongside a corner of Number Three Basin, a serious fault had been found in the after boiler.

'Another week by the look of it, Sub,' said the Captain cheerfully, as he prepared to rejoin his wife in her hotel. 'I've telegrammed the First Lieutenant and told him not to hurry back. It'll be good experience for you. You've done very well.'

'Thank you, sir.'

Young lit his pipe. 'We mustn't let Number One feel indispensable, you know. I've telephoned the doc,' he added from the side of his puffing mouth, 'he's taking the few extra days too.'

James nodded philosophically. Deprivation of the society of the surgeon left him only the company of Oakley, the gunner, from among the wardroom officers. Oakley was in fact a torpedo specialist, an older, embittered and solitary officer for whom James had no particular liking.

In the following days there was little for James to do. The ship was ready for sea apart from the damage to her boiler tubes. This, being part of the esoteric mystery of the engine room, was the province of the Tiffy, or Chief Engine Room Artificer, and James was kept in the traditional dark. Of course the Chief ERA reported daily, obfuscating his report in carefully selected technicalities James strove to understand. He kept himself busy by his rounds, chivvying the duty bosun's mate into licking the upper decks into a semblance of their pre-war, yacht-like order and painting out the heads. In the evenings he sat reading or drawing in the wardroom while *Iroquois* lay ignored in a corner of the basin. The odd visits from other ships' officers dried up when they learned that the ship-keepers were a crusty Gunner (T) and a wet-eared sub who dabbled in painting. There were no free drinks, no parties to be had aboard *Iroquois*.

One evening, shortly after the shrill pipe of the still and the descending note of the carry-on had pierced the calm autumn air and the ceremony of sunset had marked the end of the working day for the ships lying in the dockyard, the gunner invited him ashore.

'Fancy a drink, Sub?'

James looked up from his book. Oakley stood in the

wardroom doorway in civilian clothes. His face wore an expression of lonely supplication. James smiled, closed his book with a snap and got up.

'Why not? Give me five minutes.'

'Don't go ashore much,' volunteered Oakley as they walked through the dockyard gate and headed for Military Road where the bright lights of public house saloons splashed out over the pavement. 'But I like a few drinks before we go off to sea again.'

'Yes,' James agreed insincerely.

'You've got a girl, haven't you? I've seen you reading her letters.'

'Yes.' He did not want to gossip about Stella. He had not told Vera about her, let alone his mother. They would not have approved. Martins did not marry trawler skippers' daughters. Besides, it had scarcely seemed appropriate to mention any kind of future happiness in the gloom of The Reddings.

'Don't get married,' said Oakley, preoccupied with his own thoughts and hinting at the roots of his misanthropy. James thought guiltily of his mother.

'This'll do.'

Oakley turned in through a pub doorway. The upper panel was frosted glass and a hubbub of noise greeted them, along with a gust of stale air.

They elbowed their way to the bar. James had found he enjoyed the warm, demotic atmosphere of public houses. No great lover of ale, he had learned to drink it in those few short days in Hull when he stripped down *Girl Stella*'s six-pounder pop-gun and bought the cooperation of her resentful gunners with a pint or two of the stuff. The evenings with Stella had been worth the acquisition of a bad habit.

But it was the cheerfulness and the noise he truly enjoyed, in spite of the fact that much of the bonhomie was false and its deterioration into violence frequent. His youth and obvious social class usually protected him, though once he had been asked what an officer was doing in such a place. The maternal intervention of the barmaid had saved him. She had given him a leering smile and told him, with a rolling eye, that it was all right by her if he stayed all night.

46

He had thanked her politely and avoided that particular pub again, but the incident had etched itself into his imagination and he had considered what it would have been like had he been braver.

Oakley thrust a glass into his hand, said 'Cheers', and swallowed half a pint at a gulp. Oakley, too, seemed happy in the gay, proletarian surroundings. He suppressed a belch, leaned his back upon the bar and regarded the throng.

There was another group of officers disguised in mufti in defiance of regulations, but no one would bother them with the insulting white feather, nor take them for conscientious objectors. 'Conchies' did not invite trouble in the public houses of Chatham. The rest of the clientele were ratings and marines, too busy in the pursuit of oblivion or women to object, this early in the evening, to a handful of officers wetting their whistles.

'Bloody war's changed a lot,' remarked Oakley, draining his glass and nodding at a corner table. For a moment James thought the gunner, like himself, was ruminating on their breaking of regulations; but the two women at the table were a more obvious source for Oakley's remark.

'Perhaps they are on the game,' he said. Oakley turned to the bar and slammed his glass down. James refilled it for him. 'They don't look it,' he added; for all his innocence he was by now well able to identify a whore when he saw one.

'No, but they don't look like fish out of water either,' Oakley said sagely.

James furtively studied them. They were about nineteen or twenty years old and wore coats and hats. The nearer of the two sported a fur tippet. She had a fine-boned face and toyed with her glass in a detached way that suggested aloofness, though her eyes, shadowed by the sloping brim of her hat, watched the crowd closer to the bar. Her glance passed over him, then returned to stare. He felt the force of a predatory nature and it thrilled him with a prickling response so that, blushing, he picked up his refilled glass and laughed louder than was necessary at some ribaldry Oakley made.

He dared a second look, only to find her still staring at him. He hesitated, then swigged his beer, meeting her insolent gaze over its rim. He felt a small sense of triumph as she spoke to her companion; the two laughed and the fur collar rippled with the lift of her shoulders. Then she looked directly at him, robbing him of his assurance.

Confused he said to Oakley, 'Tiffy says he'll be finished in a couple of days.'

But Oakley was not listening. He stared unashamedly at the two women. James experienced a wave of relief. The unspoken conversation had been directed not at himself but at his older neighbour.

'Bugger Tiffy,' said Oakley, 'come on.'

James felt the gunner's hand beneath his elbow and the distance between bar and table vanished. There were two empty bentwood chairs and Oakley was drawing one back.

'Do you mind if we join you? I'm David and this is Jim.'

The two women shrugged and silently indicated that it was a matter of supreme indifference to them. James sat next to Oakley, between the gunner and the woman with the fox-fur collar. She was extraordinarily good looking in a conventional English way, he thought, with light brown hair, fine drawn features and a square jaw. Her blue eyes regarded James with a mixture of curiosity and amusement. He coughed awkwardly. Resting her chin on one white hand, she moved her empty glass imperceptibly forward with the other. James took the hint.

'Would you like a drink?' he asked, escaping to the bar with a sense of relief. Waiting to be served he risked a single glance over his shoulder. Oakley was deep in conversation with the ginger-haired woman, whom James had almost ignored. Fox-fur was swinging her foot and watching him so that he felt again that thrill of danger and fear that drew him back like a magnet.

'Jim's our hero,' Oakley said with a familiarity that presumed long and intimate friendship and indicated he had revealed they were both naval officers.

'Oh, I wouldn't say that,' James spluttered, aware of the mockery in Fox-fur's expression.

'Really?' she said in a cool, well-spoken voice.

'Yes; he escaped when the *Indefatigable* blew up at Jutland.'

'For God's sake . . .' James wanted no reminder of that apolcalyptic event, especially at such a moment as this.

'So you're a survivor, are you?' He thought the disdain had gone out of her voice. The blue eyes regarded him with a new interest. 'It shows . . .'

She sipped her drink, leaving the enigmatic remark hanging between them, as though it was a sufficient reason for her bold appraisal earlier. Oakley turned again to Ginger. She had a fleshy attractiveness, in contrast to the fine-boned looks of Fox-fur.

'What d'you mean?' James asked, emboldened by the beer.

She shrugged and set down her drink. 'Survival can be a painful business,' she said, compounding the riddle. She was gazing down at her drink, turning it slowly round as though it was a clairvoyant's crystal. An intuitive suspicion crossed his mind; there was something of Vera's brittle grief in her manner now.

'I'm sorry.'

She looked up sharply, her eyes bright. 'Why should you be sorry? It's the war. I just wish' – she paused and looked round the bar – 'that people didn't act as though it was enjoyable.'

'Yes,' he said, feeling hopelessly out of his depth, just as he had done at The Reddings. 'Were you married?'

'No. Engaged.'

'Was he in the army?'

She nodded and drained her glass, expelling her breath, her eyes half closed and he saw the shadow over her.

'I am sorry,' he repeated, and found his fingertips touching the skin of her wrist as she toyed again with the glass. She suddenly grasped his hand; the faintly mocking expression was back in place, her voice cool and self-possessed. As she spoke she let go of him.

'What ship did your friend say you were from?'

'Oh, the *Iroquois*, an old destroyer,' he said, disappointed the conversation threatened to become mundane. 'Are you doing war work?'

She gave a short laugh which showed a prettiness about her mouth. 'You could say that.'

He frowned, slightly irritated that she had dismissed the brief moment of intimacy and resorted to patronising him. 'Is that amusing?'

49

She sighed. 'No. It's not amusing.' She sat back as though deciding something. 'What's your name?'

'James Martin. And yours?'

'Emily Plunkett.' He almost laughed; such remote women did not have names like Plunkett, surely. 'I'm a nurse. I've been with the army in France. I'm on leave, just for a few days. Angela, my cousin' – she indicated Ginger opposite – 'lives in Rochester and I'm staying with her. It's too far for me to get home.'

'And you don't want to go.'

'How did you know that?'

'Had a similar experience myself. My cousin was killed when my ship blew up; I was scared stiff of facing them at home. You see, I lived with him. My mother's a widow and we all lived together. He was like a brother.'

'It must have been awful.'

'No worse than being in the trenches.'

'No, probably not. The whole thing's hideous. I never knew what Dr Johnson meant by patriotism being the last refuge of scoundrels, but I'd like to put some of the incompetent fools who engineered this war into the front line for five minutes.'

'*Engineered?* You think the war was engineered?'

'Of course! There's no logical reason why half the population of Europe should want to wipe out the other half.'

James considered the novelty of this point of view. It was unfamiliar in the gunrooms of the fleet which had recognised the inevitability of a test of strength with the Imperial German Navy on *Der Tag*, the Day, as Surgeon Lieutenant Wilmott had called it. Had that 'inevitability' truly been a matter of engineering, as Emily suggested?

'What else is an arms race but engineering? To make battleships you have to make the conditions for their existence. Metaphorically and literally the argument holds good.'

'You're not a pacifist or a suffragette are you?' James regretted the words as soon as he spoke them. The steel glint in her eyes was intimidating.

'If you're asking whether I believe in peace and votes for women, what do you think?'

'I'm sorry, I had no right . . .' He floundered in confusion, glancing at Oakley and seeing no rescue there, he and Angela being deep in self-absorption. He found it impossible to guess what they were talking about. 'Is your cousin a nurse too?'

'Yes.' She seemed disinterested now he had revealed his gauche inexperience. He found he profoundly regretted her loss of attention. Her eyes wandered round the bar.

'D'you smoke?' he offered, wanting to re-establish contact with her.

'Occasionally.'

He pulled out the packet of cigarettes he had taken to carrying around. As she bent over the lighter flame he said, 'I'm sorry. I didn't mean to walk rough-shod over your sensibilities.'

She blew a plume of blue smoke out and smiled. 'My sensibilities, eh? That's a pretty speech for a place like this.'

'I meant it, though.'

'Well, well . . .'

He watched her lips round the cigarette and felt the erotic tug of her. Suddenly she stubbed out the cigarette, picked up a pair of gloves and stood.

'James and I are going for a walk,' she announced to Angela and Oakley. 'Don't miss the last bus, Angie.'

Outside, a chill breeze had risen. Emily thrust her arm into James's and began to walk purposefully towards Chatham Hill. A tram rumbled past them, leaving its trail of noise to emphasise the silence between them. He did not ask where they were going; the beer and Emily's urgent tug on his crooked arm made him breathlessly reckless. She drew him uphill until they reached the grounds of the naval hospital.

Emily stopped in the shadow of a laurel bush and turned towards him, pushing herself against him.

'Kiss me.'

He felt her arms round him, and sensed that predatory hunger with which she had first set eyes upon him. Their lips brushed, brushed again, and then he felt her probing tongue and surrendered, his desire rigidly apparent. She drew back and he thought he had offended her, but she tugged at her coat, opened it and thrust herself forward again.

51

He could feel her body now, the soft resistance of her breasts, the low mound of her belly pushing against him with a gentle rhythm. His hands went round her back, pulling her towards him with a sudden access of passion so that he forsook her mouth and moaned into her hair, his mind a blur of images and impressions. He felt her mouth on his neck and earlobe and became slowly aware that she was trying to say something.

They were leaning back into the laurel bush and his hands were on her breasts now, his heart leaping with delight, for they were breasts such as young men dream of and through the fabric he could feel a delicate tumescence to match his own awkward engorgement.

'Your coat, James, your coat . . .'

They were down on the grass, with the dry scrunch of fallen laurel leaves, drawn apart for a moment in order that they might couple more effectively. Fox fur and Burberry lay under them as Emily loosened her dress and James tore at his trousers. He felt her knees grip his flanks as he lowered himself, stabbing with clumsy urgency at her.

'Gently, my darling,' she whispered, the endearment sealing an intimacy which seemed to him, in that frantic moment, to make significant their hasty lovemaking. He felt her hand cool on him, guiding his inexpertise while she enclosed him and they moved as one until it was over.

She half rolled him off her so that, shrivelling, he slithered from her and they were apart again.

'Who is Stella?' she asked, and he knew from her voice that she was crying.

'Oh, God, I'm sorry,' he said, pushing himself up on one elbow.

'Please stop apologising. You've no need to. I used you as much as you used me.'

'But I love you.'

She sniffed back her tears and began to laugh. He could see the low undulations of her stomach. 'Oh, James,' she said, 'I'd just given you credit for being a man and you turn out to be a boy after all.'

He would have felt stupid, even motivated to reply angrily, but she reached up and pulled his head down and kissed him with a tenderness he did not expect.

52

'What do you think I was doing in a place like that pub? You have been John to me . . . only John could not have done that in the last week of his life, poor devil.'

James dully made sense of what she was saying.

'I don't mind being Stella.'

He became aware of the incongruity of their surroundings and the chill breeze from the south-east. The trams rumbled with a curious persistence.

'Can you hear them?' Emily asked as she sat up and began to straighten her dress.

'Hear them?' he asked uncertainly.

'The guns.'

CHAPTER FOUR
The Convoy

'*Longbow* signalling, sir.'

James had already spotted the stuttering dot of light from the low silhouette of the senior officer's destroyer. Out on the starboard wing of the convoy with a pale feather at her dark bow, she cut back across the path of the sluggish merchant ships. The duty Yeoman had received half the signal before he got Lieutenant Commander Young awake out of his deck chair.

'Smoke sighted to southward, stop, investigate, stop.'

The Captain groaned. 'Very well, acknowledge, Yeoman. Ring on full speed, Sub.'

'Aye, aye, sir.' James bent to the wheelhouse voice-pipe. 'Full speed ahead!' The distant jangle of telegraphs was followed by a blacker emission from their three funnels as Young took his ship in a tight circle, then across the rear of the convoy, a dozen ships of neutral and British nationality, wallowing westwards from the Naze of Norway with cargoes of iron ore and other raw materials.

Wearily Young lifted his binoculars. 'I wonder what bright spark spotted smoke on a night as dark as this?'

No one answered the Captain's rhetorical question. Instead James asked, 'Action stations, sir?'

'No,' replied Young, his glasses sweeping the horizon ahead, 'let the watch below get a bit more kip . . . what about a cup of kye for those of us who are up, eh?'

The cocoa when it came was hot, sweet and fortifying. *Iroquois* was making thirty knots in a moderate sea, her long lean hull cleaving the waves, her stern settled well down with a huge white tail rearing up behind her while the bow waves fanned out on either side. Astern, she left a triple streak upon the black sea. It was bitterly cold, a freezing midwinter night of brilliant starlight. To the north the faintly luminous aurora traced a lambent curtain across the sky. James joined the Captain at the rail, his glasses sweeping the horizon, his eyes focused just above its line so his retinae might catch the merest irregularity.

'Can't see a bloody thing, can you?'

'No, sir.' He swept back again, still nothing; reversed the sweep, this time traversing more to the east of south. 'Yes, sir; four points to port, maybe five. One, two, three . . .'

James swallowed hard. He had seen something like that before, those tiny pyramids under their canopy of smoke. He heard the Captain's sharp intake of breath. He too had seen nemesis.

'Make to *Longbow*,' Young dictated, never taking his glasses from his eyes, 'three cruisers bearing south-east, am resuming westwards course . . . hard a starboard! Reduce to half speed!'

As *Iroquois* swung away from the three sinister shapes, the Captain lowered his binoculars. 'Well, Sub, I think we'd better join the party. Action stations and then kye all round.'

The alarms shrilled through the ship and figures appeared on the bridge, jostling him below, to the forward four-inch gun and the ignorance of local control. He knew the enemy might not have seen them, that Young had eased speed and turned away to reduce the likelihood of their having done so, but it seemed unlikely. Those three predatory outlines were suspiciously positioned for a casual interception and the progress of the convoy would have been observed passing through the narrows out of the Baltic.

'Four-inch closed up, sir.'

'Say *forward* four-inch, Sub,' came Ennis's cool, patronising tones.

'Forward four-inch closed up, sir, loading AP and training left full elevation.'

'Very well.' At least Ennis would not rebuke initiative. James brought the gun onto the approximate bearing of the enemy.

'Here come *Longbow* and *Cyclone*,' said Edwards as the

55

other two escorts raced across the convoy to interpose themselves between the threatening ships and the vulnerable merchantmen.

'It ain't bleeding U-boats we're up against then, sir?'

'No, Killick. I think they are cruisers.'

'Bloody hell!'

'Holy Mary, Mother of God . . .'

'All right lads, steady there,' Edwards said with a gruff and almost tender concern, and James was glad of the leading hand's stoicism. Since he had discerned those pyramidal shapes he had felt an uncomfortable fluttering in the pit of his stomach. He breathed in, sucking the freezing air into his lungs and hunching his shoulders in his duffle coat. Thank God he had been on watch and was sensibly attired. Some of his men, fresh from their hammocks, were already shivering.

He was about to ask permission to let them stand down a moment and get warmer clothing when the shells plunged with a ripping of the air and threw up great fountains to starboard of them. *Iroquois* heeled as they turned in towards the fall of shot. There was an awful similarity in the turn events were taking to a summer's afternoon nearly two years earlier.

'*Morituri te salutant*,' muttered James, fighting a rising panic in his gut.

'Sub!'

He was beside the voice-pipe in an instant. 'Sir?'

'Now listen carefully, Sub, it's pretty bad. *Longbow* wants us to draw the enemy fire and get in a torpedo if we can, sort of diversion while the convoy scatters. We'll be going in with *Cyclone* for company. Let me know as soon as you can see the target and we'll give you local control. Do the best you can and good luck.'

'Aye, aye, sir.'

For a blank and terrible second James stood on the sloping deck and stared at the hanging cover of the voice-pipe. He had distinctly heard the Captain snap his end shut. They were dismissed; as good as dead.

He staggered as *Iroquois* heeled further under full port helm.

'Train ahead,' he shouted at the gun, remaining beside the

voice-pipe in a kind of catalepsy, uncertain whether his knocking knees would support him.

He thought of freezing in the sea that ran like black glass alongside them, thought of Stella and how he had sullied her memory and their love with the sordidly physical affair with Emily. He could never again invoke his sexual innocence to stave off fate, and the superstition made his blood run cold.

And yet there had been more to his union with Emily than the mere animal coupling it appeared when compared with his feelings for Stella. He found some comfort in this; it occurred to him that it was not unnatural to be frightened and Emily would understand his fear.

He staggered back to the gun, the ship's wind tearing at his duffle coat.

'Going to create a diversion, are we, sir?' Edwards asked. 'Give the bloody convoy time to scatter?'

'Yes,' he answered shortly, moving towards the sight optic and searching for the enemy ships.

'Bloody convoys.' Behind him he heard Edwards complaining, expressing the reserve common to diehard naval thinking about the wisdom of merchant ships sailing in close order. James could see the sense in it, though not in their present circumstances, which left a slow-moving concentration of ships at the mercy of fast, heavy units of the German fleet.

On balance, however, the advantages outweighed the drawbacks: the U-boat had decimated imports of food, reducing the corn stocks of Great Britain to a mere six weeks' reserve at one point. Merchant ships grouped in convoy and escorted by destroyers had proved a successful means of combating the submarine menace. It was tough luck they had run into powerful surface raiders.

'Train left ten . . . steady, elevation twenty . . .' He could see the enemy clearly now, an isosceles triangle of darkness topped by a feather of smoke. He kept the gun training left and then right as *Iroquois* wove a reciprocal course designed to fool the German gun-layers who would be aiming their weapons from the sophisticated stability of a fire control top.

The isosceles triangle blossomed points of orange fire and a second later *Iroquois* staggered under the impact of a hit. James, concentrating on the reduction of the range, was not immediately aware of the mighty hiss of steam scalding the torpedomen amidships, for the image of the enemy cruiser was looming ever larger.

'Stand to,' he yelled. 'Shoot!'

He retched violently as the cordite filled the gun shield with the opening of the breech and the clattering ejection of the charge. The bang and clang of reloading formed a background to his nervous adjustments of the gun. *Iroquois* staggered again, the impact of the hit shaking the gun mounting. James swallowed bile and gritted his teeth, concentrating on his task and avoiding the humiliation of vomiting.

'All ready, sir,' prompted Edwards.

In the sight optic the cruiser bulked large, her whole side erupting in the flaming discharge of her broadside. A brilliant orange glow lit the interior of the gun shield. James felt the very deck beneath his feet buckle like a rucked carpet. He waited for the explosion, frozen into immobility. Behind him men were screaming and the distorted deck was beginning to tip as the ship heeled. He saw only stars in the gun sight and slowly turned, astounded at what confronted him.

The loading numbers were missing, so was the bridge superstructure that rose abaft the gun position. Instead the dull gleam of bare and jagged metal stood up like crookedly supplicating fingers straining towards the stars. Tosher Hughes sat dumbfounded on the deck. His head was bleeding and another man was spreadeagled unidentifiably beside him. From beyond the wreck of the bridge a white and hissing cloud roared up into the night. James stood stock still, not believing his eyes yet somehow acknowledging what he had known in his heart was inevitable. He seemed paralysed by terror, unable to do anything.

Someone was shouting, an incoherent torrent of abusive oaths. He looked down. Tosher Hughes, his mouth a dark hole in his face, his face slashed by the dark stain of blood running down from a scalp wound, sat swearing at him.

Hughes knew it was his fault, that was why the Ordinary Seaman was abusing him. James sat down, very suddenly, the lurching deck hard and cold beneath him.

Then, above the wind, above the noise of escaping steam

58

and above the tirade of foul invective Hughes continued to mouth at him, James heard the sudden tearing air that marked the arrival of another shell. The impact and instantaneous explosion lifted his prone figure bodily from the canting deck and flung it down again, jarring every bone in his body.

The shell had followed its predecessors into the engine and boiler rooms, but James had no way of knowing the blast was able to escape without transmitting itself to the destroyer's magazines. He lay awaiting death, certain now that further struggle was futile.

'Christ, you bastard, the fucking ship's going . . . she's fucking sinking! For Christ's sake don't just fucking lie there. Hey, you bugger, help me, don't leave me!'

Iroquois did not blow up, she lay wallowing, settling deeper in the water. James noticed her forecastle was climbing improbably up into the sky, for he could see the horizon above her bridge and across his line of sight the low, dark shape of the German cruiser passed not two miles away.

'Hey! Wake up, you sod! You can't leave me here to die!'

Hughes was clawing his way up the deck and James felt his trouser leg plucked with urgent jerks.

'You bloody officer, bastard. Bloody Sublieutenant Martin, damn you . . . help me!'

James shook his head, drew a deep breath and sucked cordite into his lungs.

'Oh, shit! You fucking pig . . .'

The vomit trailed across Hughes's face like ectoplasm and slowly James came to himself galvanised by panic. He was not going to die, not immediately anyway. He stood shakily on the now steeply angled deck and reached his hands out to Hughes.

The man had a broken leg and somehow James got an arm beneath his shoulder and managed to drag him round the smashed bridge front.

The water was already washing in over the maindeck. The long rows of cowl vents told that already the stern was well under water and the remains of a single funnel amidships spoke of the mortal wound the *Iroquois* had suffered. A figure in officer's uniform groaned at the twisted foot of the

59

bridge ladder and a group of men were trying to get the folding boat off its chocks on the port side.

A wave washed aboard and the awkward thing lifted clear.

'Hold the painter! Take a turn while we get the bloody thing opened . . . come on, bear a hand, for Gawd's sake.'

A leading seaman named Knowle seemed to have taken charge. James dragged Hughes towards the boat as, with a splash, it went clear of the ship, then jerked alongside on its painter. Three or four men scrambled in.

'Here, take Hughes,' James yelled, and strong arms reached out. The boat dropped away and Hughes half fell and was half yanked into it. Water swirled round James's feet as the boat surged back again.

'Come on, Sub,' someone shouted, 'there's only you left.'

The wounded officer groaned again and James turned. He could not see the man's face but the double braid and white muffler identified him as Ennis. James waded through the rising water as *Iroquois* settled further with a sudden shudder of her broken hull. He grabbed Ennis beneath the shoulders and pulled the inert body towards the ship's rail. He had no idea how they managed to get the First Lieutenant or himself into the folding boat without wrecking it on *Iroquois*'s twisted rail stanchions, or how they managed to get clear of the sinking ship. All James recalled afterwards was a sequence of impressions as he relinquished hold of Ennis, struck briefly out for the boat and then felt something drag him downwards. He fought clear, blindly struggling with the demonic strength of a terrified man; then, miraculously, strong hands grabbed him and he was hauled over the side of the flimsy boat and collapsed spewing in its bottom. When he had recovered sufficiently, he hauled himself into a sitting position and stared about him. Waves reared up and tossed the lightweight boat about. There was no sign of the *Iroquois*, only a low smudge of smoke to mark the trail of the German cruisers as they struck at the helpless convoy.

It seemed colder than ever at dawn, although this was due to a gradual awakening from the head-lolling semi-sleep they had endured during the last hours of the long night. Hughes

60

was stiff with cold, his hair matted with blood, his mouth open. Ennis was still alive, breathing noisily with no obvious sign of a wound, but a face ashen with pain.

Leading Seaman Knowle sat in the stern of the boat and glared red-eyed at the rest of them. His lips moved and James realised guiltily he was counting the survivors.

'How many, Knowle?'

'Twelve, sir.' Knowle licked dry lips. 'How d'you feel?'

'I'm all right.'

'I forgot. You've done this before; getting used to it, I dare say.'

'You can get used to most things, they say, but I don't want to do this again.'

The false, brittle humour had confronted them with the reality of their situation.

'What d'you reckon are our chances, then?'

James considered the matter. They were wet and freezing cold; there was no food or water in the boat; there was a set of oars but in the confusion of abandoning ship they had lost two of the crutches. He pulled a wry face.

'Not very good,' he said, finding now, tossing up and down while the wind cut him to the bone, that he no longer feared the end.

'Still,' said Knowle, 'while there's life there's hope.'

The Leading Seaman moved stiffly, cautiously working his way forward, looking into the face of each of the dozen men then shaking them fully awake.

'Come on you bastards, wake up!'

James watched him for a moment, detached, indifferent. The boat lurched uncomfortably, its flimsy canvas and wood-strutted sides working with the motion of the sea. Knowle was a reproach to his own inertia; *he* ought to be stirring the dying men, not Knowle. He roused himself with an effort. It no longer mattered, but it was better to die doing something.

'Tosher! Wake up Tosher, you toe-rag . . . you can't fucking die, mate.'

'Piss off.'

'Come on, you bugger, wake up!' Knowle shook Hughes so his blood-brindled head wobbled like a doll's, stirring a resentment in the supine man. Hughes made a feeble

61

attempt to ward off Knowle. The Leading Seaman moved on, into the bow of the boat.

'Sir?' James shook the First Lieutenant gently, fearing him to be dead already. 'Geoffrey, wake up! You can't go like this. You're still alive . . . fight for it, man!'

'That's it, Mr Martin, bully 'em. Call 'em all the names you can think of.' Knowle was damning a small man in a singlet whom James recognised as the cook. He was blue with cold and it was some moments before Knowle realised he was dead.

'Poor sod. I'll heave him over, sir.' It was a statement, not a question, a means of lightening the boat and increasing their chances of survival by a margin.

'Come on, Geoffrey. Remember your girl. What was her name?' James tried to recall the signed name across the photograph in Ennis's cabin. It was incredible how difficult it was to think. 'Geoffrey, remember Drusilla, eh? Remember Drusilla?'

Knowle was coming aft again, stepping gingerly over Hughes. 'Tosher, you lazy bastard, wake up!' Hughes lolled his head and Knowle, sensing he was fighting a losing battle, was driven to a frenzy of desperation, refusing to be beaten. He fell to violently shaking the Ordinary Seaman as James continued to burble the name 'Drusilla' into the First Lieutenant's ear.

Hughes stirred and opened his eyes, focusing them on the First Lieutenant. A dawning comprehension showed on his face and slowly a grin cracked his mouth. A low gurgle that, James realised, was an attempt at laughter bubbled from his mouth.

'Drusilla? Is that the name of the Jimmy's girl? Bloody hell.'

'That's better,' said Knowle approvingly, turning to the man next to Hughes. It was Goodrich, a small, huddled bundle of misery. 'Here, wake up, Pinocchio. You're too young to turn your toes up yet. Your mother'll give you a bleeding hiding if she cops you a stiff . . . wake up!' The violence of Knowle's assault on the boy threatened to overset the boat, but Goodrich stirred resentfully. 'That's better. Now you just stay awake you little bubble-nosed cunt!'

*

62

Three other men died during the day and the sun was already westering redly when Hughes pointed to the east.

'Look! A ship!'

A small steamer with a cloud of black smoke rising from her tall funnel was ploughing towards them. It seemed an endless and almost impossible task to strip off Knowle's shirt and hoist it on the loom of an oar, but their sluggish efforts were rewarded.

The black-hulled, three-island steamship, with her well-decks stacked high with a deck cargo of sawn timber and the Norwegian flag painted on her topsides, came to a stop just upwind of them. White water boiled under her counter then died away as she drifted down towards them. A pilot ladder and cargo nets were thrown over the side and big tow-headed men in checked shirts clambered down to help the able-bodied aboard. Several were too weak to move and these they swung aboard with a rope, Ennis among them. Fifteen minutes later, wrapped in blankets, the handful of survivors huddled on wooden stools in the ship's galley.

'You all right now,' said the cook, 'fair dinkum, I reckon.'

The Antipodean colloquialism, picked up in a lifetime of ocean wandering, made them laugh even though their teeth chattered on the mugs of soup they each held.

CHAPTER FIVE
Stella

'What d'you mean, you're going away for a few days? Don't you understand you're wanted here?' Vera made up the fire and turned back to her cousin. 'You're the man of the family now, James.' Her voice was bitter, and he held his peace. 'We may have to sell The Reddings. It's Aunt Anne's. Where are you going?'

'Geoffrey Ennis asked me to stay with him.' It was only a slight distortion of the truth. Ennis had indeed asked him to stay, out of gratitude for what Ennis conceived to be a selfless act in preserving his life; it would be a long time, however, before Ennis left hospital to host any visit.

'I suppose it's his sister.'

'His sister? What are you talking about?'

Vera rose, crossed the room and opened the bureau. The superscription on the letter she held out was in an unknown feminine hand.

'Aren't you going to open it?'

'Not at the moment.' James tucked the letter into his jacket pocket.

'Don't you have to get yourself new kit?' Vera persisted.

'Yes. But I've a few days' survivor's leave.'

'You're pretty good at surviving.'

'Vera!'

'I'm sorry; that was unforgivable.' She crossed the room and looked up at him, reminding him of the Vera whose budding breasts he had once squeezed. He put his arms around her and felt her sobbing.

'I'm sorry you lost Tom,' he said.

She sniffed and pulled back from him. 'You knew?'

'You made it pretty obvious . . . look, I know things have been bad . . .'

'Bad? They've been insufferable! I don't know how your mother stands it.'

'She's had a lot of practice. Aunt Anne . . .?'

'Is impossible. One ceases to feel sorry for her, just sad about the whole thing. We were so happy before the war.'

'We only know that now, though. Before the war we were orphans from the storm. Well, you and I were, anyway. Tom wasn't. He owned the birthright.'

'Tom might have owned the birthright, as you put it, but he felt the same as you and I.'

'He never felt the same as *I* did, or do now,' he said with sudden venom.

Vera pushed him away. 'He's *dead*!' She put her hands up to her face, her eyes filling with tears. 'You're not. Don't you know how many men, *young* men, are dead? Kitty Fanshawe lost two brothers in the last offensive; Billy Roundtree's dead, Eric Bellman's dead, Raymond Barnes and David Bastable are dead –'

'That's what I mean,' he interrupted, shouting her down. 'Don't *you* understand? They're dead and I'm not.'

He flung himself into a chair and stared at the fire. For a moment Vera stared uncomprehendingly at him. Then she sat in the chair opposite.

'What do you mean?' she asked quietly.

'It's pretty obvious, isn't it? They're dead and I'm alive. All good chaps, volunteers mostly, except for Bastable. He always wanted to be a soldier and join the Diehards. Well, let's hope he lived up to the Middlesex's regimental motto.'

Vera frowned. 'You mean . . .?'

'I mean, Vera, I don't deserve to be alive. All my peers are dead, and by some fluke I'm alive; a survivor. Not once, but twice. I can't tell you how awful those hours in that cockleshell boat were. A whole convoy decimated, every one of the escorts wiped out, less than a dozen survivors from the destroyers. Good men, Vera, bloody good men.'

He leaned forward and covered his face with his hands. Tears streamed out between his fingers. He felt her arm across his shoulders. 'You're a good man too, Jimmy. You deserved to live; someone has to.'

'No!' He shook himself free. 'That's not true. I don't deserve it!'

'Don't be silly.'

He shoved her roughly aside and stood up, wiping his eyes. 'I let men down. One of them said so, when we got ashore.' He could still hear Goodrich whining in the adjacent room of the YMCA where they had been accommodated after the Norwegian ship had landed them at Leith. 'He said I was paralysed with fear . . . said I did nothing and my gun could have put several shells into the enemy.'

'Does it really matter, James? You were sunk by cruisers. Even *I* know that means you were overwhelmed. What would one or two more shots from your little ship's guns have done?'

'That isn't the point,' he snapped. 'You should also know' – and he gestured round the room – 'that the tradition of the Royal Navy is to go down with guns blazing.' He seemed to deflate, continuing in a quieter voice, 'Tom would have been steady. The truth is I'm a coward. I was terrified and failed to carry out my orders to the letter.'

He misinterpreted Vera's sympathetic silence for disapproval and it stirred a defensive bitterness in him. How could she understand? She, like the public at large, had been so fed on the digestible pap of patriotism that she was blind to the hellish truth that war was not worth its spoils. Boy Seaman Jack Cornwell had died at his gun aboard HMS *Cheshire* and it had seemed this act had satisfied the British in the absence of an overwhelming victory at Jutland. They had given Cornwell a posthumous Victoria Cross. 'What matters my death if England lives?' *Pro patria mori*, his father's death . . . a great and glorious thing. Sublieutenant James Martin had dishonoured the Royal Navy.

'*That*, my dear Vera, is why you, and mother, and Aunt Anne will have to manage without me. If you have to sell this place,' he said, looking round the room, 'I won't make difficulties. It is too full of memories, anyway. Now, if you'll excuse me I have a letter to read.'

He left her alone by the fire, went to his old room and flung himself on the bed. The letter was from Emily. He had no idea how she had obtained his home address, but the

66

consideration vanished as the explicitness of the letter stirred him.

It is a terrible thing to be in love, but good to have a lover. I want you again and again, as long as your fountain is inexhaustible . . .

Hiring the motor car was an impetuous act which put the lie to Emily's assertion that to love was terrible. James arrived in Kingston-upon-Hull with an overwhelming sense of escape and freedom. He had been suffocating in The Reddings, a fact which his mother had sensibly acknowledged, for she had made no protest when he had told her he was going away for a few days.

'I think the rest and the change of scenery will do you good, dear,' she had said. 'You're looking very peaky.'

Moreover he was free of those terrible and gloomy preoccupations that obsessed him, and in such a mood it had taken only a moment to react to the 'motor car for hire' notice in the garage window.

'Nobbut funerals, lad, and most of them in France. No call for weddings, and that's what I bought car for, people being particular about weddings hereabouts.' The garage proprietor had agreed to let him collect the vehicle the following morning and he had booked into an hotel then walked to the Anlaby Road, his heart hammering in his chest.

He had forgotten about Emily; she was no more than a sweetly casual memory, for all the erotic appeal of her letter. If she gave herself that easily to him, James reflected uneasily, he could not expect to occupy her thoughts to the exclusion of others. Besides, though she had answered his profound physical need, Stella's beauty haunted him with a stronger magnetism than Emily's explicit availability.

He found the house, behind its privet hedge, and knocked, stepping back nervously. Mrs Bawden opened the door, her astonishment plainly turning to pleasure.

'Why Mr Martin . . . James, do please come in.'

She fussed round him, taking his arm and drawing him into the hall. 'My husband's away at sea just now, but Stella is here.'

He saw her emerge from the kitchen at the end of the passage, wiping her hands upon an apron.

'James?' In the dim hallway he tried to read her expression, suddenly apprehensive at her reaction to his unannounced appearance, but her smile dispelled any doubts. She stepped forward, recollected herself, took his hand and drew him into the warmth of the kitchen.

'Let's be having your coat, James,' said Mrs Bawden, bustling round with a sense of achievement. She had said nothing further of her aspiration to her husband, but the notion of an admiral's nephew as a son-in-law had bulked large in her dreams. 'How long will you be in Hull?'

'I've booked a room in the Albany for two nights.'

'The Albany . . .'

'Yes, and I've hired a car. I thought we could go for a drive tomorrow.' He threw the remark out generally, including Mrs Bawden in the invitation.

He accepted the cup of tea Mrs Bawden made from the kettle on the hob.

'You'll not be wanting me along. Stella, can you take a day off?'

'Oh, I never thought. How stupid of me,' he said, irritated with himself.

'It's all right. I'm sure Mr Biggins will not object to a day's absence.' She smiled at him again and he knew she meant she did not care what Mr Biggins thought of the matter. 'There's such a shortage with the war.'

'What do you do?' he asked.

'Stella's in an office,' Mrs Bawden explained proudly.

'Mother, don't exaggerate. I work as a clerk at the fish dock. It's not very exciting.'

He became lost in the minutiae of her life, joined them for their evening meal, enjoying its simplicity, and sat in the kitchen sketching Mrs Bawden by gaslight while he told them of the disastrous loss of the convoy.

'I thought the convoys were supposed to be a success,' Stella said. 'Didn't the Prime Minister insist they were introduced?'

'Yes,' James said, concentrating on his drawing, 'and they are a success as far as reducing the losses from U-boat attacks are concerned. But we were unfortunate in being caught by three cruisers on a sweep north along the Danish coast.'

'Seems to me you're a lucky man, James . . . May I see?' Mrs Bawden held out her hand.

'Everybody seems to think that,' he said flatly, handing over the drawing for her approval. Mrs Bawden studied it, then passed it to Stella.

'Do I really look like that?'

Stella nodded. 'Exactly like that,' she said.

'Well, you'd better draw Stella's portrait, James. I'm sure you'd prefer it.'

He turned to Stella and she looked at him with a warmth and affection that stirred him deeply. 'Just relax. Sit back and tilt your head a little . . .'

The silence was wonderfully soothing. The gentle hiss of the gas, and the kettle on the glowing range, made a snug cocoon of the room. After a while Mrs Bawden rose and made another pot of tea, leaning over James's shoulder to see what he had done. As they sipped the tea and James deprecatingly announced he could not capture Stella's likeness, the clock on the over-mantel struck ten.

'I had better be going. Will you come for a drive tomorrow?'

'Of course.'

'I'll call about nine fifteen.'

The day was fine though tendrils of mist lay in the vales as they drove north towards Beverley over the Wolds. The rushing air was sharp, for the Lanchester had a rattling turn of speed, but the sunshine was brilliant and the garage proprietor had provided extra blankets.

'I've only done this once before,' shouted James wrestling with the wheel as they approached Beverley.

Stella clutched at her hat. 'That's obvious,' she called back, laughing.

They stopped on the summit of a low hill and looked down upon the ancient town with its minster towers gleaming in the low sunlight. James slipped his arm across Stella's shoulders and they sat in companionable silence.

'What matters my death,' James murmured, half to himself, 'if England lives.'

'That's a strange thing to say.'

'Right now, looking at the view, I can actually say it with

conviction. I read it, on a poster or something, exhorting us to patriotic endeavour.'

'I had forgotten about the war.'

'I wish I could. I had done, almost, until I sat here and thought about the view; then it came flooding back.'

'Poor James.'

'Don't pity me, Stella.' He turned to her and she to him and their lips met. When they drew apart from the kiss there was nothing more to be said. James let off the handbrake and they descended the hill into Beverley.

They ate at an inn, before a blazing fire with a bottle of pre-war Chablis to accompany the nonsense new-found lovers talk of, with eyes only for themselves. The afternoon was well advanced when they emerged, hand in hand, and James wound the starting handle while Stella settled herself in her seat.

The warmth of the sun had drawn damp from the level ground north of Kingston-upon-Hull and dense fog coiled across the landscape. James slowed to a prudent crawl, welcoming the delay, unwilling to let the day end. He felt the gentle pressure of Stella's head upon his shoulder.

'Are you . . . have you many beaux?' he asked awkwardly, for the information was suddenly, sharply important.

She lifted her head and gazed at his profile. 'There's a clerk at Biggins' Brothers, and a couple of men from the fish-dock. Then there is a third hand on the *Cape St Vincent* and a mate on the *Star Procyon*.'

'Seriously?'

'If they are to be believed, yes. The clerk at Biggins' Brothers very seriously.'

'Oh.' He watched the long curve of her smiling mouth in the misty twilight.

'But none quite like you, James,' she said, and her voice had a breathless, impatient quality that he had heard before, though not from Stella.

He found the rutted entrance to a field and pulled off the road, turning to her as the engine died. Her coat was open and his arm was about her waist as she yielded her mouth, easing back in the leather seat. He was twisted half on top of her, his hand moving urgently up to the softness of her breasts and down again towards the upward pressure of her hips.

They broke apart for a moment, staring at each other with an intensity of indecision that ended in a simultaneous movement of mutual acquiescence.

'I love you, Stella; I loved you the moment I first saw you.'

'I love you too, my darling. I've never felt this for anyone before.'

And afterwards, as he stared into the wraiths of vapour that swirled about the motor car and held Stella close to him while their heartbeats subsided, he resolved how best to lay the ghosts that haunted him.

CHAPTER SIX

Special Service

'You must understand,' said the thin-lipped Captain, leaning back in his chair and revolving a pencil between thumb and forefinger of each hand, 'that you risk being shot if you are captured by the enemy. We have critics at home who consider us as operating on the very fringes of international law. The enemy will regard you with no feelings of mercy.'

'Are you aware of the case of Captain Fryatt?' added the second man sitting behind the desk. He was much younger than the thin-lipped Captain, and wore the cuff lace of a lieutenant commander in the Royal Navy. Intuitively James knew the success of the interview depended upon the impression he made on this man.

'I am, sir. He was the master of a Great Eastern Railway packet who rammed a German submarine. As a noncombatant the German government labelled him a pirate and when he fell into their hands they shot him.'

'And what are your sentiments about such legal quibbles?' asked the Captain.

'It seems, sir, that the enemy have already lost any claim to legality themselves by their opening of unrestricted submarine warfare. It would be reasonable to take whatever measures we could devise to protect our merchant shipping. That is one of my reasons for volunteering, sir.'

'Are there other reasons, Sublieutenant Martin?' asked the younger officer.

James had anticipated the question as soon as he had been summoned for the interview. His love for Stella had changed everything. It seemed to have given him a stake in the world, and although he still burned with the shame of cowardice it had reconciled him to human fright and filled him with a desire to be more than a mere pawn in the terrible game of war. By volunteering for 'special service' he felt he might be able to expiate the sin of inaction on *Iroquois*'s sharply tilting deck, to rehabilitate the name of Martin in naval circles, to avenge Tom, and to prove himself worthy of Stella.

'I have been blown up and sunk, sir. On neither occasion did I feel I had been able to . . .' He faltered, recalling the terrible moment of *Indefatigable*'s explosion. How could he say 'retaliate' when he meant 'acquit himself properly'? The Captain stopped twiddling his pencil and regarded him closely.

'Well, to . . .?'

And suddenly he thought that the real reason for volunteering was a subconscious desire for oblivion, to seek obscurity and escape the obligations laid upon him by Tom's death and Vera's bitterness, by his uncle's suicide and his mother's lonely martyrdom. And, worst of all, the possible consequences of his conduct with Stella.

'Hit back?' prompted the Lieutenant Commander.

'Yes, sir.' The truth was too complex, too personal.

'How do you feel about working in unorthodox surroundings?' asked the Captain, who was jotting a note on the file in front of him.

'You mean out of uniform with possibly non-naval personnel, sir?'

The captain nodded, watching him gravely again over the twiddling pencil.

'I volunteered, sir. I accepted that as being part of the arrangement.'

James thought of the trawlermen of the *Girl Stella*. His reasons for abandoning the mainstream of naval life even under the conditions of warfare demanded explanation to a man of the Captain's stamp.

'You have some idea of what this special service entails, do you?' the Captain asked.

'Yes sir,' James said. 'Decoy vessels – Q-ships.'

'We're an odd lot, Martin,' said Lieutenant Commander Wyatt, 'and we carry on in a pretty odd way, as you'll see.'

He leaned back in his first-class seat, took a cigarette from a silver case, tapped both ends and put it in his mouth, slipping the case away and producing a lighter in a smooth series of movements that reminded James of an actor's mannerisms. The impression was enhanced by the plus fours that Wyatt wore, alongside which his own Norfolk jacket was tweedily dull. Wyatt gave an overwhelming impression of self-confidence.

'All a bit of an act really,' Wyatt went on, crossing his legs and blowing smoke at the carriage roof as the train pulled out of Edinburgh's Waverley station. 'Don't want to say too much, but we're the eccentric end of the service. Bunch of odd men out really.' He blew more smoke at the roof and studied James through the blue mist that hung in the air. James began to feel uncomfortable under the scrutiny.

'Are you an oddball?' Wyatt asked at last, 'I sensed you might be at the interview. Captain Blood didn't want you, but I persuaded him. Illogical, but I had a hunch.' There was something vaguely unpleasant in Wyatt's tone; as though he had done James a personal favour and might want it reciprocated one day. Even the use of a nickname for his fellow interviewer seemed more than just a casual presumption.

'Thank you, sir,' James said awkwardly.

'Ah, you'll stop that. I'm a merchant Jack now, remember, and not a very prestigious one either. No bloody Cunard or P and O *wallah*, just the skipper of a West Country ketch, my handsome.'

Wyatt finished his sentence with a mock-Cornish accent and puffed more smoke at the compartment roof.

'You're too clean-cut, too obviously RN. Stop shaving, let your hair grow and get some muck under your nails. You might have just been appointed First Lieutenant of *Q 67*, but you must think of yourself as the Mate of a one-hundred-ton, parish-rigged Appledore ketch. You've avoided service in the trenches because you're consumptive, so start coughing.'

Wyatt paused and James realised the instruction was an order. Acutely embarrassed he coughed obediently, drawing from Wyatt a look of amusement that was as unnerving as his earlier scrutiny.

'Very good, my handsome,' Wyatt said archly, extinguishing his cigarette and lighting another. 'The rest will follow. We've only ten days to get the ketch to sea. Incidentally, don't expect to get any mail, not until we get to Queenstown, anyway. They make sure the boys in the battle-wagons get it regularly to keep them sweet, but we, I'm afraid, are rather different.'

James thought of Stella, and how he longed to hear from her.

'Anyway, you're footloose and fancy free, aren't you? Too young for serious affairs, eh?'

James nodded, remembering the small lie he had told at the interview. Perhaps it was true, he thought, unable to throw off entirely the spectre of Emily.

'Good,' said Wyatt, leaning forward and patting his knee, 'best way. Now, an RNR chap called Bawden reported you were a dab hand with a six-pounder.'

'Well,' said James, glad at the change of subject, 'I can strip one down.'

'And the Commander's report from the training cruiser speaks highly of you as a gun-layer.'

'Yes. I can lay a twelve-pounder.'

Wyatt puffed vigorously. 'That's all I ask of you: to lay a twelve-pounder within seconds of sighting your target, and hit with the next shot.'

His Majesty's Decoy Ship *Q 67* lay in Scapa Flow alongside the repair ship *Cyclops*. Across her stern she bore her original name, *Celandine*, and her port of registry, Appledore. Her hull had been painted black some years earlier, but her topsides were scuffed, her rigging bore signs of neglect, and even furled the sails showed patching.

The equinoctial gales rolled mist and low scud over the islands and the anchorage they enclosed. Rain swept across the Flow in dull curtains, interspersed with brief periods of lightening sky. Gulls and skuas wheeled over the grey water in their endless quest for food, subsisting largely on the refuse dumped from the idle battleships, cruisers and destroyers of the Grand Fleet who lay with steam raised, week in, week out, waiting for their chance to break lances with the Kaiser's High Seas Fleet, still fearful of the Kaiser's

Unterseebooten that intelligence told them lurked unseen beneath the Pentland Firth.

The great battle, the *Entscheidungsschlacht*, had yet to be fought but opinion in Scapa felt that, with the Tsar's army in disarray on the Eastern Front, the Germans might prosecute the war in the North Sea with more vigour. So the officers of the Grand Fleet continued to tend their sparse vegetable gardens and hack rounds of improvised golf in the teeth of south-westerly gales while their men played football and exercised. Occasionally they sailed for a practice shoot.

In the midst of this suspended animation, *Q 67* quietly made ready for sea, slipping out through the boom across Hoxa Sound for all the world on a coasting voyage from Kirkwall, with no perceptible connection with the naval base at Lyness. At her wheel stood a tall, lanky Scotsman in a black oilskin, beside him, puffing continuously on a briar pipe, stood Lieutenant Commander Wyatt. He too wore an oilskin, and the untidy locks of a damp wig could be seen beneath the crown of a small peaked cap. He balanced easily on the grating beside the helmsman as the *Celandine* moved clear of the boom and lifted to the swell. On the foredeck three men were hoisting the outer jib, for the wind was light and in the north-west, the interval between depressions in which, if they were lucky, they would have sunshine and a fair wind.

Celandine leaned to the extra canvas, and the grey northern waters began to sluice along her lee rail as patters of spray lifted over the weather bow.

The three men came aft from belaying the jib halliard. Wyatt removed his pipe.

'Take that old flag down,' he said, jerking his head at the frayed red ensign at the gaff, his West Country accent now an affectation with a sinister purpose.

James, dressed in guernsey and sea boots under flapping black oilskins, did as he was bid.

'Bend on t'other bugger,' added Wyatt. James unfastened the grubby red duster and rolled it into a bundle. 'Don't do a damned thing navy-fashion,' he recalled Wyatt saying. 'Don't even furl the ensign properly, just bundle it up and stow it in the locker.'

Every move they made, their mode of address, their

clothes, even, to a point, their attitude, had to simulate the easy-going atmosphere to be expected on a West Country coasting ketch.

But the point up to which this charade was to be taken had to be clearly understood. 'T'other bugger' was His Britannic Majesty's white ensign, the colours of the Royal Navy whose swift hoisting transformed the *Celandine* of Appledore into the decoy vessel *Q 67*, and justified her opening fire upon an enemy.

James bent the white ensign on the halliard, made sure the slippery hitch would render and unfurl the flag at the right moment, then tucked it neatly away at the base of the mizenmast. He cast a look at the boat chocked on the main hatch. Old fenders and deck scrubbers appeared to protrude from it, as though it provided the ketch's slovenly crew with a handy stowage space for such items. In fact they were all false, details almost lovingly created by Wyatt whose theatrical sense, James knew, was lethal. At the touch of a lever beside the helmsman, powerful springs split the false boat in half. Its starboard and port sides fell open, revealing the twelve-pounder that formed *Q 67*'s main armament.

This subterfuge was a grim game played for high stakes. In the opening years of the war the Kaiser's submarines had had their own technical teething troubles, but had emerged as a serious threat to merchant shipping. They had taken an increasing toll, breaking the supply of food and raw materials essential to Great Britain, and by 1917 had had the effect of almost entirely throttling the nation. Against opposition from a number of quarters, the government of David Lloyd George had insisted the convoy system be introduced. Destroyer screens, like the one Vice Admiral Martin had improvidently dismissed in the English Channel, were thought to provide cover against submarines and the development of the depth charge had given them a means of attacking after the *Unterseebooten* had dived, extending the arm of retribution beyond the haste of quick gunfire and the headlong dash to ram.

There had been other attempts to thwart the Kaiser's sea-wolves. The need to protect the British supply lines to France had resulted in a boom defence of nets and mines across the Strait of Dover. But the ruthless young men of the

Kriegsmarine circumvented the obstacle and had to be lured to their nemesis by decoy ships, specially fitted merchantmen, manned by volunteers, whose task was to look helpless, to panic, even to abandon ship with the skipper's wife, cook and parrot, while the submarine surfaced and went through the legalities of approaching the merchantman to sink it with gunfire after allowing its crew to escape in their boats.

When the rusty tramps belched fire at the German corsairs, the High Command accused the British of acting illegally, of flouting the so-called laws of war. With the sinking of the *Lusitania* and American involvement in the war, the Kaiser's decision to wage unrestricted submarine warfare revived the energy of his young officers. Desperate for reputations, emboldened by the greater reliability of their boats and cheated of prizes by the convoy system, they attacked the lone coasters that perforce sailed without naval protection. With this revival of the menace to trade came a counter-revival of the decoy, or Q-ship. To this broad strategic picture, which was well known to James and had been behind his decision to volunteer, Lieutenant Commander Wyatt now added tactical theories of his own.

'I'm damned sure,' he said to James and the engineer who maintained *Q 67*'s hidden diesel engine, 'that the Huns are supplying the Irish Republican Army with weapons, opening another front with a bit of speculative gun-running.'

He unrolled the Admiralty chart which showed the whole of the British Isles, spreading it out on the table in *Celandine*'s small, panelled saloon where the pale yellow light from the oil lamp suggested a cosy intimacy in which they might have been planning a yachting trip.

'So I'm going to trail our coat down the west coast of Old Erin and see if we can't unearth a U-boat or two.'

Wyatt sat back on the settee, lit his pipe and watched their reactions through clouds of aromatic blue smoke.

The engineer, a naval artificer before volunteering, expressed his concern that their fuel tanks were inadequate for extended passages. Wyatt waved the objection aside.

'We sail. I might use your iron tops'l, Chief, when I'm engaging.' He turned to James. 'Jimmy, any questions?'

Calling Sublieutenant Martin 'Jimmy' appealed to Wyatt's

78

sense of the theatrical because the diminutive form of James's name doubled as naval slang for First Lieutenant and had the advantage of serving very well for the mate of a West Country ketch.

James shook his head. 'No.'

It did not matter to James where they went, only that they met the enemy.

Wyatt was pleased with his second-in-command. James Martin's quiet introspection hid an active mind and an energetic body. James showed a natural aptitude for handling the big ketch, an assiduous application to the maintenance of the guns and an easy manner with the men. They were a close-knit bunch, an odd-ball collection of professionals and part-time sailors who, volunteers to a man, had dispensed with the straitjacket of naval discipline. For underlying the scruffiness, the casual behaviour and the studied negligence with which they worked the ketch southwards through the Minch, was the predatory awareness of being a lure.

Whatever the equivocal reasons that had prompted James to volunteer for this special service, he found an almost wistful happiness aboard *Celandine*. There was something of nostalgia about it, an odd kinship reminiscent of Bawden and the crew of the *Girl Stella* which combined with his relief at escaping the irksome restraints by which he felt the Royal Navy had sought to crush his natural spirit. And though there was an adolescent desire to avenge Tom, he was also aware of an ability to strike at the enemy on his own terms, free of the shadow of his cousin and the obligations laid upon him by his dead uncle and the whole weight of naval tradition. He felt he had his own personal reasons for seeking action: the very real instinct of fighting with the advantage of surprise, and the deep-seated need to wipe out the shame of fright that others had labelled cowardice. To these reasons Wyatt had added another, revealed by James's sketches of the Western Isles: Sublieutenant James Martin was by nature a romantic.

It was difficult for James to resist the land and seascapes through which they passed. He thought a consumptive could also be artistic and attempted to capture the play of light and

79

shadow as showers, clouds and patches of brilliant sunshine garnished their passage past the Hebrides. The long fingers of the sea lochs wound eastwards beneath beetling hills that were dour purple one minute and vivid green the next. To the west the hummocks of the Uists and Benbecula faded under curtains of rain, only to emerge steaming in the sunny spells.

Celandine sailed steadily south, romping along under her big gaff mainsail, mizen and headsails. Her decks were shiny with water and the clear, soft note of a steady, quartering breeze sang in her weather rigging. Her crew pottered about her deck, ever watchful for the telltale feather of water that marked the periscope of a U-boat studying them before surfacing to sink them by gunfire, for they were too poor a prize upon which to waste the expense of a torpedo.

Wyatt put in to Lough Foyle on the northern Irish coast and allowed his crew a run ashore.

'Is that wise?' queried James, thinking of the incorrigible old sweats he had as his gun crew, two marines named Blyth and Whitaker, both of whom had reputedly 'bad' characters.

'Worried about them talking?' asked Wyatt from behind his habitual screen of tobacco smoke. 'Don't; it's what I want 'em to do. Let it be known that we're taking a cargo of munitions from Derry to Queenstown and we might bait the trap if there's any substance in my theory.'

'And if there isn't?'

'If there's no Boche U-boat off Rathlin Island, where the transatlantic track runs in the North Channel and Liverpool Bay, then we amble down the west coast and round the Fastnet for the southern approach to Liverpool. If the Huns haven't got a boat on patrol there then they don't deserve to win the war.' Wyatt looked at James. 'Why d'you ask?'

James shrugged. 'I'm not sure really . . . except I'd hate to have wasted all that time working on the guns with Whitaker and Blyth.'

'They also serve who only sit and wait,' joked Wyatt.

'They used to say that at Scapa, I believe,' replied James, 'but the truth wears a bit thin in the face of what's been going on in Belgium.'

'Don't worry, Jimmy. I'm confident you'll get your own back for being blown up.'

'You think that's what I want?'
'Well, isn't it?'

It is not pleasant to admit that in fact you are no better than the rest, James thought. Wyatt's uncanny directness unnerved him and gave him food for thought as, despairing of smoking a U-boat out of hiding off Rathlin, they sailed south, round Achill Head and down the west coast of Ireland. Off Bantry Bay the wind swung south westerly and freshened so they were obliged to reef and stand off shore under shortened canvas while the Irish coast fell slowly to leeward, forbidding now that the filigree of white that had bordered its cliffs was transformed into a smoking barrier of breakers and sharp-toothed rocks.

Grey spume-streaked seas roared at them while the wind tore at their spars and sails. *Celandine* lay over to the gale, struggling to windward as she pitched, driving into the waves and shooting spray high over her weather bow. Her lee rail buried itself and green water sluiced dangerously across her waist.

Beneath the hatch, on the steel platform mounted in the hold, Blyth and Whitaker, James's gun crew, covered the dully gleaming weapon from the runnels of sea water that drove through the imperfect jointing of the dummy boat above. The gun, with its oiled steel and brass fittings, its traversing and elevating gear and the yellow rack of ready-use shells and charges, seemed possessed of a menace that was undiminished by the waning enthusiasm of the men whose task it was to bring it within range of the enemy. As *Celandine* battered her way through the third day of the gale and the onset of night depressed their spirits, Wyatt's men decided they were unlucky, that the prize they sought would elude them, and they were on a fool's errand.

'This ain't no bleeding way to fight a war,' grumbled Blyth, as he struggled into his coffin-like bunk.

'It's the best war their lordships can find you, Blyth,' said Wyatt, entering the cramped forecastle with a bottle of Pusser's rum. 'You can splice the mainbrace with my compliments.' He looked round the dingy space as the expectant moons of faces emerged.

'Ta, Skipper.'

81

'But don't let me hear you talking like that again,' snapped Wyatt, his voice suddenly cold. He held the bottle until Blyth had clambered out of his bunk and seized it. 'Understand?'

James had no way of knowing how Wyatt maintained his apparently unshakeable confidence in the ultimate success of their mission. He supposed it stemmed from the fact that so much planning, so much attention to seemingly irrelevant details, could not be accomplished without the inner conviction of climax. But at times Wyatt seemed not to care, and James considered the matter perhaps a further manifestation of his commander's odd theatricality. Perhaps they were just a pair of odd-balls, destined to survive while men who had never thought to court excitement by anything so dangerous as volunteering died in their thousands on the Western Front.

On the morning following the passing of the gale *Celandine* lay rolling in a monstrous swell ten miles south of the Fastnet lighthouse. The wind had died to a fitful breeze that failed to fill their sails and steady them and they wallowed sloppily with the gear banging about, gaffs creaking on their vangs and the canvas slatting aloft.

As the grey dawn broke, it revealed a misty horizon which, before sunrise, had produced a fine drizzle. Having stood the middle watch, from midnight to four in the morning, James was turned in and had finally dropped off to sleep. He woke suddenly with Wyatt bending over him. The pressure of Wyatt's finger was still on the side of his head, just in front of the ear. It woke a man to a perfect awareness without startling him.

'Action stations!' snapped Wyatt, and was gone.

James pulled on boots and guernsey and made his way forward through the doorway cut into the hold. Whitaker and Blyth were already there.

'AP up the spout, sir,' reported Blyth, his reversion to a Royal Marine, even an improperly dressed Royal Marine, the metamorphosis of an instant. Above their heads they could hear the clumps of the 'panic party', led by Able Seaman McLeod. There was a lot of shouting and running about, a charade of live theatre rehearsed and directed by the resourceful Wyatt. James nodded to his two men, unplugged the voice-pipe and put his mouth to it.

'Closed up,' he said into it, his voice low. At the other end he could hear Wyatt grunt acknowledgement. The Lieutenant Commander was lying on the deck above, hidden from enemy observers, but studying their target through a long slit in the bulwark planking.

'U-boat, starboard side, coming in at an angle of about forty-five degrees; men down on the casing and the gun's trained on us. Present bearing, starboard sixty . . . range is going to be damn near point blank, but we're rolling. Don't fudge it, Jimmy, or we won't be friends any more.'

Wyatt's voice was terse, the joke humourless.

'Aye, aye, sir.' James passed the information to his men. In the gloom of the hold, lit by bull's eyes in the deckhead, the gleaming gun barrel traversed as far as the restrictions of its hiding place permitted. Hands ready on the traversing gear, Whitaker waited. Blyth, another round cradled ready, stood beside the breech; James bent to the sight.

They could hear the thump-thump of the U-boat's diesel engine through their own hull, while alongside the bump of the *Celandine*'s second boat, lowered from its stern davits, told where the panic party were abandoning ship.

'The Boche is watching us.' Wyatt's disembodied voice floated out of the unpolished bell-mouth of the voice-pipe and James, his heart beating heavily, found time to marvel that such an accumulation of verdigris would not have been tolerated on the *Indefatigable*. But beside him the steel and brass of their gun shone dully with its thin film of oil.

They heard a faint shouting, then McLeod's voice in reply: 'Hold your bluidy horses. We're coming as fast as we can, but ma Mate's a wee bit arthritic.'

A lupine grin spread across Whitaker's face. They all knew the pretended arthritis was an embellishment derived from their run ashore in Londonderry. Seaman Holland, temporarily promoted Mate for the purposes of deceiving the enemy, had demonstrated the ability to walk like a rickety cripple when very drunk.

'Stand by!'

Wyatt's voice tensed them again. James felt no fear, though he knew Wyatt's warning meant that at any second

Celandine's ageing wooden sides might cave in from the U-boat's shells. But this time he was no passive part of an imperfect machine outmatched by a better. This time was very different.

'Prepare to train right!'

There was a sudden snick and instantly daylight flooded the hold. With a clatter the sham boat fell apart. Whitaker's hands whirred on the traversing handles and the gun barrel swung. James, eyes to the sights, saw a brief blur as *Celandine*'s main shrouds flashed across his line of vision, followed by grey sea.

'Fire at will!'

Wyatt's permission was the formal order dictated by the rules of engagement. It indicated their commander had whipped the white ensign aloft and tugged it free of its slippery hitch, though in the windless morning its appearance would be difficult to detect from the U-boat.

The sudden crash of a hit forward was followed by the concussion of the U-boat's gun, the shell passing through the ketch's wooden sides. The long cigar-shaped casing of the U-boat swung across James's line of sight. He shouted to Whitaker and the traversing swing slowed, then stopped. James could see men on the enemy's conning tower; he spun the elevating wheel, laid his gun at the base of the grey steel shape and squeezed the trigger.

Beside him the crump of the exploding charge and hiss of the departing shell were almost incidental to the concentration he was paying to the target, adjusting the gun as *Celandine* rolled and the relative aspect of the two vessels altered. He saw the bright yellow flash of contact while the gun's recoil mechanism absorbed the shock of its discharge, for the range was point blank. The stench of cordite wafted over them and he felt the gun jar as Blyth hefted a second round into the gun and slammed the breech shut. Beneath his poised finger James felt the action automatically cock the trigger.

'Ready sir!' Blyth shouted, but James was already squeezing the trigger. Again the crash and hiss, followed by a white plume of water alongside the submarine that had, at its heart, the yellow of a hit just below the U-boat's waterline. Again the devoted attention to the subtly shifting target, the orders to Whitaker, the wait for Blyth, and his own hands busy compensating for the ketch's roll. James felt *Q 67*, the quondam *Celandine*, shudder and shake as the Germans retaliated. He was vaguely aware of water entering the hold, then Blyth bellowed his readiness and he sent a third shot into the U-boat. He was less confident of the damage done by that third shot, so circumscribed was the circle of his vision.

They had despatched a fourth round before James was properly aware of why there was a subtle alteration in his victim. A shift in perspective caused him to take his eye from the sight for a second. The submarine no longer lay on the surface in equilibrium: she had begun to list towards them, apparently shortening the height of the conning tower, and he could see its commander exhorting his men and waving a pistol. As he waited for Blyth's assurance that the gun was reloaded and the twitch of the cocked trigger beneath his crooked finger, he saw a further foreshortening as the U-boat turned towards them so that he could see her own gun. He seemed to be staring down the barrel as a duellist might. He noted, with a sublime detachment, that now he confronted death he felt no fear. His mind was lucid, even possessed of a fierce joy. Death called every human in the end; there was nothing very remarkable in it, and he could take with him the knowledge he was no longer afraid, that Stella could remember him with pride . . .

The clang of the closing breech block recalled him. 'Ready sir!'

James saw the mushroom of smoke, saw the expanding circle of red and yellow fire with the black dot of the shell at its core. He had read somewhere that you could see the shell that hit you. Perspective enlarged it as it covered the trajectory towards you. In that split second of intelligence, he pressed the trigger again. Beside him the gun roared.

He seemed to sit quite still for a long moment, though it was no more than a mere splinter of time. But to James's distorted perception it was filled with action and impressions. Somewhere to his right, partly hidden by the hatch coaming, Wyatt was yelling something about 'good shooting', his words half drowned by the chatter of his heavy machine gun raised above the cap-rail on a tripod. On the submarine another machine gun was replying, but the U-boat was listing heavily now, and more men were coming out of her conning tower and scrambling down onto her casing; some had already jumped into the sea. There was a sluggishness about the ketch too, the sloshing movement of water within her deadened her roll, disturbing the cargo of cork and timber designed to keep *Q 67* afloat even when full of holes.

But at the same instant that these facts impinged themselves upon his consciousness, the air was filled with a roar. James felt his body, confined as it was, squeezed then plucked at. Whitaker, sitting alongside him beyond the gun barrel, seemed torn from his post as the shell passed overhead so close that they felt the heat of its passage on their skin and in their lungs. James gasped and fell to a fit of unfeigned coughing.

'Christ! Not now, Jimmy! Shoot! Shoot!' Wyatt was screaming at him, but James was alone. Blyth was no longer at the breech of the gun, instead he lay dazed beyond the gun-mounting.

James struggled to the breech where shell and charge lay ready. He heaved them into the gun and closed the breech, surprised how much his arms ached with the effort he had expended. He moved to the traversing handle and swung the gun five degrees, ducked under the gun barrel and levelled it, pressing the trigger so that crash and hiss followed in satisfactory sequence. The echoing impact of the explosion on the submarine's casing was the last *Q 67* fired.

'She's going . . . she's going. Check your fire!'

James climbed breathlessly from the gun position onto the deck. *Celandine* was low in the water and trimmed by the head, but Wyatt was grinning at him and both men turned to stare at the enemy boat. Instead of the grim outline of the Krupp gun, a bizarre steel flower seemed to bloom on the U-boat's deck, and that deck was tilting, tilting at an ever increasing angle until she reared her tapering stern with its hydroplanes and screws and rudder so they made a sharp angle with the sea.

In front of them the rail exploded in a cloud of splinters. Bullets whined past them and James saw the U-boat's commander braced against the after rail of his conning tower, pistol in his hand. Wyatt fell back, his hand to his shoulder.

James grabbed the heavy Vickers machine gun Wyatt had been firing. It swung easily on its tripod, the belt of cartridges still half full. The U-boat commander jerked like a puppet, his chest smashed by the hail of bullets James unleashed.

The U-boat was sinking fast, sliding into the grey sea to be swallowed like the pretty little *Iroquois* and the mighty *Indefatigable*.

James's eyes fell on the heads and waving arms of the German sailors in the water. It was not right they should survive, for the men of the *Indefatigable* had not survived, nor had the majority of those on the *Iroquois*; besides, they would not want to survive. Survival, he knew, was a burden, and he thought of his shipmates and the boys who had died aboard the *Tremendous* and the *Hogue*, *Cressy* and *Aboukir*.

The bullets sputtered across the water, throwing up vicious spurts. The gun juddered in his hands as shots struck the helpless enemy seamen and the grey sea was tinged with a spreading stain of blood. The weapon stopped at the end of the belt. Suddenly his knees were shaking. Beside him Wyatt sat up with a groan.

'Give me a hand.'

They leaned exhausted on the rail, their eyes glazed like those of dead fish. Someone pressed a field dressing onto Wyatt's shoulder and he groaned again as it was tied. His eyes wandered out over the water.

'Jesus Christ,' Wyatt said appalled, 'did you . . . did you have to?'

James did not hear Wyatt. The echoes of the stuttering machine gun reverberated in his ears and beyond Wyatt's now wigless head with its boyishly tousled hair, Tom was looking at him and smiling, his face fading in the mist.

James found himself staring at the sea. A film of oil was welling up in the swirl left by the sinking U-boat and across its dark stain McLeod's panic party were rowing back to the ketch. Odds and ends of wreckage turned slowly, a wooden grating and an empty ammunition box.

'Well, you got your bloody U-boat, sir,' James said tonelessly.

Looking at the oil and the red tinge, Wyatt nodded. 'Yes. It's bloody all right.'

James held out his hand. The gesture was, he thought, appropriate, but it succeeded in being merely incongruous. 'Congratulations. She's only an old West Country hooker, but she's done more than any battleship.'

Wyatt looked at the outstretched hand with repugnance. Terrible apprehensions were forming in his mind. To kill in the heat of action was one thing, to kill, no, to *massacre* in such cold blood was utterly beyond the pale. He stared at the young man before him, revolted where once he had felt attraction, aware that if word of this got out it would be associated not with the name of Martin but that of Wyatt, the Commander of *Q 67*. There had been earlier incidents, and men's reputations had foundered on them. They were black, ugly deeds. War was a gentleman's occupation and Wyatt was damned if his career was going to be terminated by the outrageous conduct of a boy!

James saw the horror in Wyatt's eyes and lowered his hand, guessing its cause. 'You wanted a gun-layer,' he said his voice expressionless.

'But not a bloody *murderer!*' Wyatt hissed, his hand to his shoulder.

'If they had all got on board they could have overwhelmed us,' James snapped, his tone almost insubordinate, his logic inescapable. But Wyatt knew James had not shot the swimming Germans for so cogent a reason. It came to him that he himself might actually have encouraged James Martin's conduct and the thought repelled him.

'You wanted your fucking revenge,' he began, but James had turned aside to catch the thrown painter of the panic party's returning boat.

'You wiped the bastards out then, sir,' said McLeod clambering over the rail, and Wyatt was shocked that McLeod addressed him.

'Fish some debris out of the water before you stream that boat astern,' he ordered coldly, turning away. They would have to take some evidence into Queenstown for the Admiral, and in the absence of any prisoners . . .

'D'you want my engine, sir?' asked the engineer, nodding aloft at the lack of wind in the slatting sails.

88

'Yes,' Wyatt said with bitter vehemence, eager to leave the stink of oil and the dispersing tinge of men's lifeblood that disfigured the surface of the sea. He wondered if James Martin would dream often of the morning's work, sure that he himself would.

But Sublieutenant Martin stood beside the *Celandine*'s wheel while it dawned upon him that Tom was avenged and he was no longer nauseated by the stink of cordite.

They reached Queenstown next day and Wyatt, his wound properly dressed, made his report to the Admiral commanding. When he returned he brought with him a bag of mail. James seized his own handful of letters eagerly. Vera wrote to tell him they thought The Reddings would soon be sold; his mother sent her love. There was a letter from Emily, enclosed in a second letter addressed to him in Vera's hand. In it Emily begged James to write.

But there was also a letter from Stella which he had left until last, though the postmark was weeks earlier. As he read it James forgot Emily's desperate appeal for it dispelled every other thought from his mind.

Having taken life with such savagery to sever the cords binding him to the past, James Martin discovered he was about to become a father.

CHAPTER SEVEN

The Maverick

'Why did you do it?' Wyatt asked.

The question hung in the stuffy air of the saloon like the clouds of smoke Wyatt puffed from his endless chain of cigarettes, having abandoned his pipe with his disguise. James put down the tumbler of whisky and tried to focus his eyes and bring Wyatt's face into a single image. The Scotch endowed him with a wisdom that told him they were well past any state of happy euphoria over their victory, and sliding into a dangerous drunkenness. Wyatt would never have asked the question sober; he would have maintained a truly British silence about the incident, at least for a decent interval, whatever his inner turmoil.

But the whisky, of which they had drunk a considerable quantity judging by the ullage in the bottle that stood between them on the cabin table, had loosened Wyatt's tongue and exposed his innermost preoccupations. James had been thinking about Stella. The more he drank, the less he feared Bawden's reaction or his mother's reproach. In a savagely joyful way it satisfied him too, to know that no matter what now happened to him in this damnable war, he would leave something behind him, which was more than Tom had done. Unless you counted grief, and that was something much devalued by its present proliferation.

It dawned on James that Wyatt was his superior officer. Indeed he still wore the uniform in which he had earlier made his report to the Admiral, and the light from the oil lamp sparkled on the gold cuff lace.

'Why did you do it?' he repeated.

Beyond the fuggy saloon the rumble of the salvage pump

kept the inflow of water at bay, though *Celandine* would not sink with her cargo of cork and timber. And somewhere forward her crew noisily shared a couple of bottles and drank to victory and oblivion.

'Why did I do what?' James asked.

Wyatt looked at the young man with ponderous concentration. There had been something about Sub-lieutenant Martin that he had felt made him the right man for *Q 67*, something intangible and beyond his reputation as an able gunner. Wyatt, with his feeling for the theatrical, had sensed a quality of implacability in him which had seemed a definite asset in manning his ship. James Martin had performed exactly as Wyatt had planned, hitting the enemy submarine with a hail of well-directed shells, and Wyatt was pragmatic enough to know the actuality usually fell short of the intention. Perhaps it was the very fulfilment that made James's subsequent behaviour so reprehensible. For Wyatt it was inconceivable that anyone could exceed the script he had so assiduously written, especially so personable a young man as James Martin. Wyatt choked on the thought.

'You know bloody well *what*.'

'I told you at the time,' said James, 'they could have overwhelmed us if they had all got on board. Besides, they were the enemy we were to seek out and destroy. Isn't that the watchword of the Royal Navy? Isn't that what Nelson taught us, to remove the threat by annihilating it?'

'Nelson also prayed we might be magnanimous in victory.' Wyatt's tone was pompously sententious.

'As an adulterer, Nelson was a poor moralist,' James said, relishing his own argument. 'It's only an historical sophistry to apply the values of 1805 to 1918. We fight a dirtier way today, a more scientific and logical way. The Huns intended sinking us; we turned the tables on them and they lost. Who knows?' he said, slurring his words in sudden bitterness, 'it may be our turn tomorrow.'

There was something profoundly shocking about the way young Martin spoke; an unfeeling coldness that turned Wyatt's repugnance at James's act to an active dislike of James himself. Wyatt, imbued with naval tradition and the creed of the imperial zealot, had sought to outwit the odious, underhand methods of the enemy's new weapon. He saw in James the very type of man he conceived the enemy U-boat men to be and his own initial attraction seemed now perverse, a consideration that fuelled his dislike.

It again occurred to him that he himself had called this monster into being and the thought made him shudder. The dubious exploits of the Q-ships had not been universally hailed in high places, their methods were often considered as un-English as the enemy's. James Martin had marred his moment of glory and it could never be redeemed. The command Wyatt had so enthusiastically assumed now seemed less prestigious. The nightmare consideration that this young man might have compromised him, perhaps jeopardised or even wrecked his career, confronted him in all its personal horror.

'I don't think there is going to be a tomorrow, Sublieutenant,' Wyatt enunciated carefully, reasserting a superiority he felt James Martin had temporarily usurped. 'We're not fit for sea without a dry-docking and a refit.'

James drifted away to thoughts of leave and Stella, and the whisky insulated him against too miserable a contemplation of the reaction of other people.

'That's good news,' he said, adding bluntly, 'I'm going to apply for special leave.'

'What the devil for?' asked Wyatt.

'I've got a girl pregnant, sir,' James replied, his head swimming, 'and I'll have to get married.'

Wyatt looked at him with increasingly contemptuous distaste, as though his dislike was justified by this despicable confession. It suddenly blinded him to his own innermost sentiments about James. The flamboyant character of Lieutenant Commander Wyatt could be as spiteful as it could be generous, and the lingering sense of his subordinate's actions lodged in his heart as an abiding hatred.

Afterwards the word was leaked out. It was not then called an 'atrocity', merely a hint of somewhat dishonourable conduct on the part of Q 67, and when people in naval circles gossiped they were apt to assert strenuously that it was not Colin Wyatt who was responsible. Colin had done a brilliant job, actually; absolutely first class. In fact he was badly wounded by machine-gun fire as he engaged the U-boat he accounted for. They gave him a medal for it. No, it was Colin's First Lieutenant who let the side down. Nauseating business really: he shot up the Hun survivors after they had thrown in the towel and were swimming towards the decoy ship. Mind you, he was a bit of an oddball. His guardian was old Admiral Martin, the one who lost the *Tremendous* at the beginning of the war, remember?

What happened to him? The last heard was that he had to get spliced to a trawler skipper's daughter. Some trollop he'd got in the family way . . . yes, really, a trawler skipper's daughter.

James had no excuse to delay a meeting with Bawden, feeling that a stormy confrontation with Stella's father was preferable to facing his mother, acutely aware he had broken his promise to her. He did not fear her reaction as he had once feared the reaction of his uncle to the details of Tom's death, but he wished to have resolved the situation with Bawden, to have squared matters as decently as he could before seeing his mother.

Bawden met James in his hotel room in response to his telegram. He was carrying a bundle rolled in an untidy piece of newspaper. For a guilty moment James had the ludicrous impression it was a gun.

'Well, lad, I didn't think you'd do this to us.' Bawden's face was dark with menace.

'I'm sorry, sir, sorry for what I suppose looks to you and Mrs Bawden as . . . as appalling manners.' He paused as Bawden's mouth twitched dangerously, conscious that he was choosing his words badly. Swallowing, he pressed on: 'Quite simply, sir, Stella is the most wonderful girl and I'm deeply in love with her.'

'Have you thought about class?' Bawden cut in.

'Class? What do you mean?'

'You're not our class, lad. It may not mean much to you right now but it'll matter later. One of you is going to be bloody unhappy then. Mayhap it'll be you, and you'll deserve it, but you've the edge on my Stella. She's to be wife to you and go wi' *you*, lad; happen she won't make ideal Navy wife, feel out of it when Sublieutenant Martin's posted to Malta on a pittance o' pay, or maybe she'll hold back your chances of promotion because she talks broad and Admiral's missus only asks *ladies* to take tea. *That'd* make Stella unhappy and I won't have my lass unhappy, Martin, so you take damn good heed o' what I'm saying.'

James felt anger rise in him. He had stood when Bawden entered the room, now he took two steps towards the bluff Yorkshireman.

'I don't care!' he snapped. 'I'm not *typically* Navy, and I know what you think of stuffed shirts. I grew up with an Admiral, I had a dead naval hero for a father and I'm not in any kind of awe of gold braid, Bawden. For God's sake understand that! I have no naval friends, I'm virtually penniless, though I shouldn't admit it to you, but if it makes you feel better, you could buy and sell me three or four times over! It may seem an odd thing to say, but I feel more at home with people like yourself . . . and, damn it, I love your daughter.'

They confronted each other as the evening slowly darkened the anonymous hotel room, adding a dimension to the silence that was the beginning of reconciliation between the two of them.

'Aye, it seems we both love her, lad,' said Bawden diffidently. 'A father's love is different, but don't doubt its strength.'

'Of course not,' mumbled James. 'Is she all right?'

'Turn up bloody gas,' Bawden said, ignoring the question and seating himself. 'You are going to marry her, lad,' he said in a flat tone that made of the words neither question nor statement.

James turned from the gas jet as the room was bathed in a pale glow. 'Of course! Did you think I wouldn't?'

'I don't know what I thought, lad. You had us in right sweat. When you didn't write it hurt Stella more than anything.' He looked at James then, as though his neglect had been worse than the act of intercourse.

'I'm sorry. I didn't know. I was on special service . . .'

'Well, no harm's done by a bit o' delay,' Bawden said. 'You're here now, and maybe that's th' main thing.'

He tore at the crumpled paper parcel to reveal a bottle of whisky. When two glasses had been found he half filled them, passed James a tumbler and raised his own.

'I'll drink to you then, and to Stella, though I could ha' murdered you a while back.'

James raised his glass silently and realised his hand was shaking with relief. Bawden sniffed, then fumbled in his pocket for his pipe with a wry smile on his face. 'I'll tell you sommat before wife says owt . . . cheers . . . You called it appalling manners. In my day it was th' ultimate sin, but plenty of us young lummocks committed it.'

'You mean . . .?'

'Aye, lad, I did same wi' Stella's mother. Stella was a love-bairn herself.'

'Then you . . .'

'We understand, lad, but it don't make it any easier. Forgiving's a bit different. Anyroad, the fact that you'll be likely to take her away will make it easier for her.' He puffed on his pipe, regarding James through the smoke.

'She'll live at The Reddings, sir, if you and Mrs Bawden don't mind.'

'She'll be *your* wife, lad,' Bawden said bluntly.

'How is she?' James repeated.

'Worried about you, but she's well enough otherwise. It'll be born in autumn, but I expect you'll have guessed that for yourself.' He poured a second glass for both of them. 'Some women look right lovely when they're expectin',' he added in a low voice, 'I mind her mother.'

James could think of nothing to say and they sat for a moment in silence, sipping the Scotch. Then Bawden tossed off his glass and stood up.

'It's Tuesday night; you can marry Saturday. We've made most o' the arrangements, except your leave.'

James recalled Wyatt's frigid valediction: 'I'll be applying for your transfer, Mr Martin.'

James got to his feet. 'That'll be all right. But when can I see her?'

'You can't. Not before wedding, that's flat. She's not here anyroad. We sent her to stay wi' my sister for a few days. You'll have to be content wi' that.'

He reached The Reddings the following evening in time for dinner. Afterwards he took his mother aside to tell her.

95

'I already know, James. Mr Bawden seems a very pleasant man.'

'You know? But Bawden said nothing about having told you,' he said in astonishment.

'They were concerned. They did not know where you were. There were arrangements to be made.'

James realised his ignorance, remembering the necessity of calling banns.

'She shall live here with us and have her baby here if she wishes to, James,' she said, taking his arm. He was no longer a child, she thought, not even a boy. After what he had endured the news had not surprised her. There was one thing bothering her, though. 'Do you love her?' she asked.

'Of course,' he replied. 'She's beautiful, mother. I'm sure you'll like her.'

'I didn't ask what she looks like. She wasn't a . . .'

'No, mother, no!' He wanted to tell her he had known Emily too, and that he knew there could be a difference, both for him and for the girl. In the end he could only say, 'It's quite all right, mother, she isn't cheap.'

She stroked his hand and her calmness mollified a little the remorse he felt in her presence. 'I do regret something.'

'Oh?'

'I'll be breaking my promise to you, my promise not to marry.'

'A lot of things have happened since then,' she said, 'to all of us.'

Oddly, it was Vera who expressed the doubts and gave James the rough time he had expected from other quarters.

'For God's sake,' she had said, her face much older than he recalled, 'what are you going to do with a girl like that for a wife?'

'You haven't met her.'

'I'm not sure I *want* to meet her. Look James, we've a right to expect an end to shocks and worries, and now you present us with this problem.'

'Why is it a problem? All right, she's expecting a child, my child, but I'm to marry her so surely that ends the problem?'

Vera shook her head. Jealousy, embitterment and prejudice provoked her.

'Why not?' he asked.

'Well because . . .'

'Because what? She's not our class, is that it? No, she's not our bloody class! She's the daughter of a trawler skipper. That's what worries you, isn't it? Not whether we want to marry. It is, isn't it?' James stared at the silent Vera. 'Good heavens, Vee, don't you see your very silence admits the awfulness of what you mean? Why does everybody talk about class? This sort of thing is happening all the time; it's the war, it's changed a lot of things. Oh, God, I'm sorry . . .'

But Vera had already run from the room, and Tom's shadow intruded once more.

The next morning he sent a hopeful telegram to Geoffrey Ennis whom he thought to be on extended leave: *Best man needed Saturday Hull stop Dress war-paint stop Papoose due stop*. The flippant reference to the old *Iroquois* was a measure of James's desperation. He had not expected Ennis to agree with any enthusiasm, nor to reply with any warmth at the news, but Geoffrey telegrammed by return: *Congratulations stop Least I can do stop red indian custom after life preserving stop have teepee on big-chief's hunting ground for squaw and brave stop*.

Ennis's gesture was more than the repayment of a debt. Since the loss of the old destroyer they had corresponded, becoming friends of a kind, and after he had made an enemy of Wyatt, James valued Geoffrey's kindness all the more. When they met at the Albany Hotel on the eve of the wedding, and Geoffrey joined James, his mother and Vera, his cheerfulness dispelled an awkwardness sustained by Vera who had not wanted to come. Only Harriet's insistence that the occasion should be marred by no more than one act of impropriety had persuaded her.

The wedding was quiet and attended by a few close friends of the Bawden's in addition to the Martin contingent. There was no arch of swords for bride and groom to emerge under, but Mrs Bawdens' social pretensions were crowned in unplanned circumstances by Geoffrey Ennis. Newly promoted to Lieutenant Commander and fully recovered from his wound, he wore his acres of braid and sword with an assurance that showed that, although her son-in-law only boasted the thin lace of Sublieutenant, the new member of

97

the Bawden family possessed influential friends.

'Lucky fellow,' Ennis whispered in his ear as they both turned and watched Stella enter the church on her father's arm. James found he could not look at her. Instead, Mrs Bawden caught his eye, her own brimming with tears. He turned away, staring at her husband and it was the sight of Bawden's sober suit and gleaming boots that struck him with the irreversible importance of the occasion. Suddenly the sword at his own hip seemed incongruous.

A moment later she was beside him, veiled, and in white as James had naively expected, and he found himself trembling, a lump in his throat, so that he had to cough before uttering his marriage lines. Then she had lifted the veil and he was gazing into those wonderful eyes and smiling at her as she smiled at him.

Afterwards, when they were man and wife in the eyes of the church and the world, Geoffrey charmingly soothed any ruffled feathers in the Bawden camp.

'His people have an estate in Somerset,' Mrs Bawden confided to a relative at the modest reception in a back room of the Albany, 'and James and Stella are honeymooning in a cottage there.'

His duty suavely done, Geoffrey paid a deferential court to Vera which pleased James in a smug way, a way that a man might be forgiven for on his wedding day. Drusilla, Geoffrey's former girl, seemed to have been forgotten.

'She doesn't approve of me, does she?' remarked Stella, clutching his arm and tossing Vera her small bouquet. It was a gesture that pleased Mrs Martin and suggested her son's choice was not mistaken.

The docking of His Majesty's Decoy Ship *Q 67* resulted in the drafting of her crew and the fulfilling of Wyatt's threat of transfer. James and his wife spent only three days in Somerset before orders from the Admiralty recalled him and he brought Stella up to London and The Reddings.

The whisper about the destruction of the U-boat had no immediate effect on his career. Since the story made no appearance on paper it had no official existence; nor had its slow poison yet seeped insidiously into the full network of naval rumour. Instead it was just a snippet of what the Royal

Navy called 'scuttlebutt', the gossip exchanged when men congregated to drink.

The Admiralty's orders attached James briefly to the staff of the Flag Officer at Dover and he kicked his heels in an office shuffling paper in connection with the fuelling of troop transports and minesweepers. It was here that he received the news of his son's birth, obtaining a few hours' leave to see Stella and her baby. Standing by the bed he felt supremely happy, seeing in the wrinkled face of the tiny child, a good omen for the future.

Across the Strait of Dover the war ground to its close and in the heady moment of victory there was one final posting for Sublieutenant James Martin. He found himself hurriedly appointed liaison officer aboard an American cruiser, the USS *Schuyler*. He suffered a certain amount of good-natured ragging by the Americans, but found he liked their informality. It disguised, he discovered too, its own class system, and he found it difficult to become friendly with any of the Annapolis-educated young officers for whom Britain, not Germany, was the traditional 'enemy'. But he struck up a friendship with a lonely engineer lieutenant named Mav Garcia, a clever Hispanic from San Diego.

'Why do they call you "Mav"?' James asked, 'when your real name is John?'

Garcia smiled sadly. 'My *real* name is Juan,' he said, 'and my grandmother was a pure Pueblan Indian. They call me "Maverick", a Texan nickname for a strayed steer. You see, Jim, I don't really belong to this ranch.' Garcia gestured round the wardroom of the *Schuyler*.

'Maverick,' James repeated, testing the word and, recalling Wyatt's hostility, wondered whether it could be applied to himself. He carried Garcia's address away with him after his short stay with the Americans.

The purpose of his brief appointment was to facilitate the cooperation between the Royal Navy's Grand Fleet and representative units of the United States Navy at the formal surrender of Germany's High Seas Fleet. The awesome double line of allied warships had met their quondam enemy at sea with their guns loaded in case of treachery. Standing apart on the *Schuyler*'s navigating bridge, feeling himself something of an unnecessary luxury to the competent

Americans, James experienced a moving moment as the Kaiser's vanquished fleet passed between the twin columns of the victors. The last time he had seen these ships had been seconds before the explosion of the *Indefatigable*.

The imperial German ensign was hauled down for the last time and a few days later the humiliated Germans were escorted north to Scapa Flow, held as a bargaining card to be used in the Peace negotiations at Versailles. *Wehrlos, ehrlos* – disarmed, dishonoured – the German warships lay rotting at their anchors for months until they were finally scuttled by their demoralised crews. This act seemed the final extinguishing of Germany's maritime ambition.

Britannia, the press trumpeted, continued to rule the waves. For the Royal Navy its distant blockade of the Kaiser's fleet, even its Pyrrhic victory of Jutland, fully justified its existence. The early disasters were forgotten and Kit Craddock's defeat was wiped out in the afterglow of the Falklands triumph, when the long arm of the British Admiralty reached the length of the Atlantic and smote von Spee with all the old élan of Nelson.

James was ordered home as soon as his duties aboard the USS *Schuyler* were complete, to await their lordships' pleasure on the understanding that his commitment to 'special service' remained valid. With Stella and their child to support, and faced with the inevitable prospect of the Navy reducing to a peace-time establishment, he felt lucky to be so favoured.

In the winter of 1918, as the euphoria of victory faded and the troops returned home, the enormity of the cost in human lives began to be more generally appreciated. There was a lot of talk about the war having been the last war, the war-to-end-all-wars; but already the influence of events in Russia was reverberating across Europe. Bolshevik revolution had broken out within the German High Seas Fleet in its base at Wilhelmshaven as Germany fell, humiliating further the officers responsible for its surrender, and there were dark rumblings in other places.

At The Reddings they fussed over the baby and worried whether they could keep the house. With the optimism of youth James was confident they could, somehow or other. He waited happily for his new job, writing to Ennis and encouraging him to pay court to Vera. *You know*, he wrote, thinking of his own small part in the victory, *I don't think it was the blockade of the High Seas Fleet that was our greatest naval achievement. I think the defeat of the German submarines was more significant, and a closer-run thing. Vera sends her best wishes.*

Geoffrey wrote back in agreement: *And don't underestimate either the airplane or the tank. Though the latter can't do the Navy much harm, the former could be a real menace. Give my kind regards to Vera, Stella and your mother.*

As he read Geoffrey's reply he smiled. He recognised conventional additions when he saw them.

CHAPTER EIGHT
Cold Wind From Russia

'It's lovely here.'

James looked up from his drawing. Stella's face was shaded from the hot June sunshine by a straw hat decorated with a blue ribbon which fell over its brim and down onto her shoulder.

'Oh, you've moved!'

He put down the pencil aware he had caught her white muslin dress and the deck chair in which she sat with a pleasing economy of line.

'Ssh. You'll wake his lordship.' Stella put out her hand and peered into the cradle set beside her.

James watched her. 'You're happy here, then?' he asked.

'Of course,' she said, turning from the baby to her husband.

'I couldn't bear it if you weren't.'

'Dear James. Let me see.'

He handed her the drawing. 'You were dozing. I didn't think you were going to move for a while.'

'I wasn't dozing,' she said, 'I was sitting quite still. I didn't want anything to change – ever. It's so very peaceful and . . .' She shrugged, her voice trailing off. She gazed the length of the garden. '*Will* you have to sell the house?'

They both studied the warm red brick with its heavy ivy covering. The young leaves trembled in the warm breeze.

'I don't know. Strictly speaking it's Aunt Anne's house, and you know how matters stand there. Anyway, I don't know whether we'd be able to sell; things aren't the way they were before the war. What do you think of the drawing?'

'Eee, you're bloody clever, lad,' she said in her broadest Yorkshire accent.

102

'Don't ever stop talking like that.'

'Vera thinks it's awful.'

'Did she say so?' asked James, astonished at his cousin's effrontery.

'She doesn't have to. She wrinkles her forehead. She thinks it's prejudicial to your career. She cares a lot about your career.'

'She must have been talking to your father,' he said with a hint of bitterness.

'What do you think?' She looked at him solemnly with her green eyes. He sensed her insecurity, an insecurity compounded by the new-found responsibility of the child.

'I love you, Stella. It's quite simple: nothing more or less than that. I can't answer for Vera because she had expectations that were dashed by Tom's death. I don't see how she could have married her cousin, though people do it, but his death removes any quibbles and merely makes her bitter. I'm glad to see Geoffrey making a fuss of her, but I suppose she's jealous of you. The fact that you come from a different background makes it difficult for her to accept.'

'A *humbler* family, don't you mean?' Stella said ironically. 'I overheard your mother use that expression.'

'There's not much humble about *your* mother,' he said, grinning. 'It's all a lot of nonsense anyway. If the war taught me anything, it's that people are just people and you like them or dislike them or you don't care one way or the other. It hasn't got much to do with what backgrounds they come from unless it really interferes with the relationship.

'I've always felt odd because I was an orphan, I suppose. Mother and I were accepted here on sufferance. I grew up feeling a bit alien. Part of that was always playing second fiddle to Tom; Tom would have been first violin even if our respective positions had been reversed, because he was bred to the Royal Navy. He was a classic Englishman.'

'No, he wasn't.'

James frowned; Stella's tone was assertive. 'What do you mean? You never knew him.'

'He was not what you thought, you know.'

'I don't understand.'

'He wasn't your uncle's son, James. Aunt Anne told me everything. I think she assumes, sometimes, that I am some kind of family servant, the kind you confide in. Anyway, she told me. Your cousin Tom was the son of a married friend of your aunt's; she married your uncle . . .'

'To legitimise Tom?' James looked at her in astonishment. 'Good God!'

'Did you never think of them as an odd match?'

James digested the information. The shock of it, far from lifting a weight, seemed to lay a heavier obligation on him.

'No, never. When one is young, one accepts the world as it is. I suppose the Admiral never knew?'

'I shouldn't think so. Your mother doesn't miss much but I shouldn't think Vera knows, though she might have found out. It could explain her feelings for Tom.'

'And her heartbreak.'

'You won't tell her, James, will you? It would only open old wounds, particularly now Geoffrey seems to be showing a mild interest.'

'No, of course not . . .'

They sat in silence for a while. It pleased James that Geoffrey Ennis was attracted to Vera. He was a good deal older, but it would somehow redress the balance in the family and help make good the awful damage of the war if anything came of it. They were, after all, a naval family, and their lives mirrored the fortunes of the service that nurtured them. As for the difference in age, with the decimation of a whole generation of young men amid the churned clay of Picardy and Flanders, such irregularities were becoming commonplace. He somehow saw his own marriage to Stella in this light.

To survive, society, and the Royal Navy in particular, had to become more democratic, to open its doors to new blood as the United States Navy was already doing in commissioning men like Juan Garcia, men of ability and talent. The Royal Navy needed to preserve its old threads of tradition, threads like the Martin family itself which could trace its ancestry back to the establishment of the great naval dynasties of the Napoleonic Wars; but it needed to be as open and eclectic as it had been then, when a country parson's son with a searing Norfolk accent could find immortality as Viscount Nelson of the Nile. What it could not afford was to cultivate tradition for its own, revered sake; that way lay atrophy and mummification.

104

'Here is Vee,' said Stella, breaking into his train of thought. She walked down the garden, a tall, slender figure, her long skirt swirling about her. She was smiling and James thought she looked happier than she had done for a long time.

'I thought you'd bring us some tea,' James joked.

'No, only news.'

'Good news, I hope.'

'Yes.' She sat on the grass beside him, tucking her skirt under her knees and smoothing the grass as though it was the pile of a carpet. 'Geoffrey's coming to dinner. He's been appointed to a ship in Admiral Cowan's fleet.'

'What does that mean?' asked Stella.

'This Bolshevik business in Russia,' explained James. 'Cowan's fleet is going to the Baltic; intervention is the name for it. I'm not sure it's a good idea.'

'Does that mean you wouldn't want to go?' Vera asked sharply.

'I'll go wherever their lordships send me, Vee,' James replied coolly. 'I'm simply not in favour of our involvement.'

'James is a naval officer,' said Stella supportively.

Vera lowered her eyes. She seemed to regret any implied criticism, for she quickly added, 'Geoffrey says there's a cold wind blowing out of Russia and Cowan's being sent as a draught excluder.'

Eager to recover their earlier mood James and Stella laughed and the noise woke the baby to a grizzle. James rose and lifted his son from the cradle. The child's face reminded him of Bawden and the screwed up eyes were those of Stella.

'It's all right, little man,' he murmured, then said to Stella and Vera, 'he wants *his* tea, you know, and *he* won't wait!'

They no longer habitually dressed for dinner at The Reddings. The reduced circumstances of the household (which could now only boast an inefficient teenaged maid) dictated this, while Aunt Anne's condition rendered it impractical.

Aunt Anne spent most of her time in silent introspection. There was the occasional irrational outburst, upon which either Vera or Harriet Martin would take it upon themselves in an unspoken rota to soothe and console. Once or twice

105

they had found her crouched motionless over some broken object, a vase or statuette, contemplating its shattered shards with a curious expression of horror, bewilderment and satisfaction. The doctor, a young man, had dismissed this behaviour as unimportant, something he called an 'association of ideas', whatever that might mean, for nobody saw in it anything other than another symptom of her derangement.

But Aunt Anne's madness did not quite alloy the pleasure they all derived from that dinner. Fortunately the Admiral had bequeathed a stock of fine claret and Harriet Martin had discovered a certain enjoyment in cooking. As Geoffrey Ennis remarked, her lamb cutlets 'melted on the tongue'.

Ennis had arrived in high spirits as sailors do upon the eve of their departure, looking forward to the challenge of the future and unmindful of those they leave behind them. His mood was infectious, and Harriet was pleased to see the youngsters enjoying themselves, relieved the bad times were past. They were a family again, she thought, and then, with a mild shock, she was the oldest member of it! The idea was uncomfortable and demanded diversion.

'What are we to make of these Bolshevik revolutionaries then, Geoffrey?'

Ennis turned his sleekly handsome blond head with its grey-blue eyes, his forehead wrinkling into a frown.

'Bit like Robespierre's lot, I suppose, Mrs Martin. Lot of twaddle about *liberté, egalité* and all that, but pretty adept at the fratricide. I believe the whole country is in an uproar, but the Whites seem to be doing quite well. The Yanks and Japanese have intervened from the Pacific coast, the Cossacks are playing the devil round the Caspian and Black Seas, and we're doing our bit in the Baltic and the White Sea.'

'I'm not sure we're wise to get involved,' James put in, repeating his misgivings of the afternoon.

'But James, what about the poor Tsar and his family?' objected his mother.

'They say there isn't much hope for the Tsar, I'm afraid,' Ennis said.

'But his poor children, that little boy,' said Stella, acutely conscious of the vulnerability of children.

106

'It's Russia's problem,' said James. 'We did the same when we executed King Charles the First; the French did it with Louis the Sixteenth. It makes turning the clock back more difficult. I don't see much difference.'

'But this is 1919, James,' said his mother.

'Ask the Russian peasants or factory workers what 1919 means to them.'

'James has been reading that awful man Ransome in the *Manchester Guardian*, haven't you, James?' sniped Vera, 'I found a copy in the study.'

'Sedition, James! Infamous conduct,' laughed Geoffrey, who did not want the conversation to become political.

'I think Ransome's rather good,' said James, catching Ennis's mood. 'I suppose the Navy's always sorting out someone else's problems. It's a great British tradition, intervention, sticking our nose in, call it what you will. Anyway, here's to your new posting, Geoffrey.' He raised his glass. 'A very successful commission and a speedy return.'

They toasted Ennis, then Stella and the baby; they toasted James in anticipation of his own eventual posting, followed by Harriet on the excellence of her lamb cutlets. Then Geoffrey raised his glass to Vera because, as he said, she was pretty enough to deserve a toast drunk in her exclusive honour. As the laughter died away Mrs Martin put out her hand to her sister-in-law.

'And Aunt Anne,' she said, 'for being so frightfully brave.'

'Here, here!' They raised their glasses again, slightly sheepish at their merriment, and turned to Aunt Anne.

Hearing her name and confronted with their faces, the poor woman felt constrained to reply.

'I read the *Manchester Guardian*,' she said timidly, and the oddity of the remark kept them staring intimidatingly at her.

'I'm sure you do, Anne darling,' said Harriet, recovering first, 'now let's all –'

'It's influenza, you know,' Aunt Anne went on, her eyes wide. 'Influenza.'

They looked at each other, embarrassed, then Geoffrey asked, 'Will you play for us, Vee?', and they moved into the drawing room where Vera settled herself at the piano and Geoffrey coughed beside her. The others sat and waited.

'Not Stanford's *Sea Songs*, Geoffrey,' pleaded James. 'He sings "Drake was in his Hammock" every morning while he shaves,' he explained.

'No,' Ennis said grinning. 'Something for us.' He looked down at Vera.

'Tinkle the ivories then, Vee,' James demanded, and Stella motioned him to silence.

Geoffrey sang 'Me and My Girl' to Vera's accompaniment, and during the applause his hand touched hers. James and his mother exchanged glances and Aunt Anne, her head lolling forward, jerked awake with the word 'Influenza!'

James and Vera saw Ennis to the door. 'Good luck, old man,' James said. They shook hands and James left them alone. There was no announcement that night, but it was clear to James from Vera's expression as she rejoined the others that Geoffrey would propose when he returned from the Baltic.

'She'll accept,' he said quietly to Stella as they prepared for bed, 'and I'm pleased for her. She can worry about Geoffrey's career instead of mine.'

'Yours,' joked Stella in her exaggerated accent, 'is blighted by unsuitable wife, lad.'

But it was not the case. James's own departure occurred only three days later, a hurried summons that brooked no delay: he learned that he had been selected for 'special operations'.

'What does that mean?' asked Stella, her eyes brighter than ever.

'Oh, nothing much by the look of it. I've got to report to a place in Essex; bit of a malarial swamp, I gather. Very hush-hush.' He took her in his arms. 'You'll be all right here.'

'Oh, I know, but I wish you weren't going so soon.'

'Orders, darling.'

'I understand. A trawler skipper's daughter can say her farewells without hanging on your arm weeping.'

They kissed, and he held her for a long time. 'Look after my son, darling,' he said at last.

'Look after my husband,' she whispered, moving her body against him.

'God, I love you, Stella.'

'Right sir, full throttle.'

The grimy figure of Artificer Hain emerged from the engine compartment hatch. The noise of the big Thorney-croft engine mounted to a roar. James felt the rudder kick, so he had to grip the wheel as the coastal motor boat increased speed and the crests of the little wavelets rippling the surface of the River Blackwater advanced towards them with a regularity only obvious at speed. On either side the marshy banks of the Essex coast fell back. To starboard, behind a low sea wall, the ancient and lonely chapel of St Orthona broke the line of the horizon, nestling in a corner of a ruined Roman fort. To port, fronting the low promontory of Point Clear with its squat Martello tower, the irregular quadrilateral gaff sails of a pair of Brightlingsea smacks worked out of the Colne with the ebb tide under their keels.

Hain pulled himself out of the hatch, grinning with triumph. The removal of his bulk released more noise and James gestured to the hatch which Hain closed.

'Think you've cured the problem this time?' James asked, still having to shout. Hain nodded but showed his fingers crossed. 'Fuel feed,' he mouthed.

The CMB bumped slightly now, as they passed out into the open waters of the Wallet and the Eagle buoy shot astern.

'You could drive this thing over a field of wet grass,' remarked James as the rushing air tore at his hair. Tears were drawn from his eyes as he felt the sheer thrill of commanding so much power. His elation was a mixture of personal and professional pride which seemed a vindication of his survival; a complex, somewhat shameful rationa-lisation that now saw in his preservation an almost mystical significance: Tom had not been the legitimate heir to the family's tradition. He and his son were. He had been home once, on weekend leave from the secret naval establishment on Osea Island. Stella looked radiant while the boy had begun to toddle uncertainly, and James thought him a miraculous little being. They had called the child John, partly because it was a simple name and partly in honour of Juan Garcia whom, in some curious way, James hoped his son would emulate in what he conceived would be the universal meritocracy of the twentieth century.

And the Royal Navy, contracting though it was, had almost answered his aspirations with this posting. The new-fangled motorboats entailed adapting the diesel engine for marine use in something the engineers and scientists called 'hydroplanes'. The analogy with the new aerial technology gave the temperamental CMBs an up-to-the-minute *cachet* intoxicating enough to any young and dashing naval father.

'Well, sir, what do you think? Caspian or Baltic for us?' The question was bellowed by Hain in his ear. The Admiralty had managed to transport a number of CMBs overland to the Caspian Sea where they were operating in support of the White Russian counter-revolutionaries; and in the Baltic another flotilla was based in a Finnish yacht club from where they carried out periodic sorties to run agents in and out of Petrograd. Working their boats up, James and Hain were part of a second wave who only awaited orders for their deployment.

James turned the boat in a long sweep, aware she skidded with the centrifugal force of the alteration of course, the wheel kicking madly in his hands. They were almost abeam of Clacton and the sea was rougher, shaking the boat so that, from time to time, the propellor moved into less dense water and raced alarmingly.

'She'd handle better armed,' shouted James.

'We ought to do a run with a dummy loaded, simulate the weight.' Hain jerked his thumb aft. The CMB's principal weapon of attack was a single torpedo. It was mounted behind them in a tube that pointed astern, which meant they had to manoeuvre close to an enemy before delivering a lethally Parthian shot, relying on their speed both to arrive undetected and to get away unmolested.

But their satisfaction was changed to mutual anxiety as the pitch of the engine abruptly changed. The descending note was depressing, the roar dropped to a rumble and then that too died away. The CMB lost way, its smooth, powered plane ceased and it lurched uncomfortably upon the surface

110

of the sea, throwing its crew about while the stink of diesel oil promoted an unmanly nausea.

'Why the hell did I volunteer?' grumbled Hain, pulling back the engine hatch.

Philosophically James jammed himself into a corner and awaited events. It was not the first time they had suffered a breakdown.

The steam picket launch attached to the Osea Island establishment towed them in at sunset. Impotently waiting for the repair Hain failed to achieve, James had been doing some calculations. The engine problem was obviously going to delay them further, and by the time the boats were made ready, crated and shipped to Helsinki, or Turku-Abo, the season would be too far advanced for much action in the Baltic. Cowan's fleet would have to withdraw to avoid being iced in, so it looked like the Caspian for them.

He felt a mild irritation he should not have thought of that before, and wondered if Hain, who was a bright chap, had realised it. Perhaps they had just been too busy trying to sort out the engine; it was getting a bit tedious. If their colleagues were having anything like half the worries running in and out of Bolshevik controlled waters, they must be wetting their pants with more than spray up in the Gulf of Finland.

The trees of Osea were black against the blood-red sunset, the jackdaws cawing loudly as they tied up dispiritedly to the wooden jetty and walked to the HQ hut to report. The CO looked drawn and worried when James marched in and saluted. James was rather touched with his concern.

'I'm sorry, sir, bloody thing –'

'Martin,' the CO broke in, lifting an envelope from the papers on his desk, 'I gather it's pretty bad news. I've been told to give you leave.'

He went back to the jetty and sat on board the CMB where the persistent stench of diesel kept the mosquitoes and gnats away. There was enough light to read the scrawled capitals of the telegram, written with a dispassionate hand, the hand of a middleman, a word-broker, a teller of horrid truths . . .

REGRET STELLA PASSED AWAY LAST NIGHT STOP BABY AND YOUR MOTHER UNWELL INFLUENZA STOP VERA

He stared unseeing at the river's surface. The tide was on the ebb again, gurgling at the piles of the jetty and tugging gently at the boat's moorings. It ran smoothly seawards in a series of whorls and eddies, grey and cruel in its indifference. He was mocked by the happiness and elation he had felt earlier in the day, and as the tears started from his eyes, blotting his vision with the realisation of his loss, they seemed at first, against the background of the river, like the bobbing heads of defencelessly swimming sailors.

CHAPTER NINE
The Windjammer

The daylight was fading as James Martin, swathed in an ill-fitting black oilskin and carrying the brass sidelights, fought his way up onto the forecastle. Astern of the heavily laden barque a pale streak of bilious sky appeared briefly between a lowering overcast and the heaving irregularity of the horizon.

The sidelights, one glowing ruby red, the other green, their glims magnified by heavy lenses, were dull with verdigris. If he had trimmed the wicks properly they would survive the night, otherwise they would be blown out in an hour. Bracing himself against the swooping scend of the ship he fitted the sidelights in their respective places and secured them.

'All alight!' he holloaed into the wind, and saw for a moment the upraised arm of the Second Mate, standing silhouetted against the ochre sky before a great sea rushed up astern of the ship.

James turned forward, took up his position as first lookout and settled himself to his lonely vigil. The Clyde-registered four-masted barque *Socotra* was running north-east, heading out of the Roaring Forties, cutting obliquely across the southern Indian Ocean on her way from Cardiff to Hong Kong with a gutful of Welsh steam coal in her wallowing hull. With the wind on her port quarter and her double topgallant sails furled, she raced along under reduced canvas, dipping her bow while the sea surged up to within a few feet of James, boiling round the tawdry figurehead, then stabbing her spike bowsprit at the sky so that, as she began her next swoop downwards, James felt the pit of his stomach rise sickeningly.

113

But it was a familiar inconvenience, one that he accepted if not willingly then with the knowledge that he had volunteered for it, eager for its cold comfort. And he had endured this endless, stultifying routine of four hours on and four hours off duty, of helm and lookout, of rust chipping and painting, of sail shifting and heaving at brace, tack and sheet for nearly four years. He had laid aloft day and night, in stark terror on the first few occasions, to beat half-frozen canvas into submission so the gaskets that reefed and reduced *Socotra*'s sail area could be knotted round the heavy cloth. He had gone without sleep when the cry for all hands turned the watch below from their bunks and the length of time necessary to accomplish their task had sent the other watch below on its completion, and he had endured the bad food and inadequate water that made British merchant sailing ships notorious the world over, their owners a by-word for meanness, parsimony and indifference.

All this catalogue of deprivation he had accepted because it exhausted him; because when he turned in wet and cold he fell instantly asleep and because, even when engaged in the lonely duty of lookout, he had learned the sailor's trick of allowing his mind to slip into limbo, a trick made easy by the diet and the tiredness.

And yet the savage, unremitting routine, dictated not so much by the greed of ship-owners as the implacable waging of war against the elements, filled him with a profound satisfaction, a satisfaction which dismissed those urgings of conscience that implied he had run away from his responsibilities. It was not his fault; the Geddes Axe, as it was popularly called, had fallen upon the Royal Navy to chop off its inessential brushwood, and the rumours circulating about the Decoy Ship *Q 67* and the events subsequent to her sinking of a German U-boat had gathered like a little cloud over his name. He had not gone to the Caspian, his absence attending Stella's funeral had caused him to miss the boat, and his later appointment to a cruiser had been short-lived, terminated brutally by official notice of redundancy. At the time it did not seem a very terrible blow; he did not suffer alone and nor was Stella's death his only bereavement. In the influenza pandemic he had lost his mother as well as his wife. Only his son had recovered, to be

114

looked after by Vera. Vera had refused Geoffrey Ennis; she had, she said, contracted obligations that made any thought of marriage an impossibility. Stella's child was henceforth her own.

That was, perhaps, cause enough for James to suffer pangs of conscience, but he had sensed Vera was glad of the excuse; it underlined her earlier love for Tom and seemed to be the affirmation of fate to tend her tiny nephew.

He received letters from her occasionally, acknowledgements that she was receiving his paltry allotments and, most recently, the welcome news that she had at last settled the fate of The Reddings.

You will be glad to know, she had written, *that I have found a purchaser for The Reddings, a man named Briggs who, rumour has it, is a war profiteer. I know he owns six steam ships and I believe they have made him rich. We will be removed when you return. Geoffrey has found us a house near Harwich. It is not above fifteen years old and came cheap as the owners were naval people who have been forced to sell thanks to that awful man Geddes.*

So Geoffrey was still a friend, which was surprising. Geoffrey had not been booted out of the Navy, but then Geoffrey had not had an uncle who lost a battleship, nor had he machine gunned a ruthless enemy.

Anyway, the house is on the coast and Johnnie will grow up within sight and smell of the sea. He is very well and I thank heaven he never knew his mother . . .

Did he not? James recalled the dark head nuzzling Stella's full breast, and shied away from the thought with practised ease. Stella belonged to a hermetical, private part of his life. He was not yet ready to dwell on her memory; what mattered now was to survive and Vera's clumsily well-intentioned phrase seemed almost cynical, suggesting little John lived under a strict and uncompromising regime.

Such a frigid childhood would not make him vulnerable to life's disappointments, James thought, when he allowed himself to think of these things at all.

By midnight, when James's watch was tumbled out of the forecastle again, he found himself on the wheel. The *Socotra* rushed through the water, the hiss of the sea joining the

115

moan of the gale in her rigging. The wind piped a dozen notes in her fabric, from a thin whistle in the rigging screws to a deep booming in the weather stays. Aloft, the differing diameter of chain sheets, of wire braces, lifts and halliards, produced a variety of howls that formed one vast diapason. This noise was not constant, but varied in pitch as *Socotra* ascended in the following sea and had as its counterpoint the crash and roar of the waves as they raced up astern, threatening to overwhelm the barque, except she outran them and they burst under her lifting counter and foamed up along her sides, sluicing in over the port rail and filling her waist, only to exit through the starboard wash-ports which opened and closed with a discordant clunk.

As he felt each sea lift the stern James instinctively turned the wheel, bringing *Socotra*'s stern to it, avoiding a broach which would slew the ship broadside to the tumbling wave crests. He was aware, as the watch drew on, of the increasing difficulty he was having in keeping the barque on her course.

A figure loomed up in the darkness and peered into the orange halo of the binnacle light.

'Getting a bit mulish, is she?' asked Mr Bushnell, the *Socotra*'s Second Mate.

'Got a bloody mind of her own, sir.'

James did not resent the respect due to Bushnell as an officer. His early experience with men like Bawden had taught him the foolishness of despising men who commanded ships without the benefit of a Royal commission. It was a foolishness he had encountered several times in the Royal Navy, but since that service had abandoned him he had transferred his allegiance. He was not jealous of Bushnell's status as an officer, for he had deliberately chosen the path of seaman for himself.

Bushnell grunted and walked forward. James could see him staring aloft, and then he called an apprentice and sent him below to speak to the Captain.

'We'll take the main course off her, mister,' ordered Captain Short 'and the mizen tops'ls.'

'Aye, aye, sir.' Bushnell began bellowing down into the waist, where the rest of the watch, saving James on the wheel and the lookout forward, huddled for shelter.

116

Short stumped aft and stood next to James. The *Socotra*'s Master was a taciturn man whose longest sentences were orders such as those he had just given. James had seen him reeling drunk, but only in port, and only the day after they arrived, when the tension of a passage and the relief of arrival might be allowed any man.

'Keep her steady now,' Short said as, amidships, Bushnell and the watch were starting the main sheets. Through their very boot soles they could feel the flog of the heavy canvas as it no longer contained the driving force of the gale. Master and helmsman could hear the shouted orders beyond the poop rail. Then they could see the great sail, grey in the gloom, gradually gathered up under its yard by the clew lines, and the dark shapes of the men going aloft to furl it.

'Easier?' asked Short.

'A little, sir.' James still struggled with the helm as the *Socotra* continued to threaten a corkscrew motion to port which could still result, if he was careless, in her broaching-to.

A larger wave hustled up under her stern and the deck canted steeply. The poop seemed to lift, rearing into the sky, the waist disappeared under a welter of water and the forecastle and bowsprit seemed to skid into the black depths ahead. The wave slammed against the rudder, a physical blow that, despite the low gearing of the steering, transmitted its energy to James as he applied counter helm. For what seemed like an age, *Socotra* continued her pitch-poling movement, apparently determined to turn end over end like a child rolling head over heels down a hill. At last the rudder bit, the wave passed on and the poop sank with sickening suddenness. Stabbing now at the sky the bow rose and the fore-course drew the ship onwards. Mr Bushnell dragged himself up the poop ladder. Even in the dark James could see the water pouring off him. He would have been alone in the waist, coiling down the clew garnets as the watch furled the sail above his head.

Beside him, James heard Captain Short give a low, merciless chuckle. 'Wet work, mister.'

'Aye, sir,' replied Bushnell philosophically. 'Mizen topsails now, sir?'

'Yes, Mr Bushnell, if you please.'

The *Socotra* steered much easier once the mizen topsails had been furled. James reported the fact to the Captain, expecting him to go below again, but Short remained alongside the wheel. After a few moments he said, 'You've been on the ship nearly four years now. That's enough time to sit for your ticket. You could do it in Hong Kong.'

The idea had never occurred to James. He had joined the *Socotra* as a seaman, if not to avoid responsibility then to lose himself in the vastness of the ocean among the other sea tramps and vagabonds that made up the crews of the few remaining British windjammers. He was lost for words, but common courtesy demanded he said something.

'Yes, sir,' he managed lamely.

'Think about it,' said Short, moving forward. 'You're wasted here.' And then he was gone and James stood alone at the wheel, the gale flapping the oilskin about his lean frame and shrieking 'second chance' into his ear.

'Bushnell reckons we'll raise Wang Lan lighthouse before dawn.' Able Seaman Wren brought the news into the forecastle while the members of the starboard watch lounged through the second dog watch. It was an evening of fine weather with the *Socotra* carrying sail to her upper topgallants, above which she bore nothing, her royal yards having been removed some years earlier for reasons of economy. She leaned easily to the breeze which, it being late September, was a favourable, south-west monsoon wind. Smudges of steamer smoke on the horizon marked the presence of other ships, an indication of the trade routes converging on the entrepôt of Hong Kong, and they had been passing through fleets of Chinese fishing junks since that morning, further evidence of the vast country on whose borders the British colony was but a tiny enclave.

'Be up Nathan Road tomorrow night then, lads,' said Able Seaman Todd, rubbing his hands in anticipation. 'Up the rags for a short time, eh?'

The thought of slaking their lust silenced them for a few moments, then someone asked, 'What are you going to do for money? Old man won't give us a sub.'

Todd had already thought of this. 'Sell these,' he said, drawing from a canvas ditty bag pieces of scrimshaw work, a pair of ships in bottles and some neatly done rope-sennet work.

'Who's going to buy that crap?' asked Wren. 'Every Jack's got a heap of that garbage.'

'Tourists. Them rich Yanks . . .'

'Them rich Yanks'd rather buy ivory carvings and them laquer things and camphor wood chests. Not that crap.'

'He only wants enough cash for a short time, Birdie,' put in a third man, using Wren's predictable nickname. 'You know, a little Chinese bint, not one of them pieces of white shit that cost the earth and have doses up to their ear 'oles.'

'What *I* want,' said Copplestone, 'is one of them Russian women. Bloody princesses and duchesses, and Gawd knows what, some of them.'

And the conversation followed its idle way into a discussion of the price of debauchery. James lay on his bunk and stared at the deck-head above him, shutting his ears to the words of his watch mates. Talk of women, even as detached as the unfortunate drabs that brought the seafarers of the world their brief, joyless moments of release, inevitably revived his own memories. He thought of Stella's warm body, and then, because he had the facility of switching his mind forcibly off thoughts of his true love, he let himself be stirred by distant and lascivious recollections of Emily. Where was she now? And what would she say if they met, him a washed out merchant Jack with not much more than the shirt on his back to call his own?

He wondered whether he should take Captain Short's advice. Four years was enough to atone for those obsessively haunting events in which he had had a hand, and enough to mourn Stella, though he would mourn her as long, in Emily's unforgettable phrase, as his fountain was inexhaustible.

No, that was nonsense. He would always love Stella as long as there was breath in his body, but he thought now, for the first time in four years, that he did not want to end up like these men. He liked them, the odd rag-tag collection. Birdie Wren whose aggressively tough exterior concealed a soft heart and whose comments were a kind of cross-grained, big-brotherly advice to his watch mates; Micky Todd, a merry-eyed mischievous man who never wasted a

119

thought on tomorrow; Tommy Mackay, big, loose-limbed, with the intellect of a simpleton and the strength of a carthorse, and Sven Haraldson who had run away from the Baltic island of Bornholm at the age of nine and inexplicably made this elderly rust-bucket of a lime-juice barque his home.

James sighed. He had more in common with *Socotra*'s apprentices, middle-class boys aspiring to become officers. He had helped them with their studies, shown them something of the intricacies of determining longitude with sextant and chronometer, or working a traverse, in preparation for sitting their Second Mate's examinations at the Board of Trade. He supposed Captain Short had got wind of his knowledge and abilities, for he had never spoken of his past to anybody on board beyond admitting that he had served in the Royal Navy during the war.

Whatever the reason behind Short's advice, the old man was proposing a rather decent thing, James thought. In releasing him from his articles, Short accepted he would have to find a replacement. Granted, such things were not difficult in Hong Kong, but British ship masters were not noted for such consideration for their crews, and Short had hitherto shown no signs of breaking the mould. To James, with his shadowy faith in fate, Short's suggestion seemed a manifestation of cosmic forgiveness.

The next morning, with Wang Lan lighthouse a white column astern lit by the rays of the rising sun as the *Socotra* lay with her main sails backed to the mast and waited for tug and pilot to tow her in through the Lye Mun Pass, James Martin, rated AB, requested his discharge in Hong Kong.

Captain Short nodded his approval. 'I've had my eye on you for some time,' he said, 'and I'm glad you've decided to take my advice. You don't belong in the fo'c's'le and men who don't belong there only go one way.'

Being a man of few words he did not enlarge further but James knew, but for Captain Short, he had been on the brink of the abyss.

Part Two – Fire
1929-1945

'And after the fire, a still small voice.'

First Book of Kings, Chapter 1, Verse 19.

CHAPTER TEN
Old Friends

'Officer come see you, sir.'

From his desk James grunted acknowledgement of the quartermaster's announcement. As Chief Officer of the SS *Poyang* owned by the China Independent Steam Navigation Company of Hong Kong, there was almost always someone clamouring to see him, particularly in the ship's home port. The officer, be he customs, immigration or police, could bloody well wait until he had finished allocating the consignments of cargo arriving alongside in accordance with his rough cargo plan.

'Cases of bicycles for Shanghai,' he muttered, reading the next boat note dumped on his desk by his last visitor, the Chief Tally Clerk, 'for number three tween deck.' He scribbled the abbreviation on the note. Outside the derrick winches clattered, hissing steam into the already humid atmosphere of Hong Kong harbour. The *Poyang* was encircled by merchantmen from all corners of the globe lying at their mooring buoys, each surrounded by junks, sampans and lighters, their crews coming and going along with the washer-women, tailors, cobblers, barbers, sew-sew women and fortune-tellers who pandered to them. Ferries crisscrossed the busy harbour, setting the smaller craft bobbing, while every hour or so a merchant ship arrived or departed. This concentration of activity, bounded by the hills of Victoria Island, Kowloon and the New Territories, filled the air with a hum and buzz that never ceased, day or night.

'James?'

Chief Officer James Martin finally looked up. He did not

123

recognise the figure in the doorway at first. The white tropical uniform with its impossible imperial bloomers for shorts, the three gold bars of commander on the shoulder epaulettes and the face shadowed by the cap peak was unidentifiable. The stranger raised a white shod foot over the seastep, entered the cabin and removed his hat with the familiar anchor and crown of the Royal Navy.

'Geoffrey!'

James was on his feet in an instant, pumping Ennis's hand delightedly and drawing him beyond the desk into his cabin proper. He gestured Ennis to the chintz-covered settee, ensured the fan was adequately trained and rang the bell for his steward.

'Two beers, Wong, or would you rather have a gin?'

'Beer will be fine.'

They sat for a moment, staring at each other, then Ennis said, 'I suppose long-time-no-see, is the appropriate thing to say,' and the ice was broken.

'My God, it *is* a long time,' agreed James, 'and I suppose I'm to blame for that.' James broke off as the beers arrived. He felt suddenly guilty, guilty of neglect, of relying too heavily on Vera and of indirectly spoiling the romance between Ennis and his cousin. He sighed.

'Look, Geoffrey,' he said, when the steward had gone, 'I'm really grateful for all your help and support. I'm sorry you and Vee didn't get together.'

'I don't know why you're apologising. You had a rough deal, but it was Vee who refused me, you know.'

'Yes, but it was largely on account of Johnnie.'

'Was it? Or was it on account of that blighter Tom? I never met him, and it seems a trifle irrational to dislike a dead man, but I cordially disliked his memory. Cheers.'

Ennis was grinning; he only half meant what he said, but James knew the extent of Tom's posthumous influence only too well.

'He was quite a fellow, Tom; one of nature's golden boys. Matter of fact I still feel pretty sore about him sometimes, which is damn stupid when you consider he was blown up over ten years ago. Shows the perversity of the human soul, eh? Anyway, Vera wrote and told me you'd married.'

Ennis nodded. 'Yes, in twenty-four, girl called Drusilla

124

Trelawney. Old Cornish family. We've a two-year-old daughter.'

'Congratulations,' said James, 'and on the brass hat.' He indicated Ennis's commander's braid. 'Where are you now?'

'In the *Peterborough*.'

James recalled the cruiser lying off the naval dockyard. So Geoffrey was second in command and well on his way to captain and admiral, James thought with a stab of mixed regret and jealousy. Geoffrey, cheated of Vera, would have married well; an old Cornish family would be in the best traditions of the service, and surely Drusilla had been an old flame? Not for Geoffrey Ennis the daughter of a Hull trawlerman!

'You've done pretty well considering the pounding the old service has had,' he said quickly, lest Ennis guessed what he was thinking.

'God, haven't we? You've no idea, Jimmy. Oh, I know you caught it from Geddes's bloody axe and we lost a lot of good chaps, but we could always recall you fellows to the colours *in extremis*. No, it's the ships; of course, we had a lot of old rubbish to clear out, the pre-war battleships and so on, but we dispensed with seventy-odd cruisers and over *two hundred and fifty* destroyers! Can you imagine it? And most of *them* were sold! You and I know that in any future scrap submarines and aeroplanes will be a big problem, and to protect our surface fleet, not to mention merchant ships like this one, we'll need destroyers or something damn like 'em.'

It was clear Ennis was on a favourite soap box. James was not sure he would rush to join up with the alacrity that Ennis seemed to take for granted, but he was nevertheless interested in a conversation that touched the subject he once knew so much about.

'D'you think there's going to be another war?' he asked. 'I thought the Washington Treaty would stop any chance of that.'

'Huh!' exclaimed Ennis. 'All very laudable, and due credit to our American cousins for initiating it, though it was that pair of Japanese battleships the *Matsu* and *Nagato* which frightened them enough to do it. I think the Yanks are right to be apprehensive of the Japanese; what's your view? You've been out here long enough.'

125

James shrugged. 'They certainly snapped up the German possessions in Shantung and they have imperial ambitions to rival our own. What's more, they reckon to have a better title to bits of the Far East than ourselves.'

'You sound as though you agree with them.'

'Well, if you make a vogue of imperialism you shouldn't be surprised if others flatter you by imitation.'

'That doesn't sound very patriotic.'

'Oh, come on Geoffrey, times are changing. I'd have thought that would have been obvious to even the most tradition-rooted officer after the General Strike you've been through.'

Ennis was uncomfortably silent.

'Anyway,' James resumed, 'you don't think this Washington Treaty's going to hold?'

'No, the limiting tonnages are already being broken. The Japanese did it first with the aircraft carrier *Akagi* and were promptly followed by the United States, and I mention this in confidence because we pay lip service to both governments' assurances that the ships are within the limits. Both the *Saratoga* and the *Lexington* are over the top, and latest indications are that the new Jap carrier, the *Kaga*, is about five thousand tons in excess of the agreement.'

'So the whole thing's a farce?'

'More or less.'

'What about us?'

'We stick to the rules. All our carriers are lightweight and within the limits. So far I suppose their lordships consider the Americans and the Japs can indulge in their own arms race for a Pacific theatre war.'

'We've still got a stake in the Pacific. Hong Kong here, Malaya, Borneo, not to mention the purely commercial interests and investments we've got in China.'

'The trouble is, James, we can't afford to keep up any more. We only managed in the last scrap because of American loans; so as long as Germany's on short commons, we can let the Yanks take the weight hereabouts.'

James digested this intelligence, but Ennis was in full flood.

'A friend of mine in the *Kent* had a look over the Jap cruiser *Myoko* and he dismissed any ideas we might have that the little yellow men are lagging behind us in hardware. He said the *Kent* was a bloody luxury liner by comparison.'

'That's rather your fault, isn't it? – if that isn't being too tactless.'

'*My* fault?' frowned Ennis, detecting the acidulous tone in James's voice. 'I don't follow you.'

'Well the Navy always insists on a high bullshit factor in its ship design, doesn't it? Big quarters for the officers, lots of brass, spit and polish, all part of the philosophy of keeping a fighting service on the top line. We didn't have any of that in *Q 67* and she was one of the most efficient fighting ships I've been in.'

'Yes, I've heard all about *Q 67.*'

'And what does that mean?' James drew himself up in his chair.

'I did a staff course with Colin Wyatt. He's a captain now. Your name came up and he told me about the chaps in the water.'

'He would . . .'

'Look, I'm not judging you, James, damn it I –'

'I know, I know. Geoffrey, you've been a brick. I'm sorry. I really do appreciate what you've done, especially for young Johnnie.'

'I've told Vera we could get him into the Royal Hospital School next year. It's pretty close to where they're living.'

'Yes, Vera told me, and I'm grateful.'

'You've had rotten luck, James, and I'm still fond of Vee. I hope you don't think I'm meddling.'

James felt a lump forming in his throat. Somehow Geoffrey's concern and thorough decent-mindedness shamed him, shamed him just as the lingering and persistent story of his shooting the swimming German sailors did.

'I'm aware I'm regarded as something of a bad lot in some quarters,' he said, 'but I've rebuilt my life after a fashion. This' – and he gestured round the cramped cabin with its insistently English chintz furnishings and gleaming brass port dogs – 'is a real home, not a bolt hole. I'm sorry it snookered things for you and Vee, but I was no good to Johnnie on my own.'

With a curiously archaic slap of his knee, Geoffrey Ennis dismissed these maudlin sentiments. 'Forget it, Jimmy. I

127

came to see how you were, make my number now the *Peterborough* is stationed here, and to invite you to the wardroom tonight. It's fortunate you are in port; we're at home to old chums.'

'What, *merchant* chums?' asked James mockingly.

'Old chums are old chums, damn it.'

'I don't think I could stand cheerful Charlestons played on wheezing gramophones wound up by idle snotties who forget their job halfway through the evening.'

'I think we might roll out a few real women for you, Jimmy, if you've a mind to dance.' Ennis rose and picked up his hat.

'I wouldn't know how to.'

'You'll come?'

James nodded. 'If I can get away.'

'I see you still dabble.' Ennis paused by the cabin door and studied a watercolour which showed a pagoda overlooking a stretch of river in which a steamer, presumably the *Poyang*, lay at anchor.

'Foochow, on the Min River.'

'Try and make it, old man.'

James saw Ennis to his boat, and though he grinned cynically at the naval launch with its smart crew and a snotty at the helm, its boat hooks tossed in the formula approved of by the Royal Navy and its brasswork gleaming as it edged aside the Chinese *wallah-wallahs*, the sight caught at something within him, plucking a nostalgic response that was almost painful.

As the launch curved away from the foot of *Poyang*'s gangway and Geoffrey gave a casually warm wave, James found his vision slightly blurred.

HMS *Peterborough* lay at a buoy off the dockyard, her eight-inch guns sealed by the bright buttons of tompions, a huge jack flaunting over her bow and the chain securing her painted white.

James's *wallah-wallah*, a small boat with a rattan awning under which he sat, flew the house flag of the China Independent Steam Navigation Company. It was, James thought, a rather pale and worthless imitation of the style of the Royal Navy. Nor did his civilian suit, lightweight linen and made for him in forty-eight hours by Tommy Lee Tailor Company, make any kind of impression on the young midshipman deputed to meet the wardroom's guests at the head of the cruiser's gangway.

'Mr Martin, Chief Officer of the SS *Poyang*,' he announced, meeting the disdain in the boy's face and wondered how did the Navy do it, generation after generation? And then decided that he was being ungracious, especially as he was accepting the Navy's hospitality.

'Ordinary Seaman Hopkins'll show you where to go, sir.'

Ordinary Seaman Hopkins did as he was bid, his accent revealing he was Gorbals Glaswegian.

'Here's the wardroom, sorr.'

'Thanks, Hopkins.' James drew back the curtain from beyond which came a terrific babble of voices. Glasses chinked and the predictable tones of a rag-time dance tune fought a losing battle with the din.

The room was crowded, the atmosphere heavy with tobacco smoke. Wilting white uniforms sporting gold braid and bearing brick-red faces were interspersed here and there with the bright colours of a dress and the flash of a bored smile.

It suddenly struck him that neither the faces nor the conversations changed, and neither did the loyal boredom of the women. This might as easily have been a wardroom party in 1919 as one in 1929.

'I told the blasted Buffer that if he thought I was falling for that old trick . . .'

'Andy Watts? Know him? Good God man, I went through Dartmouth with the blighter, beat him at every sport and the bloody Admiralty decided he should have his own ship before I did. Lucky bugger got a destroyer. Oh, we know Andy, don't we, Susie?'

'Yes, darling . . . d'you think I could have another gin?'

'I'll get it for you, Mrs Adams. Gin and what?'

'Gin and *anything*, Malcolm, there's a good boy.'

'Susie Adams?'

'Yes, and young Malcolm Curtis . . .'

'What, that young two-ringer from Staff?'

'So they say.'

'Don't believe it, though old Adams is a bit of a fart.'

'He wouldn't miss a slice off a cut loaf.'

James made his way round the wardroom, privy to roared bonhomie and stage-whispered gossip.

'I spy strangers . . .'

Nothing had changed. The large, unlovely woman who seemed to be at every wardroom party caught him by the sleeve. She would be something at Admiralty House, or in the Governor's office, a spinster with nymphomaniac leanings and an enthusiasm for boys in uniform, a collector of priapic scalps, as James had once heard her unfortunate type called. Evasion was too late, James felt his sleeve savagely plucked.

'Tell me your name and I'll get you a drink. I'm Fiona McRae.'

'How d'you do? James Martin, er, a gin and bitters.'

The wardroom steward was bidden with practised ease, then Miss McRae turned her attention to her catch. 'You're not RN, eh?'

It was like an accusation and accompanied by a quizzical frown.

'No, I'm a friend of Commander Ennis.' James cast vainly about for Geoffrey.

'Any friend of Geoffrey is a friend of mine!'

James swallowed the gin and bitters too quickly. Fiona McRae was pushing herself against him, though whether it was due to the press of people surrounding them or to her own bodily prompting he was not certain, because for all her size and plainness Fiona McRae sported a voluptuous bosom she disdained to hide under the flat fashions of the day.

'These are such intimate and jolly occasions, aren't they?' she said smiling, her face flushed and perspiring, her shoulders rising in a shrug.

'I haven't been to one for a long time.'

'You're in commerce, I suppose?'

'Yes, and you?'

Fiona laid a finger alongside her rather large nose. 'Cipher work; hush-hush.'

'Ah, the faithful government servant, eh?' said James, attempting a blundering levity after his second drink.

'I'm *devoted*,' said Fiona, though what precisely she was devoted to was not clear. It was clear, however, that she was more than half drunk and the rapidity with which his own glass was being refilled made him suspicious.

'I do love these parties,' Fiona babbled, 'and *Peterborough* is such a super ship.'

James realised that a group of young officers, sub-lieutenants mostly, were encircling them. Their intention to get Fiona roaring drunk was obvious. He was just considering how to detach himself when rescue arrived.

'Mr James Martin?'

He turned. A lieutenant commander of about James's own age confronted him.

'I'm First Lieutenant, Bill Nugent.'

'I remember you at Dartmouth. Fencing champion, weren't you?' They shooks hands and Nugent drew him aside.

'Sorry you got landed with the fair Fiona.'

'My own fault; walked into it, rather. She won't be alone long, if I'm any judge.'

'Those young buggers'll give her what she wants, I've no doubt. Whatever happened to love?' Nugent raised his harassed eyebrows. 'Commander's been delayed ashore with the Captain. He asked me to look after you. I've been woefully neglectful, but come and meet some people.'

James was thrust into a little group none of whose names he caught and who were too intently talking among themselves to do more than acknowledge his presence. He stood on the fringe, suddenly wishing he had not come. He no longer belonged here, was no longer part of what they talked about. He even felt a revulsion towards their single-minded obsession with the hardware of war.

'Look we *gave away* the *Lion*, scrapped her to comply with the Washington agreement, and while we still think we're playing a game of cricket, the rest of the world is building like mad.'

'I agree, David, but I'm not sure we should put many more eggs in the battle cruiser basket. The *Hood* . . .'

'Oh, sod the *Hood*.'

The vehemence of the conversation disturbed him and he turned away again, bumping into a woman and spilling his drink down her dress.

'I'm terribly sorry. I –'

'My God! James? Is it really you?'

131

She was so pallid that James thought she was about to faint, and put out a hand to steady her. She leaned towards him and he felt the pressure of her body. For a moment he failed to recognise her, for her skin was browner, her face faintly marked by disappointments. But the structure of her bones gave her the durable beauty that survived the ravages of time and circumstance. As she steadied herself and the colour came back into her cheeks, her identity dawned on him.

'Emily!'

'Oh, my dear.' She was breathless, looking up at him, her smile beguiling, lighting her face with an expression of pure joy. 'Oh, James . . . my dear, let's get out of here.'

She was pulling him and he followed, not seeing the press of people through which they forced their way.

'Where's Emily?' Lieutenant Commander Nugent asked a few moments later.

'Gone off with that civvie chap, in the linen suit.'

'Blast! The bugger always was a bit of a bounder.'

Beyond the wardroom the painted steel alleyway with its cable trays overhead and the bare lights and hum of dynamos bore the faint aroma of perfume. James thought at first it was Emily's, until they passed an open cabin. The door curtain was imperfectly closed. He caught a glimpse of a massive thigh and an urgently thrusting pair of shirt-tails, grunts amid surrounding sniggers and laughter. Fiona McRae was presumably rounding off the evening in the manner to which she had become accustomed.

On deck, the night air was cool. The ceremony of colours was over and *Peterborough* glowed with decorative fairy lights. At the foot of her gangway *wallah-wallahs* waited for customers and all around the lights of Hong Kong and Kowloon glowed in the darkness.

Emily had a flat near the military hospital. During the rocky *wallah-wallah* passage ashore and the taxi ride following it, neither spoke a word. In the taxi she clasped his arm. James, his mind in a turmoil, felt an upsurge of tenderness for her and put his arm around her shoulders. But as the cab slowed outside her block of flats, Emily disengaged herself with

132

almost brisk purposefulness and ran inside while James paid off the cab.

Outside the door she fumbled for her keys, her face hidden in shadow, and he was not certain whether the sniff she gave was one of annoyance at her own clumsiness or the fighting back of tears.

And then they were inside. She shut the door and grabbed his arms, drawing him towards her with a terrible, irresistible urgency.

But he had no need to resist, fate had stripped him of obligations and Emily's eager mouth awakened a sudden violent hunger in himself. They tore at each other in the ferocity of their passion and they met not as flesh against flesh, but bone against bone.

It was briefly over and they lay in the hall amid a tangle of clothing, breathlessly listening to the thumping of their hearts.

'We really ought to try and do that more slowly,' Emily said softly. She still clung to him, reluctant to let the moment pass. Then, very quietly, she began to cry. James rocked her gently, stroking her hair until her sobs subsided; then he lifted her up, and carried her through into her bedroom.

'Why did you never answer my letters?' she asked at last. 'Was it because' – she propped herself onto one elbow so she could watch his face as he answered – 'because of the way I . . . the way we were before? In Chatham? Did you think I behaved like that with every man I picked up?'

He met her eyes. 'Partly. It frightened me a little; you were the first, you see . . . and I could see nothing to recommend me.'

'Oh, James. It was true I wanted you that night, but surely you realised from my letters that I . . . that you meant something more than just a fuck?'

The word, so often and senselessly upon the lips of seamen, struck him like an accusation. 'I'm sorry. I should have replied. The truth was I was getting married.'

He told her about Stella, about the drive to Beverley and the confidence Emily herself had given him; he told her about the pregnancy and marriage, and about Stella's death in the influenza epidemic in which he had lost not only his wife but also his mother.

'So, you've a little boy?'

'Not so little, I believe, though I'm ashamed to say it's years since I saw him.'

'Don't you want to see him?'

'Yes, perhaps now; but for a long time I knew he would only remind me of his mother.'

'So it wasn't entirely a question of having to marry?' Emily said shrewdly.

'Well, we *had* to, in the conventional sense, but that isn't what you mean, is it? No, I wasn't trapped. I . . . I loved her, you see. She was very beautiful and sweet natured.'

They fell silent, and then Emily asked: 'Hasn't there been *anybody* else?'

He pondered the question for a moment, and then decided he owed her the truth. 'Not for a long while. I ran away, really, after the Navy kicked me out. I wasn't much good after Stella died . . . anyway, I shipped out as a seaman on a windjammer.' He gave a short, self-deprecatory laugh. 'Bloody quixotic really. No future in it; when the old man told me to leave in Hong Kong and take my Second Mate's certificate, I presented myself at the offices of the Board of Trade here, passed the examination, joined China Independent and worked my way up. Now, God help me, I rejoice in the title of Master Mariner. But that wasn't what you asked, was it?'

'No.'

'You're too busy on a sailing ship to think of anything except sleep, and the damned things keep you at sea most of the time. But when I joined China Independent I had begun to regard life as more or less normal again. I'd stopped thinking I was going to end up an admiral or some other kind of hero out of the *Boy's Own Paper*. The war killed that kind of sentiment in me.' He looked at her. 'And I suppose you dispelled the dream that women were all damsels chained to rocks awaiting the arrival of Perseus.'

'Go on. Don't make excuses.'

'I had a . . . a relationship with a Chinese girl, a bar girl. You know the type, a semi-professional.'

'And?'

'It was pretty businesslike and in the end we drifted apart. After Stella . . . oh, I'm sorry, I didn't mean –'

134

She hoisted herself into a kneeling position, slipped out of her remaining deranged clothes and sat astride his knees.

'What about you?' he said, his hands running over her belly to her breasts, her full fleshy breasts he remembered so well. They were wonderfully firm and her body was lithe and lovely under his caress.

'When you abandoned me, you bastard,' she said, her head falling forward so her hair hung about her face, 'I came out to Singapore, still with the army.' Her head fell back and all he could see was the column of her throat and the jut of her chin. 'Six months ago I accepted a posting here.'

She lifted herself onto his tumescent member with a sigh, her hands pressing him beneath her, pinning him down by his shoulders. He reached for her breasts, almost brutally as she rode him with increasing violence, tearing at him with the motion of her loins.

'Oh, you, you bastard James . . .'

Then he was driving up to meet her, more angry than he had ever been, mindlessly, stupidly angry with an animal ferocity that brooked no interruption, even though there flew through his mind a series of images that had nothing to do with love. Their climax was simultaneous and they fell apart, to lie panting alongside each other.

Emily broke the silence. 'When I saw you in that pub . . . I can't explain it, but I knew the meaning of the biblical expression. My bowels yearned for you. I don't know what it was about you . . . you seemed different, as though you had suffered as I had suffered. Despite the fact I had just lost a man I thought, hoped somehow . . . how stupid of me . . . that you could take his place.' She paused, then added bleakly, 'So when you did not write, I was desolate.'

The word hung between them and in the silence acquired its true meaning, echoing the poignant loneliness of every human soul.

'I'm sorry,' he whispered at last and, turning to her, began to kiss her with a tenderness he had last felt for Stella. 'I'm so very sorry.'

CHAPTER ELEVEN
The Devil's Children

For two years James Martin's life possessed a stability and peace he had not known since those few brief months before Stella's death. He maintained a small flat in Kowloon where he and Emily lived when *Poyang* was in her home port. By tacit agreement the question of marriage never arose; Emily was infertile, a circumstance she had come to regard with mixed feelings, though she never spoke of it. She was not, she admitted to herself, the maternal type, nor did she seek for anything in her relationship with James beyond the deep contentment their union brought her. She was too worldly to believe in happiness and during his absences she continued to be what fate had ordained, a thoroughly professional nursing sister, cursed and loved by the servicemen she tended, unembarrassed by their indiscreet illnesses and roughly tender to those whose sickness made them children again.

Those officers who had known her in Singapore, or pursued her because they had heard she 'did a turn', found her now coldly irresponsive. She would play tennis with them, a sport she loved and which kept her body in enviable trim; she would dance, but all other intimacies were discouraged.

'Is she a Sapphic?' one rebuffed and puzzled subaltern asked.

'No,' he was told, 'she's canoodling with a bloke on one of the merchant ships.'

'*Merchant* ships?' sneered the young officer, shrugging his shoulders in disbelief.

For James their affair was a pleasing recreation that made

his existence worthwhile as he and the *Poyang* worked their concurrent destinies up and down the Chinese coast. From Hong Kong to Amoy, Foochow and Shanghai; up the yellow Yangtze Kiang to Chinkiang and Nanking, and back again. It was a regular trade in which they carried every kind of cargo, including people, for the *Poyang*'s capacity for passengers was mostly the renting of deck space for the indigent Chinese coolies who went from one work place to another in accordance with the demands of the free economy then prevailing in that large, ramshackle and decayed state.

The Nationalist government, natural heir to the republic bequeathed by Sun Yat Sen upon the dissolution of the Manchu Empire, was still in the throes of usurpation by independent warlords, impudently styled generalissimos who sought to carve autonomous kingdoms for themselves at the point of the bayonet. In addition, the emergence of a Communist alternative to Nationalism was sapping the peasants' support for General Chiang Kai Shek, while Japanese economic involvement in Manchuria was rapidly being converted to military occupation with the seizure of Mukden in September 1931. These complexities diverted the Chinese government's attention from its grave internal problems.

Amid this confusion the shipping companies and business houses, largely operating from the sanctuary of International Concessions wrung from a supine Manchu government at the beginning of the century, made considerable fortunes. And although their individual servants might have, from time to time, been at considerable personal risk (a risk lessened by the periodic appearance of British gunboats specially built for the rivers of China) they too made a comfortable living, no matter how lowly.

A Chinese quartermaster tallying the coolies aboard the *Poyang* at Nanking was capable of accepting a small bribe to overlook the embarkation of an extra young man eager to reach Shanghai where the International Settlement, with its own police and laws, lay outside native Chinese jurisdiction and offered employment. For the Chief Officer of the ship such kick-backs, or *cumshaw*, were proportionately greater and formed part of everyday business practice. Almost any contract involving the ship, whether for caulking her decks, painting her funnel, cleaning her holds or supplying provisions, incorporated a percentage of appreciation to its originator. Of course, if the Chief Officer of the *Poyang* wasted too much of his owner's potential profit he might find himself discharged onto the beach, but a modest syphoning (and all things are relative) was condoned.

While James was modest, he was no puritan. His changed way of life demanded a little more free spending. In distant England there were his motherless son's school fees to pay, plus the upkeep of The Lees, a neat detached villa that stood on the clifftop at Dovercourt. And there was Vera who, once a month, sent him a letter and sometimes a photograph in return for her allowance, spinning out her bitter existence harbouring God knew what regrets in the wilds of parochial Essex.

John, she wrote at the beginning of the Michaelmas Term, was doing well at school. Not exceptionally gifted mathematically he was holding his own, shone at history and was a first-class cricketer. His house master did not think he would have any trouble passing for the Royal Naval College at Dartmouth. Vera added that 'he had his father's artistic talent', and appended a postscript appealing for her cousin to come home and at least see the boy. John's photographs made him look disturbingly like his mother.

During HMS *Peterborough*'s Far East commission James had met Geoffrey Ennis several times. They too kept up their sporadic correspondence and from time to time met in places other than the Crown Colony. In the Customs Club at Chinkiang they had enjoyed a game of billiards, but more often they ran into each other in the Jockey Club at Shanghai. *Peterborough* frequently lay at the mooring buoys in Garden Reach off the Shanghai Bund. Sometimes, if he was not too pressed, James would take a sampan down river when *Peterborough* berthed alongside Holt's Wharf at Pootung to join a shooting party after snipe in the adjacent rice paddies. Back in Hong Kong he and Emily would challenge Geoffrey and a brother officer to a game of tennis, and afterwards take them to dinner. Usually they ate at a restaurant, sometimes Emily would cook.

'I'm awful at this,' she would invariably protest as she served the first course, though it was clear that, despite herself, she rather enjoyed the intimacy of the occasion.

'After wardroom cooking, Emily,' Geoffrey would say, 'your cuisine is delicious,' and they would laugh at the rather feeble joke with the deep pleasure of good friends.

'Anyway, it's good for James after the rich food on the *Poyang*,' Emily added one evening.

'China Independent looks after its chaps better than their lordships, does it, old man?' said Geoffrey, with one eyebrow raised quizzically.

'You know damn well it does,' grinned James. 'You've been eager enough to sample it in Shanghai. What's more it is part of our pay. Not like you poor mugs having to cough up for your grub.'

'Can't have the Navy sponging on the payers of income tax,' Emily said, then Geoffrey asked, his tone suddenly serious:

'Don't you miss the Navy at all, James?'

James put down his soup spoon and toyed with the stem of his wine glass. The others fell silent. 'Yes,' he said eventually, 'in some ways, I do. The camaraderie, for instance, the sense of belonging. But what I do now is useful, indeed necessary, and I'm not ashamed of it.'

'I didn't mean . . .'

'I know you didn't mean anything unkind, Geoff, but there is a touch of implication in the question. Actually, since I was chucked out of the Andrew, I've thought a good deal about it. Working on the China coast gives one an odd perspective, I suppose, but here we don't see the Royal Navy as the protector of the realm; more the buttress of our commercial interests. That's the role it has always played in the East and I think it is emphasised by the presence of other foreign navies. You know what the Garden Reach looks like at Shanghai? We call it "Warship Row" with the Japs, the Americans, French, Italians and ourselves, all showing our respective flags. I think the Navy is demeaned by it, and I find it rather reprehensible.'

'You sound like a pacifist,' scoffed Lieutenant Bedford, Ennis's tennis partner.

'No,' replied James, keeping his temper, 'but I support

139

the League of Nations as an essential forum for the resolution of world differences. I cannot see why every man of goodwill should not join me in that. Crude and intimidating flag-waving ought to be out of date, don't you agree?'

'But we're there to protect British interests in Shanghai,' persisted Bedford.

'Oh, I know *that*,' snapped James, 'and I concede my own hypocrisy in working for a company that trades advantageously under the British flag, even though it is co-owned by a Chinaman, but in answering Geoffrey's question I have to say that this perspective diminishes my regrets at no longer serving in the King's Navee.'

'A sort of mild disapproval of our oriental activities, d'you mean?' asked Ennis mildly.

'Yes, exactly,' said James, smiling and refilling their glasses, 'reciprocating your equally mild disapproval of my involvement in *trade*.' He gave the last word a pejorative ring.

'I don't really see,' said Emily, gathering the soup plates, 'how anyone who went through the war could view any form of military machine without a certain amount of misgiving. *My* perspective supports James. *I* still mop up the casualties, even in peace-time.' She paused, seeing the frown on Bedford's face. 'You know, Charley, the breakdowns due to loneliness and separation, the odd dose of clap.'

Ennis rocked with silent laughter as Emily withdrew to the kitchen, grinning at his discomfited colleague. James rose to help her fetch the main course. 'She's a forthright girl, Charley,' Ennis said in a low voice, 'and she *can* cook. Won't have a servant either.'

Ennis's approval of Emily often made James uncomfortable. He was aware that the conventional Geoffrey thought their irregular union bad form.

'You should marry that girl, James,' Geoffrey advised one day as they enjoyed a drink at the China Fleet Club.

'We're hardly children, for heaven's sake.'

'What is she, a couple of years older than you?'

'Yes, but that's not what I meant.'

'You can't grieve for a whole bloody lifetime.'

'No, I know that. It's not grief, Geoff. I can't marry Emily because, well . . .' He hesitated and looked at Ennis, wondering if he could understand. 'It's not love, you see, not like I knew and felt before.'

Ennis bowed his head and for a moment James thought he was laughing into his drink, that his own confession marked a lapse into such unbecoming conduct that this stuff-shirted naval officer could not comprehend the heart of his maverick friend.

'Yes, I do understand, Jim; but sometimes second best is all life is going to offer.'

And looking at Ennis, James recalled Vera's refusal and wondered if the union with the landed Drusilla was itself a marriage without love.

'A dance band?' James stared incredulously at the Purser.

'Yessir! The Shanghai City Stompers.'

'Never heard of them.' *Poyang*'s harassed Chief Officer turned back to his desk.

'They're pretty famous. The lead singer's a peach.'

James threw down his pencil in exasperation and turned to the Purser. 'Robin, they're just another parcel of cargo, but as they're first-class cargo they're your concern not mine, so please don't bother me about a bloody dance band, there's a good fellow.'

Crestfallen, the Anglo-Chinese officer turned away. 'I thought you'd like to know.'

James gazed after the departing Purser. He sometimes felt older than his thirty-one years. Self-imposed exile aboard the *Socotra* had divorced him from the brittle post-war gaiety and the dance-band crazes which had swept west from America, via Europe to the Far East. It was not surprising Shanghai boasted its own 'City Stompers'. The place was not China, but a western city, a cesspit, according to some, rivalling Chicago in its wickedness, but an oriental Paris to others. Like so much in the East, it depended on your point of view. James smiled to himself and picked up his pencil.

'Sir?'

He looked up at the Chief Tally Clerk. 'Oh, hullo, Chief Tally, how's that consignment of engine parts?'

'Jus' arrive 'longside, *Dafoo*, I get discharge very quick from *Astyanax* and tranship in junk.'

141

'Well done, that's excellent.' James rose, stretched and stared out of the porthole. The Blue Funnel liner *Astyanax* had only arrived at Hong Kong an hour earlier.

'Number three hatch all finish, number one maybe half-hour more,' added the Chief Tally Clerk.

'Very good, I'll send word to the Captain.'

'Capt'in Ross already come on board; 'bout ten minutes ago.'

Captain Ross was eager to be off and James found him already on the bridge.

'I've told the Second Mate to make certain all the derricks are stowed, mister,' he rasped in a broad Scots dialect which twenty-five years' service on the China coast could not moderate. 'There's a typhoon warning just come in.'

James looked across to the Storm Signal Station at the tip of the Kowloon peninsula. Below the white yard on the signal mast he could make out the black specks of the storm signals.

'Going to make a dash for it, are we, sir?'

'That's it. Get east and then north into the Strait, we should miss it.'

James grunted agreement. Ross was a very experienced seaman and James trusted his judgement. If the typhoon was heading for Hong Kong it would dissipate as it passed inland, by which time they would be sixty, seventy miles to the eastward and heading for the Formosa Strait.

'We've almost finished cargo. There are only a handful of deck passengers, thank goodness, twenty-five labourers on their way back home to Shanghai, and this dance band.'

'If it does come on to blow, we can put the coolies in the tween decks.'

'Yes, there's room in number four.' James noticed a man waving from the foredeck. 'Second Mate's signalling he's finished cargo, sir.'

'Good, get the hands to stations, then. We'll secure the deck as we leave.' Captain Ross seized the brass handle of the engine room telegraph and swung it violently back and forth. From below a faint jingle came which was repeated with a loud jangle on the bridge instrument: stand by engines.

James cast a glance at the sky. Grey cumulus banked up to

142

the south with, above it, high mare's tails of trailing cirrus catching the late afternoon sun. To the north, over the blue-green hills of the New Territories and a more distant China proper, fleecy white clouds jostled in a blue sky that spread patches of sunshine and shadow on the landscape. There was certainly a change on the way. He stood at the top of the bridge ladder and raised the whistle to his lips, blowing the piercing single blast that would bring the Chinese seamen out on deck to their stations.

James met the Second Mate at the head of the gangway. The junior officer had just circled the ship in the company's *wallah-wallah* to read the draught and handed James the chit recording it.

'Thanks Bill; heard about the typhoon?'

'Yes. I met the old man as he came aboard.' The Second Mate cocked an eye at the sky above the Peak. 'Taking a bit of a chance, isn't he?'

'He knows the coast pretty well. You think familiarity breeds contempt?'

The Second Mate shrugged. 'Ours just to do and die.'

'Morbid bugger . . . hoist the gangway then.'

'No, no sir, not yet . . .' Both officers turned to see Robin Chan emerge from the accommodation. 'First-class passengers still to come aboard.'

'What, your bloody dance band?' asked James.

'Yes. Company advertised five o'clock sailing, it's only half past three.'

'*You* can go and tell the old man, Bill,' said James. 'Perhaps you can persuade him to change his mind about sailing. I'll go and tell the Bosun to start squaring the derricks.'

'Thanks very much,' said the Second Mate sarcastically.

James was coming forward again, returning to the bridge after seeing the deck secured, when he heard the quavering note of a muted cornet. Through the cacophony that filled the air of the harbour, a compound of rattling steam winches, shouts and orders, boat engines, sirens and the swish of the wash of a myriad small craft, the note of the instrument warbled clearly. A *wallah-wallah* approached the side of the *Poyang*, bare now of junks and lighters, and in its stern stood the cornet player. It was over two hours since

Captain Ross had rung his engines to stand by, and James could guess the state he would be in for he was a man used to obedience, a stern Calvinist with fixed ideas on how a ship should be run and the importance of its Master. Not that he was a tyrant, far from it, but long exercise of authority and assumption of responsibility had made Ross brook no thwarting of his will, and to be delayed by so vapid a thing as a dance band was more than the old Scot could tolerate.

'Do we have to pander to the De'il's chillun, eh, Mister Martin?'

'I was surprised you hadn't given the order to sail, sir,' James said drily, winking at the Second Mate behind Ross's back.

'The Company had contracted to embark the passengers, mister,' Ross said sharply, 'and you well know ma sentiments aboot loyalty to the Company.'

'Aye, sir,' James agreed noncommittally, wondering casually whether Ross occasionally let China Independent have precedence over God himself.

'Look at them! Drunk, o' course . . .'

James joined Ross on the bridge wing and they stared down at the gangway. The cornet player remained in the stern of the wallowing motor boat improvising a solo that marked the wavering tread of his fellow musicians as they made their unsteady way up the ladder. From beneath the *wallah-wallah*'s rattan canopy they saw two young women emerge unsurely. One of them motioned the cornet player to get on board which, after a short delay, he did, his fellows cheering him from the ship's rail. Three of Robin Chan's stewards nipped down the gangway and swiftly gathered bags and instrument cases. Finally, they all waited for the two women to embark.

'Bluidy fine gentlemen that lot are,' muttered Ross. He rarely swore and it was a clear indication of his exasperation. Below the two young women in skirts entirely inappropriate to the climbing of ship's gangways, struggled to scramble on board unaided.

'For heaven's sake,' seethed Ross, fuming at the protracted and farcical delay. Then Robin Chan raced down the swaying steps, put out his arm and handed one of them aboard. The sight of his own Purser exchanging pleasantries

144

with her as she paused to giggle a few steps up the ladder was too much for Captain Ross now that he had one of his own subordinates to bawl at. 'Mr Chan! Will ye quit havering and get those confounded women on board!'

At the Captain's outburst the remaining girl looked up, teetering wildly on her high heels. For one heart-stopping moment James thought he was staring at Stella.

James went through the ritual of departure in a daze. The uncanny resemblance of the girl had profoundly disturbed his tranquillity and he was possessed of violently conflicting emotions of curiosity and repugnance.

Once the *Poyang* had cleared the approaches to Hong Kong he went on the bridge to relieve Captain Ross with mixed feelings of relief and disappointment. The ship was rolling easily as a low swell surged up from the southward, but the steady breeze was from the east. The cloud had now overcast the sky and Ross was staring at it, shaking his head and still fulminating over the delay.

'Tell me, Mr Martin, can ye see anything *useful* in the existence of a dance band, eh? Confounded parasites!'

James grunted. 'I must admit, I expected them to be Chinese,' he said, still thinking of the girl who so powerfully reminded him of Stella.

'Chinese? They are White Russians,' Ross snapped dismissively, adding, 'and in furst class! The De'il's chillun, Mr Martin, and they'll be half seas o'er the whole bluidy passage, ye mark my words!'

'Perhaps that's preferable to them playing their jazz,' said James abstractedly.

'Aye, you're right; it's nae goin' tae be the quick passage ah reckoned on, mister.'

'No,' agreed James, listening to the painful thud of his disturbed heart.

James was relieved at eight o'clock and went below. He stood for a long time at the head of the handsome teak staircase from the officers' accommodation to the promenade deck. If he hoped to hear the strains of syncopated jazz, he was disappointed. Captain Ross had made it quite clear, through the medium of the Purser, that he forbade such ungodly behaviour. What he did hear – the sound of over-loud laughter and the chink of glasses – caused him to pause, wrestling with his conscience.

Prescience, or instinct, compelled him to acknowledge a feeling of inevitability about his circumstance. Had he foreseen it in that gin-induced confession to Geoffrey Ennis just before *Peterborough* completed her Far East commission? Had he denied Emily in order to make a fool of himself over a scarcely glimpsed face?

He knew, however, without any doubt, that if he descended to the passengers' lounge (as he had every right to do, armed with a warning about coming bad weather) he would not leave without . . .

Without what?

He started down the staircase.

'Ah, sir . . . may I present the famous Shanghai City Stompers?' Robin Chan waved an airy hand at the group in the lounge. Judging by his flushed face, Robin was doing his best to catch up with his passengers. 'Yessir, famous, world renowned. In Hong Kong they made a record . . . for an American company.'

'Really?' James was trying to catch the girl's eye. She was partly turned away from him, talking to one of the musicians, and had not noticed his presence. 'An American company?'

'Yes, RKO. Drink?'

Robin Chan's eyes glittered with excitement and reflected glory.

'Gin and bitters please.' A sense of anticlimax filled James. 'So they're famous, eh, Robin? Heroes of the twentieth century? Dance bands and film stars.' He sighed and leaned on the bar, speaking in a low sardonic voice, aware he was masking his disappointment. 'There were different heroes in my day.'

'Times change, Mr Martin.'

'I thought all the best jazz bands were negroes,' James said, accepting the drink.

'We are *white*, my frien'.'

James felt an imperious hand on his arm. He confronted a tall, bearded man whom he recognised as the cornet player. The man reeked of alcohol and sweat.

'White Russian, you understand? Very white!'

146

'I understand.' *Poyang* gave a slow, seemingly endless roll and the Russian fell back a pace, then grinned and held out his hand.

'Me, Yuri. Play cornet.' James took the outstretched paw. 'This Vassili, guitar; Arcady, piano and clarinet; Nicolai, clarinet; Anton, drums and percussion; Valeria saxophone and vocals.'

The girl had looked up and was staring at him. He felt a strange void in his stomach. No, she was not a bit like Stella and a wave of relief surged through him, as though reason had dispelled some namelessly primitive fear. But she was incomparably lovely.

Her hair, cut in an Eton crop that framed her face, was jet black. Her face was thin, with high cheek bones that hinted at Tartar ancestry, her mouth wide and expressive, but it was her eyes that melted him, set under arched black brows they were of an intense and vibrant green.

'And Sonia, our lead singer.'

Never taking his eyes off her, James gave a little bow and said, 'James Martin. I am the Chief Officer of the ship and I came down to warn you we are expecting bad weather.'

'You mean, bad more than this?' squeaked Valeria, a brittle blonde in a sheath dress of silk which had clearly been copied by a Chinese dress-maker from a movie magazine.

'Oh, yes,' said James, still looking at the girl called Sonia.

'Then we had better go to bed, Arcady,' Valeria shrilled, and they all laughed.

'You like jazz and good music, Martin?' asked Yuri, and James saw Robin Chan turn away with an amused smile on his face.

'I, er, don't know much about it, I'm afraid.'

Yuri's beetling brows knitted in disbelief. 'Don't know about jazz?' He turned to the other members of the band. 'Hey, this Martin, don't know about jazz!'

Valeria screeched with outrage and the others joined in, adding their wild drunken laughter until even Robin Chan could no longer control himself. James felt a fool, tossed off his gin and slammed the empty glass on the bar.

'Thanks for the drink,' he said curtly, and made for the lounge door. Just then *Poyang* fell into the trough of a swell that caught him off balance. He lurched against the

147

bulkhead, provoking more gales of laughter as glasses slid and Yuri, with exaggerated abandon, allowed himself to fall into an empty chair. Amid the shouts and whoops of derision, James failed to hear the girl with the green eyes say something in Russian.

Daylight next morning found James back on the bridge, keeping the morning watch. The wind had shifted ominously into the south-east and increased to gale force. Great grey tumbling seas reared up on their starboard quarter as they headed for the Formosa Strait. The *Poyang* pitched and rolled, alternately ascending with an accelerating motion, then slowing as her stern fell into the trough of the succeeding wave. James had slept badly, his body tossed in its bunk by the worsening conditions, his mind aflame with impossible thoughts. He had dreamed in fits and starts, of Stella and of love, of Emily and sexuality; but always he woke abruptly thinking of the Russian girl who lay in her own bunk two decks below.

Now he stared morosely through gritty eyes at the monstrous sea. The shift in the wind, the increasing steepness of the seas and the falling barometer convinced him of the worst. He cocked his head, listening to the slow rise of the wind-noise in the stays and funnel guys; it crept steadily upwards towards the roar of storm force, while the grey fractus that overcast the sky seemed to lower just above the wildly circling mastheads.

In the wheelhouse the Chinese quartermaster struggled with the wheel, fighting at the same time to keep his balance as *Poyang* rolled. James cast a glance around the horizon, already blurred by flying spray, then over the lashed derricks and the taut, wet hatch tarpaulins, the lifeboats and the upper decks of his charge to check all was secure. Then he stared again at the sea.

It seemed to him, on that wild grey morning as he braced himself and fought off fatigue and the depression left by his dreams, he had no alternative but this miserable, bitter existence; he had no right to expect more and even Ennis's suggested 'second best' might be too good for him. He had lost Stella and gained Emily; he had machine gunned German sailors as they struggled in the water and yet

148

survived the war himself, a prey to bad conscience. No longer could he soothe himself with the juvenile consolation of having avenged Tom; no, vengeance was truly and properly the Almighty's instrument. It was better for him to eke out his life in this solitary way. He would not go home in answer to Vera's pleas, for it was better never to see his son, or let his son see his own father. Here, on the bridge of the *Poyang*, he was at home, content to play his small part in mankind's defiance of the sea and nurse the ageing steamship to her destination, untroubled by regrets for Emily's sterile bed. They had been thrown together in the awful aftermath of war but she was, he admitted coldly to himself, no more than the repository of his useless seed. If the sea had preserved him after Jutland it had done so for Stella's sake, not for his; and perhaps the explosion of *Indefatigable* had indeed torn his soul from his body, just as the virus of influenza had shrivelled his heart.

So he must stop the foolish fantasies about the Russian girl and wake up to the brutal reality of the morning and the prosaic struggle of his ship. With an effort he shook himself free of the lingering effects of the night and climbed up the sloping deck.

In the wheelhouse, as the quartermaster tugged and swore at the wheel, he reached for the voice-pipe, blew into it and then put the bell-mouth to his ear. He heard Ross stir and grunt interrogatively.

'Mate, sir. Wind's rising fast and the glass is plummeting. From the wind direction I'd guess the typhoon's recurved before hitting the coast.'

He transferred the bell-mouth to his ear and heard Ross's disembodied voice: 'I'll be up, mister.'

James had resecured the brass whistle and clipped the voice-pipe to the bulkhead when *Poyang* shuddered and flung her bow high into the air where it hung as the ship rolled violently to port. From aft came the thunderous roar of a torrent of water. In an instant James was on the bridge wing staring anxiously astern and deluged with the spray whipping forward with the speed and viciousness of bird shot. Abaft the accommodation *Poyang* was inundated with water; green-white it streamed from her poop, cascading into her after well-deck and foaming about the base of her main-mast. James could feel the hull protesting as its inherent buoyancy fought to rise against the deluge of the huge sea that had curled over her stern and broken over her.

Slowly, aided by the lull in the sea's energy which always followed a large wave, the ship shook herself free and her after-part appeared like a half-tide rock. A length of mooring rope streamed away, followed by a chicken coop whose occupants squawked even as they drowned. In the wheelhouse the hand-cranked telephone from the engine room rang. James leapt to answer it, apprehensive that one of the mooring ropes torn off the poop had fouled the propeller and left them defenceless in the sea.

'You all reet up there?' asked the Second Engineer, his Geordie accent heavy with concern.

'Just about. What about you?'

'Aye, got half the China Sea down bloody ventilators, but I enjoy an occasional paddle. One of my firemen got a wee bit burnt, but he's all reet.'

Captain Ross loomed in the wheelhouse door. 'A lump running, mister,' he said as James put down the engine room telephone.

'Aye, sir. We've been pooped; no ill effects in the engine room, though one of the firemen's been burnt.'

Ross shuffled to the forward windows. 'They're used to that.'

'The Second says it's not serious.'

Ross spoke to the quartermaster in Cantonese. Visibly chastened, the unfortunate Chinaman stopped grunting and drawing attention to the effort he was putting in to the steering.

'We can still outrun the worst,' said Ross, turning forward again to stare out over the grey, streaked waste of the sea. 'I don't want to heave to unless I'm compelled,' he said, then added laconically, 'I'll take the bridge; you have a look round.'

It took James an hour to carry out his survey of the upper decks. An hour of perilous dashes from refuge to refuge, of ducking behind winches or deckhouses as green seas broke on board, sluicing the well-decks in particular with irresistible torrents of water. He clung on until his arm muscles cracked with the strain and the sea tore at his lower body, soaking him from head to foot. On the poop he looked apprehensively astern. The after-extremity of the ship rose high out of the sea and shook as the thrashing propeller raced in unresisting air. He felt his stomach cleave his throat as the stern fell shuddering into the following trough and the surface of the sea rose to the sheer strake, then lapped the very lip of the poop. The spray was whipped from it and tore at his body like the fingers of demons in a nightmare.

But no damage had been done. The *Poyang*'s fabric strained and protested, the rivets screeched and the steel work clicked appallingly as she twisted and rolled and pitched, but she was a good ship, a stout ship, and her hatches had held against the onslaught of the pooping sea. Wearily he made his way back to the bridge, the water pouring from his oilskins and wet clothing and adding to the film already running hither and thither across the matting in the wheelhouse.

'She's all right, sir. Nothing loose bar some crockery in the saloon. The boats are secure.'

'I'll finish your watch. Go down and get dried out.'

James grinned. On the old *Socotra* he would have continued his watch sodden and had to turn into his bunk in the same condition. He nodded his thanks to Ross and went below. On the boat deck, just as he was about to enter the accommodation, he noticed something moving across the deck, a precipitate, uncontrolled movement downhill as the *Poyang* lurched into a heavy roll to starboard. He ran aft.

'What the . . .?'

Between the lifeboats, half hidden by the luffing davits, the figure cannoned into the rail and he heard the 'Ouff!' as the impact drove the air from the lungs. Wildly James reached out and caught a flailing arm, jerking the figure towards him as *Poyang* completed her roll and flung herself to port.

The Russian girl pressed against him, sagging in his arms as he fought to keep his balance. Her face was greenishly pallid and almost slimy from the sweat of fear and seasickness. Tangled locks of her black hair stuck across her face, matted with traces of vomit, and he felt her shudder, eyes closed in complete surrender as she retched over him.

151

He twisted round and pulled one arm across his shoulders and half dragged, half carried her forward, lugging her over the sea-step into the officers' alleyway. Finally, breathless and exhausted, he laid her on his rumpled bunk and stood looking down at her while he regained his composure.

Even in disgusting disarray she was beautiful as she lay inert, eyes shut, shivering slightly like a frightened animal. James took a damp flannel from beside the wash basin and wiped her mouth and soiled hair. Once she opened her eyes and he seemed to be staring into the sea itself, for in the gloom of the cabin their intense green was muted and greyed.

He smiled reassuringly. 'Everything is all right,' he said softly, and realised the expression had been overused that morning, but signified a mixture of anxiety and relief, of fear and hope. She closed her eyes again, her breathing became regular and he thought she might have drifted into a light doze. Standing up he took off his oilskin, stepped out of the cabin and hung it on a hook in the alleyway. There was a pounding of feet on the companionway from the promenade deck and Robin Chan's worried face appeared.

'Mr Martin!' he almost sobbed with anxiety. 'Miss Starlenka seems to have been lost overboard. The pantryman saw her go on deck and one of the sailors says he saw her on the boat deck. I've just telephoned the bridge and Captain Ross says there's no one up there now.'

'She's all right, Robin,' James cut in, aware that once again those reassuring words had been trotted out. 'She's sick as a parrot and in my bunk. You should take better care of her. Leave her there for the time being. Send her up some tea.'

Relief spread over the Purser's face like a blush, and he turned below calling words of gratitude over his shoulder. James went back into his cabin suddenly anxious to make the most of the few moments more he had with the girl. She lay as he had left her, pale and motionless. The shivering had stopped and he was certain she was asleep. Very slowly he reached out his hand and gently pushed stray hair off her forehead. Reluctant to withdraw it, he let it trail across her cheek and, bending over her, he lightly brushed her forehead with his lips. As he straightened up she sighed,

152

slipping into deeper sleep, and when Wong arrived with the tea James drank it himself. He was still sodden and cold and the girl's presence made it awkward for him to change.

Instead, as *Poyang* bucked and rolled, he opened his sketch book and picked up a soft-leaded pencil. The stiff cartridge paper ruckled from his dripping hair as he sought to capture the girl's likeness.

CHAPTER TWELVE
Chrysanthemum Warriors

Sonia Starlenka and the dance band left the *Poyang* on her arrival at Shanghai. The ship was white with encrusted salt, patches of rusty steel showed where the abrasive power of the wind had stripped the paint, and her guard rails were bent and buckled under the onslaught of the sea. But passengers and cargo were unharmed and the former thanked Captain Ross with an effusiveness that the old Scot found embarrassing. James busied himself with the arrival of the agent's runner and the wharfinger of the Hongkew wharf, deliberately avoiding the painful business of saying goodbye. He had barely made the acquaintance of Sonia Starlenka before he realised she lived under the protection of Yuri, the cornet player. He had no right to complain of the arrangement; it was identical to that which he himself enjoyed with Emily and doubtless a good deal happier. Yet in the weeks following her departure he could not shake off her image, nor banish from his mind her shy thanks when she woke that stormy morning. Nor did it help that Robin Chan maintained an interest in the band which, following the release of their record, were enjoying a popularity in the city's night-spots. James would rather have had Sonia Starlenka disappear into the anonymity of Shanghai than to learn she could be found at Joe Farren's, or the Del Monte. Fortunately the duties of Chief Officer made it difficult to get shore leave and the *Poyang*'s frequent occupation of a buoy in mid-river was an added discouragement. But Robin Chan, mad about jazz and with his head turned by Valeria's corn-gold hair, could not be stopped from his dogged enthusiasm.

The *Poyang*'s schedule was a relentless reality and autumn passed into an uneasy winter. Vera's correspondence was remarkably well-informed about Far Eastern affairs. In her Christmas letter, after her report on John's progress, she expressed her misgivings.

We are all watching the ambitions of the Japanese with concern. The cynical occupation of Mukden and the installation of their puppet-emperor in Manchuria is seen here as an indication of their imperial aspirations. It worries us, too, that the League of Nations seems unable to support the Nanking government and while the socialists rail against our gunboat diplomacy, you must be glad to see the Royal Navy . . .

Vera had included a photograph of herself outside The Lees. Thin and spinsterish, her hair drawn back, she still reproached him about what she saw as James's defection from the Navy. It did not seem to matter that he had been kicked out of the service; in Vee's perception, the fact that he relied upon its ships made his subordination somehow shameful.

James spent New Year's Eve with Emily. They returned in the early hours of 1932 from a party held at the home of one of the hospital doctors. James was aware he had drunk more than was good for him as they let themselves into his flat.

'God, James,' said Emily, lighting a cigarette and throwing herself down in an armchair, 'you are drunk.'

'I know. I'm sorry.'

'I don't know what's wrong with you tonight. You were bloody unpleasant to young Sangwell. I think the poor devil wondered what he'd done.'

James fought an upsurge of rising bile. 'For Christ's sake . . .' Emily stubbed out her cigarette, rose and walked through into the bedroom. James stood stupidly at the window, watching the lights of distant Victoria across the black, shining waters of the harbour. He felt awful. Young Sangwell had asked if he was Emily's husband. He recalled snapping the unfortunate man's head off with a curt order to mind his own damn business. It was not the sort of thing decent chaps said on New Year's Eve.

Emily reappeared with a pillow and an armful of blankets.

'I don't want you throwing up over me,' she said tossing the bundle of bedding into a chair. 'You're sailing tomorrow. I thought we might have . . .'

He turned from the window and something in his face stopped her. Something of the awful, hurt appeal of the first glimpse she had had of him in the Chatham pub was there, but overlaid with something else, something she could not explain but which was not the drink, except the drink had exposed it. For a moment she confronted a stranger, and the realisation came as a shock. Then her training reasserted itself and she briskly led him to the chair, settling him and covering him with the blankets. Seated, she knew, he was less likely to choke on his own vomit. As he closed his eyes, she brushed the hair from his clammy forehead. 'Don't ever leave me, you awful bastard,' she said, turning out the light.

'There's a reduction in the transhipment cargo due to the Chinese government boycott on trade with the Japs, but we won't be affected very much. In fact I anticipate an increase in the volume of consignments to Nanking.'

James nodded. The agent's runner was a newcomer, a young man from England come out to learn the trade before taking over a directorship in London. 'All grist to our mill, eh, Mr . . .'

'Powell, but please call me Mike.' He handed James a wad of boat notes.

'Thanks. I don't suppose it'll stop Shanghai from waltzing,' he said with a sigh.

'Hope not,' said Powell, 'there's a terrific singer at Kirilov's.'

James was only half listening, his mind already occupied with resolving the eternal problems of cargo stowage.

'She used to be with the Shanghai City Stompers, but now she's gone solo.'

James froze. His heart suddenly hammered in his breast. Forcing himself to sound casual he asked, 'Blonde or brunette?'

'Neither; hair black as the ace of spades.'

James looked up sharply. The young man's enthusiasm was obvious. 'At Kirilov's?' he asked.

'Yes, halfway along the Rue Chu Pao San, on the French side of the boundary.'

'I know where Blood Alley is . . .' After Powell had gone he could not stop himself thinking of Sonia beneath a spotlight, singing amid the cigarette smoke in Kirilov's, being ogled by seamen and the bachelors of the *taipans'* business houses. Nor could he plead the difficulty of getting ashore, for *Poyang* lay at a berth on Hongkew wharf, and a rickshaw ride would take him to the door of Kirilov's in twenty minutes or less.

It was raining when he left the ship. On the wharf, illuminated by the clusters hung over the side of the *Poyang*, greasy puddles of water reflected the lights and rippled in the chill, late January wind. From the adjacent godowns bales of cotton piece goods were rolled out and hitched onto *Poyang*'s cargo runners. The clatter of the steam winches and chatter of the coolies were accompanied by the swaying bales and the bizarre shadows they threw as the derricks snatched them aboard.

The rickshaw trundled smoothly towards the Bund, passing the formal gardens, lamplit now, that backed the principal landing place. Here launches, junks, sampans and agents' boats congregated as the nightly tide of free-spending sailors washed ashore. Men from the merchant ships and the warships lying off in the stream, men in search of excitement and relief from the dull monotony of their lives. The rickshaw turned inland, passing into the narrow canyon between the great buildings that lined the Bund, huge monoliths of European architecture which indicated here, in the very heart of China, other nations dominated the infrastructure of the huge city. The rickshaw bounced gently along the boundary between the International Settlement proper and the French Concession and into Blood Alley, as the Rue Chu Pao San was colloquially known.

Outside Kirilov's stood a huge, bearded man wearing a *papenka*, baggy trousers and boots. His coat bore the looped frogging of the Don Cossack and he cast an experienced eye over James as he turned from paying off the rickshaw coolie.

Inside, once past the hat-check girl and the notice that respectfully requested patrons to deposit their side arms with their coats, the interior was dark, the only light radiating outwards from the bar where an elderly Russian with sad moustaches and an elaborately embroidered peasant's shirt presided over a small staff. Judging from the glows of cigarettes, the side booths were already crowded. At the end of the long room a low stage was illuminated and the fading applause and flapping of curtains indicated an act had just finished. James made his way to the bar and occupied one of half a dozen vacant stools.

'Drink, *Barin*?' The sad-moustachioed Russian confronted him. The man's eyes stared like those of a dead fish from fleshy pouches. 'Sergei Petrovich, *à votre service*.'

'Gin and bitters, please.'

Sergei returned with the gin and aromatic bitters. 'Is Mam'selle Starlenka singing this evening, Sergei Petrovich?' James asked, sipping the drink and lighting a cigarette.

'Ah, the *Barin* has heard of the lovely Mam'selle, eh?'

James glared at the barman. There was something in his sarcastic tone he did not like. He put both elbows on the bar and drew on the cigarette. 'Is she singing tonight?'

'Later, *Barin*. You must be patient.'

'Mr Martin?'

He swung on the stool. Robin Chan, dressed in a dinner jacket and very *à la mode*, smiled at him. 'May I present Mai Wong?'

The Chinese girl was slender and wearing a long *cheongsam*, the skirt of which was daringly slit above the knee. The Purser had clearly transferred his affections from the blonde Valeria. James offered them a drink.

'We have a table; would you care to join us?'

'That would not be fair, but thank you.'

'Have you come to see Sonia?' Robin asked. There seemed little point in denying it.

'Yes. I heard she had gone solo.' James repeated Powell's expression.

'She's a crooner, now . . .'

'Sonia friend of yours, Mr Martin?' asked Mai Wong.

'Er, not exactly.' He stubbed out his cigarette, feeling slightly uncomfortable.

'I tell her you here?' Mai Wong's concern was touching

until James realised her motivation was professional, that she worked in Kirilov's and was only doing her job.

'Thank you, no. It will not be necessary.'

'All right; we go back now, Robin?' She tugged gently on the Purser's arm. Robin leaned forward and hissed confidentially, 'Watch the barman, he's a faggot.'

James grinned. Robin's concern for his innocence was more amusing than his escort's, for Robin genuinely thought he spent too much time on board to possess the sophistication to survive an evening in Kirilov's.

'Thank's, Robin, but I already discovered that.'

A peasant trio in brilliant scarlet shirts occupied the stage. Two dropped to their haunches, hands on hips in preparation for a *trepak*, while the other strummed three or four chords on a *balalaika* before launching into an energetic dance tune that had the two booted 'cossacks' twirling and kicking within inches of the nearest tables.

'See you later,' mouthed Robin, allowing Mai Wong to lead him to their booth. James turned to his drink.

'Are you alone tonight, sailor?'

The woman smelled heavily of musk and wore make-up that failed to disguise the fact she was nearer fifty than forty. Her mass of luxurious black hair owed more to artifice than to nature, and curling black hairs peeped insolently from beneath her ample armpits, mocking the elaborate décolletage of her low-cut gown. Both it and its wearer had seen better days.

'You have cigarette?'

He went patiently through the ritual, stirred in spite of himself and in spite of her. The touch of her hand on his as she guided the flame of his Ronson onto her cigarette was a signal of her availability. She would be easy to reject later and he was vaguely glad of her company, if only to keep away greater and lovelier temptations flitting about the lights of the bar. He called to Sergei, saving her the trouble of asking and himself playing the game to the hilt. 'Champagne for *Madame, La Princesse.*'

'*Chéri.*'

He felt her hand on his thigh and gently pushed it aside. Catching her eye he said, 'Drink it slowly, princess. I am neither a rich nor a generous man.'

159

She smiled ruefully, and he saw the genuine woman behind the pretence. 'Nor are you a fool,' she said.

'And don't think you can flatter me. I could buy half a dozen river girls for the cost of that sugar water.'

'Sergei serves my "champagne," ' she said archly, 'with a little vodka.'

'You look remarkably good on it. How long have you been in Shanghai?'

She made a *moue* with her over-rouged lips. 'That is not a gentleman's question.'

'Who said I was a gentleman?'

'You are an Englishman.'

'Ten minutes ago I was a lonely sailor. Where do you come from?'

The woman crushed her cigarette into the brass ashtray on the bar and James immediately offered her another. She lit it brusquely and blew the smoke at the low ceiling. 'Petersburg. I have been in Shanghai for ten years. My husband was a naval officer who ended up a dead soldier in Chelyabinsk fighting for Kolchak against the Bolsheviks. I have had two children, both of whom are now, thank God, dead. My name is Natalia and I am a countess.' She dragged viciously on her cigarette and the tip burned fiercely so that half an inch of grey ash appeared as she continued. 'Now I am a whore. I find my cunt useful and the doctor assures me I have not yet caught syphilis.'

He grasped her bare arm and stared into her brimming eyes. Already mascara was running in the lines beneath her lashes. 'I'm sorry,' he said and produced a handkerchief.

The *trepak* concluded in a stamping of feet and wild applause. The woman dabbed at her eyes with a degree of practice and the dark rimming only became more accentuated in the half-light of the club.

'I *am* sorry,' he repeated as the applause died away, but the woman Natalia merely shook her head and turned towards the stage. The trio were decamping and a solitary Chinese in evening dress appeared. From the opposite wings a piano was pushed on stage, a stool was produced and, with an elegant sweep of his coat tails, the Chinese pianist sat in the light of a single spot. Very quietly, so the chatter of the clientele reduced in line with the volume of noise from the

160

piano, he began a slow, lugubrious tune in a melancholy, minor key.

Then suddenly she was there, standing swaying in a second spotlight, her slim figure sheathed in a vermilion *cheongsam*, the silk shimmering in the light, taut over her flat belly and rising seductively over her breasts to encircle her neck. As she moved, her voice caught the notes with an unexpected huskiness and the skirt of the long dress parted from ankle to hip, exposing a long, bare leg. The effect was electric; even Natalia, who must have seen the sight a hundred times before, had her hands clasped ecstatically beneath her chin. For James it was devastating. He hardly heard the words, so intent was he on watching her body and her beautiful face. The hair was still bobbed, and long jet earrings glittered below the lobes of her ears. But – or so it seemed to him – it was her green eyes that held him. Though they had reminded him of Stella, they no longer did so, for they were uniquely Sonia's own.

James did not understand the song's words, guessing they were Russian, but they started tears once more in Natalia's eyes and the haunting air was eloquent of exile and longing for the past. As the applause died away, Sonia stepped forward off the stage and the pianist struck up a different tune. James knew it, another song of broken dreams, but from a different corner of the world.

'Buddy, can you spare a dime . . .' Sonia sang, moving sinuously from one table to another, the indigent lament oddly apt, thought James, for the glamour of the *cheongsam* suddenly looked tawdry, almost the dress of a servant, she put so much pathos into her performance.

He longed for pencil and paper, for she was feline in her progress round the dance floor, her face that of a beautiful cat . . . a beautiful alley cat, like the gamin beggar children on the streets outside.

She concluded the song on stage, her back to the applauding audience, her incredible eyes pleading with them over her right shoulder.

'*Magnifique*,' Natalia whispered beside him.

Then Sonia stood behind the pianist as he played the opening bars of 'Always'. Her hands caressed his shoulders but she looked at her spellbound admirers with the fictional impression that it was *their* shoulders she stroked.

'I'll be loving you,' she sang, pushing her pelvis forward, into the small of the pianist's back and then, very slowly as her husky voice dragged out the reprise 'Always' she exposed her right leg from hip to ankle, resting her knee on the side of the piano stool.

'Jee-sus!' said an American sitting nearby.

'With a love that's true . . . always.'

As the song ended he found Natalia looking at him. 'She is beautiful, yes?'

'Yes,' he agreed simply, 'she is very beautiful.'

'She is living with me,' Natalia confided, as though she gained a degree of prestige from the fact. 'Her boyfriend beat her. Now she is like my daughter.'

'She must break many hearts,' James said, finding it easy to speak frankly to this woman and glad Sonia had broken with Yuri.

Natalia smiled triumphantly. 'Oh yes, many, many hearts.'

They finished clapping. Sonia had gone, disappeared behind a swirl of dusty velvet curtain and James felt filled with an awful emptiness, an almost desperate sense of anti-climax. Sergei was calling for 'Natasha,' and Natalia exchanged a few words of Russian before slipping from the bar stool and disappearing in the shadows beside the stage.

'Another drink, *Barin*? And one for *Madame La Princesse*?' Sergei raised his eyebrow over the matriarchal title like an accent of sarcasm.

His tone had its effect. James stood suddenly, ground out the last of a seemingly endless succession of cigarettes, and declined.

'You are leaving *M'sieur*?'

'Yes,' he snapped.

'*Mam'selle*, will be disappointed,' Sergei pouted, but James failed to grasp the significance of his remark. Instead he stood at the hat-check counter after collecting his coat, momentarily irresolute. Making up his mind he asked the flat-faced Chinese woman, 'Where does Madame Natalia live?'

The woman shrugged. 'I no tell customer. You go with Madame Natalia to hotel. You ask her where she live.'

James fingered twenty dollars. It was his last note, a preposterously high sum for the trifling information he wanted. 'You give me proper address. Write proper fashion.'

'No can write.'

The woman's illiteracy came between her and her cupidity. Her eyes glittered in contemplation of the crinkling bank note and James felt a shameful self-revulsion at what he was doing.

'You wait. One minute.'

She vanished for a moment, then reappeared with a square of card. 'You find now all right.' She held out the card, her other hand reaching for the note.

James returned to the ship, turning over the card from Kirilov's Russian Nightclub as he stared unseeing at the emaciated back of the rickshaw coolie. In pencil was scrawled by an unknown hand the address of a flat in the Yangtzepoo district.

The rain had stopped but a fog was rolling off the Whang Pu river.

He woke to the sound of gunfire. Uncertain whether or not he had been dreaming, he lay staring at the rivets of the deck-head. Then, in a rush, he recalled meeting Captain Ross on his return to the ship the previous evening. Ross had confided that there were disturbing rumours from the north. Japanese soldiers had been seen on the right bank of the Yangtze Kiang. In his ambivalent state of mind James had failed to grasp the significance of this. The movements of the Japanese as they arrogantly trampled over the independent sovereignty of China had ceased to shock. Now the sudden reports of heavy field artillery came again and James was out of bed in an instant.

It seemed the whole of Shanghai had been immobilised in that hiatus, praying it had been mistaken and then acknowledging the worst. He could hear the shouts of coolies, the screams of women in the sampans in midriver as they pointed excitedly at the pall of smoke rising over the roofs of Chapei. James met Ross on the bridge where both men sought a view of the city through their binoculars. The river curved east round Pootung Point, running along the

163

frontage of Yangtzepoo beyond the Soochow Creek and the British consulate. Just beyond the borders of the International Concession lay the sprawl of Chapei, a flat alluvial plain covered with the dwellings of the Chinese beyond the North Railway station and the lines to Ning Po and Nanking. Above this grey skyline slowly lifting clouds of dirty smoke rose into the morning air as the salvoes of Japanese shells exploded with a delayed crump.

'They've got a spotting plane up, look!' James shifted his binoculars to where Ross pointed and saw a small aeroplane turning lazily above the Chinese city. 'Or a bomber.'

'Oh God . . .'

'What's the matter, man?' Ross turned disapprovingly, irritated by his Chief Officer's blasphemy. 'Are you unwell?'

Some quirk of the light northerly breeze that drifted over Shanghai brought with it an unmistakably unsettling stink that, by its very unfamiliarity, overlaid the myriad smells rising from the teeming city.

The day passed in an unreal manner. The crump of artillery fire went on at intervals, accompanied by sporadically chattering machine guns. There was a noticeable reduction in the commercial traffic in the river; junks and sampans remained tied up and even the launches of the steamship companies seemed less willing to stray far from the Bund and the Customs jetty. The boats of the warships were hoisted inboard and parties of blue-jackets could be seen removing the tompions from gun muzzles and the canvas jackets off their breeches. From time to time a turret would train and its gun elevate, but the warships were under strict orders not to interfere and as long as the Japanese were scrupulous in confining their artillery bombardment to the native areas of the city and avoided the International Settlements and Concessions, they had no right to intervene.

Alongside, *Poyang* and one or two other cargo ships loaded piece goods, antimony and tung oil as though nothing unusual was happening, but as the day wore on the normally industrious Chinese labourers began drifting away. Old China hands had survived these 'troubles' before and were philosophical.

164

'It'll soon blow over,' said Ross in the saloon at dinner. 'Ah was here in twenty-five when a coolie was killed by a Japanese foreman. There was a big anti-foreigner demonstration, mostly students shouting '*Nakuni*-out' slogans and the police opened fire on them. The police were British-officered and it made us unpopular for a wee while, but they soon forgot about it. O' course,' he added conversationally, helping himself to vegetables from the saloon steward, 'the warlords up-country made the most of the newspaper photographs to whip up sentiment against us. But thousands were dying in their own internecine strife, women drowning themselves to avoid rape, children being sold into brothels or slavery . . . Is something the matter, Mr Martin?'

James shook his head and resumed his meal. An uncomfortable vision of swimming German sailors had passed into his mind's eye.

'Ah, Powell, d'you bring us news?'

They all stared at Powell as he entered the saloon. He was dishevelled and bore a package which he offered to Captain Ross.

'Canna that wait until ah've finished ma dinner?'

'I was told to deliver it personally, Captain, it's diplomatic mail.'

'Ah can see that!' Ross snapped, halting the inexperienced young man from further indiscretions in front of the Chinese saloon staff. 'But you've no need to barge in here . . .'

'I'm very sorry, sir, but I have to get back.' Powell's face had gone pale and his voice had a dangerous edge in it. Ross's *sang froid* was clearly irritating him. 'I don't think you understand what is happening, sir.'

'How the devil can ah when the agent's runner doesn't show up until after sundown? It's only a bit of bother, son, there's no need to panic.'

'I'm not panicking. This is diplomatic mail through from Nanking and the British consul wanted it put directly aboard a British ship in case the Japanese fail to respect the boundaries of the Concessions.'

'Then why doesn't he put it aboard a destroyer?' countered Ross, visibly angering.

165

'Because,' explained an exasperated Powell, 'the warships are to be held here to act defensively if required.'

'The situation will be changed by tomorrow morning.'

'There's a whole bloody Japanese army north of Chapei, Captain Ross, and they haven't come Shanghai-side to play *mah-jong*!'

Stunned silence greeted this news and the rude manner of its delivery was overlooked by all but Ross, who had lost considerable face in front of his Chinese stewards. It became obvious that Powell did not exaggerate, for the noise of the bombardment had become continuous.

'What exactly are the orders you are bringing me?' asked Ross with a forced dignity by which he meant to circumvent Powell's cheek and attribute his insolence to the management of China Independent itself.

'Sail as soon as possible, of course!'

'There's no "o' course" about it, son!' roared Ross. 'We've a boiler blown down and it'll take twelve hours to raise steam. Ah've no' completed loading.'

'I don't think we're going to get our full cargo, sir, not if we wait a week,' James broke in, embarrassed for Ross and Powell both of whom, he could see, were separated by more than a generation's age difference. 'Do we get an escort as far as Woosung?' he asked Powell.

Powell shrugged. 'I believe the consul was liaising with the Senior Naval Officer.'

'We'll have to have at least the identification of British nationality,' he said to Ross. 'Union flags on our sides. We can get those done this evening and be ready to slip at dawn. I'll ballast number five double-bottom tanks.'

Ross expelled his breath and glared at Powell from below his brow. 'We'll leave at daylight.'

Powell nodded and, in his wake, James rose from the table. 'I'll get cracking.'

Outside the saloon Powell was detained by an anxious Robin Chan. As he went in search of the Bosun he heard Powell, his voice strained, explaining the extent of the Japanese attack. 'This is no "incident," ' he was saying, 'this is a full blown attack on Chapei at the very least.'

Pausing on the boat-deck after ordering the painting of

166

the tarpaulins, James stared in the direction of the northern suburbs. A bright glow lit the sky, with here and there lurid flashes and the delayed concussion of guns. Again he smelled cordite, but it no longer made him queasy.

Robin Chan met him in the alleyway; the Purser was in an agitated state.

'What's the matter, Robin? We're getting out of here in the morning.'

'It's Mai Wong.'

'The Japs won't dare touch the Concessions, not with all those warships sitting in the Garden Reach.'

'She doesn't live in the Concessions, she lives in Chapei. I'm worried sick.'

'She means that much to you, does she?' He need not have asked the question for the state of Robin Chan's mind was obvious. 'You want to get her out?'

'The agent tells me the Kuomintang soldiers are putting up a stout defence, but' – Chan shrugged – 'if those Nip bastards get through . . .' He could not bring himself to say it, but it was not necessary. Ross had touched upon the subject already. 'Kirilov keeps most of his girls in an apartment block on the edge of the Settlement, near the North Station.'

'*Most* of his girls?' A cold feeling of apprehension was clutching James's heart. 'Don't some of them have their own apartments?'

'Yes, but Kirilov's the landlord. You're thinking . . .'

'Of Sonia Starlenka, yes.' James went into his cabin, rummaged in his suit pocket and pulled out the card. He thrust it at the Purser. 'Where's this?'

'That's Kirilov's place.'

'Bloody hell!' James stood irresolute for a moment, then he stripped off his uniform. 'Get a taxi! I'm coming with you!'

There were a few people about, but the absence of foreigners on the Bund was evidence that shore leave from the ships lying in the river had been stopped. A few street vendors and the patient queues of rickshaw coolies waited

167

hopefully but, though the lights burned brightly in the clubs and business flats, they also blazed, long after closing time, in the banks and *taipans'* offices.

What movement there was seemed confined to the sleek passage of dark motor cars and taxis, several bearing the plates of the diplomatic corps. Uniformed officers of the Shanghai Municipal Police were also out in strength.

The taxi sped along the Bund, past the banks and the Astor hotel, past the British consulate with its imposingly turbanned Sikh guards and over the Garden Bridge across the Soochow Creek. It then swung north, through the American sector where the residential quarter gave way to the industrial area of hosiery factories and textile mills crowding the bank of the congested waterway.

'Don't be fooled by all the glamour at Kirilov's,' Robin Chan explained as the taxi cornered wildly and the red glow in the sky drew nearer. 'The *cheongsam* Sonia wore last night belonged to the nightclub.'

James recalled the poignant image of the Russian girl's vulnerability, somehow emphasised by the lascivious dress. Sonia, far more than the ageing Natalia, was a marketable commodity in the *demi-monde* of Shanghai. How much greater was her exposure to the Japanese soldiery? He knew he *had* to get her out of Shanghai.

The gable end of a brick-built factory had collapsed into the street and the area was littered with broken glass. They were stopped near the North Station by a police checkpoint. James knew the far exit of the station led not onto the ground of the International Settlement, as did the nearer, but onto the soil of China itself. Beyond the station was a battle zone.

After a brief remonstration with the Shanghai police, they were allowed through. Chinese soldiers were to be seen now, dressed in grey-green cotton battle dress, some wearing field dressings and squatting exhausted beside the creek. The taxi turned inland, the driver slowing and looking over his shoulder as though wanting instructions and enthusiasm. Fires could be seen burning beyond broken walls and shattered windows. Gangs of Chinese coolies swung bucket chains from the muddy creek and the air was filling with acrid smoke. The explosion of mortar bombs popped the ears and a heavy shell landed not far away, rocking the taxi on its suspension. James could hear the screams of women and children, and here and there little groups of them huddled hopelessly, the flickering of the fires lighting up the dull resignation in their frightened faces. The odd dichotomy summed up for James the patient suffering of the Chinese: the personal terror borne with a racial courage that humbled him. At the same time it fuelled his resolve to find Sonia Starlenka.

At the sight of a manned and sand-bagged machine-gun post, the taxi skidded to a halt. The driver jabbered something at Robin Chan.

'He says he'll wait half a mile back by the police post if we pay him now.'

'Aye, aye. This is no time to haggle.' James pressed a ten dollar note into the Purser's hand and stepped out into the road. A Chinese officer rose from the machine-gun emplacement and waved him back, shouting. Chan got out, paid the driver and the two of them stood there as the taxi reversed, then swung away with a squealing of tyres. Chan exchanged words with the Kuomintang subaltern, then grabbed James's arm.

'This way, come on.'

They ran into a side street. High walls surrounded Chinese houses built round internal courtyards, well-to-do houses which seemed to cower in silence. Then a dog barked and somewhere a man was shouting. The sudden concussion of artillery was painful to the ears, though no shells fell near by.

'He said,' puffed Robin, referring to the Kuomintang officer, 'that we're well back from the front line.'

'I was twenty miles from the front line when I was last blown up,' replied James grimly, fighting a rising fear now the spurious shelter of the taxi was far behind.

'I didn't know . . . which ship was that? Not one of China Independent's?'

'No, at Jutland . . . bloody battle cruiser.' They paused briefly at a cross roads. Opposite a row of tenements flanked an alleyway strung with palely fluttering rows of washing. James wondered how many people cowered in terror behind the closed shutters. The occasional glimmer of light and the underlying swell of indeterminate human noise rose and fell, broken now and then by an identifiable noise, the weird piping of a caged thrush, or the crying of a child.

'This way.'

The stinking darkness of the alleyway engulfed them. These were the homes of the industrial workers, the men, women and children who toiled in the foreign-owned silk, hosiery and textile works. The comparative silence of the quarter was oppressive, as though the inhabitants held their breath, effacing themselves as things of no account to the Japanese officers directing the bombardment.

James and Robin pressed on and, at the same instant, the Japanese artillery shifted its target.

There was a sudden ear-splitting crash and a wave of searing heat flung them to the ground. The thunderous collapse of masonry threw shards of disintegrating brick and the thick, suffocating dust of stucco and plaster upon them. Choking, they clambered onto their feet, grabbing at each other for reassurance and support. The gritty filth scoured their sweating skin and settled in their mouths so they spat and coughed and swore. All about them the cowed population gave vent to their fear. Screams, wails and shouts rent the air, the voices trailing from the crescendo of pure terror to the soft, nerve-shattered paralysis of horror. In the darkness, deprived of proper sight, they were assailed by the overwhelming stench of explosives, insanitary living conditions, excrement and urine.

'D'you know where we are, Robin?' James shouted at the pale blur of Chan's face.

'I did just now, before that shell landed. Wait, here . . .'

He stumbled forward, the plaster dust on his arms and shoulders ghoulishly outlining him. 'Yes, here, over here.'

The doorway stood open, the dim flight of stairs barely perceptible. An enamelled number plate was screwed to the adjacent wall.

'This way.'

The building was full of dust and noise. Doors opened and closed, dark shapes pushed past them in the stairwell, shrill, outlandish voices passing in a swirl of skirts, wafting air stale with cabbage water and musk. It was a moment before he realised they were all women, large Caucasian women who spoke Russian, and the shriller, smaller Chinese and half-caste hostesses from Kirilov's.

'Mai Wong! Mai Wong!' Robin was racing up the stairs ahead of James, shouting and elbowing aside these women, dodging their wild slaps as he threw them off, ignoring their invective.

James felt one of them grab him. She attempted to peer into his face. 'You police?' she asked repeatedly. 'You help me?'

He thrust her aside. 'Get out!' he commanded. 'The building next door has been shelled.'

But such a rational explanation was ridiculous. In a second he was beseiged. Lights were reappearing and he found himself surrounded by a dozen women who were, or had been, outstandingly good looking. A few steps higher he caught sight of Natalia. She had seen who he was, and paused indecisively on the stairs. He fought off the others and struggled towards her. Natalia came to herself, disbelieving her own luck; she swung on her fellows, swearing and beating them off.

Then, as another shell landed close by, the lights went out again, the air was filled with renewed screaming and James felt his arm seized.

She was muttering in Russian, low sacred words of relief, drawing him to her so he had to grab her shoulders and force her to listen.

'Natalia! Natalia, listen. I want Sonia, Sonia Starlenka. Where – is – she?'

An oil light flared on the landing and James saw the look of shock cross Natalia's face. The gobbet of spittle hit his cheek and he squeezed her shoulder with his hand and shook her violently.

'Stop that. Take me to Sonia! Take me to Sonia and I'll get you both out of Shanghai!'

The bearer of the oil lamp swore at them for blocking the stairs, but by its light he saw Natalia's face fall in acquiescence. She turned and led the way upwards. James wiped the spittle from his cheek and followed. They met Robin and Mai Wong on the top landing. He carried a bundle.

171

'I'll wait by the taxi,' the Purser called.

James followed Natalia across the landing and through the door she held open. He passed her rigid figure and into the room beyond. He did not see Sonia at first, for the glassless window of the apartment looked out across a hellish scene of red devastation. Fires raged, throwing into sharp contrast the pitch black of intervening walls. Periodically glass exploded and the rain of shells and mortar bombs blew yellow-white blossoms amid this inferno and, momentarily distracted by this awesome sight, James's artist's eye likened the moment of explosive impact to the bloom of a chrysanthemum.

And then he saw her as she moved in nervous response to a heavy shell exploding not half a mile away. She must have seen him at the same moment, for he could hear her gasp and saw her put out her hand to the wall for support.

'Miss Starlenka?'

'Natalia?' he heard her ask uncertainly.

'Yes, I'm here,' the older woman answered in English. 'Your friend has come.' Natalia shut the door. 'Do you have your lighter?' she asked James, bending over the table. They coaxed an oil lamp into life and James was aware of an air of hostility between the two women.

'Your friend has come to take you out of Shanghai.'

'I will take both of you.'

'That won't be necessary. Do you have a cigarette?'

He found the crushed remains of the packet they had shared the previous evening and shielded the lighter flame dancing in the hot wind that blew in through the smashed window. As he pocketed the Ronson he found Sonia beside him.

'You can take us away? In your ship?'

'Yes, both of you, if you hurry.' It occurred to him that at any moment the Japanese might cease their bombardment and launch an infantry assault. God only knew what the time was. He had lost all track of it and Ross would sail when he said he would, missing officers notwithstanding.

But, in the way of women, they seemed not to grasp the urgency of the matter and to his astonishment Sonia sat herself down in an armchair.

'I saw you last night, with Natasha. When I was singing.

172

After I finish I send message to Natasha; ask her if she make business with you. She say no and I come speak with you, but you gone.'

'I, er . . .' James turned to Natalia. She too had sat down, her legs crossed and her cigarette held between red-nailed fingers. The look in her eyes was accusing. Embarrassed and anxious he cast his eye about the room, taking in briefly the evidence of a past life, the samovar and heavily draped table, the single, cherished photograph of a family group.

And the two beds, each with their segregating curtain.

More shells thundered outside and the whole building shook. 'We must go,' he urged, 'now!'

They rose obediently. Sonia was smiling. 'We have good journey now,' she said simply, turning to a chest of drawers and beginning to throw clothes into a suitcase.

'It is an old Russian custom,' explained Natalia, 'to sit before going on a journey.'

'Ah. You must pack, quickly!'

She shook her head. 'Where will you take us? Hong Kong? Singapore? What will I do in those places that I cannot do in Shanghai?' She stared out of the window, silhouetted against the fires and the chrysanthemum explosions of the shells. 'I can always find myself a Japanese officer . . .' Her voice trailed off and when she turned back to him she was choking with emotion. 'What is your name?'

'James,' he replied, feeling utterly helpless.

'James,' she repeated, testing the name and nodding approval. 'Look after her, James. Last night we quarrelled over you, but now you must look after her. She has been like my daughter.'

Natalia took a tiny ornament from a shelf and pressed it into the younger woman's hand.

'*Niet.*'

'Take it!' Natalia commanded, swinging round on James. 'Take her, go!' James picked up Sonia's ancient suitcase and grabbed her arm. He paused momentarily by the door. Natalia stood beside the window, her shoulders shaking. He dragged Sonia out onto the landing.

'Natasha? Natasha!' She stumbled after him, calling over her shoulder as he pulled her gently towards the stairs.

And then they were picking their way along the foetid

173

alley, no longer deserted but thronged with a milling and uncertain crowd driven from their homes by Japanese shells and bombs.

CHAPTER THIRTEEN

Sonia

'Who *is* she?' hissed Emily, staring furiously at the closed door.

'Her name –'

'I know her bloody name. I want to know what she's doing here in our . . .'

'*My* flat, Emily,' he said, angering. 'She's a refugee.'

'She's a tart you picked up in Shanghai.'

'She's got nowhere to live, for Christ's sake! The bloody Japanese shelled the street.'

'Nowhere to live? With a face like that!'

'Don't be a tediously jealous bitch, for God's sake.'

'Oh, but I am, James,' Emily said, lowering her voice menacingly. 'A very jealous bitch.'

'Look, Emily,' he said, trying to be reasonable, 'you've nothing to be jealous of. I've not been to bed with her.'

'I know that, you fool; you're saving her for something more permanent, Jimmy-boy. She'll end up as your wife, that's obvious!'

'Emily, don't –'

'Emily, don't what? Emily, don't be stupid? Is that it? Because it's *you* that's stupid. What are you going to do with her when you're at sea? D'you think she's the type to sit and knit comforters for you?'

'Emily –'

'Christ, James, you bastard. I wanted you the first moment I set eyes upon you. I never asked a thing of you more than you were prepared to give, I've lived with you for three years, been more than devoted to you, and now it's "Emily this is *my* flat." '

175

'Emily, I'm very tired, and it's late.'

'It's late all right; too late!'

He did nothing to stop her leaving, but stood stock-still, staring at the closed door to the lounge. Slowly he turned the door handle and slipped into the darkened room. From the window he could see the black waters of the harbour reflecting the light of Victoria on Hong Kong island. He recalled standing in the same place in the first hours of the year, closing one eye to focus his drunken vision on the same scene. Now everything had changed.

But had it? No, it had been wrong then, and gone on being wrong. He had not admitted it to himself before and only did so now because Emily had confronted him with himself. He had been too intent on burying his head in the sand, of avoiding the truth, of hiding behind his mask as Chief Officer of the *Poyang*, enjoying the favours of Emily's body.

But it had never been the same since he had set eyes on the Russian girl.

She was asleep on the settee. There was enough light to illuminate her pale face. There *was* something feline about her, a smooth and supple quality that influenced her character as well as her body. What did he know about her?

Nothing.

Yet Emily had suggested marriage and even as he had rounded on the unfortunate Dr Sangwell six weeks earlier some similar resolve had been forming in his subconscious. Marriage?

It would solve the immigration problem.

It would solve the riddle of his life's pointlessness.

But what of *her*? It was ridiculous to think she felt anything for him. What little she had had he had torn her from in Shanghai. And what had she been in Kirilov's? Merely the singer; the crooner, as Robin Chan had called her. Or had she, like Natalia, been a whore?

He flung himself disconsolately into an armchair. On the settee Sonia stirred, stretched and woke. Suddenly she sat up, looking about her.

'It's all right. I'm here, you're quite safe. You're in my flat in Kowloon, remember? You were very tired when we got off the ship.'

176

She brushed a hand through her hair. 'Oh, yes. I remember.' She relaxed, sinking back onto the settee.

'You fell asleep.'

'Somebody came. Who was she?'

'She?'

'I heard her voice, I think. Was she your girlfriend?'

'Yes, but she's gone now.'

'Because of me?'

'Yes.'

James took a deep breath. There was little point in beating about the bush. Sonia, whatever she had been in Shanghai, was no innocent.

'She will not come back, Sonia, as long as you are here.'

'Then I . . .'

'I do not want you to leave. You may stay as long as you want to. In fact,' he ploughed on, emboldened by her silence and the dark hollows of her eyes watching him from the pale oval of her face, 'I want you to stay forever.'

'James . . .' She reached out a hand and he almost crawled across the carpet to take it, sitting on the floor beside the settee so their faces were level.

'I – I do not care about the past, Sonia. My own past is not very pleasant, not very good.' He wanted to explain, but the need to simplify his language kept him faltering, so that she broke in.

'Please, James, we do not make our lives. We only live them as best we can. In Shanghai my mother die. Yuri he take me to nightclub one night and when my mother die he say we can live together. Other Russian people live together; our old life was dead. In Shanghai we make new life. We hear American music, jazz. One day, we say, we will all live in America. Today we have no money, so we will make American music and soon we will be able to go and live in America.'

She paused, gently stroking James's hand which she held between her own.

'But it is not so easy. We have good jazz band, we make money, but then Yuri and Arcady . . . they drink too much, sometimes smoke opium, Valeria too. Then Yuri get very angry. Have you got cigarette? I leave him. Kirilov offer me job as singer. I have to eat, James.'

177

'I understand,' he said quietly, lighting her cigarette.

'Natalia Drubskaya save me. She say I am like her daughter. She take me to her apartment.' James thought of the wretched one-room flat the two stateless women had called their 'apartment'. 'She very kind to me, very kind . . . but not like my mother. You understand, James?'

'Yes,' he said, 'I think so.'

'Then you say you want me. You bring me to Hong Kong.'

'Shanghai is not safe.'

'Nowhere is safe for White Russians except America.' She said it matter-of-factly, and he missed its significance in his English preoccupation with the past.

'And Hong Kong.'

'Maybe.'

There were silent for a little, then he asked, 'Where did you live – in Russia, I mean?'

'I was born in Vyazma, but I lived for a while in Moscow. My father was journalist, writing for liberal newspaper. He was arrested once by the OGPU, but did not like the Bolsheviks. He went out one day when there was rioting. There was shooting. He came home covered in blood. We call doctor, but late that night my mother sent for me and my sister Katya. My father was in bed and my mother was crying. He held our hands. "No more English lessons for you, my darling," he said. He was proud of knowing English. When my father was dead, we moved back to Vyazma. There was much disturbance during the fighting. For a long time the White army was near us, then, when they were beaten, we moved east, along the railway. In Khabarovsk we met Americans. They told us to go to America; there were Russians in the American soldiers, you understand? Men with Russian names, German names.'

'Yes, I understand.'

'It was very bad. Katya died. It was my fourteenth birthday when we buried her. I cannot remember the name of the village; only that the station master's wife gave us soup. My mother got a job when we reached Vladivostock. The two of us were happy, but it was not for ever. Soon some ships came into the harbour. Mother said we must leave. I do not remember anything about that time now,

178

except seeing American soldiers going onto their ship. We came to Tientsin and then Shanghai. It was like Moscow again, only we were poor . . . That is all.'

She recited her life dry-eyed, as though it no longer touched her and was too remote. Yet at the same time he admired her detachment. She was a survivor; she knew how to bury pain, to live on vague dreams of America and subsist from day to day.

'And you, James? What is your story? Tell me about your girlfriend.'

When he had finished she drew him towards her. It was the first time they had kissed, for aboard the *Poyang*, under the eye of a disapproving Ross, Mai Wong and Sonia had travelled as passengers. For a languid moment he allowed himself to be drawn, to succumb to the unbelievable softness of her lips and the fragrance of her hair. But the murmurings of her voice aroused him, told him she acted not out of compassion but something more urgent.

She made no protest as he fondled her breasts, only sighing with muted pleasure and moving her hips with a slow, demanding insistency. Trembling, he moved his hands lower, and she clung to him with a tenacity that incensed his passion as he struggled free of his clothing.

Letting him go she released herself and lay naked, irresistibly wanton with outstretched arms. Her white flesh gleamed softly as she parted her legs. He sank upon her, the lubricious passage swallowing him in the erotic perfection of the little death.

Much later he lay beside her on the bed. Unlike Sonia he could not sleep, prevented by a guilt borne on the scent of Emily's perfume that pervaded the pillows. He was troubled by the way he had treated Emily, but equally unable to deny the incredible feeling of contentment the sleeping Sonia had brought him. To terminate the delicate sensation of happiness seemed more callous than the means by which he had acquired it and, in the end, his conscience was eased by the knowledge that Emily had left him of her own free will. She was part of the past; Sonia belonged to the future.

The *Poyang*'s owners took advantage of her disrupted schedule to send her into dry dock. Shored up in the Taikoo graving dock, her rusty sides were scrubbed down and repainted, her boilers cleaned and she was pronounced fit for a further four years' service by a Lloyd's surveyor. Such activity might have heavily involved the *Poyang*'s Chief Officer had not another circumstance occurred. Whether or not one believes in providence, it was to prove fateful to James Martin, altering his life in two important ways.

The event was the death of Captain Arkwright of the *Shantung*, the newest ship in China Independent's fleet. When, in haste, the command was offered to Captain Ross he declined, arguing he was too old to transfer from the *Poyang*. He advised the directors of China Independent to select another man, naming his own Chief Officer as a suitable candidate. Unexpectedly, James found himself called to a modern office block in Victoria where, amid dark rosewood panelling and the subtle scent of joss 'the respected Chang' and Messrs Moncrieff and Angus, co-directors of the company, offered him the command of the *Shantung*.

'It is customary for our newest ship to be the command of our senior master, Mr Martin, but in view of the wide dispersal of our fleet and the unforeseen nature of the situation we now find ourselves faced with, we are considering yourself as the most suitable candidate for the *Shantung*.'

'Thank you, sir,' James said to Moncrieff, the chairman, and a formidable figure in his high wing collar and frock coat.

'You are highly recommended by Captain Ross, Mr Martin.' James bowed to 'the respected Chang' who stood at Moncrieff's left shoulder. Rumour had it that Chang was incredibly wealthy, but his plain, dark blue gown and skull cap gave no indication of anything beyond a comfortable prosperity.

'Well? D'you accept?' snapped Angus, the aggressive junior member of the board.

'Gratefully, sir . . . gentlemen.'

'She arrives the day after tomorrow,' went on Angus. 'Her Master may be relieved on arrival. You've three days here in Hong Kong to discharge and load for Japan.'

'Very well, Mr Angus.'

180

He had reached the boardroom door when Moncrieff said in a low voice, 'Is it your intention to marry, Captain Martin?'

James paused, his hand on the brass handle of the door. Turning, he faced the formidable trio, aware that the *Shantung* carried three dozen first-class passengers and her master should therefore be a model of rectitude.

'We have heard gossip, Captain.'

'The matter is in hand, gentlemen,' he said.

'We would not be averse to your wife travelling with you, Captain, if she so desired,' soothed Moncrieff. James suppressed his smile, aware that the old Scotsman's regard for the moral welfare of his passengers was not exaggerated. He disliked his officers philandering, and knew a captain with his wife aboard to be an excellent guarantor of his crew's good behaviour. The frosty eyes of Angus revealed that perhaps he knew Sonia Starlenka was not quite the woman his partner imagined.

'As I say, gentlemen, the matter is in hand.'

Walking down the hill towards the ferry landing, James pondered his predicament. The unexpected promotion ought to have made him happier than it did, and he leaned morosely on the rail of the Star ferry as it churned the yeasty and teeming water of the harbour in its crossing to Kowloon.

Emily's prediction looked uncannily accurate, though what Sonia herself would say to the notion after so abrupt and curious a courtship he could only guess. As for Emily herself, a discreet enquiry had revealed she had accepted a vacant post in Singapore and left hurriedly two days earlier on P and O's *Strathnaver*. He himself knew only that he could not live without Sonia, that she filled the void left by Stella in a way Emily never could. Still musing, he took a rickshaw up Nathan Road to the flat where, for the past week, he had lived with the lovely Russian, enjoying a few days' local leave before rejoining *Poyang* in the Taikoo dockyard.

She was in his arms the moment the door was closed. He pulled himself away from her with gentle insistence, sitting her on the settee on which they had first declared their mutual attraction.

'Sonia, listen. It is important I speak to you.'

She drew back, her face suddenly serious and he suffered a moment of panic, of inadequacy at trying to establish any claim over her. He got up and moved to the window, his mind a whirl of doubts and misgivings.

It was not what *she* had been that troubled him. He was far beyond the boyish prejudice which sought to enslave a single female for his exclusive use; Emily had cured him of that. It was his own sense of damnation, the feeling of unworthiness that had marred his survival at Jutland which returned to him now.

He stood miserably uncertain recalling Emily's own, desperate letter. *It is a terrible thing to be in love*, she had written, then added, *but good to have a lover*.

How right she had been, poor Emily, and how shabbily he had treated her. No matter how he consoled his conscience with the thought that she had repudiated him, he felt the prickling guilt of shame when he considered the end of their affair. But Emily had never seemed to need him; she was a friend, never a dependant, and James was compelled to face the unpleasant fact. It had seemed somehow a diminution of his manhood.

It was all so very different with Sonia. Her submissive beauty captivated him and persuaded him her very loveliness was a danger to herself. The world would take advantage of her as, indeed, it already had. In getting her free of the shambles of Chapei she was already bound to him in a way which seemed more fated than fortuitous.

'What is the matter, James?' Sonia asked anxiously, jerking him back to the present. 'You are going to ask me to go away.'

'No!' He swung from the window. 'No, of course not.'

Her face was pale, insecurity plain in her expression and he shook his head vigorously. '*Niet*, no, never.'

He was too old to bury himself again, as he had before aboard the *Socotra*. Jutland, his survival and the action with the submarine off Ireland had surely been expiated by the loss of Stella. Besides, the young took these things too much to heart. The individual human soul was not of much importance, China had taught him, and happiness, as his mother had said, only existed in retrospect.

If Sonia brought him pain, it did not matter. She was

staring at him, her red lips slightly parted as though trying to kiss him across twelve feet of Tientsin carpet and he felt himself trembling.

'Will you marry me, Sonia?' he asked. 'Come and live with me on a new ship? In a few years we will retire to live in England.'

'Not America?' she said, smiling and holding out her arms to him, wanting him to come to her and end the agony of her uncertainty. And as he kissed her he wondered how, or when, he would be called to account for the good fortune no man truly deserves.

Old Captain Ross proved correct about the duration of the 'trouble' in Shanghai. Just as he had predicted, it blew over after a couple of months of bitter fighting. Old China hands conceded grudging praise to the unexpectedly dogged resistance of the Chinese forces, but there was much head-shaking over the growing power of the Japanese in Manchuria and their aggressive attitude to China.

James and Sonia (married that spring of 1932 by special licence and the good offices of the Anglican padre of the Mission to Seamen) watched with dismay the western powers preserve a nervous but united detachment from what were, reprehensibly enough, considered local native squabbles.

'It is worse than in Russia,' Sonia said of China's creaking and abused republic. 'Soon there will be much trouble from the Kuomintang or the Bolsheviks.'

'Or the Japanese,' agreed James, alarmed at the concessions granted to Japan at the London Naval Conference in the matter of submarine tonnages and the walk-out of their delegates from the League of Nations.

He was in a good position to watch units of the Imperial Japanese fleet as the *Shantung* was frequently in Japanese waters. The ship had become something of a legend in a minor way, proving popular with the expatriate British, American, German and French communities in Shanghai who annually migrated to avoid the August heat of the Chinese city. Passengers clamoured for berths aboard the SS *Shantung*, especially the younger set, eager to join in the entertainments provided and organised by the exotic Mrs Martin.

183

If James had harboured any doubts about Sonia's ability to settle to the routine of a ship master's wife she soon dispelled them. She proved, with her exceptional grace and beauty, her thick Russian accent and eccentric English, a glamorous attraction and in the rat-race of the Shanghai commercial *milieu* the story of her dramatic rescue and subsequent installation aboard the *Shantung* was seen as a true romance.

The fact that there were hundreds of her unfortunate countrymen and women rotting stateless in the open prison of the International Settlement in Shanghai did not diminish her appeal, for she was real evidence of a storyline which reflected the popular myth then being promulgated by Hollywood films. She was not married to a rich man, but the lifestyle aboard the *Shantung* was sufficiently luxurious to convey that impression in the few days her passengers were embarked. Thus the jazz band, the cabaret bar and the alluring presence of Sonia herself helped make her husband's command an almost instant success. Such was the prestige of the *Shantung* that China Independent's management turned a blind eye to its origin. It had not been quite what they had in mind when they urged marriage upon Captain Martin, but there was no doubting its profitability.

Most important to James was the fact that Sonia herself was never bored. She had grown accustomed to a life of some flamboyance, fed on it with the deep insecurity of the former refugee, and purred with feline contentment whenever James complimented her on the success she had made of his career.

With what James learned was a characteristically impetuous generosity, Sonia repaid Natalia Drubskaya's kindness by insisting James retained the Kowloon flat and installed Natalia there for as long as she wished. James could refuse her nothing, not even her occasional overindulgence in what he came to call her 'Russian evenings' when she and Natalia would get hopelessly drunk and reminisce in their native tongue.

On these nights James would cross the harbour and take himself to the China Fleet Club where, Geoffrey Ennis and HMS *Peterborough* long having departed at the end of their commission, he was reminded of the awful loneliness of bachelorhood.

The contentment of his marriage and the absorption of

command made him dismiss from his mind all thoughts of returning to Britain for some time. The only clouds on his horizon were the increasingly hysterical letters from his cousin Vera, with their constant reminder that in England dwelt a son who was reaching manhood without knowing his father.

CHAPTER FOURTEEN

The Return of Ulysses

Geoffrey Ennis stepped out of the taxi into a sleeting rain. Hurriedly paying off the driver he crossed Regent Street and entered the Café Royale. It was not his choice of a rendezvous but, under the circumstances, was probably the best place in central London.

'Over here, darling!'

He caught sight of Drusilla's wave and her ridiculous hat, waved back and made his way through the tables. Even a month after the event, the Café Royale still seethed with the euphoric mood which had gripped London since Mr Chamberlain had returned from Munich waving his piece of paper. People no longer had quite so much faith in his assertion that he had secured 'peace in our time', but were prepared to enjoy life from day to day, conscious that at least for a while immediate danger had been diverted. Anyway, Christmas was approaching and judging by the look of things Drusilla had taken advantage of a rare foray to London to buy presents.

She kissed him on the cheek as he sat down. 'Had a good day, darling?'

They were as different as chalk and cheese, Ennis thought sadly, shaking Vera Martin's hand. Drusilla blonde, bubbly and superficial, and poor dear Vera a desiccated spinster, her hair in earphones and wearing an out of fashion dress that utterly obscured her otherwise handsome features.

'Hullo, Vee,' he said, stumbling through the ridiculous nonsense of small talk. 'How are you? Is John with you?'

'I'm fine, thank you. John promised he'd be here by four.'

'It's only five past,' said Ennis, looking at his watch as he

186

offered Drusilla a cigarette and took one himself. 'No vices, Vee?'

Vera managed a wan smile, then her face lit up. 'Here he is,' she said, and they turned to watch Sublieutenant John Martin weave through the tables. He was clearly somewhat sheepish about wearing uniform in public.

'He *is* a good-looking boy,' said Drusilla, expelling a blue plume of smoke from her rouged lips.

'I expect he'll be nervous,' said Vera, her own pallor an obvious indication of her misgivings at the outcome of this meeting.

'Understandable,' muttered Ennis, rising and extending his hand. 'Good to see you again, John.'

'And you, sir . . . Aunt Dru, Aunt Vee.'

They sat smiling at each other, and Geoffrey ordered tea and scones.

'I was at the Admiralty this afternoon, John,' he said. 'I've made a formal application for you to join me on *Shrike*; your TAS specialisation was a great help. Too many of your generation still specialise in gunnery.'

'It was father's advice to go for it. He says the submarine will pose the biggest threat, if there's another war.'

'Do we have to talk about war? We've been promised peace,' said Drusilla, grinding out her cigarette and adding with typical tactlessness, 'how often did your father write to you?'

'Every quarter,' put in Vera. 'I insisted on it.'

'I wonder what his wife's like?' Drusilla rattled on.

Geoffrey glanced at his watch again. 'They should be here by now, but with this rain I expect the traffic . . . what's the matter, Vee?'

Vera had half risen from her seat and her face was dead white. Geoffrey swivelled in his chair. They were standing by the door, James in a dark blue suit with a sopping trilby in his hands. Beside him stood a slender, elegant woman with a small brimmed hat. She wore a tight black costume and was smiling at the doorman. She had clearly made an impression, as he was fawningly folding a large umbrella.

'Well, well, well,' said Drusilla, rolling her eyes at the young John, 'quite a stepmother, my boy.'

Both Ennis and John stood as Vera sank back into her

seat. Ennis waved and caught James's eye. Most of the clientele of the café watched Sonia as she walked over to them.

'My dear James,' Ennis said warmly, holding out his hand.

'Geoffrey! And this must be Drusilla. How d'you do . . . And Vee, my dear, how good to see you.' James paused and Geoffrey could see he was nervous. 'This is my wife, Sonia.'

Ennis watched Drusilla's cool handshake and Vera's stern scrutiny, and then he bent his head over Sonia's hand, aware that she was extraordinarily beautiful.

'I did not know Englishmen kissed hands,' she said, and then turned to John. 'And you are John, yes? Will you also kiss my hand and call me Sonia, please?'

It was a masterly little performance and broke the ice perfectly. Geoffrey had not entirely trusted Drusilla's motives in arranging the reunion in so fashionably public a place, but it worked. As the three women sat, indulging their mutual and barely disguised curiosity, James Martin greeted his son.

The young man reminded him of Bawden. He had the same well-built frame and direct way of looking at one. It somehow disappointed him now, after the years that had passed, to find he had shed his mother's looks.

'My dear boy.'

'Father . . .' The boy's eyes were hazel, and very serious, the eyes of an introvert, James thought.

'You'll have a lot to talk about later,' Geoffrey said in an overloud voice, 'but first tea, and then we'll plan the evening.'

The men sat late in the hotel lounge. Drusilla, by prior arrangement, had scooped up the women, confident that Sonia had had a tiring day. They retired early, Drusilla to help Sonia unpack and worm out of her the details her curiosity demanded.

'Good trip home?' inquired Geoffrey as they settled to cigars and brandy.

'Very pleasant. We came on the *Glenearn* from Singapore. Fine ship.' James looked at Geoffrey and then at John.

'I won't outstay my welcome, Jimmy,' Geoffrey said, leaning forward and gently knocking the ash off his cigar, 'but I'm afraid I couldn't do you much good at the Admiralty today.'

'Too old, I suppose,' said James. 'Or was it that other business?'

'Wyatt's there. He remembered your name. I'm sorry.'

James sighed. 'It's more or less what I expected.'

'I'm not entirely convinced there's going to be trouble, you know.'

'For God's sake stop using euphemisms, Geoff. Of course there's going to be another bloody war. You have absolutely no idea of the scale of Japanese activity. There's a full-blown war going on in China now. Shanghai, barring the International Settlement, fell last November and they took the Kuomintang capital Nanking a few weeks later. What the bastards did there defies belief,' James said, his voice low and passionately intense. 'Rape is too mild a word with a quarter of a million dead.'

'And you're no longer for peace at any price?' asked Ennis with a wry grin.

'I feared the worst for China when Japan left the League of Nations, but at least I felt we could keep out of the quarrel. Now, with the Germans following suit . . . no. I felt – we felt, Sonia and I – that it was better to come home and see if there was something useful we could do.'

'I never really thought you were a pacifist.'

'Only because,' retorted James with a trace of bitterness, 'you know about the circumstances of . . .' He trailed off, throwing a quick glance in John's direction. Ennis forestalled further dialogue and rose to his feet.

'Well, I'll leave you two to chat. I'm sorry about the Admiralty, Jim.'

James shrugged. 'Perhaps I'll go and see Wyatt myself.'

'Oh, I don't think I'd bother. Good night.'

James and John sat in silence for some moments, then James said, 'I suppose I've been a bloody awful father.'

John managed a smile, a rather embarrassed smile, but it suddenly transfigured his face and reminded James poignantly of Stella.

'I never really thought about it in those terms,' John said.

'It, er, seems rather a pretence, then. Shall we regard ourselves as friends?'

189

'Rather than relatives?'

'If you like.'

'Aunt Vee deserves better, you know,' John said. 'She never once criticised you to me, though I think she thought you had abandoned us both.'

'To be candid, John, the truth of the matter was that I had. I had to earn a living and keep Vee and yourself, but I suppose abandon you was more or less what I did.' James paused, then added, 'I *was* pretty cut up to be chucked out of the Navy.'

'Grandpa's still alive. *He* wasn't so diplomatic about you.'

'Does he know I remarried?'

'I don't know, but it wouldn't hurt to go and see him. Grandma's still pretty active.'

'Your mother,' James began, staring down at the last of the brandy, aware that it and the wine with dinner had loosened his tongue, 'was a very lovely person. I wasn't much older than you when she died.'

'You were the same age.'

'That war had a lot to answer for,' he said, 'in terms of social turmoil. If there's another, which seems likely, there'll be a hell of a lot more distress. Just before the last one broke out, my mother made me promise not to marry during the war. I didn't keep my promise and I wouldn't be fool enough to extort any such thing from you, but consider the matter well if you want to do it.' He tossed off the cognac. 'Anyway, how *is* the dear old Andrew?' he asked.

'Uncle Geoff's asked for me to join him on *Shrike*, working up on anti-submarine work. You see, I took your advice and made it my specialisation.'

'Good. I'm glad you listened. Don't ever serve in a capital ship.'

'Well,' said John frankly, 'I *was* intending to do gunnery, but then when the civil war blew up in Spain we did an analysis of the effect of the Italians' submarine offensive against Russian ships supplying the International Brigade, and I realised that the threat to any supply line is often the determining factor in a campaign.' John's voice was serious. He had not overindulged in drink as James and Geoffrey had done.

'Ever since I was blown sky high at Jutland,' James said,

190

aware of a surprising twinge of pleasure at capturing the boy's interest, 'I've had doubts about the wisdom of a naval career.'

'It *is* a family tradition, father.'

'Yes . . . yes, it is, isn't it?'

'It's a pleasant house, Vee, and with a fine view, too.'

James stared from the rear attic bedroom window of The Lees. The shallow water of Dovercourt Bay stretched south-east to the distant Naze with its high, red-brick tower, and cumulus clouds raced across the blue sky alternating patterns of shadow and sunlight on the sparkling sea.

'It's not The Reddings, but it's comfortable enough.'

James put his arm round her thin shoulders as they stood at the window.

'You're a good sort, Vee,' he said in a low voice, 'and I truly appreciate what you've done, both for John and for me.'

'I didn't really have much alternative.'

'You could have married Geoffrey.'

'Don't be silly. I didn't love him. I liked him, but I didn't love him and he was ten years my senior.'

'Eight,' James corrected. 'Anyway it's a jolly nice house.' He released Vera's shoulders and sensed her relief. 'There's plenty of room for all of us.'

'Yes,' said Vera sharply, 'there is.'

'Look, Vee –' James began, but Vera interrupted him.

'She doesn't like me, you know.'

'Don't be silly. How do you know?'

'One just does, James. I'm not a fool, so please don't patronise me.'

'I'm sorry.' He wondered where Sonia was and then caught sight of her below them in the garden, playing with Vera's King Charles spaniel. 'She's got a lot more in common with us than you might think: a decent home disrupted by war and revolution. It's a bit like us and our being dispossessed of The Reddings. There was no future for her in Shanghai.'

'Singing in a nightclub,' Vera said contemptuously. 'Is that why you married her? Because you felt sorry for her? Just like Stella . . .'

'What d'you mean?' he asked.

'I liked Stella, she was a down-to-earth creature, but I often thought there was an element of condescension in your affection for her.' Vera's tone was level and venomous, and she stared straight before her.

'Vee, that's unforgivable,' James protested.

'Is it?' she asked, turning on him. 'Geoffrey wrote to me and told me you were living with a perfectly decent girl in Hong Kong and he had high hopes of you marrying her. I'm not an old maid enough to disapprove of you having a common-law wife in a colony, but when you throw over a girl of your own type for –'

'Vee!' James snapped, 'I owe you a lot, more than I can ever repay, but don't lecture me. You could have married Geoffrey, he's "our type", whatever the hell that out-moded phrase means nowadays, but you didn't; you let him marry Drusilla who reminds me of a well-bred horse. It's plain he's not happy. He as good as admitted it once in Hong Kong. Why d'you think he kept up the friendship with you, wrote to you, advised you about getting John into Dartmouth, eh? Without Geoffrey, the boy would not have got the commission you so earnestly desired for him.' The tears welled up in her eyes, 'Vee,' he said soothingly, 'you *loved* Tom, and that was bloody silly. You would never have married him, but you loved him. As far as I know, you still do.'

She was nodding and said, 'I *do* understand, you fool, but why, oh why do *you* have all the good fortune?'

In the succeeding weeks even this imagined good fortune seemed to have deserted James. He wrote repeatedly to the Admiralty, both generally to the secretary, submitting a lengthy paper on his observations of the Japanese navy and the efficiency of aerial attacks carried out on the environs of Shanghai and shipping in the Whang-pu and Yangtze rivers, and also personally to Captain Wyatt, who, he discovered, was employed on the staff of the Second Sea Lord.

Wyatt's reply was disconcertingly frosty. James did not hold it against him, but realised the service, in retaining Wyatt, was continuing to foster a notion of the perfect naval officer as being a gentleman cricketer. He was more distressed by the official reply to his paper. It was addressed to plain 'Mr Martin'.

'I signed it as "captain",' he complained to Vera and

Sonia over the breakfast table, ' "former master of the SS *Shantung*", but I suppose some damn fool in their lordships' pay deemed that to be presumption of the worst sort.'

'So they won't give you a job?' said Vera, helping herself to toast.

'Doesn't look like it, does it?'

'You'll have to seek employment in the merchant marine again, then,' said Vera, her lips pursed disapprovingly.

'There's one last chance. The Navy were recruiting deck officers directly from the merchant service, but I expect I'm too old.'

'You'll have to find something.'

James looked from Vera to Sonia who sat stirring her coffee and saying nothing. 'Things aren't desperate. We've a little money left. If the Admiralty would drop this silly pretence of playing the government's song for them and pretending that scrap of paper Chamberlain brought back from Munich was worth anything, then maybe we'd get somewhere.'

'Why don't you write to Mr Churchill?' Vera suggested. 'That's what I'd do.'

James stared open-mouthed at his cousin, then began to laugh. 'My God, Vee, what are you trying to do? *Start* a bloody war?'

'You can laugh if you like, but we lobbied and lobbied and got the Air-Raid Precautions Act through the House of Commons and a rearmament programme that has given the Navy two new battleships, new battle cruisers and escorts.' Vera stood and began to clear the table, waving the maid out of the way. 'That's more than you can say for your colonial types sitting on their verandahs drinking gin slings.'

Despite his pleas to the Admiralty, James Martin had not truthfully come home to fight a war, but to avoid one. He could not expose Sonia to the unavoidable risks which shipping on the China coast now ran, for the all-out aggression of the Japanese would, sooner or later, involve the so-called neutral powers. Nor was he sufficient of an imperialist to sit smugly in Hong Kong or the International Concessions in the purblind belief that Hirohito's chrysanthemum warriors would continue to respect the white

193

man's preserves. He was only too well aware of how the white man had obtained them in the first place, for his own father had lost his life storming the Taku forts and the Japanese had already sunk the American gunboat *Panay* and fired on HMS *Ladybird*.

Moreover, his thinking had long ago divested itself of the childish preoccupations of British superiority. His experiences both during and after the Great War were persuasive enough. True, he had not lived through the upheaval of the National Strike or the worst of the Depression, but the privations and lowly status of an able seaman on a windjammer had rid him of the tedious arrogance assumed by his countrymen and women abroad.

He had seen the moral bankruptcy of such an attitude in common with many of his generation, whose more frivolous reaction was to have plunged into fads such as spiritualism. As much of their attitudes stemmed from a desire to make reparation to those of their fellows who had died in the war, as from a desire to repudiate the hypocrisy of the established church. But more serious souls embraced socialism as the only way of building homes fit for heroes, and volunteered to take up arms again to stem the tide of fascism in Spain.

If James lagged unconcernedly behind Robin Chan in his knowledge of jazz and was late in experiencing the lascivious joys of crush-dancing, he had understood why the Oxford Union had voted against fighting for King and Country. War, as his mother had hinted years ago, was never 'a great and glorious thing'.

Unlike Vera, trapped by her adolescent love for Tom and rooted in a world that had vanished in 1914, who still believed in the power of the British Empire as an agent for universal good, he had seen the terrible manifestations of modern war and dreaded its occurrence in Europe. But despite the impression that Britain had had nothing more on its mind than the abdication of its King-Emperor, Vera's letters had kept him informed of developments in Spain. The activities of Germany's Condor Legion were but one example of fascist intervention, but dramatic enough to make him aware of the dangers presented by Hitler and Mussolini, which seemed but a pale imitation of what the Japanese were doing in China.

194

'It seems,' he said one evening as they sat over their coffee, 'that Europe is in danger of destroying itself in the same way as China is being destroyed. Italy seizing Ethiopia was like the Japanese taking over Manchuria; then Hitler annexing the Rhineland and marching into the Sudetenland paralleled Japanese high-handedness in Shanghai in thirty-two.'

'Japan is so greedy. Formosa she took from China, and Sakhalin and Port Arthur from my own country,' put in Sonia.

'They're new countries, you see, Vee,' James continued. 'Oh, I know you wouldn't strictly speaking call Japan "new", not like the comparatively recently unified Germany and Italy, but it is *newly* industrialised, a thing the Japanese accomplished with astonishing speed.'

'Most of their industrial *matériel* comes from us,' Vera said dismissively.

'That's only partially true and an argument I've heard before, but it shouldn't make you underestimate them. You saw on the film newsreels Madame Chiang appeal for help against them. You didn't see what they did in Nanking.'

'They are absolute bastards, Vera,' Sonia said and James smiled inwardly as Vera winced at the crudity.

'But that only make things worse, don't you see? Hitler hasn't finished expanding the German frontiers and, hell's bells, we even *helped* him,' exploded Vera.

'What d'you mean?' queried James.

'The Anglo-German naval agreement signed three years ago actually *broke* the Versailles Treaty by allowing Hitler a navy nearly half as big as ours! And it wasn't the only international agreement His Majesty's Government has been setting aside in this eternal policy of appeasement.'

'And that's why you wrote to Mr Churchill, is it?' James asked.

'That's how to deal with a bully, isn't it? You have to make a stand somewhere.'

'So you think war's inevitable?'

'Absolutely,' said Vera with conviction.

James reached out and patted Sonia's hand.

'At least we're a family again, Vee. It's what you wanted, isn't it?'

'You see, Vera,' Sonia added, impulsively clasping James's hand, her strange green eyes huge and expressive, 'although I will always be a Russian in my heart, I am also British now.'

'Yes,' said Vera coolly, 'I suppose you are.'

During the winter of 1938 and the following spring, James and Sonia lived quietly with Vera at The Lees. James pottered about the garden and, as he had done years earlier at The Reddings, cleared gutters and repainted window frames.

Among the local sea-faring community which manned the railway packets, the pilot cutters and the steam tenders of Trinity House, they found an eclectic collection of seamen with a corresponding variety of wives. Sonia appeared less exotic than she might have been elsewhere in the country, and they had a pleasant, if uninspiring, social life.

There were contacts with the Royal Navy, too, for there was almost always a pair of sloops attached to the training establishment at HMS *Ganges* and a periodic flotilla of destroyers would steam in from exercises in the North Sea to moor to a trot of buoys off Shotley. HMS *Shrike* was among these visitors, and the three of them visited Geoffrey and John, enjoying the wardroom hospitality on a summer evening in late June.

'It's a lovely estuary,' said James as he and John smoked cigarettes on deck while the sun set behind the distant spire of the Royal Hospital School.

'Yes. I always loved it, even when I was at school there.'

'Didn't you enjoy school?'

'No, not really.'

James watched his son, waiting for more, only to be disappointed. He experienced a deep pang of intense regret that he had missed all of John's boyhood, followed by a deep compulsion to do something, no matter how small, to rectify his appalling neglect.

'In my experience, John,' he said slowly, 'one never finds exactly the right moment or exactly the right words to express oneself properly to people to whom, I suppose, one owes some such explanation, or confession. Even with women it can be difficult, as you may already know.'

He was interrupted by the shrilling of the bosun's pipe and the tannoyed call for the upper deck party to stand by for the ceremony of sunset. Beside him John shifted awkwardly and pitched his cigarette over the taffrail.

'It's all right, father,' he said as the colour party came aft and fell in across the quarterdeck. 'I quite understand.'

Half relieved, half irritated by the intrusion of naval ceremony, James said, 'Mind if I stay?'

'Not if you stand to attention,' John said, smiling.

As the high piping note of the still floated out across the smooth waters of the harbour James stood behind his son, watching him salute as the white ensign slid down the staff at the precise moment the sun dipped below the distant trees. He stood ram-rod stiff as they had taught him at Dartmouth and, though he had tried for a long while to avoid it, there was something inevitable about standing again on the deck of a British warship.

The descending note of the carry-on humanised them again. 'I think I could stand another gin, my boy,' he said as they turned forward.

Astern of the moored sloop, a pair of oystercatchers flew low over the ebbing Stour, piping their own ritual calls. John stopped briefly to watch them.

'I always think it's such a sad sound,' he said, continuing his way back to *Shrike*'s tiny wardroom from where the banal air of 'Tip-toe Through the Tulips' wheezed out of a portable gramophone.

There was something uncannily like 1914 in that long, hot summer. James borrowed a small yacht from a neighbour already called up in the first wave of naval reservists and took Sonia sailing on the Walton Backwaters and the River Orwell. Under the hanging woods of Pin Mill they sometimes lay at anchor, James painting in watercolours and Sonia stretched out in the sunshine.

'I'm bored, James,' she would say, winking, and they tumbled gaily below, to make love in the impossibly narrow bunk while the boat moved gently in the tide and the water chuckled softly under her bow. Afterwards they liked to revive themselves at the Butt and Oyster public house, drawing up their clinker tender beside the huge bulk of the sprit-sail barges on the hard.

It was, James knew, an idyll, slipping through their fingers, but furnishing him with the memories that, in the months ahead, should bring him the retrospective happiness he had come to treasure.

But there were moments of regret, too. Taking John's advice, he wrote to Bawden, explaining he was back in England and had remarried. The old skipper replied, his fine, copperplate hand disfigured by the rheumatism endemic among elderly fishermen. The bluff Yorkshireman was brutally frank:

I see little point in your coming all the way up here, he wrote. *We have seen a little of John, our grandson, but to see you after all these years would only wake up old memories that we have spent many years trying to forget.*

James burnt the letter. Bawden, too, thought his signing on the *Socotra* was an act of cowardice. He tried to explain something of this to Sonia.

'It is not good for you to look back, James. You only see what you have done out of – oh, what do you call it?'

'Out of context?'

'Yes. We do not blame ourselves for acting in this way at the time. Afterwards we blame only ourselves, forgetting the reasons why we did it. This old man blames himself for letting you marry his daughter.'

'Perhaps,' James said, unconvinced.

'Anyway, if you had not come to China,' she said, 'we might never have become . . .'

She lent across the settee and kissed him. That much, at least, was true.

Towards the end of August he knew his resources were dwindling and he would have to seek regular employment. As the tension in Europe mounted he had been compelled to register for military service under the Conscription Act, indicating his preference for the Royal Naval Volunteer Reserve, but his overtures had been ignored.

'Surely they can make *some* use of me,' he said to Vera at breakfast one morning. 'I can't help feeling I'm being black-balled.'

198

'They'll find a job for you when the time comes,' she replied, studying the *Daily Telegraph* with her customary intensity. 'And I think it will be quite soon now.'

'I'm not sure I can wait any longer. I daresay they'll want volunteers to man merchant ships.'

'Surely you can do better than that,' Vera said, indignantly, crushing the newspaper. 'A Martin has served in the Navy since before Trafalgar.'

'Don't be such a ridiculous traditionalist, Vera. There's no dishonour in serving on a merchant ship.'

'Maybe, but it's not the same.' Vera lifted the paper again and James thought what a tragedy her life had been. She had aged prematurely and was quite out of step with her generation, acting like some pre-1914 patriot. Then it occurred to him that John, whom it was clear she regarded almost as her own child, was shortly to be exposed to the same risks as Tom. She had erected a sort of living monument to her lost love, only to find providence might be merciless enough to replicate his fate.

He wanted to say something kind and reassuring, then Vera said abruptly, 'Where is she?'

'I do wish you'd call her Sonia,' he sighed. 'She's in the bathroom; she'll be down in a minute.'

Vera dropped the newspaper again. 'She's pregnant, isn't she? She's been late down for over a week now.'

Sonia came into the breakfast room at that very moment. Her white silk peignoir was soiled and her face the colour of paste. James jumped to his feet.

'My God, Sonia, what's the matter?'

'You are wrong, Vera,' she said weakly, as James caught her. 'I just have miscarriage and lose my baby.'

CHAPTER FIFTEEN

Cry Havoc . . .

James did not hear Mr Chamberlain's broadcast on the sunny Sunday morning of 3 September 1939. He was sitting beside Sonia's bed reading to her when Vera came in.

'We're at war,' she said simply, and sat on the end of the bed.

James felt Sonia's hand grip his own. 'When will the air raids start?' she asked nervously.

'Yes,' Vera said, standing up, 'we are a bit exposed here. We ought to get an Anderson shelter put up in the garden. How are you feeling?'

'A lot better,' Sonia said.

'Good,' Vera said. She moved to the window which overlooked the garden and James watched her angular figure, knowing she was mulling something over. 'James,' she said after a while, 'when you have been called up and Sonia and I are alone' – James caught the quick, resentful glance she threw at Sonia – 'I would like to do something for those Jewish children.'

The refugees had been arriving for weeks past, sent by their desperate and trusting parents from the Reich to a safe haven in England. Currently they were held in the neighbouring holiday camp, pathetic, lonely creatures.

'I thought, perhaps, when Sonia is better, as she knows what it is like to be a refugee . . .'

'Yes,' James nodded with relief. The prospect of leaving the two women alone had worried him. With some task to share in common, they might learn to like each other. 'You would help with that, wouldn't you, darling?' he said to Sonia.

'Yes, of course. In a few days . . .'

200

'Yes, yes, you must rest now. The doctor says that's all you need.'

'Thank you, Vee,' he said later, when he and Vera were alone, 'that was thoughtful of you.'

Vera brushed his plaudits aside. 'Oh, I can't sit and do nothing. Anyway,' she added with a rare smile, 'I'm good at taking in foundlings.'

Next morning they learned of the sinking of the liner *Athenia* and the news put James in a foul mood. He fulminated about the U-boat menace and expressed his deep resentment at not having been called up.

'I thought,' Vera goaded him, 'you were all for "jaw, jaw" being better than "war, war".'

'Don't be bloody silly, Vee!' he raged in exasperation. 'It's too late to hope. All I want now is *do* something!'

'Go and join the Special Constabulary,' she said sharply, 'or the ARP.'

He was staring open-mouthed when the door bell rang. On the doorstep the telegram boy held out a buff envelope. James tore it open with a pounding heart.

'Bless my soul!' he exclaimed.

'What is it?' Vera stood in the doorway to the breakfast room.

'Any reply, sir?' the boy asked.

'No . . . no, not at the moment.' James found a shilling in his pocket and tipped the youngster, then, shutting the door, handed the telegram to Vera.

'You have to go?' Pale as a wraith, Sonia stood on the landing in her nightdress.

'Yes,' he said.

'Where?'

'It says,' read Vera, ' *"If you still enjoy voluntary disguise report office of Naval Assistant Second Sea Lord Admiralty London forthwith stop Wyatt."* '

'I don't understand,' pleaded Sonia.

'It's the department of the Admiralty that controls the appointment of officers,' Vera explained knowledgeably. 'Geoffrey obtained John's appointment to *Shrike* through it. Well,' she said to James, 'you've got what you wanted.'

'Have I?' he said, wondering why Wyatt had sent for him.

*

'Mr Martin to see you, sir.'

James glowered at the Wren Second Officer. '*Captain* Martin, if you don't mind, young lady,' he growled.

'Ah . . . well, well, sit down Martin, do.'

Wyatt waved towards a chair, his black reefer cuffs glittering with the four lace rings of a full captain. From the left tumbled a theatrically stuffed cream silk handkerchief.

'Thank you.' James did as he was bid, wryly noting the lack of a handshake. Wyatt had clearly not forgiven him for dishonouring the flag and James was determinedly unrepentant.

Wyatt, his thinning hair slicked back smoothly over his round skull, his expression bland and self-confident, drew a file towards him. Opening it he lifted a page or two and James recognised his own letters.

'I'm afraid "*Captain*" is out, Martin. I see you were master of the SS *Shantung*, but a commission in the Reserve might put a few noses out of joint. However, I think we might take you on as a two-and-a-half in the Wavy Navy. How does Lieutenant Commander, RNVR sound?'

'Good enough,' replied James noncommittally. It was what he wanted.

'Right then,' Wyatt said looking up from the file, 'because I've delayed your call-up deliberately, until I felt we had something appropriate to your peculiar talents.' He lit a cigarette.

James sat silently, aware Wyatt was not even attempting to veil the sarcasm in his voice.

'I wanted to be sure,' resumed Wyatt, after the pause had lent weight to his words, 'because the last time I backed you against opposition, things didn't go quite as I imagined they would, did they?'

James stared Wyatt down. Wyatt returned to the file. 'I've been reading your analysis of the military and naval capabilites of the Japanese. It seems your form of warfare is very much in vogue.'

'Damn it!' James snarled, half rising from his chair. 'You have no right!'

'*Sir*, Martin. No right, *sir*, is what you should have said.' Wyatt waved his left hand airily, so that the handkerchief fluttered at his wrist and James wondered how he could once have liked and respected the man. 'Anyway, I see you are also of the opinion that the Japs are capable of overrunning Hong Kong.'

'I think,' said James, regaining his self-control with difficulty, 'that is very likely.'

'Not a very patriotic thought, is it?'

'I don't see the argument, *sir*. Military analysis, albeit unfavourable, is not inimical to patriotism.'

'When I was with the naval delegation to the London conference,' Wyatt said smoothly, 'the Japanese continued to profess considerable admiration for British institutions and have copied many of –'

'Imitation might be the sincerest form of flattery, but it is flattery nonetheless and the purpose of flattery is not concerned with indefinite inferiority. But this is not what you have called me here for, is it?'

'No, Martin, it isn't. You were born, bred and trained as a naval officer; now the country is calling in its investment.' He held up his hand. 'And before you get on your high horse I'm giving you command of a battleship.'

'Is this some kind of joke?' James's face flushed at the complacent smile wreathing Wyatt's jowls.

'Well, yes it is, I suppose. Actually your command is officially to be known as "Fleet Tender D" for Delta. You will be attached to Force W and operate in the first instance from Rosyth.'

'What the hell are you talking about?' snapped James, his patience at an end. 'Is this another Q-ship, or what?'

'Oh Lord, no.' Wyatt shook his head with exaggerated vigour and ground out his cigarette. 'This is a dummy ship, a mock up. Very theatrical: plywood, paint and canvas. You were, I recall, something of an artist, so it should be just up your street. Paint-on details, you know the sort of thing: torpedo booms with all the chiaroscuro of a Rembrandt and no substance at all, portholes and rivet heads . . .'

'But what . . .?'

'Before you scoff, Martin,' Wyatt said with an edge in his voice, 'consider this is the personal brain-child of the First Lord.' He gestured at the wall implying the proximity of Mr Churchill in an adjacent room. 'He advocated it in the last war and it worked well. We had the battle cruiser *Queen*

Mary blockade the commerce raider *Kronprinz Wilhelm* in Norfolk, Virginia, until the Americans interned her. The *Wilhelm* had succeeded in sinking nearly sixty thousand tons of allied shipping. The only thing was the *Queen Mary* was a phantom, a sham, a dummy. A White Star liner suitably adapted to deceive from a distance. Savvy?'

Wyatt leaned back and lit another cigarette. He was about to return the silver case to his pocket when he thought better of it and held it out.

'Smoke?'

James helped himself, his mind a whirl. The idea was intriguing, he had to admit, and independent command, in whatever form, had its merits for a man of his age and experience; but doubts and questions crowded into his mind. Wyatt, however, was like one of those Kleeneze salesmen with a foot in the door, and went remorselessly on as soon as his cigarette was alight.

'Furthermore, you will doubtless recall the *Audacious* and the scuttlebutt surrounding *her* sinking. She foundered off Malin Head after hitting a mine, but their lordships gave out she had made Londonderry for repairs. Something very like the *Audacious* was to be seen knocking about until the end of the war. Actually, it was Canadian Pacific's old steamer *Montcalm*.'

'Ingenious, but that was during the last war. Things have changed a good deal.'

'Ah, I was wondering when you were going to ask what their relevance is today. Well, as you know, we've been rearming, but we need more time. Anything that buys us time, particularly if it costs little and can be arranged quickly, is of value to us. Mr Churchill's idea is brilliant because it fulfils these criteria admirably. Moreover, even if it becomes known we are deploying these phantoms, the enemy still has to decide if their reconnaissance or their intelligence has accurately identified the reality or the dummy.'

Wyatt waved his hand dramatically. The flourish produced a curl of smoke from his cigarette and the flamboyant ripple of his silk handkerchief. Afterwards James thought the effect might have hypnotised him and robbed him of his sense.

'But they are not to act as decoys?'

'Not as Q-ships did, no. They will act according to circumstances. Perhaps be deployed with units of the fleet, as they were at the Dardanelles, to give the impression of greater force; or to lie at anchor convincing aerial reconnaissance that Force W, representing capital units of the fleet, is helplessly at anchor in Scapa, for instance.'

'Thus drawing a weight of enemy concentration upon us,' extrapolated James.

'Of course. And as you have good knowledge of merchant ships combined with a somewhat rusty appreciation of naval methods, we've hand-picked you for the job of commanding the pseudo-*Royal Oak*.'

'But . . . .'

'To do this,' Wyatt went on, ignoring James's interruption, 'you will travel to Harland and Wolff's at Belfast and take over Fleet Tender D for Delta, alias the SS *Königsburg*, formerly owned by the London and Lithuanian Steamship Company.'

'What about armament? I presume we'll have some anti-aircraft weaponry?'

'In the last war, the phantoms were fitted with wooden mock-ups. Lengths of pipe led below. These pipes went to a central boiler where old engine room waste was dumped. Under fire this lot was lit up and each gun mounting boasted a set of bellows. At action stations, the crew used to run round jumping on the bellows and emitting puffs of black smoke from the "gun muzzles".' Wyatt smiled. 'I'm told it was jolly realistic.'

'I hope this time round we can do a bit better,' James said drily.

'Oh, good heavens, yes,' Wyatt said. 'We've got it marvellously controlled now by electricity.'

James was appalled. 'You mean . . .?'

'I mean they're dummies, Martin; phantoms. Oh, you've got a handful of Lee-Enfields for self-defence if you're boarded, and the tween-decks are filled with empty oildrums to give you plenty of time to abandon ship. All our stockpiled twelve and six-pounders are allocated to proper merchant ships. Now, your written orders are with Second Officer Darby in the outer office. Congratulations on the commission, Commander, and good luck.'

'What about machine guns?' said James standing slowly.

'Surely we mount a few machine guns?' he asked, finding himself shaking hands with Wyatt.

'Oh, no,' said Wyatt, his eyes cold, 'especially no machine guns.'

Their eyes met and James was filled by a tardy but bitter regret that he had so easily been trapped. When he had gone Wyatt returned to his desk.

'Cry havoc,' he quoted blithely to himself, 'and let slip the *dogs* of war.'

And sitting down he mopped his forehead with the cream silk handkerchief.

The aftertaste of the interview with Wyatt preoccupied James in the next few hours, overshadowing his farewell to Sonia. Alone in the train to Stranraer he read again the newspaper containing the King's speech to the Empire, convinced by now that German aggression was indistinguishable from that of the Japanese and could no longer be condoned. In the same newspaper in which the King denounced the 'primitive doctrine that might is right', Herr Hitler had assured the world through President Roosevelt that there would be no bombing of civilians. Almost alongside it was a despatch reporting the death of fifteen hundred men, women and children after an incendiary air raid on the Polish town of Katowice.

James sighed in despair. After the horrors of the Great War he had fervently hoped mankind had learnt its lesson. In that had lain his opposition to intervention in Russia. Something of this hope had helped ease the bitterness of dismissal from the Navy; for one could not make so radical a change in human affairs without affecting individual security. He had been further convinced of the utter madness of war from his contacts with the seamen on the *Socotra*, who told him of the cynical profiteering that had been practised by ship-owners, men who put profit before the lives of their crews and hotly opposed the introduction of the convoy system until faced with national disaster in 1917. It had seemed such a terrible waste, and he watched from a distance as the Navy reverted to its peace-time role, shedding its small ships in favour of battle wagons – ships like the *Repulse* and *Renown* which had spent so much time

206

in dockyard hands that they had been nicknamed *Refit* and *Repair* – he knew no lessons had been learnt and the opinions of most of the anti-submarine lobby had been ignored. True, the Anglo-French anti-submarine device 'asdic' had been introduced in 1937, but with it had come the Admiralty's proud boast that 'the submarine should never again present us with the problem we were faced with in 1917'.

There was, James thought, an excess of pride in the statement that invited a fateful tumble. The U-boat offensive had started the day war broke out with the sinking of the Donaldson passenger-liner *Athenia*. Together with the bombing of Katowice, it confirmed the mendacity of Hitler's professed concern for civilians. The Admiralty had had its comeuppance a fortnight later when the aircraft carrier *Courageous*, sent to sea with a screen of destroyers to hunt U-boats, was herself a victim. Her sisters on similar missions were hurriedly recalled. It seemed a repeat of Admiral Martin's fiasco.

Such falls from grace, James ruminated morosely, toppled individual as well as institutional pride, and Wyatt's attitude had persuaded him that he himself was being set up for such a degringolade. Did this improbable command of a stick-and-canvas battleship argue for Wyatt's malice, or the genius of Mr Churchill?

Lashing rain greeted him at Belfast. Above the sheds and cranes of Harland and Wolff's, the upperworks of the spurious *Royal Oak* were impressive enough. Closer-to they were much less convincing. The large grey areas lacked detail to deceive for long.

He reported to the Senior Naval Officer, but he was out on his rounds and he made his number with Mr McCloghran of the Naval Construction Department. 'Sure, you can go aboard and have a look round,' McCloughran said when asked.

The rain had eased to a drizzle and a single glare of sunlight cast a rainbow across the clouds, terminating above the gleaming slate roofs of the huddled houses of Belfast. The sight stopped him in his tracks. He wanted his watercolours and the sight of the crammed and crowded dwellings reminded him of that childhood glimpse of Tyneside.

He was not a pretentious man, for all that he had commanded a ship, nor was he self-important. Command, he had learned, was a privately humbling experience sustained by its own, unique tradition. But the sight of those houses acted upon his adult mind as powerfully as those on Tyneside had upon his immature consciousness. They were eloquent of aspiration, of family ties and obligations, of love and hope.

He *had* volunteered, he thought, running up the ladder to *Königsburg*'s sham bridge, for this rum command. He *had* vacillated enough in his private convictions, for God's sake; *and* loved three women since he had pleaded with fate to let him survive the *Indefatigable*'s exploding to know the pleasure just once; so what in heaven's name was he whining about?

He stood on the compass platform. Above his head stretched the phoney fighting top with its fire-direction platform and long horizontal tube that represented a battleship's range-finder. Behind that rose the trunks of grey painted pine trees, the tripod mast and signal yards of a capital ship.

Abaft the bridge *Königsberg*'s original funnel had been enlarged with sheet steel and around it clustered searchlight platforms and anti-aircraft armament, plywood gunshields with broomstick barrels. Several old merchant-ship lifeboats acted the parts of admiral's barge, launch and gig on chocks amidships, with a real whaler hoisted in davits for the abandonment that must surely follow any kind of determined attack the Germans made.

James looked forward, down onto the imposing array of A and B turrets. Superficially the gun houses were creditably realistic, but if, with a darker shade of grey, he limned in a door or two, complete with securing dogs and a streak of rust . . .

His mind began to seethe with possibilities. He would have to be careful about scale. McCloughran had said the dummies were five-sixths the size of the real thing, as the merchant hulls available were far too short to simulate the full length of a battleship. Perhaps, James thought wryly, he could request a draft of short men.

He began to descend to the false upper deck. He dreaded

208

to think what would happen when they hit a heavy head sea, for in addition to having had her sides extended by sponsons to increase her beam, the *Königsburg* had to sit several feet lower in the water to conform with the freeboard of a capital ship. To achieve this her lower holds were filled with shingle ballast.

All this would make her vulnerable in a seaway. Considering the pros and cons of his crazy ship, James returned to the office of the Senior Naval Officer.

'Good to have you with us, Commander Martin,' said the SNO in welcome, going on to outline the general arrangements made in respect of his unusual squadron. 'It looks as though you're going to be completing well in advance of the other three ships. D'you feel happy about proceeding independently to Rosyth? You'll have an anti-submarine escort of a trawler.'

'It can scarcely be worse than the Yangtze under aerial attack, sir,' James said dismissively.

'Yes . . . well, the forepart of your ship is empty of any accommodation, as you probably noted. It gives the men a chance if you hit a mine.'

'What about an aerial attack, sir?'

'There are protected citadels in the original accommodation and there's a rather clever device –'

'That emits puffs of convincing smoke. Yes, sir, I've heard about that. I just wondered if we could come up with a Lewis gun, or something a bit like it not made of cardboard.'

'I'm afraid not, Martin,' replied the elderly officer with a pained look on his face.

Philip Burton had been a retired chief petty officer nearing the end of his time on the reserve list when his call-up papers arrived. He had not been madly enthusiastic about rejoining, having already served twenty-one years in the service and in his retirement he developed an enthusiasm for the twin delights of leeks and pigeons. The one he raised with a revolting witch's brew, the other he raced with devoted wonder. When the call to return to the colours arrived, he quietly went out to his pigeon loft and wrung the birds' necks. For the duration he had privately decided to revenge himself on Adolf Hitler. He was, therefore, slightly disenchanted to be posted to 'Fleet Tender *Delta*' and to be told he was being sent for his experience as his commanding officer was a Lieutenant Commander from the volunteer reserve.

'A bleedin' two-and-a-half with two circuits of the Isle of Wight in a ruddy yacht by way of sea time,' he complained to an ageing chief artificer whom he found on the train destined for the same ship.

'So you're going to be Yeoman of Signals are you?' the Tiffy asked.

'That's what the draft chit says.'

'On a fleet tender?' The Tiffy scratched his head. 'They told *me* there was a bloody engineering lieutenant aboard,' he said. 'Don't make any sense to me.'

'What sort of a bleedin' warship is this?' the drafted men asked incredulously as they boarded Fleet Tender *Delta*, looking round at the interior of unpainted canvas and wooden battens, and discovering underneath curious deck fittings that looked oddly unnaval.

'Ere, it's a bleedin' Q-ship, like they had in the last show!'

'It ain't, but it's one where you'll get *Quaker* oats for breakfast, mates!' they were sarcastically told by those already on board.

'We're fittin' out specially for conscientious objectors; any of you blokes conchies?'

'Conchies?' asked the outraged party, dumping their kit bags and gas masks in a heap on the deck.

'Yeah, Quakers, or what not? 'Cos if you ain't you soon will be. You'll be quaking all right when Jerry's bleedin' dive bombers take a shine to yer. Oh, an' on those days you get baked beans for breakfast.'

'Baked beans?' asked the puzzled and gullible newcomers.

'Yeah, baked beans.'

'Why?'

'Because, lads, fartin' is our only *offensive* weapon.'

Thus, with time-honoured ribald sarcasm, Fleet Tender *Delta* acquired a complement of forty officers and men, but James's meticulous attention to detail was the catalyst that transformed them into a ship's company.

'I think you're taking things a little too far, Martin,' the

SNO of Force W said when James submitted another requisition. '*Delta* is already completed to the official specification and I'm happy for you to get on your way. I don't think we need to count exactly how many scuttles *Royal Oak* actually has.'

'Begging your pardon, sir, but I disagree,' James reasoned. 'Most of my crew are old sweats, men in the last years of their reserve period, three-stripe men with twenty-odd years to their credit, most of it in peace time. What they remember about their time in the service, sir, is bull. It used to horrify me how much energy was wasted on it in the Grand Fleet, but somehow it acted as a soporific. Things don't look right to an old sailor if they're not tiddly. Fleet Tender *Delta* might be up to spec, but a few of these refinements will be good for morale. Besides, I hear the real *Royal Oak*'s in Scapa; our arrival in Rosyth should look as much like the genuine thing as possible.'

The SNO nodded and smiled. 'You've made your point, Martin, but don't snaffle *all* the paint . . . oh, and do you really need the rum butt from the local drill ship?'

'Yes please, sir. We don't have one, and on fine days I want to issue spirits on the upper deck.'

'Look, you've made your case for verisimilitude, but issuing rum on the upper deck . . .'

'In case a U-boat is watching.'

'But you've only got forty men, for heaven's sake!'

'I think the Earl of Peterborough only had twenty in the War of the Spanish succession, sir. When he had the enemy's envoys in his tent discussing the terms of a truce he made them march round and round outside.'

'I hope you're not being facetious?'

'I more or less asked the same thing at the Admiralty when this appointment was disclosed to me, sir. I was told the matter was deadly serious.'

The SNO sighed. 'I think you have me cornered there, Martin.'

'About it being deadly serious,' James persisted while he had the advantage, 'have you got my application for Lewis guns?'

'Please don't raise that again, Commander.'

*

211

Chief Yeoman of Signals Burton found he rather approved of his captain. Scuttlebutt revealed Lieutenant Commander Martin had trained as a regular officer before being chopped out of the Navy by the Geddes' axe. While the captains of Fleet Tenders A, B and C were retired regulars, running their ships from their cabins, it was more usual to find Lieutenant Commander Martin wearing a boiler suit and hanging over the side on a bosun's stage painting the 'eyebrows' round a scuttle, or improving the shading below a housed anti-torpedo net boom, so that from only five yards away you could not tell that the thing was false.

'D'you ever do amateur theatricals, sir?' he asked once.

'Me, Chief? No, why?'

'I just thought you must have painted scenery some time.'

Chief Yeoman Burton was impressed by the trouble his commanding officer took, and as he got to know him grew to like him. As the senior signalman, Burton was the confidential recipient of all official communications and was thus in close contact with James.

'The skipper's all right,' he would announce to the Chief and Petty Officers' mess.

'Never mind about the skipper, what about the ship? What's she *for*, for Gawd's sake?'

'I'm not absolutely sure about our role,' James said as he addressed the wardroom on the first evening of their commission. 'This morning we hoisted the white ensign and are officially a unit of His Majesty's Fleet. It is clear we are to be sent to Rosyth and there, or elsewhere for all I know at the moment, we pretend to be *Royal Oak*.'

He looked round at the officers lounging in what had once been the quondam *Königsburg*'s officers' dining saloon. His First Lieutenant was an elderly RNR officer who, by the state of his nose, had a liking for spirituous liquors. Clearly Fleet Tender *Delta* was a convenient backwater for a man who looked a potential danger to his own side, rather than to the enemy. There were two additional sublieutenants RNVR, both inexperienced but both supplied as watch-keepers, and an engineering lieutenant from the Reserve who had, like James himself, merchant ship expertise.

'Our main purpose is not to take the offensive, or even the

defensive for that matter, but to confuse intelligence. Our presence anywhere might, just conceivably, alter enemy planning; and even when it becomes known that we exist, doubt as to whether we or *Royal Oak* is the phantom might also deter the enemy.'

He looked round, hoping he sounded convincing. He resumed, speculating.

'The old R-class battleships are being deployed with ocean convoys as protection against surface raiders, and if times get really hard I suppose it is possible we might be asked to do our bit there. I really don't know, but it gives us something to aim for.'

He went on, outlining his extravagant plans for deceit, raising a laugh and a smile and being asked to stay on in the wardroom afterwards for a drink.

'Got to get our priorities right, sir,' growled the First Lieutenant.

'Quite right, Number One,' said James looking at the heavy jowls of his subordinate. 'Have you got a second uniform?'

'Course I have, sir. I've got four of the bloody things; used to be in the Cunard Line.'

'Four?' James queried incredulously.

'Yes sir, a bezzy, a chatty, a nightie and a scruffy.'

When the laughter had died away James said, 'Get your number two uniform fitted up with rear admiral's braid, and if anyone else has a gash reefer jacket they have my permission to promote themselves. A couple of commanders would be handy, and any number of lieutenants.'

'What about scrambled egg, sir?' asked one of the sub-lieutenants eagerly.

'There's a tin of gold size outside my cabin, but don't overdo it. Only on *extra* uniforms. I want at least one set of proper rig for each of you in case we are inspected by a real admiral.'

'Damn funny way to win a war.'

'Who said we were going to win?'

'Damn fun trying though.'

And for three days it was just that, damned good fun; three days before the pun backfired and nothing was funny any more, but all became hard, unremitting labour.

213

HM Fleet Tender *Delta* let go from Harland and Wolff's and headed directly to sea. It was just after dawn and a light mist disguised her departure. Nevertheless, if only to establish his precedent of pretence, James had Lieutenant Crosby-Milne RNR dressed in a rear admiral's jacket on the upper bridge and flew the appropriate red and white flag from the masthead. Outside, in the choppy grey waters of the North Channel, they were met by HM Armed Trawler *Barbella*. The trawler dipped her ensign and took station ahead as their anti-submarine escort.

'I think you can go below now, Admiral,' said James, and Crosby-Milne's flabby and rubicund features looked crestfallen.

'I was just beginning to enjoy myself,' he said. 'Going to send a signal to that bloody trawler to follow senior officer's motions.'

The two men shared the joke and an uneasy friendship got under way.

At ten knots, with the stokers toiling below to maintain steam, they headed north towards the Minch.

'I last came through here in a Q-ship,' James said that evening as he shared the four-to-eight with Crosby-Milne. To starboard the outline of mountains rose dimly against the horizon, ahead the sea lay like a sheet of lead.

'I was in the *Glitra* when the last show blew up, doing my time for my master's certificate before joining the Cunard.' James smiled in the twilight; Crosby-Milne seldom let any opportunity pass to inform one that he had served in the Cunard Line. James supposed it lent a ruined life a certain credibility. 'She was a little nine-hundred-tonner and we were brought to by a bloody U-boat off the Norsky coast. First British ship to be stopped by one of those damned things, you know. The Huns came aboard, gave us ten minutes to take to the boats then smashed the engine cooling inlets. She went down and we watched her from the boats, but d'you know what I remember most?'

'Go on.'

'The first thing they did when they got aboard was send a rating aft to strike the ensign. It was a pretty tatty thing, but this officer had it brought up to the bridge and waved it under the old man's nose. As I say, it was a smoke-soiled old

214

rag and only the day before I'd overheard the old fellow tell the mate not to change it. I suppose he thought a bit of muck might confuse the issue of our nationality, or perhaps he was just being tight-fisted. But when that bloody German was holding the frayed bunting, it seemed like something else. We were horrified when the swine tore it up and spat on it.'

'Magic symbols,' James said quietly, 'totems. Odd how one comes to think of them. We sank a U-boat,' he added.

'What? In your Q-ship?' Crosby-Milne asked.

'Yes.' He paused. 'We shelled it and when they abandoned it I shot up the survivors in the water.' He found the confession extraordinarily easy to make.

'Bloody good job you did. So many fewer now.'

'D'you think so?' James looked keenly at Crosby-Milne. The puffy face was a pale blur, in the gloom, but it was clear there was more to Crosby-Milne than met the eye.

'Of course! Don't get sentimental about war. Once you're drawn into it, a fight is a fight and you've only two options, to win or lose. It makes things nice and simple.'

'My CO didn't feel quite like that.'

'Thought you'd let the side down, dishonoured the flag, eh?'

'Yes. He went to enormous lengths to perfect the *ruse de guerre*, but believed in playing strictly to the rules.'

'There was a lot of that bloody nonsense in the last war. Hypocritical rubbish! Nelson's maxim, "seek out and destroy", is the best advice I know, but afterwards follow his advice again: "Be magnanimous in victory." If the Allies had been a bit more magnanimous at the peace talks in 1919 we wouldn't have left Germany in a state ripe for an Adolf Hitler. It was the politicians who got us into the last war, and they've done the same again. I lost two brothers on the Somme. I don't blame the Hun for shooting them, it was dog eat dog by then, but the real shits were the incompetent fools that let things get that far. Now it's happened again and we've got an embittered enemy to fight. If they could hate us enough to spit on a filthy old ensign in 1914, how d'you think the bastards feel about us now? I'd seen it all coming. That's why I joined the Reserve.'

'Yes, there was a certain inevitability about it. I saw it from an eastern perspective.'

'Oh, the Japanese won't amount to much. They're too busy in China and would never dare challenge the Yanks. We'll be all right if Mussolini keeps his nose out of things. The French will help us contain him in the Med. Yes, we'll survive – if you keep shooting Huns, sir.'

Crosby-Milne's sudden reversion to strict formality ended his avuncular dissertation.

'I would if we had a few machine guns,' James said pointedly.

'Bit of a lame duck, aren't we?'

'Quack, bloody quack.'

James had timed his passage of the Pentland Firth to coincide with a favourable tide, so even at the slow speed they were reduced to in the fog they debouched into the North Sea at nearly ten knots.

To the south of them the granite rampart of Duncansby Head marked the north-east corner of the British mainland, while to the north lay the lonely islands of the Orkneys surrounding the old Grand Fleet's anchorage. But the low fog, pierced by the blaring horn of the lighthouse on the headland, blinded them and it was with considerable anxiety that James consulted his chart and finally agreed with Sublieutenant Watson that the sound of the foghorn was sufficiently far astern to warrant an alteration of course southwards.

'Don't be too eager to believe your ears, Mr Watson,' he cautioned. 'Fog has the property of being able to deceive your sense of direction and, furthermore, the proximity of high cliffs will act to form echoes. You could be hearing that sound from a quite different bearing than the true one.'

'I see, sir.'

'Don't worry, you'll soon develop your sixth sense. Now, where's *Barbella*?'

'Just crossed the bow, sir,' said the bridge lookout, a keen, but elderly seaman.

'Very well. What's your name?'

'Davis, sir.'

'Keep your eye on her, if you can.'

'There she is, sir!'

They could see the trawler, a grey wraith, her bow flying

high with its raised forecastle and gun platform, adding to the murk with a pall of smoke belching from her raked funnel. Her appearance, ghostly as it was, tugged at his heart-strings, for she was so like the *Girl Stella* that it hurt.

'He's coming round to starboard, sir!' shouted Watson excitedly.

'Yes.' James had snapped his glasses up to his eyes. 'Stop engines!'

Below the wooden platform, in *Königsburg*'s real wheelhouse, the jangle of telegraphs sounded remotely. On *Barbella*'s tiny bridge wing a bright bead of light began stuttering at them.

'Signalman!'

'Here, sir.' Burton's voice was calm and he was already reading the signal.

Barbella swept across their bow, then heeled as her helm was out over again and she turned back to port, to return across their course two cables further on.

'What's she doing?' Watson asked of no one in particular.

'Half ahead!' James ordered. 'Well, Chief?' he said to Burton.

Behind him Crosby-Milne, alerted by the telegraph bells, had come up to the bridge. 'He's carrying out an asdic sweep,' he explained to Watson.

Burton turned to his captain. '*Barbella* signals: "Submarines reported your area." It's from the Admiralty, sir.'

'Yes, I know that. Shouldn't we have received the same signal ourselves?'

'Yes, I suppose so sir. Shall I . . .?'

'Not now, we'll look into that later.'

'Aye, aye, sir.'

'So you see they're bloody important ships, Watson,' Crosby-Milne was saying, 'and I'm surprised we haven't seen a lot more of them around here. In the last war the approaches to Scapa were littered with Patrol Service auxiliaries.'

'Well,' said Watson, pleased to adduce some knowledge about modern warfare, 'they've got defensive underwater loops to protect the anchorage now. They detect any steel object passing over them.'

'Hmm,' growled Crosby-Milne sceptically.

'Fog's lifting, sir,' reported Davis, and they were rewarded with that abrupt and spectacular atmospheric change that can dramatically end low visibility.

'That's a relief, sir,' remarked Watson.

'Perhaps,' said James, scanning the horizon with his glasses. 'If there is a U-boat about, he'll have no trouble seeing us now.'

'I wonder if we'll come to welcome fog?' asked Crosby-Milne quietly.

No U-boat disturbed their tranquillity, and with *Barbella* still dancing attendance they hove in sight of Stevenson's elegant tower on the Bell Rock and then the Isle of May, where a destroyer ran in close, her officers staring with undisguised curiosity and a precautionary dipping of her white engsign. By the evening they were gliding up the Firth of Forth with the great cantilevered girders of the bridge etched black against the sunset.

'I think we'd better strike your flag, Admiral,' James said to Crosby-Milne who nodded ruefully, while beside them Burton took their instructions from the flag ship, his aldis lamp chattering in the gathering dusk.

'It's a bit chilly,' said Sublieutenant Watson.

'Signal from Flag, sir,' reported Burton. James passed the pencilled chit to Crosby-Milne.

'Plot our anchor berth on the chart and lay me a course, please.'

While he waited, James pondered the second part of the message, 'Report to FOIC on arrival.'

'*Barbella*'s detaching, sir,' prompted Burton, his aldis nestling expectantly in the crook of his left arm, his right on the handle and trigger.

'Very well. Signal to *Barbella*: "Nice making your acquaintance stop hope it is over by Christmas stop." '

As Burton clattered away James called the anchor party out and steamed to his anchorage. It was almost dark and the *Königsburg* seemed indistiguishable from the grey shapes that lay quietly at their moorings.

'*Barbella* replies: "Some hopes stop good luck stop." Not very original, sir.'

'No.'

'There's a picket boat approaching, sir,' reported Watson.

218

'I think they've sent transport for me. Better have the pilot ladder put over the side.'

In the absence of a gangway, James scrambled down the rope ladder and jumped aboard the picket boat. A midshipman, his white collar patches catching the glimmer of a green sidelight, saluted him.

'I'm to ask you to report to the duty staff officer, sir. You are the Captain, aren't you, sir?' The boy looked puzzled, casting his eyes down to James's volunteer braid.

'Yes,' he answered curtly, and sat himself down as the picket boat picked up speed.

'Lieutenant Commander Martin reporting.'

He was shown into an office where a middle-aged Commander sat at a desk illuminated by a table lamp.

'Sit down, Martin. I've very bad news, I'm afraid. It's for your ears only at the moment, but it does throw some doubts about the deployment of Fleet Tender *Delta*.'

'Sir?' James frowned.

The Commander rose and lit a cigarette, offering one to James. As he bent forward to light it, he said in a low voice, 'The *Royal Oak*'s been torpedoed and sunk. A U-boat penetrated the Scapa defences and' – the man sighed – 'we lost damn near a thousand men.'

James sat in silence. The fun was over. The war had begun in earnest. And suddenly he wanted more than just machine guns.

CHAPTER SIXTEEN
Kristallnacht

The shadow of war had come early to Dovercourt. Contacts with the continent were close, the crews of the Harwich ferries brought home stories of German ambition, and many of the town's menfolk served in deep-water merchantmen. One, aboard British India's SS *Neuralia* transitting the Kiel canal, had witnessed Nazi brownshirts dynamiting a synagogue. The arrival of destitute Jewish children had therefore come as no surprise. Their parents, disturbed by five years of increasing anti-Semitism on the part of the Nazi government, had sensed worse horrors to come after *Kristallnacht* in November 1938. Those able to afford the bond and fare sent them out of the Reich with promises of seeing them again soon. They were brought to Dovercourt in special trains and the ferries of the Great Eastern Railway Company, and accommodated in a bleak, wind-swept holiday camp set behind the sea defences bordering acres of salt marsh.

Their arrival came as a welcome preoccupation for Vera. With John finally serving in the Royal Navy, her life had lost much of its purpose and neither the bossing of the maid, nor the exercising of a King Charles spaniel, could fill the void. Her life seemed suddenly pointless, so she joined the local committee set up to bring some measure of comfort to these unfortunate children while their 'temporary' immigration was being processed and foster homes were found for them. Moreover, only James's announcement that he was at last returning home from China with his new bride had prevented Vera from accepting two or three of them into the house earlier.

To Vera such an act was not one of charity, merely a means of being useful. Having long ago cast aside any consideration of personal happiness expressed in the conventional institution of marriage, she had clung to her consoling teenage passion for her lost cousin and enshrined her love for Tom in the effort she put into John's upbringing. She had ceased to think of John as an adoptive charge, but, with the self-deception of the lonely, ascribed a closer relationship, devoting all her energies to his welfare.

She dismissed James with a mild contempt. He had, she thought, run away from his obligations: he could have tried a little harder to remain in the Navy, and even had this not worked it was unnecessary of him to defect so spectacularly to the merchant marine and then immure himself in China. There was, to Vera's forced maturity, something peevishly adolescent about his behaviour.

And yet even this contributed to her own determination. She was proud of her family, proud of the Martins as a naval clan. Tom's death had been a tragedy, but one to be borne with fortitude, to be woven into the fabric of family tradition. He had given his life that others might live in freedom and Vera was not ashamed of that, for Tom's sacrifice gave meaning to her own life. It was her duty to bear the loss, and Vera was not one to flinch from that. In the circumstances she had found herself in at the time of the Armistice, it was impossible to join in the prevailing gaiety and abandon going on around her. Self-abnegating, she became old before her time.

As John grew and left home for the Royal Hospital School at Holbrook, she filled the void of his absence with letter writing. Apart from John and James, she corresponded with Geoffrey Ennis, with whom she remained on good terms despite her rejection of his proposal, and also with more public figures. She became a keen observer of the political scene, devoured avidly *The Times* and the *Daily Telegraph*, and her letters kept her correspondents abroad well-informed. She was hawkish, a supporter of Mr Churchill, confident that appeasement only delayed the inevitable and lulled the public into a false sense of security.

Increasingly embittered, headstrong, opinionated and almost sexually desiccated, Vera was intolerant and

221

unprepared for sharing a house. When she had welcomed James and his wife she had known she might have to do just this, but the onset of war, predicted and expected though it had been, had caught Vera at one disadvantage. To Vera the exotic and beautiful Sonia was an irritating nuisance. The two women had nothing in common.

For her own part Sonia was bereft, beset by the trauma of her miscarriage, lonely and desolate at losing James so soon after arriving in yet another strange country. Not for the first time in her life she felt abandoned, so apparently heartless and shrivelled a companion was Vera. Brusque, matter-of-fact and coldly logical, it was inconceivable that Vera was almost the same age as herself. In Sonia's imagination, Vera possessed the influence and power proper to an aged *babushka*.

But there were other factors that increased Sonia's sense of isolation. As she recovered from her illness, she found herself the centre of a small, parochially intrusive inquisition. Despite the fact that, married to an Englishman, she was on the National Register as a British citizen, and would explain to anyone who doubted the matter and cared to listen that she was anti-Bolshevik, a White and a refugee, the opportunist Russian attack on Poland made her an object of suspicion in the neighbourhood. This misunderstanding, silly though it was, upset her and kept her indoors. Even here Vera's pointed endorsement of Churchill's condemnation of Russia's 'cold-blooded policy of self-interest' only served to make her feel more and more alone.

Thus, when Vera introduced two Jewish refugee children to The Lees, Sonia's spirits were further depressed. The sight of their sad, intelligent eyes was a painful reminder of her own flight, a reminder she did not want, for in marrying James she had thought her escape from such events complete. She attempted to explain this to Vera, but found her unsympathetic.

'I did not expect you to be so selfish,' said Vera, staring at Sonia in disbelief. 'After all, they are not so very like you were.'

'Of course they are like I was! It is terrible, terrible. But how can you expect me to *live* with them?'

'Because they are unfortunate,' railed Vera, who failed

utterly to comprehend the cause of Sonia's distress. 'Because we have plenty of room here, because you, as much as I, need something useful to do. Is that not enough?'

'Yes, of course,' replied Sonia desperately. 'It is impossible that you can understand.'

'You think you are the only one who has suffered? Life cannot all be singing in a cabaret,' continued Vera with a relentless lack of tact.

Sonia bit her lip, lost for words in English to express her frustration. She had not wanted her life in England to reflect her past; she sought freedom, to break the mirrored confinement she foresaw with Vera and the Jewish children. But she was not unkind to them; she took them to tea in the Cliff Pavilion from where they watched the grimy colliers and coasters rounded up by escorting sloops, *Shrike* amongst them, forming the East Coast convoys started by the Admiralty three days after the outbreak of war.

Occasionally John would steal an hour's leave with them, but as the autumn wore on his visits became rarer.

'I do wish he'd find time to call,' Vera complained.

'He will be very busy,' said Sonia, and Vera bit off her reply with the irritating reflection that Sonia had the advantage of having sailed on a ship. 'He will be tired after the sea patrols.'

And then, on 21 November, the destroyer *Gipsy* blew up on a mine in the very entrance of Harwich Harbour and the realities of the war struck home. Thirty men died, many of them local. Their bodies were washed up along the beach. Vera grew increasingly irritable worrying about John.

As the cold of a bitter winter settled on the east coast of England, Sonia's spirits revived a little. The invigorating chill, the hard light and heavy frosts reminded her of Russia, and though the memory was poignant it conferred upon her eyes a luminous beauty that enchanted the two young Berliners. They found common ground in their escapes, and compared with Sonia's the fears that had beset the German children's train ride across Europe seemed to fade. Sonia discovered a surprising gift for regaling her young listeners with her own adventures.

'You should write a book,' snapped Vera one freezing December afternoon, as she came stamping in from the garden where she had been chopping wood.

'Oh yes,' said Ruth, her dark eyes aglow with enthusiasm.

'And I will make the pictures for you,' said her brother Joachim eagerly.

'He is very good at making the pictures,' agreed Ruth.

'Perhaps Ruth is right,' Vera said later as, with blackout curtains drawn and a wood fire hissing in the grate, the two women huddled round the radio. 'Writing a book would keep you occupied.'

'You think I am not working enough?' Sonia asked.

But Vera did not reply, for the Home Service news was announcing the scuttling of the German pocket battleship *Graf Spee* outside Montevideo following an action with three British cruisers. Her efforts, cast in doubt a week or two earlier with the news of the loss of the *Royal Oak*, now seemed vindicated. England's bulwark was still, thank God, the Royal Navy.

'What a wonderful Christmas present!' she said jubilantly, her eyes shining.

And for a moment she shed her cares and looked like the girl Geoffrey Ennis had fallen in love with twenty years earlier.

Thirteen-year-old Ruth Jahn began to menstruate three days before Christmas, 1939. Awakened by discomfort and then horror, she left her bed in search of relief, terrified at the mess she dimly perceived she had made of her sheets. In the breakfast room she sat shivering from cold, her hands pressed into her lap staying the bloody flux with a crushed page from *The Times*.

Sleeping fitfully, Sonia had heard the girl go downstairs from her attic bedroom. Fully awake now, Sonia could make out sobs of distress and, pulling her silk wrap about herself, she followed.

'What is the matter?' she asked, switching on the light. The look of abject misery on Ruth's face was mixed with the guilt and horror of discovery. The red mess between her thighs told its own tale.

'It is nothing, wait. I will get something.'

When she returned from her room, Sonia took the girl into the kitchen, knelt beside her and helped her clean herself, finally handing her the sanitary towel.

'I am so . . . so ashamed,' Ruth mumbled as Sonia turned away and put the kettle on.

Sonia smiled. 'It is nothing. I understand.'

'I do not think Fräulein Martin would understand.'

Sonia looked at the girl. Her huge, dark eyes were brimming with tears but she was attempting to smile back, making a brave face. Sonia felt a wave of tenderness and compassion for the young woman, an overpowering sensation that again brought her to her knees alongside Ruth and compelled her to put her arms around the girl. Uncertainly, Ruth reciprocated; her head fell onto Sonia's shoulder and she felt the older woman stroke her hair. She was unable now to stop her crying. The tears welled up in heaving sobs and she wept out of loneliness, unhappiness and fear, fear of a world that was alien, held out no hope, no future and no love. The only emotion fate had drawn from her in recent weeks was ambivalent uncertainty, for she was unable to rid herself of the image of her father's anguished face as he laid upon her the great obligation: 'Look after your brother, Ruth. Look after little Joachim.'

Whether her father had said this because she was the elder or because she was the girl she had been unable to decide. Joachim seemed not to understand fully what had happened. He was only nine. But tonight *she* understood, tonight she had become a woman and knew what her father had truly meant.

'I am so sorry.'

'It is all right,' said Sonia in her low, crooning voice. 'I know what you are feeling. It happened to me like this, in a railway station.'

'Oh.'

'You understand why?'

'Yes, my mother told me. You are very kind.'

'When I was younger, I lived with a women called Natalia. She was kind to me.'

Sonia fell silent. She had not thought of Natalia for a long time and squatted, lost to the present, holding the Jewish girl in her arms.

'You are very warm,' said Ruth, looking at Sonia's pensive face under the harsh glare of the electric light, then

225

added in a whisper prompted by Sonia's obvious detachment, 'I shall never be beautiful like you.'

'Mmm?' Sonia was recalled to the present. The powerful emotive tug of Ruth's lonely plight had metamorphosed into something less comfortable, for thoughts of Natalia had stirred other memories.

'You will find a nice young man, perhaps an Englishman like I did.'

'No, I do not want to marry, to have children. It is terrible.'

'Come,' said Sonia suddenly, pulling away from the girl, 'you will catch a fever. You must go back to bed.'

As she stood, Sonia knew in a prescient moment that something had begun that night. She had felt the young body of Ruth against hers in a womanly embrace, but it was in their drawing apart that both sensed something other than mutual comfort.

'It will be different in the morning,' she said, putting out the light and watching Ruth's pale form head for the staircase. Sonia was trembling and knew the fragile barrier that exists between people had shattered between her and Ruth. It would be very different in the morning.

At Christmas Vera gave Joachim a violin. They had discovered the boy had been learning to play and among the gifts donated to the refugees Vera had found the instrument. Her partiality for the young boy was marked, though unsurprising. Sonia gave Ruth the tiny porcelain figurine that Natalia Drubskaya had swept from its place in the Shanghai flat. When she had joined them in Hong Kong, Natalia had insisted Sonia kept it.

'Oh,' smiled Ruth as she examined the curio, 'it is wonderful.'

'It was the only thing a friend of mine brought from her home in Russia,' Sonia said, and their eyes met in the unspoken accord that so disturbed Sonia.

'I suppose it is all right to give Jewish children Christmas presents,' Vera said later, as the two of them toasted their stockinged feet before the fire and drank a last glass of sherry.

'I do not see any harm in it,' Sonia replied.

'I wish something would happen,' said Vera, after a pause.

'*Happen*?' queried Sonia sleepily.

'With the war . . . nothing seems to be happening. Except at sea, of course.'

'I hope nothing *ever* happens,' said Sonia, rousing herself and making ready for bed. 'Nothing.'

The cold of the bed sheets wakened her and she lay longing for the feel of James's body beside her. Reminiscing, she felt herself aroused, then sat up guiltily as a quiet tap on her bedroom door interrupted her train of thought.

'Can I come?'

Ruth's face peered round the door. She advanced to the bed.

'I . . . I have come with a present.'

Dimly, Sonia perceived a soft, white handkerchief which Ruth held against her cheek. She felt the warmth of Shantung silk.

'It was my mother's,' Ruth said.

'No, no, I cannot take it,' Sonia protested.

'Please,' the girl insisted. 'It is for you.'

Sonia took the square of silk with its delicate perfume, then threw back the bedclothes and drew Ruth into bed. The girl rested her head on Sonia's shoulder and Sonia stared at the ceiling stroking Ruth's hair.

All about her the glass of her confinement was shattering.

CHAPTER SEVENTEEN
Fortune of War

'Aircraft green five five!'

Lieutenant John Martin hit the klaxon button with reflexive speed as he swung from studying the smoking collier on *Shrike*'s port beam. Sweeping his binoculars to starboard, he glimpsed only the eternal grey of a North Sea overcast as the sloop, guarding a coastal convoy, made her way north-west inside the Dowsing shoal towards the Tyne.

'Look like Junkers eighty-eights, sir. Two, no three!' The starboard lookout kept up his relentless flow of information while John struggled to spot the distant specks.

'Got 'em!' It was Ennis's voice, marking his reappearance on the bridge. He bent to the voice-pipe 'Starboard fifteen, revolutions for nineteen knots.'

'Starboard fifteen, wheel relieved, sir, Coxs'n on the wheel, revs for nineteen knots.'

'Yeoman, make to escorts "Aircraft attacking from nor' nor' east", repeat to Commodore.'

'Aye, aye, sir.' The clatter of the signal projector was instantaneous. Ennis continued his stream of orders, his eyes still glued to his glasses.

'Number One, get W/T to inform Admiralty, "under air attack." '

'Eleven miles north-west of Dudgeon,' put in John.

'Yes, with the usual preamble.'

John bent to the row of voice-pipes, calling first the wireless transmitting office and then taking the reports as *Shrike*'s complement closed up to their action stations for the second time that day. The first occasion had been in response to a signal from the Admiralty to expect an aerial attack but they had seen nothing, though several of the bridge staff thought they had heard the drone of aircraft above the clouds.

'Midships.'

Ennis steadied the heeling ship on her new heading and John finally caught the approaching enemy in his binoculars, three black dashes set high against the grey rolls of alto-cumulus. *Shrike* rolled and pitched easily as her speed increased and she ran before the quartering sea chopping up under the brisk south-westerly wind. The dashes were growing larger with an alarming rapidity. He could see the dots of engine nacelles and fuselages, the discs of whirring propellers and then the bright points of light as the bombers opened up with machine guns.

'Open fire!'

Ennis roared the order over the bridge rail and *Shrike*'s four-inch gun barked. With the sound of a thousand buzzing bees, the occasional high-pitched whine and discordant whirr, the German bullets passed harmlessly overhead, ricocheted, or tore holes and splinters off *Shrike*'s thin plating. Abaft the bridge the vicious chatter of the sloop's anti-aircraft machine gun rattled into action and John found, without remembering he had put it on, that he was wearing his tin hat.

'Port ten!' Ennis shouted to the Coxswain on the wheel and then to John, 'watch the bearing of the leading ship, I'm cutting across the head of the convoy.'

'Aye, aye, sir.' Glad of something to do to assist Ennis, John bent over the azimuth ring and brought the pointer round onto the leading vessel, a three island short-sea trader flying the blue cross of the convoy Commodore. *Shrike* was swinging towards her, cutting an acute angle across the convoy's line of advance to keep her guns bearing and throw up a sufficient barrage of shot to deter the German pilots from pressing home their attack. If they bombed the leading ship in the convoy it would throw the following merchantmen into disastrous confusion, for they were traversing a comparatively narrow channel swept clear of mines.

The thud of gunfire came from the far side of the convoy where *Shrike*'s consort *Crossbill* and the armed trawlers opened fire.

229

'Midships, steady as you go . . . steer three two zero.'

John straightened from the azimuth ring. 'Steady bearing with the Commodore, sir,' he shouted above the storm of machine-gun bullets, the noise of the approaching planes and the cacophony of their own guns.

'See if we can have more revs, Johnnie. If I come back to starboard, the after gun won't bear.'

'Aye, aye, sir.' John cranked the engine room telephone. Crackling, the Chief Engine Room Artificer's voice came up to him.

'Bridge, Chief. Give her all you've got, the Luftwaffe are here.'

'Aye, aye.'

'Aircraft breaking right, sir!'

'Chicken-hearted bastard,' said Ennis and John looked up in time to see one of the aircraft swing to its left, then flatten out towards *Shrike*.

'Spoke too bloody soon,' snarled Ennis, calling down to the wheelhouse, 'starboard twenty!'

Shrike heeled and began her turn. The stink of cordite swept back over the bridge from her gallantly firing forward gun, but its hand-loaded concussions were painfully slow. Ennis was thumping the rail impatiently as the noise of the approaching aircraft rose to a tremendous crescendo. There was one second when, just above the masthead it seemed, the whole underbelly of the Junkers was exposed and seen in detail, not as a malevolent shape against the sky, but a pale painted crucifix with its housed undercarriage and the hooded faces of its air crew looking down; and then it was gone, a diminuendo of noise, replaced by the tall columns of near misses that rose on either side of the eggshell-thin plating of the sloop, and the thunderous crump of fused high explosive.

Shrike shuddered from end to end, her long, slender hull whipping like a living thing, lifted several feet by the force of the explosions. Solid water cascaded down upon the bridge and men gasped from the shock of it.

Ennis, white-faced, leaned over the bridge to gauge the extent of damage to his ship. She seemed to have suffered no permanent ill effects and he swung round, triumphant in his relief.

'We rattled him, by God!' he roared, watching the departing Junkers climb and bank away. 'He dropped that stick on us, not the merchant ships.'

But John had no time for jubilation; he was answering the engine room telephone and receiving a damage report. As he straightened up to tell Ennis the news, the fourth ship of the column received a pattern of bombs, two exploding alongside, near misses that raised tall white splashes of water such as *Shrike* had suffered, two striking her amidships, bursting at the base of her funnel and lifting her fiddley deck in an ugly twist of steel. Smoke and steam poured from her and she began almost immediately to list, evidence that the near misses had stove in her shell plating.

'Sir, the Chief reports . . .'

But Ennis was yelling orders: 'Yeoman, make to *Lord Acton*,' 'Stand by *Glemham Hall*.' 'What's that, Number One?'

'Damage down below, sir. Chief reports fractured steam pipes and an oil leak from the starboard settling tank. He's losing pressure and won't be able to keep up this speed.'

Ennis cast a look round the convoy. The three planes, having delivered their attack, were climbing into the clouds and wheeling back towards the east. Ennis blew out his cheeks and took off his tin hat. The strands of lank hair were dark with sweat.

'Very well, reduce to eight knots. Go down and see how bad it is.'

'Aye, aye, sir.'

Ennis turned away. 'Well done, starboard lookout. It's you Chilton, isn't it?' But Chilton was incapable of answering, his lower abdomen was shot away, lacerated by splinters from the strafing fire of the Junkers bomber.

Shrike's engine room was like a scene from hell. The humid air was full of the white mist of escaping steam. It condensed on cooler pipes, bulkheads and the steel gratings and ladders that descended into the hissing turmoil. Occasionally, as he felt his way down, John was aware of flitting shapes, ratings moving purposefully among their own, familiar world. The thud-thud of hammer blows, a shouted order and a call for a 'three-quarter Whitworth' broke the insistent escape of the steam.

231

John struggled further down into the abyss. He hurried along the lower platform, passing the thrusting connecting rods and the eccentric turning of the crankshaft. At the forward end, where the control wheels, reversing levers and revolution telegraphs marked the heart of the engine room, an artificer stood by.

'Give 'em what for, did we, sir?' he asked.

'Yes. Where's the Chief?'

'In the boiler room, sir,' he said.

John stepped through the airlock. On the control platform the cool breeze from the ventilators had briefly eased the sweating he had begun the instant he entered the sodden atmosphere. Now the heat from the opened furnaces almost scalded his wet skin. He gasped momentarily, trying to locate the Chief ERA among the small group of reddened figures. Then he recognised the bald head and the half-opened patrol jacket. The Chief was staring with great concentration into the glowing maw of the starboard boiler. He straightened up and saw the First Lieutenant.

'Captain's compliments, Chief, and he'd like to know the worst.'

The Chief shook his head. 'Apart from the leaking steam pipes, sir, and they're serious enough, we've a problem with the oil feed and serious damage to this.' He patted the monstrous oval boiler end. 'I can keep steam for about six or seven knots, but it's a dockyard job.'

Back on the bridge John made his report.

Ennis was watching the trawler *Lord Acton* as her aldis light winked at them. Of the *Glemham Hall* there was no sign.

'Very well,' said Ennis, 'we must submit to our fate. We were due for a boiler clean anyway.' He sounded exhausted.

'Signal from *Lord Acton*, sir,' broke in the signalman. ' "Have on board eighteen survivors from *Glemham Hall*." '

Ennis nodded. 'Acknowledge and say, "Well done and my condolences to the master of the *Glemham Hall*." ' Then to his First Lieutenant he said, 'I have a feeling I should have sent my apologies. We let those chaps down, Johnnie; it's our duty to see the convoy safely through and we failed as far as the *Glemham Hall*'s concerned.' All trace of the earlier jubilation had gone.

'It's the first one we've lost, sir,' John said consolingly.

Ennis turned a grim face towards him. 'But it won't be the last. We hardly scratched those aeroplanes. What can one do with a slow-loading, hand-laid, single-shot pop gun against those devils, eh?' He dropped his eyes to the red smear where Chilton had stood.

'You said we rattled him. He dropped his stick on us, not another merchant ship.'

But Ennis seemed not to be listening. He had rested his chin on his hands as he peered over the bridge rail at the distant horizon. 'Yesterday's weapons, that's what we've got, and they've been practising for years in Spain,' and he stared up at the grey sky overcast which, with the coming night, laid a pall over the heaving wastes of the North Sea.

Lieutenant Martin knocked on the opened door to his Commander's cabin.

'Yes?' John drew back the door curtain. 'Ah, Johnnie, come in, come in, take a pew. Shift that bloody duffle coat . . . stand it in the corner, it's stiff enough. Like a gin?'

'Almost more than anything else in the world.'

'Almost? Ah, yes, I forget these things. You're still a young man, though I don't mind admitting a hot bath would come pretty well up on my list of priorities.' Ennis poured them two gins and bemoaned the lack of angostura. 'Bottle shot to pieces by that bloody Junkers.'

John looked at the holes stuffed with newspaper that peppered Ennis's cabin.

'Cheers.'

'Cheers, sir. We're to dry dock in the morning. I've just had word.'

'And I've just received your draft chit, Johnnie. This is the parting of the ways.'

'Oh.'

'Let's not pretend we're sorry. *Shrike*'s been a good little ship, and once the Tyne Dock and Engineering Company have had a go at her she'll go on being a good little ship for a bit longer, but neither you nor I want to stay in her. I've got the destroyer I've been pestering the Admiralty for. She's a *Havant* class, one of those we were building for the Brazilians at the outbreak. She's called *Havildar*.'

'Congratulations, sir.'

233

'Don't crow yet,' Ennis went on, 'it means I'm to command an escort group in the North Atlantic, what I've been waiting a long time for, but,' he sighed, 'they won't let me have you as my Jimmy.'

They had both known for some time they were unlikely to remain much longer in *Shrike*. Geoffrey Ennis was a fairly senior commander and many officers junior to him had been posted to destroyers. The majority of the trawlers and new corvettes then coming into service were being officered by the reservists of the RNR, former merchant naval officers who had trained periodically with the Royal Navy during peace-time. They were also filling up with officers and men of the volunteer reserve, pure amateurs, yachtsmen for the most part, while regular naval officers like Ennis and himself were leap-frogging into escort commander's berths. John knew too Ennis had been worried that he had, as he put it, 'missed the bloody omnibus', a passed-over commander left with two elderly sloops and a trio of armed but largely toothless trawlers. Both men appreciated the importance of the coastal convoys, but their ambitions sought greater challenges.

'That's a disappointment, sir,' John said.

'Yes, and I'm afraid it's a bigger disappointment than you think. You're off to a shore job.'

'*What?*'

Ennis handed John the signal. *Lieutenant J.J.R. Martin to report SNO Tobermory forthwith*.

'Who the hell is the SNO Tobermory?' John said sharply.

' 'Nother gin?' asked Ennis.

'Too bloody right.' John held out his glass.

'I bet you're glad you trained for anti-submarine warfare, eh?'

The SNO Tobermory took his seat at the head of the saloon table of the requisitioned ferry, shot his cuffs and opened the file laid before him by the writer. Then he unscrewed his fountain pen and looked at the faces about him.

'Lieutenant Martin, what's your assessment?'

John consulted the clipboard of notes before him. It was all very well for the SNO, a retired vice-admiral reinstated as Commodore, Royal Navy, to relish giving one of the crews under training a resounding raspberry, but John, as anti-submarine evaluating officer, had been as frustrated with the day's work as the First Lieutenant of the corvette in question.

'They carried out an adequate search, sir. Helm orders were a little slow in response to asdic contacts, but they made contact and held it quite well. The final run in of three of the attacks were good, though the fourth –'

'The fourth was a bloody shambles. Lieutenant Howson?'

'I agree with Martin up to a point, sir.' John listened as the submarine Commander, a lieutenant a couple of years older than himself, explained his own reaction as he had carried out his dummy U-boat attacks for the commissioning corvette to practise on. 'But none of the grenades burst anywhere near me. They were much too late.'

'So,' said the Commodore shortly, 'looks like nemesis for the *Nemesia*.'

'They were very keen, sir.' John felt impelled to say something, for there had been an odd, indefinable component missing in the day's war game. *Nemesia* had performed fairly well in the routines of preparing to tow and hoisting out her sea boat at a moment's notice. In fact the basic seamanship tasks had been better performed by the ship's company of the *Nemesia* than the half dozen other corvettes he had so far studied in his new job.

'So you think she has redeeming features, do you, Martin?' The Commodore cast a baleful eye over his young subordinate.

'So do I, sir,' broke in a lieutenant commander who, like Martin, had sat quietly on *Nemesia*'s bridge and observed her reservist Captain and his volunteer officers put through their paces.

'D'you think the Boche is going to give them the benefit?'

'No, sir, but I think we should.'

'Do you now?' The Commodore leaned back in his chair and tapped his pen thoughtfully. He fixed his eye on Lieutenant Martin. 'Well, Martin, in the manner of councils of war, we start with the junior officer present. Convince me.'

John coughed. The writer bent his head to hide his smile. 'Well, sir, her general performance in most of the seamanship tasks was quite good . . .'

'Was it? That might have been your opinion, Lieutenant,'

235

said the Commodore with heavy emphasis on John's lack of rank. 'You're here as anti-submarine evaluating officer.'

'And her gunnery was well up to scratch, sir,' put in the elderly Lieutenant Commander, unintimidated.

'Go on, Lieutenant,' growled the Commodore.

'It was her Commander who let her down, sir.'

The Commodore thumped the table with the palm of his hand so that the pencils jumped. For a second John thought he had committed some impropriety in criticising a lieutenant commander RNR.

'Exactly! Very sound, Martin. Trouble is the fellow's got an excellent file.' The Commodore's hand patted the brown cardboard file-skin with a gentler motion. 'So what's at the root of the problem?'

'Could be nerves, sir. He was a bit nervous.'

'Gentlemen, that corvette is due to join an Atlantic convoy the day after tomorrow. She failed to press a successful attack against her target and was quite unable to . . . yes, what is it?'

The signalman passed the folded chit to John who passed it directly to the Commodore. The committee, curious, watched the Commodore's reactions. He frowned, then looked up.

'This is a signal from *Nemesia* marked urgent. It says "Captain has suspected peritonitis, please pass instructions." The poor devil has been in agony with appendicitis. Martin, signal them to get their sea boat away and land him. Let the doctor know he's coming.'

John left the cabin and caught up with the signalman. When he returned the meeting had ended. Only the writer was in the room, gathering up the unused sheets of paper.

'Sir, the Commodore said to report to him as soon as you got back. He's in his office.'

Against the far window and through the frosted glass of the door of what had once been the ferry's purser's office John could see the figure of the Commodore. He was speaking on the telephone and John hesitated for a moment to allow him to finish before knocking. He overheard a few words, 'desperate remedies' and 'no time to mess about', and finally the Commodore said, 'no, no, no problem. We've two days before *Nettlewort* arrives, you can find me a replacement. Good, goodbye.'

The phone slammed down and John knocked. 'Come in. Ah, Martin. You can stop chafing at the bit. The Admiralty have approved my suggestion you take command of *Nemesia*. You'll get a signal to confirm it as soon as you get aboard. I think you've got quite a good little ship there. Go and see what you can make of her.'

'Aye, aye, sir, and thank you, sir.'

'Don't thank me, my boy. It's just the fortune of war. Oh, and Martin?'

'Sir?'

'Have you had your appendix out?'

CHAPTER EIGHTEEN

A Phoney War

The wind caused a peculiarly dismal note to sound in the wires and struts that supported the SS *Königsburg*'s spurious armour plating. Taking a turn up and down his odd bridge shortly after lunch on an early March day, James Martin considered he had never heard quite such a mournful sound. It was, however, oddly in tune with both his thoughts and his surroundings.

The windswept desolation of Scapa Flow had been their home for three weeks. For the first days they had occupied it almost alone, except for the beached hulk of Jellicoe's old flagship *Iron Duke* and the seaplane tender *Pegasus*. He had watched the wind draw its vicious little catspaws across the grey water, and seen them cut up into short, steep seas that set the odd armed trawlers and the local fishing boats bobbing uncomfortably. He had watched the curtains of rain and snow drawn across the Flow in a ceaseless panorama of atmospheric change.

James had kept his ship's company warm and active by adopting some of the routines of a capital ship at anchor and the frequent exercise of abandon ship drill. For a while this had occupied and sustained his own spirits, but they had seen nothing of the enemy who, having made an air raid on both Rosyth and Scapa in the first weeks of the war, had left them alone.

'Well,' said Crosby-Milne fatalistically, '*they* know they've sunk the *Royal Oak* and they could wreck us with a box of Swan Vestas, so they aren't going to bother with another expensive torpedo.'

'But we're now supposed to be *Ramilles*,' expostulated Sublieutenant Bristow, RNVR, who still nursed a touching faith in the Admiralty's wisdom.

To sustain his own spirits as the days dragged by James had painted a number of sensitive studies as the pale, fleeting sunshine caught the waters of the Flow and the surrounding hummocks of the islands.

Then, on St David's day 1940, the remainder of Force W arrived, three Shaw Savill liners disguised as the battleships *Revenge* and *Resolution*, and the aircraft carrier *Hermes*. Further additions took up their anchor berths – destroyers, submarines with their depot ship, three cruisers and, a week later, the battleship *Valiant* and the Navy's darling, HMS *Hood*.

In the driving drizzle of that afternoon, the grey pyramids and long, low hulls of both real and counterfeit warship were indistinguishable. James blew the raindrops from the end of his nose and continued walking up and down. Unfortunately that day not even the monotonous silhouettes of the great capital ships could tempt his pencil, for with the new arrivals had come a bag of mail for Fleet Tender *Delta*. It included a caustic letter from Vera in which it was not difficult to detect a souring of her relationship with Sonia. The pleasing news of the Jewish children was tempered by the innuendo that Vee supposed *anyone who had once worked in a cabaret would enjoy a drink*. Was his cousin being unfairly critical of one of Sonia's occasional alcoholic lapses? James wondered. Or was she alluding to a more regular habit that was becoming a problem? James was unable to judge; he knew Sonia's very Russian soul was capable of plunging into an abyss of melancholy which was difficult to tolerate. It had been different in Hong Kong when Natalia Drubskaya had been on hand.

Sonia had written, too; five passionate letters, ill-spelt but miserably sincere. They tore at James's heart and he could not avoid the thought that he had brought this anguish on himself for loving a woman for her dependence upon him. An Emily Plunkett would not have admitted such abjection, but Emily Plunkett was not Russian.

It is like living alone, Sonia had written, *cold harted without you. I wait wait but from you no letters come. The*

German children are so sad. Ruth is my friend but not like my darling James . . .

It went on, page after page of it, exasperating, heart-rending in its desperate imperfection. James sighed, turned at the end of his walk and strode back. Across the anchorage the tinny double strike of two bells, one o'clock in the afternoon, rang in rough synchronisation from ship to ship.

Reaching up, he struck the polished brass bell that still bore the legend '*Königsburg*, 1924'. 'We should be shamming a Jerry battle wagon with a name like that,' Crosby-Milne had observed back in Belfast. It was one of the minor ironies of war. It was another irony that young John had his own command already. That news, veiled by John's judicious humour to escape the censor, had arrived in the same mail bag. *I am already head gardener, tending a young bloom. I seem to have got the job without much effort.* So John, only just having reached his majority, already had command of a Flower-class corvette.

How long had his father had to wait for a ship? It did not bear thinking about. Still, James was glad for the boy, and Vera ought to be pleased, if she knew, unless she considered he should have had a destroyer!

A sudden noise interrupted his reverie. He looked up, expecting the arrival of fighter cover to occupy the vacant airfield at Hatston now that major units of the Home Fleet occupied the Flow, but the increasing howl of the aeroplane's engines had a malevolent roar. A single plane, leaving two consorts circling in and out of the cloud above, hurtled down on the anchorage. James hit the alarm bells, hoping his crew would not rush out on deck but take shelter in the reinforced citadel built amidships.

The Heinkel III flattened out and roared over his head, apparently waggling its wings in derision. It did the same over the *Hood* then, as James watched the dots detach themselves from the belly of the aircraft, it loosed a stick of bombs on a small steam ship which had brought supplies up to the base of Lyness.

'Did he think we were all dummies?' asked Crosby-Milne afterwards.

'We behaved like them,' James replied. 'Not one bloody ship let off so much as a single shot.'

'*Ce n'est pas la guerre, c'est une faute!*' replied Crosby-Milne.

A second aerial buzzing was made the following evening, but this time the ships responded, streams of tracer shells following the tail of the enemy aircraft as it droned eastwards out of sight. Reports of magnetic mines dropped in the entrance to Hoy Sound delayed the entrance of more units of the Home Fleet including HMS *Rodney* with the First Lord of the Admiralty on board.

Mr Churchill, brooking no delay, entered Scapa Flow aboard a destroyer. But James saw no more of him than he had done of the King, who had inspected the other three dummy ships before they left Rosyth.

Rodney and her consorts entered the Flow the next day and that evening the Luftwaffe paid them another visit. The cruiser *Norfolk* sustained fire damage from a bomb, but no attacks were made on the dummy ships. Nightly raids then became routine and, as the crews of the warships went to action stations every dusk, the companies of the dummies abandoned ship to huddle cravenly in a derelict farm near by, whose only roof was a soil-covered tarpaulin.

'This is no bloody good for morale, sir,' James complained to the Captain of the pseudo–*Revenge*, who was shivering with the onset of pneumonia. 'At least let us mount a few machine guns and fire back, if only for our own satisfaction.'

But a few days later the attacks fizzled out and then ceased.

'Some bloody war,' growled the frustratedly pugnacious Crosby-Milne.

A different and more terrible frustration had seized Sonia, the frustration of indecision. The forced inactivity of life at The Lees was increasingly unendurable, for Vera, acting as some censorious form of guardian, thwarted any attempt Sonia made to enjoy such social life as the town offered. The presence of Ruth and Joachim, though schooling had now been arranged for them, presented Sonia with another problem, a problem she half encouraged. Ruth found the older woman attractive, would seek out her company, perform little services and, inevitably, their intimacy assumed a less formal character. In Ruth she saw mirrored

241

something of herself and of her own girlhood, and although on Sonia's own *Kristallnacht* – the night Ruth had come precociously to her bed – Sonia had formed the resolve to leave the shelter of The Lees, Ruth held her there. Though Sonia longed for freedom, longed again for the spotlight that had in distant Shanghai conferred upon her a unique individuality, she was aware that at Kirilov's she had had the friendship of Natalia Drubskaya.

'Must we always play over again the parts fate wrote for our careless and unhappy young lives?' she asked herself, whispering the Russian words into the darkness of the alien bedroom as Ruth slept upon her breast. 'Must I be like Natasha even though I travel halfway round the world to make a new life in England, only to find a new Sonia here?'

She stroked the head of the sleeping girl. She knew now with fatalistic certainty that Ruth's active young body sought to entrap her further. Gently waking the girl with a kiss, Sonia sent her back to her own bed. She had to end this thing before it inextricably enmeshed both of them, and before Vera discovered them. Vera could not be expected to understand, let alone tolerate, this sweet and innocent passion. But how Sonia might accomplish this without hurting Ruth eluded her.

One evening, as they gathered round the radio and learned of the imminent collapse of France and the call for the 'little ships' that would extricate the British Expeditionary Force from Dunkirk, Ruth expressed her desire to help the war effort.

'A lot of woman are doing war work. They told us at school.'

'And what can you do?' Vera asked, turning off the radio.

'I can speak German,' Ruth retorted.

'You are rather young for that kind of thing,' said Vera, reaching for the newspaper.

'Well I could teach other people, help them, make them speak it good.'

'Speak it well, Ruth,' corrected Vera from behind the newspaper.

Ruth cast a despairing look at Sonia. 'I want to do *something*,' she whispered, as though Vera's dismissiveness had driven her eagerness underground. But Sonia was staring abstractedly at the fire, an idea having taken root in her mind.

Waking early to the high buzz of aeroplanes, Sonia rose and went downstairs. She had slept fitfully, refusing Ruth her bed the night before, as ways and means of implementing her plan formed in her overactive brain. In the early chill she turned over the papers in Vera's little escritoire, finding her correspondence with Geoffrey Ennis and in particular the letters that discussed the steps Vera should take to get John appointed to a ship. They mentioned the Admiralty, the Appointments Office of the Second Sea Lord, and an officer named Captain Wyatt.

Before breakfast Sonia wrote, offering her services as a British national fluent in Russian. She signed herself 'Sonia Starlenka'.

She heard nothing for some weeks and the lack of news worried her. This evident withdrawal manifested itself in an indifference to Ruth which might have precipitated a crisis had not Ruth, Joachim and Vera been totally absorbed with the aerial battle being fought out in the blue skies overhead. As they craned from the attic window following the vapour trails of the dogfights between Messerschmitt and Spitfire, tracing the downward spiral of the vanquished and the triumphal upward roll of the victor, Sonia sat consumed with worry over what she had set in train.

Eventually a brown envelope arrived marked OHMS and franked with the postmark 'London SW1'. Vera watched Sonia open it.

'Not bad news, I hope?'

'No.'

'What is it?' Vera persisted.

'Just something to do with James,' Sonia answered vaguely, regaining her self-possession as she digested the letter's contents.

'May I see? Is everything all right?'

Sonia folded the letter and met Vera's inquisition with a level stare.

'Yes, everything is quite all right. It is a private matter.'

And Vera had, perforce, to be satisfied with her answer. A few days later a second letter arrived. It was longer than the first. Sonia was asked a series of questions and asked to forward her marriage certificate. A month after volunteering her services, a third letter arrived.

'I have to go to London,' Sonia announced. 'James has a short leave.'

But Vera was not deceived. The succession of official buff envelopes had roused her suspicions, and there had not been a letter from James for weeks.

'What in God's name . . .?' Crosby-Milne stared through his glasses at the line of three destroyers entering Scapa Flow. Their silhouettes were jagged with the effects of German shells and bombs. 'My God, they've taken a bloody pasting!'

James stood silent beside his fat and wheezing first lieutenant. In his bones he had been waiting for something like this, some northern counterpart to the southern debacle of Dunkirk. In the last few days Scapa Flow had been a-buzz with rumour. The capital ships of the Home Fleet had moved in and out, their phantom doubles shifted onto their moorings to confuse the Junkers reconnaissance aircraft that flew its daily mission to glean intelligence of the Royal Navy's movements. First had come news that a submarine, believed to be HMS *Truant*, had damaged the cruiser *Karlsruhe* off Norway, then a second submarine had crippled the pocket battleship *Lützow* while, to the delight of the company of Fleet Tender *Delta*, Fleet Air Arm Skuas flown from Hatston on Orkney had dive-bombed and sunk the German cruiser *Königsberg*.

'I'm beginning to suffer a severe identity crisis,' complained Crosby-Milne jokingly.

The activity of heavy units of the German fleet off the Norwegian coast coincided with British minelaying operations designed to prevent the German seizure of Narvik. Part of the minelaying force, the destroyer *Glowworm*, was detached to search for a man lost overboard in heavy weather. Thus isolated and in thick weather, *Glowworm* ran into and engaged the German destroyer *Bernd von Arnim*. The action was terminated when the cruiser *Hipper* appeared on the scene and drove off the *Glowworm*, setting her on fire. But undefeated, HMS *Glowworm* returned to the attack, ramming the huge German warship in a gesture of sublime defiance. As she drifted away from her opponent

244

she radioed the news of the full-scale German invasion of Norway. A few moments later she exploded.

In response Admiral Forbes took the Home Fleet to sea and his destroyers were heavily engaged in the approaches to Narvik, supporting a British, French and Polish military counterattack that fizzled out, despite early promise of success. Now, as the remnants limped back to Scapa, James and his First Lieutenant watched the wounded ships enter the anchorage.

At slow speed, their wrecked decks enveloped in steam leaks, their rigging shot away and their superstructures peppered with holes, the three destroyers brought to their anchors. James called to Burton, 'Make to the leader, "Can we be of any assistance?" '

While Burton's aldis clattered away, James turned to Crosby-Milne.

'I'll send young Watson over in the whaler to see what we can do.'

'I'll go with him, if you don't mind, sir.'

'Of course not,' James said abstractedly, reaching for the small sketching block he kept tucked in the flag locker. He found the sight of those three, broken little ships profoundly moving. His pencil rasping over the coarse watercolour paper, he limned in the defiant rake of the aligned gun barrels thinking, as he had done several times since he had heard of it, of the end of the gallant *Glowworm*. It was a meaningless, almost stupid gesture, of little tactical and no strategic effect, and yet it was an incident that struck a primitive response, so primitive that it raised the hairs along the spine and brought a lump to the throat. It was what the Royal Navy expected, engagement against all the odds; the manifestation of a huge, awesome weight of tradition. No doubt her dead captain would be honoured. It was in the interests of the state to do so, but what moral burden had the man taken with him in his glorious death? If he had been imbued with the spirit of the Navy, what of the scores of men in his ship's company? Had they shared the patriotic fervour of their commander as he launched his fragile ship against so unassailable a foe as the cruiser *Hipper*?

It was the great lie again, *pro patria mori* . . . A great and glorious thing. They gave their lives, the memorials erected after the bloodbath of the last war had said. Or had them torn away.

As he completed the drawing, James thought again of the great burden of command in war; and suddenly he felt a sense of acute anxiety for his son.

Crosby-Milne did not return to the ship until just before midnight. He had sent Sublieutenant Watson and a boatload of filthy seamen and stokers across in the whaler, and the destroyer's men had been allowed the run of the former *Königsburg*'s accommodation, luxuriating in hot baths after the rigours of their operation. When his First Lieutenant did arrive back, it was in a state of inebriation. James could hear him roaring a song as he made his painfully slow way along the alleyway to his cabin. Angrily James leapt out of bed.

Crosby-Milne stood swaying outside his cabin, his arms cradling a long, angular bundle wrapped in an oily blanket. His face wore a beatific smile as he caught sight of James.

'G'd evenin', Shur. Reportin' aboard.'

'For God's sake, man, pipe down or I'll throw the confounded book at you. Get your head down at once.'

'Can't,' replied Crosby-Milne happily, 'got a lot of work to do.' He nodded at the heavy bundle. 'Got to fit these beauties.'

'What the hell have you got there?'

Crosby-Milne, sweating under the effort of holding his load, balanced it in one arm and folded back the corner of the dirty wrapping.

'Machine guns!'

For several days the clandestine fitting of the machine guns occupied them, giving them something practical to do while they digested more gloomy news. German Panzer divisions rolled past Dunkirk into France. Paris was bombed and the news from Norway told of Allied containment by the invading Germans. They were slightly cheered to hear Churchill had taken over from the ousted Chamberlain, but unimpressed by the new Prime Minister's speeches. In the aftermath of the Norwegian campaign they learned that the aircraft carrier *Glorious* had been sunk. Wrestling with an adjustment of an ill-fitting gun-mounting bracket improvised by the Engineer Lieutenant, Crosby-Milne asked how.

'I understand *Scharnhorst* and *Gneisenau* hit her,' James said.

'With gunfire?' asked Crosby-Milne, looking up from his task.

'Yes, the buzz is the *Glorious* wasn't flying air patrols.'

'Oh, Jesus. So they threw away the advantage of having eyes in the sky?'

'Or didn't appreciate the wisdom of keeping them up there,' said James thoughtfully.

'No.' Crosby-Milne grunted as he plied the spanner and finally secured the improvised mounting to his satisfaction. James leaned on the rail, enjoying a patch of sunlight that moved slowly across the Flow and illuminated Fleet Tender *Delta* in all the detail of her specious splendour.

'The problem is,' he said, 'that such an action will only increase the conviction of the big-ship lobby.'

'You really don't think battle wagons are worthwhile, do you?' Crosby-Milne struggled breathlessly to his feet.

'No, I don't. We're as effective as the real thing in the imagination of the enemy, but the real McCoy is cripplingly expensive and not invulnerable, as we discovered with the *Royal Oak*. Besides, they have a nasty habit of exploding.'

'Ah, yes,' said Crosby-Milne glancing with renewed interest at his commanding officer. 'I had forgotten.'

But James had turned away and was pacing the short walkway that had once been a compass platform. The patch of sunlight had faded, and a grey curtain of rain was sweeping down from the high rocks of Hoy.

Adolf Hitler's legions had seized Norway and Denmark at a stroke, adding further to the awesome impression of Nazi invincibility. Once again his new Kreigsmarine had bloodied the nose of the world's proudest Navy, destroying more than ships and men as its achievements ate like acid into the very fabric of tradition.

James was seized by the conviction that Britain and her Empire were going to lose this war, and he felt overwhelmed by a great weariness.

'What the hell *are* we doing here?' Crosby-Milne asked, swatting a persistent fly with a yellowing copy of the *Daily Telegraph* that announced Italy had joined Hitler's Germany to form a Fascist axis. 'The bloody frogs have caved in and now the RAF are being shot out of the sky, by all accounts.' His despairing tone echoed round the wardroom but elicited no response from the other officers. 'I mean there must be something useful we can do instead of sitting on our arses in the middle of Scapa Flow and pretending. *Pretending*, for God almighty's sake!'

'You won't be for much longer, gentlemen.' James entered the wardroom with the pink flimsy of a lengthy signal in his hands. 'We're to reduce to twenty men; half our strength are drafted, starting with the officers. Watson, you're off to join a new corvette completing at Smith's on the Tees . . .'

When it was over James addressed Crosby-Milne. 'You and I and the Chief Engineer are to stay on, Number One.'

'Bugger. Somebody's got it in for us.'

'Perhaps,' James nodded with a grim smile. Idleness might be undermining his sense of proportion, but it was surely not credible that Wyatt's malice could persist through the present crisis.

'I think I'd better get some authentic rust streaks painted down the sides of this bloody old hook-pot,' Crosby-Milne said, heaving himself to his feet.

James sat in the emptying wardroom and watched him go. Was the man all bravado, or did the fat, bibulous figure conceal a disappointed rather than a wasted life? James sighed. War was, above all things, such a superlative waste. The drafts would empty his ship. He would be sorry to lose Burton, posted to a shore job at the Defence Telecommunications Network at Lyness, but like other key petty officers he was wasted where he was. James would be left with barely enough men to maintain the ship in safety at her moorings. And she was still an asset, of that he was certain, for during a walk ashore the previous day he had met a staff officer with whom he was on nodding terms.

'Things are looking a bit bleak in the Atlantic,' the man had confided. 'The Hun's submarines are doing rather better than they should be.'

Allowing for the euphemistic phrasing that was a concession to preoccupations with secrecy, it appeared to James that disaster loomed again on the cold great waters of the Western Ocean. John was out there somewhere, but it did not do to dwell on such thoughts.

He looked round the wardroom. It was still very obviously a merchant ship's saloon when all was said and done. Beneath the sticks and canvas of an utterly useless battleship, there remained the capacious holds of the SS *Königsberg*.

CHAPTER NINETEEN
Guns and Butter

As the day faded, the sun dipping early behind the banks of cloud building to the west of the convoy, Lieutenant John Martin, RN, Commanding Officer of His Majesty's Corvette *Nemesia* came onto the bridge, acknowledged the officer of the watch's salute and occupied the compass platform that Sublieutenant Kirk, RNVR, respectfully vacated. He was grumpy and still sleepy from the unsatisfactory doze he had stolen for an hour in his sea cabin and lit a cigarette to avoid the necessity of small talk.

'Nothing to report,' said Kirk formally.

'Very well.' The equally formal reply was patently insincere. Nothing seemed very well to John's present frame of mind. He had been unable to sleep properly for several nights, despite the absence of any real alarms.

'*Havildar* signalling, sir.'

John stirred himself, stretched and nodded at the signalman's report. He took his cap off, ran his fingers through his dark hair and pulled the cap on again.

' "Exchange stations with *QPR*." '

'Very well, acknowledge.' He bent to the voice-pipe. 'Starboard twenty, increase revolutions to one eight zero.'

'My God, we're offside again.' The First Lieutenant cracked the joke that had become standard, a silly reference to the anti-submarine trawler named after Queen's Park Rangers football club, and with whom Commander Ennis regularly had one of his two flanking corvettes exchange stations at sunset. During the day, as the convoy of twenty-five laden cargo ships rolled lazily across the grey Atlantic, Ennis liked his corvettes up on either flank in

250

echelon with *Havildar* which zigzagged across the front of the westward bound convoy.

The arrowhead of three warships extended the visible horizon of the convoy and they kept a lookout for surfaced submarines as they worked their way into their favourite position for an ambush. But when darkness fell and the enemy might be expected to submerge, to surface inside the convoy and torpedo the laden cargo ships, Ennis wanted *Nemesia* ready to counterattack if the worst happened, while the echoing ping of her asdic beam might deter a U-boat from penetrating the convoy.

Nemesia completed her outward swing and turned astern of the convoy. The eerie, resonating note of the asdic quested out into the vast Atlantic, an integral part of this panorama of ships that was now thrown in sharp silhouette against the horizon. They were old ships mostly, the product of Britain's shameful pre-war neglect of her merchant marine; slow ships, too, built by parsimonious ship-owners who economised on fuel at the expense of speed. Faced with the subsidised competition of foreign ships, Britain's merchant fleet had continued to decline in numbers after the losses it had suffered in the Great War. Unaided, the owners looked to their own profits and the status and conditions of the merchant seaman, which were never high, declined accordingly. This avoidable neglect was exacerbated by the inevitable effects of the world slump. True, some of the ships that composed the convoy were new, products of a 'scrap and build' programme introduced in 1934. But this had been at the expense of berths, for two ships had to be scrapped for an owner to receive assistance for a new one, and had had more to do with providing work for idle shipyards and engineering works than husbanding the merchant fleet as the strategic reserve it now so obviously was.

But none of these facts occupied any part of John's reflections that evening. He saw, with his young eyes, the smoking funnels and the dark, lumbering hulls that carried Britain's exports to the United States in exchange for armaments under the 'cash and carry' arrangements made with President Roosevelt.

'General quarters,' he ordered, suppressing a yawn. He

251

wondered if he would ever accustom himself to going without sleep for long periods. No one, in his short grooming for it, had told him of the disadvantages of command, and he had not yet learned the art of the instant catnap that more experienced men possessed.

Through the ship the pipes twittered and *Nemesia* stirred from cruising stations to general quarters in accordance with the escort force commander's standing orders. They were new at this game, but Ennis had given it much thought and was taking no chances.

'The problem, as I see it,' Ennis had cautioned his escort commanders, 'is that our asdic doesn't detect a submarine on the surface and the intelligence reports indicate this is what the Huns are doing. Getting past us, ducking under our guard and coming up inside our charges.' He had looked round their impossibly youthful faces. The only man of his own age was the Skipper Lieutenant commanding the *Queen's Park Rangers*, and he had a young RNVR lieutenant with him as his anti-submarine specialist.

'Our first duty is always to see the convoy through, so guarding and keeping the U-boats at bay, well away from the convoy, is priority. But one or two convoys have been taking a pasting, and I want the capability of hitting back.'

They had all agreed with that, for they were intent upon aggressive defence, if defence must be their role in this war. Thus had been born their sunset manoeuvre. Being ruled offside, *Nemesia*'s First Lieutenant had called it, and the joke had stuck.

'Ship's closed up to general quarters, sir.' Lieutenant Audley Hindmarsh, RNVR, originator of the joke, ducked into the asdic compartment after making his report. In his brief stint aboard *Nemesia*, John had had little time to make the acquaintance of any of her company. Hindmarsh was the exception and John knew he was fortunate in his First Lieutenant. Hindmarsh was not the mad-keen, yes-sir-no-sir uniformed bank clerk that he had seen numerous examples of at Tobermory. Their enthusiasm was admirable but they were lightweight, ill-suited for the remorseless quality of the long battle of attrition they were unknowingly embarked upon.

Hindmarsh's ability had been conspicuous from the first moments of the embarkation of the Tobermory party. He had an easy authority that combined with an impressive resourcefulness in dealing with the problems the Commodore hurled at the greenhorn *Nemesia*.

'However did you get that collision mat organised so quickly?' John had asked him, soon after taking command and referring to one of the Commodore's favourite evolutions. 'I've seen a fully trained RN crew take twice as long.'

'When I saw the thing come aboard, I thought it might come in useful,' Hindmarsh explained, referring to the heavy coir mat. 'You see I used one once when I sprung a strake in an old boat I was sailing. It was only a spare jib, but we had a few problems getting it secured in the right spot so I worked out that if there was any lift in the sea, as there was in my boat and I guessed there would be in the Atlantic, a few odd shackles on the under-keel wires would make a difference.'

'You'll have to write an amendment to the Admiralty Manual,' John laughed. It was a valuable insight into Hindmarsh's capabilities, but it also revealed the extent of his ambition. Two years older than Lieutenant Martin, Lieutenant Hindmarsh made no secret of his desire to command and, John felt, he was slightly resentful of his own presence.

'He was a pretty good old stick,' Hindmarsh would remark, referring to the invalided Lieutenant Commander RNR whom John had replaced. 'Pity he wasn't on form during our work-up.'

'Perhaps you'll get him back after his operation,' John had said.

The rest of the ship's company were a mixed bag. A thin sprinkling of naval regulars in key positions, a leading signalman and an asdic operator, boatswain's mate, a chief engine room artificer and coxswain. They were, John knew, the backbone of his ship's company and hence his ship. He sensed they were not entirely indifferent to having a regular lieutenant in charge. The rest were a rag-tag mixture of reservists and conscripted 'Hostilities Only' ratings. Among these, James noticed with some alarm, was a failed medical student and a classics graduate.

'I can see the quack might be of some use,' James said as

253

Hindmarsh showed him the crew list in Tobermory, 'but what can we make of the second?'

'I've put him in the depth-charge party under the Leading Torpedoman. I presumed he was philosopher enough to handle that.' John grunted. 'The thing is,' Hindmarsh added pointedly, 'when it comes to real fighting, we're all pretty much amateurs, aren't we?'

John had tried not to resent the dig. To have argued he had already been under fire would have cut little ice with a man of Hindmarsh's character and would have further worsened his opinion of himself, so he let the matter go, reflecting it was ironic he could not tell his First Lieutenant that it was he who had recommended Hindmarsh to the SNO Tobermory.

'No contacts, sir,' Hindmarsh now reported, popping his head out of the asdic hut.

'Very well. Keep up the good work. *Havildar* signalled us earlier that the Admiralty thought there were three U-boats in our area.'

Above the moan of the breeze in the flag halliards and the hiss of the wake as it folded outwards from *Nemesia*'s pitching bow, the echoing ping of the asdic kept up its hunt for the hidden underwater intruder.

'We're in the wrong bloody station,' he heard someone say. 'Too much noise from the propellers of the convoy.'

'All right, Wiggins, we know you're an expert, just keep on with it.'

John smiled to himself. Hindmarsh's rebuke was pitched just right. Wiggins was a regular, a good operator but apt to resent being surrounded by amateurs, the type of old sweat who was always critical of his superiors.

John was glad Hindmarsh had choked off the adverse comment on Ennis's dispositions.

It was altogether another irony that he had found himself under Geoffrey's command again. 'Glad to have you with me, Johnnie. All we need now is your father as Convoy Commodore.'

'I think that too improbable a twist of fate, sir,' John had replied.

Ennis was somewhere in the darkness ahead of them, pleased as punch with his destroyer. 'She's fitted like a

254

blasted yacht, veneered panelling in my day cabin and no end of folderols provided for the Brazilians,' he had said. 'Well, rank has its privileges, my boy,' he had added, as John described the spartan accommodation of a Flower-class corvette.

'Cuppa kye, sir?' The smell of the hot chocolate drink was heart-warmingly domestic. It was nearly time for them to stand down from general quarters. He could drink the cocoa and try and sleep in his hutch of a sea cabin.

Turning forward, the hot drink in his hands, he wedged himself in a corner he had discovered between the angle of the rail and the battery of voice-pipes.

Suddenly the darkness ahead was ripped apart by a blinding flash of orange fire that subsided into a flickering of flame and was accompanied by the boom of an explosion. There was an angry howl as Wiggins picked up the torpedo detonation on his earphones, an instant's uncertain hiatus, and then John jerked to action as several things happened at once.

'Ring on full speed! Action stations, starboard fifteen!' He shouted his orders then alternately bent over the compass binnacle and stared ahead through his glasses. His heart was pounding as *Nemesia* increased speed, her bow lifting with a faster rhythm. Beside him the asdic extension loudspeaker pinged eerily, the forlorn note mixed with the mush of propeller races as the corvette closed with the convoy.

'Midships, steady, steer two seven seven.'

'Looks like the second tanker, third column, sir. Number fifteen.'

'That's the *Elleston*.' John leaned over the bridge front. 'Four-inch!' he bawled at the gun below him. The grey shape of Sublieutenant Kirk's anti-flash hood moved. 'Sir?'

'Fire starshell ahead.'

'Aye, aye, sir.'

'*Havildar* on R/T, sir, carry out "Cough-drop".'

'Acknowledge.'

The crump of the gun and whirr of the departing shell was accompanied by simultaneous firing from the other escorts. The slab sides of the merchant ships were suddenly illuminated by the ghoulish light of descending flares, a nightmare painting by a modern Bosch. The lanes between the column up which they advanced were empty, a waste of water churned by the opposing washes of the adjacent columns of ships reflecting the white glow of the illuminating starshell and the orange inferno of the burning tanker.

'He'll have dived by now,' muttered John anxiously to himself, concerned that the U-boat had doubled back and slipped through the rear of the convoy even as *Nemesia* entered it. He stood on the compass platform staring about him, irresolute and alone.

Ahead of them the *Elleston* continued to burn with a series of explosions as her empty tanks, imperfectly purged of gas, blew up. Gouts of flame licked the underbelly of the rising pall of smoke which hung above her, blacker than the night itself.

The bulk of the drifting tanker slewed out of control across the path of the ships astern as she broached to. The heat of her agony blew down on them, searing them in its intensity. Suddenly the order of the convoy broke down around them. There seemed to be ships everywhere, sounding their sirens as they sought to avoid collision with the *Elleston* and each other.

Then, amid this hellish confusion, as John realised with a violently palpitating heart that driving *Nemesia* into the heart of the convoy was achieving nothing, the pencil beam of an aldis lamp from one of the merchant ships to starboard of the corvette showed John in the lens of his binoculars a momentary but indelible image, a swirl of water centred on a slim grey column.

'Full ahead, starboard fifteen!' he roared, his doubts evaporating in an instant. He tried to get a bearing on the vanishing swirl and shouted for more starshell.

'Make to *Havildar* . . .'

But his words were drowned as a second ship was torpedoed on the starboard side of the column. The U-boat had indeed slipped out of the convoy, exploiting the gap left astern of the *QPR*, and had then turned, taken a peep through her periscope, and delivered a Parthian shot.

'Make to *Havildar*,' John repeated, ' "Periscope sighted to starboard of convoy am engaging." '

'Aye, aye, sir.'

Ahead the starshell showed an empty sea, but immedi-

256

ately to starboard the flare of a tramp steamer's bow loomed over them.

'Midships . . . steady . . . steer three one one.'

The steamer was blowing her whistle and faintly John heard the bellow from her bridge: 'Get out of my fucking way!'

But *Nemesia*'s acceleration carried her ahead and the steamer's bow wave cut into her wake thirty feet astern as she raced out of the northern flank of the convoy. As her questing asdic dome cleared the churned up water of the outer ships' wakes Hindmarsh's face appeared in the asdic hut door: 'Contact!'

John heard it at the same instant. The echoing transmission pipped off short, lost, then regained as Wiggins slewed the transducer at an ever decreasing angle across *Nemesia*'s line of advance.

'Moving right, sir, moving right.'

John bent to the voice-pipes. 'Starboard fifteen, slow to one five zero revolutions.'

On the surface the German submarine could outrun the slow, sixteen-knot corvette. Submerged it was a different matter. The U-boat's best speed was little better than the convoy's. This was one explanation as to why the Germans worked round the convoy on the surface, dived as it approached, and surfaced inside the escort screen to attack before retreating under water. The U-boat they were now hunting had proved greedy and come to periscope depth to launch a second attack; perhaps it would prove her undoing.

Under full helm HMS *Nemesia* heeled over. John leaned on the bridge rail trying to gauge his enemy's intentions. The U-boat was turning east, trying to draw away from the convoy as quickly as possible. Its crew would be aware of the hunt, the asdic signal sounding on the submarine's pressure hull. But the corvette was capable of a sharp turn, a turn of lesser radius than the submarine's, and John listened intently to the return echo from the steel hull somewhere below and ahead of him.

'Bearing's swinging left slowly, sir . . . faster now.'

'Midships, steady, reduce to one hundred revolutions.'

The disembodied voice of the Coxswain came tinnily up from the wheelhouse. *Nemesia* slowed and waited. The

257

indications were that the U-boat, having taken a reciprocal course to that of the convoy, would now make off at her best speed. However, with a corvette prowling overhead, she might at any moment swing one way or the other and she would do that suddenly, having lulled her hunter into the assumption that she was making good her escape.

Left or right? To port or to starboard?

'Range closing fast sir, one thousand two hundred yards . . . one thousand one hundred . . .'

'He's slowed down, slowed down quickly. He wants us to run over him.' John was sweating, the perspiration pouring off him as he strove to out-guess his opponent. The U-boat commander was cool, very cool, and probably knew it was in the last few seconds, as the anti-submarine vessel closed her target, that contact could be lost, the submarine running below the sound beam of the asdic.

'Sixty revs,' John snapped, trying not to fall into the trap. *Nemesia* slowed further, lifting to the low swells and easing through the slight sea the south-westerly breeze generated.

'Still right ahead, sir, range closing to eight hundred.' Hindmarsh's voice was tense with excitement.

Still the conundrum nagged, left or right? And to it was added a third problem. At what depth should the charges be set? A twist of the fuse by the Leading Torpedoman aft would set the three hundred pounds of amatol to explode hydrostatically at up to five hundred feet, and no submarine could go that deep. On the other hand the explosions had to be within fifty yards of their target, otherwise they were wasted. They might wound, but they would not kill. John monitored the sound of the return echo. It was fading.

'Search left and right!' he ordered.

'Bearing remains ahead, sir,' came the reply out of the asdic hut.

'Then he's diving deep!'

'Losing target, sir.'

'Sweep close left and right of the ship's head.' John strained his ears. The note was almost inaudible, already replaced by the strange resonation of an unopposed beam dissipating itself in the vastness of the ocean.

'Target fading quickly, sir.'

'Which way did you sweep first, left or right of the ship's

head?' John could hardly contain his impatience as Wiggins replied,

'Er, left, sir.'

'Confirmed, we swept left, then right.'

'Hard a starboard!' John yelled at the wheelhouse voice-pipe, then moved his head. 'Bridge, quarterdeck!'

'Sir?' Sublieutenant McQueen's voice sounded unnaturally high-pitched.

'Maximum depth settings! Six charge diamond pattern!'

McQueen was too excited to repeat the order, but through the long, meandering copper tube John could hear him screeching for deep-fused settings.

John calculated. The last contact was six hundred yards, three cables, at three knots.

'Fire depth charges,' he said levelly, turning round to watch the stern of his ship. Behind the funnel he could see the blazing *Elleston* and the jagged shape of the second ship that had been torpedoed. Starshell still arced over the convoy as it drew away from them and he realised with a shock that he had almost forgotten about the existence of those forty ships with their complements of close on two thousand men.

In the asdic hut Hindmarsh's index finger pressed the firing alarm and with a dull crump the throwers launched the depth charge pattern, more being dropped from chutes over the stern.

'One hundred revolutions, port twenty.'

John brought *Nemesia* round on a port turn, waiting for the charges to sink and detonate, and when they did he jumped involuntarily. Even in the darkness the sudden pale lifting of the sea surface astern of them was impressive. Then, in an upward surge, a column of water rose vertically into the sky to fall back amid the seething whirls of the initial disturbance.

There was a wild cheering from abaft the funnel, where the pom-pom crew, closed up throughout the action with nothing to do, yelled their heads off.

'Silence there!' John shrieked. 'Be quiet!' Hindmarsh had appeared in the doorway of the asdic hut, his face sidelit from the dim glow of the instruments within. 'Any contact?'

'No, sir.'

'Sweep round again, and keep sweeping.'

They circled the spot until dawn, the June night being short

259

in such high latitudes, but they saw nothing and heard nothing of the U-boat. At daylight John reported his lack of success to *Havildar*.

Ennis was reassuring.

' "Have breakfast with mother," sir,' the signalman reported.

'Acknowledge. Secure from action stations, Number One, and rejoin the convoy.'

Lieutenant John Martin, RN, slipped the binocular strap over his head and yawned uncontrollably. He was tired and disappointed. And, worse of all, he felt horribly outclassed.

CHAPTER TWENTY

Gentlemen Abed in England

Captain Wyatt lit a cigar, swirled the brandy round in its glass and regarded the dancers with an indulgent eye. 'The war has certainly given this place a new lease of life,' he remarked to his companion, an officer from the Admiralty's Operational Intelligence branch. 'Added a certain piquancy, don't you think?'

'Certainly shaken the barrel up a bit,' his friend agreed. 'Never seen *quite* so much available totty. Good tune, too,' he went on, crooning gently, 'what'll I do-oo, if I lose you . . .'

'Who's the stunning creature Lejeune's with?'

'Don't try and poach, Wyatt. LJ is insanely possessive.'

'All's fair in love and war, and when you have both together, well, we're all up for grabs, aren't we, eh?'

'That's as maybe, but the last chap who tried cutting out LJ's prize was mysteriously sent off to Tobruk, or somewhere ghastly. Anyway, you're too old.'

'Careful, old boy, don't be personal. Who is she? You seem to know, so share the intelligence.'

'Her name is allegedly Miss Sonia Starlenka. Russian interpreter, a White, sometime nightclub singer in Shanghai.'

'Starlenka?' Wyatt frowned, trying to recall where he had heard the name before. 'What do you mean "alleged".'

'I think she's married.'

'But not to Lejeune,' said Wyatt, waving his left hand from which floated the silk handkerchief he affected.

'Lord no,' his companion replied archly, rolling his eyes. 'Old Lejeune likes his *objets d'art en masse*; a catholic *connoisseur, mon brave*, one who collects his partners like possessions.'

'So I'd heard,' said Wyatt ruminatively. He had remembered the unsolicited letter from a 'Miss Starlenka' volunteering her services as a Russian interpreter, and recalled passing it on to the Foreign Office. He received many applications from volunteers, a surprising number of them women, and they usually alluded to some naval officer who had suggested an initial approach to the Appointments Office of the Second Sea Lord might be a quick way of breaching the ramparts of bureaucracy. It was a fact that many women thought their talents might be unique, an inaccurate generalisation, though in 'Miss Starlenka's' case no understatement. He watched her through half-closed eyes. The pert buttocks under the clinging dress, the slender waist round which Lejeune's paw was hooked, the heavy bosom pressed with that intimate concurrence that marked the couple as likely lovers led his rising glance to the sheer loveliness of the upturned face with its frame of raven hair.

'Where's the husband?' he asked, not ceasing to watch her.

'He's one of our mob, I think . . . Martin, yes, that's the name. Martin.'

'Martin?' Wyatt looked round. It was a common enough name, yet some instinct alerted him to the fact that this encounter with Sonia Starlenka was no coincidence, and although his faith in the dramatic could not admit otherwise he asked, 'Are you sure? I mean how do you know?'

'Coincidence, really. He's on one of our secret units.'

'One of the phantoms of Force W?' Wyatt said with mounting conviction.

'Yes, do you know him? I think he's the grandson, or something, of that old boy who shot himself after losing a battleship to a U-boat in the last scrap. You would remember. The *Tremendous*, wasn't it?'

'Yes,' said Wyatt, 'yes. I know the fellow.' He ground out his cigar. All the tumblers dropped into place: James Martin, the China coast and the amateur whore from a Shanghai dive. 'How very amusing!'

He leaned back, smiling inwardly, and continued to watch the lissom creature in Lejeune's embrace as she gyrated

262

slowly about the floor, oblivious to anyone but her lover.

The Heinkels found the old *Königsberg* north-east of Lindisfarne, fifty miles north of her destination, the mouth of the River Tyne. She was steaming south into a rough sea and a stiff south-westerly breeze, with an anti-submarine trawler out on either bow.

'Damn those bloody trawlers,' barked Crosby-Milne, his fingers still on the alarm bell as James reached the bridge.

'They'll betray us with their bloody ack-ack fire if they open up.'

'Bugger that, I won't be able to use my machine guns,' Crosby-Milne said, but James banged the rail in exasperation, missing Burton and a proper bridge staff which would allow him to communicate with his escorts.

'There they go!' Crosby-Milne vented his spleen into the wind as the trawlers fired at one of the curiously circling aircraft. The Heinkel peeled off, intrigued by the 'battleship's' apparent passivity as the two trawlers spewed flak skywards. 'Got sod all chance of hitting the bastards.'

James watched as his heavily built First Lieutenant grabbed the training handles of the home-made mounting. Then, realising they had no option, he turned to the bridge telephone and cranked it wildly. 'Chief? We're being investigated by Jerry aeroplanes. Keep steam up as best you can, and give that AA gunfire simulator a go, will you? Yes, now!'

As Crosby-Milne puffed and swore, dragging the barrel of the port gun round to cover the approaching aircraft, James stared aft to where, behind the huge funnel, the canvas of which was dished slightly with the pressure of the ship's wind, pathetic gouts of black and white smoke began to puff impotently into the air, an unconvincing display of futile ingenuity.

For a second he was rooted to the spot, a flash of *déjà vu* paralysing him, reminding him of Jutland and the last moments of the *Indefatigable*, and then the roar of the German aeroplane overhead jolted him back to the present. The pilot was unsure of his target, for he had pulled up and climbed steeply away, the underbelly of his fuselage showing the long grey cylinder of the torpedo. The Heinkel banked in a tight turn and then, as though suddenly certain of his prey, came roaring back towards them. Far above, his consorts, doubtless alerted over the radio, dipped their wings in aggressive intent.

'Come on, you buggers!' James heard Crosby-Milne shout as he rushed back to the bridge.

'Hard a port!' he yelled at the helsman, in an attempt to turn the old *Königsberg* towards the attacking Heinkel and comb the track of the torpedo.

A shattering chatter came from the port bridge wing and, simultaneously with Crosby-Milne's fire, cannon shell from the Heinkel thumped into *Königsberg*'s genuine plating or ripped harmlessly through her fabric armour. The bursts of machine-gun fire and the roar of the aircraft reached a crescendo of noise as James leaped for the starboard machine gun, brought it to his shoulder, threw off the safety catch and fingered the trigger.

The ship heeled, halfway through her slow turn, but the Heinkel bore from both wings of the bridge. Impervious to the stream of cannon fire, James caught the black shape in the cross-wires of the sight and joined Crosby-Milne in the madness of the moment, the methodical juddering of the heavy machine gun thump-thumping his shoulders, the discarded brass cartridges rattling about his feet as the magazine discharged itself.

Seconds later the Heinkel roared overhead, while its torpedo passed down the heeling *Königsberg*'s port side, bounced in the wake and trailed away towards the distant Northumbrian coast.

'Midships!'

'Midships, sir.' At least the helsman was still alive and a bellow from the port bridge wing told that Crosby-Milne had sighted his next target. The second Heinkel tried to compensate for the *Königsberg*'s swing to the east, but made a poor job of it. The plane never bore from James's gun, passing well clear down the port side and its torpedo was dropped more in hope than anger. But the long traverse of the ship's side had exposed it, allowing Crosby-Milne to score several hits. Wounded, the second Heinkel climbed into the grey clouds, trailing a thin plume of blue smoke.

But the third pilot was of a different mettle and aborted

his initial attack, circling the ship and calling the first to assist so they were now assailed from both sides. James slammed full starboard helm on his ship, but her slow response left them at the mercy of the Heinkels' gunfire. Of the last torpedo's track they knew nothing, save that it missed them, but the strafing of the two aircraft left the bridge a bloody shambles.

A flying piece of timber knocked James momentarily unconscious, throwing a shroud of stiff grey canvas across his face and as he came round he seemed engulfed in darkness. Tearing this aside he staggered shakily to his feet. The steel of the original bridge-wing was peppered with holes, the grey canvas of the phoney fighting top above his head hung in tatters. The wind caused a thunderous tattoo to rattle and hammer at the internal wires and rigging screws supporting it. Dazed, James clung to the bridge rail. To the southward one of the Heinkels flew low over the sea, heading east, a heavy cloud of black smoke poured from her port nacelle. High above, the third gave her cover. Mauled though they themselves were, they had driven off their tormentors.

James staggered into the wheelhouse. It was full of smoke from a fire burning in one corner. Slithering on a wet deck, he emptied a fire extinguisher as a party of seamen roused a hose through the wheelhouse door.

'You all right, sir?'

'Yes,' he gasped.

'Blimey, Charlie's copped it!'

Able-Seaman Charlie Renshaw, with the three chevrons of twenty-one years' service sewn onto the shred of serge that hung round the wreckage of his left arm, lay dead over the wheel, his body forked between two spokes and supported by the brass telemotor. His chest had been torn apart by shells and his blood washed in a red slime across the wheelhouse deck. James smelt the hot reek of it mixed with the hanging smoke and fought back the violent urge to vomit.

'Where's the First Lieutenant?' he asked through gritted teeth.

'Not too good, sir,' one of the hose party volunteered. 'He got 'it, sir, 'e's on his way down to the sickbay.'

'Oh . . . very well. One of you men take the wheel. Move Renshaw and then steer one six five.'

Slowly discipline reasserted itself. One of the asdic trawlers was signalling and, after searching for it, James trained the miraculously undamaged aldis light and blinked the response.

'Are you all right?' the trawler enquired and James, with the affected insouciance of naval training, sent back, 'Bloodied but unbowed.'

'See you in Geordie land,' the trawler responded.

'DWWP,' James replied and grinned despite himself when the trawler queried with the interrogative.

'God willing – weather permitting,' James expatiated, relieved to concentrate on petty matters while he recovered something of his composure.

He laid the aldis light on the wheelhouse deck.

'Be glad to see the Tyne, sir,' remarked the man on the wheel, his hands dark with Renshaw's blood. The almost trite normality of his words expressed a profound and fundamental relief.

'Yes,' James said, ignoring the breach of strict naval etiquette. 'Bloody glad.'

'Still, we did for one of 'em, sir.'

'Yes, we did, didn't we?'

'First Lieutenant was fairly soundin' off at 'em, givin' 'em a right old mouthful too 'e was as we came past 'im with the 'ose.'

'Did he call you up to the bridge?'

'Yes, sir.'

'I don't remember that.'

'Well, you was on the other side, sir.'

'Yes. Was the First Lieutenant badly wounded?'

'I don't rightly know, sir.'

'I'll have to go down and have a word with him later,' James said, more or less to himself, 'he did well.'

James was unable to go below until they arrived off the Tyne. It was already dark and the boarding officer from the examination vessel was apologetic. 'You'll have to anchor, sir, until daylight. We've been copping it a bit rough the last few nights. Air raids.'

They heard the lugubrious wail of the sirens, carried on

the light wind that blew offshore from the darkened coast. This was the place *Iroquois* had sailed from on her last voyage, James thought, as he waited for the launch to come out and remove their wounded. He wondered if there was any significance in the fact, any link between then and now beyond the thin thread of his own life's span; or whether the very thinking of such things drew down upon one the implacable disinterest of fate. He dismissed the reflection as they brought the stretchers on deck. It was an idle super-stition, a human conceit that sought to invest one's tiny life with some cosmic significance.

Under his blanket Crosby-Milne seemed shrunken, his eyes bright in the brief flash of light as they lifted the blackout curtain. James knelt beside the stretcher.

'How are you, old man?'

'I'll manage, sir.' James stood and confronted the doctor who had boarded from the launch. The man's face was a white blur, his eyes dark hollows, but the brief perfunctory shake of his head was clearly understood. The insignificant yarn of Crosby-Milne's life was near breaking point.

On the grey surface of the sea the wake of the departing launch left a white furrow. Its exhaust hung over the disturbed water until its dark shape was lost among the greater darkness of the night.

Thus was death, that and nothing more. James stood at the rail, staring west long after the launch had vanished. Above the cloud he heard the drone of the German bombers and then from Shields and Jarrow, and Hebburn, Wallsend and Newcastle, the sky was suddenly crisscrossed by the lancing beams of the searchlights seeking the enemy.

The crump of high explosive began and the thin lines of tracer flared upwards.

'What stupid bloody madness,' James muttered to himself.

Next morning they passed through the boom defences and into the Tyne. He remembered the steep-sided banks so well, with their crowded roofs tumbling in anarchic profusion down to the polluted grey waters of the narrow river. On either bank, squashed in a narrow littoral strip, the bustling dry docks and repair yards resounded to the skull-cracking hammer of the riveters, the gentle knock-knock of caulkers, the bang and crash of repair work to the injured ships: a steel section for a mine-damaged freighter, new shell plating for a holed destroyer, a new boiler for a bombed and salvaged cargo liner. More ships awaited repair while in the fairway others left to resume duty or, laden to their marks, detached themselves from the coal staithes still swathed in dust and made their way downstream to join the next southbound convoy to the London River.

'Ah'll say one thing for Adolf Hitler,' remarked the Geordie pilot after he had got over the shock of discovering Fleet Tender *Delta*'s real identity, 'he put an end to unemployment on Tyneside, man.'

No less incredulous, the tugs fussed alongside her at Palmer's, their big bow pudding fenders crushing the 'armour' until they found solid contact with the ship's side or the sponsons. As they backed away, while James's crew ran mooring ropes to the grimy dockside, they left festoons of torn canvas and the raw yellow of exposed pine battens trailing in the dirty water of the river. After the shelling and the ministrations of the attending tugs, James's once convincing command appeared in her true colours: an exposed sham.

'D'you think you convinced Jerry, Captain?' asked the pilot after he blew the final whistle that dismissed the tugs.

'I think we might have kept him guessing,' James replied, signing the pilot's chit, 'which was all we were asked to do. Now we're more valuable as a cargo ship.'

'Aye, there's been some terrible losses in the Atlantic, they say.' Then, changing the subject, he asked with a pat of the chart table, 'Is she the old *Königsberg*?'

James handed him the signed chit. 'Yes.'

He went down to his cabin where the yard's ship manager and the foreman-rigger waited to see him. Plans and specifications were spread on the cabin desk and an elderly, uniformed lieutenant commander of the Reserve attached to the staff of the Flag Officer, Tyne, appeared and took charge of the situation. James felt ousted, listening to the familiar chat of men used to working together.

'I'd like your men clear of the ship by this evening, Martin,' the Lieutenant Commander said when they were through. 'They can sleep in feather beds ashore tonight.'

'Most of them had their draft chits before we left Scapa,'

James said, then looked round the cabin, aware it had become, like so many cabins before it, what passed for home. 'So she's going to be reconverted to her original purpose,' he said abstractedly.

'Yes, but not her original name. Bit too Teutonic.'

'What are they going to call her?' James asked. It suddenly mattered, for he had grown ridiculously attached to the sham battleship. She had seemed singularly appropriate, a tangible equivalent to his own irregular career.

'Now she's managed by the Ministry of War Transport I believe they're going to call her *Empire Kingston*.'

'*Empire Kingston*. Very neat.' He smiled. 'That'll do. Well, she's all yours.'

James went through into the night cabin and began to pack his things.

In the hospital they told him Crosby-Milne had not long to live.

'He lost a lot of blood,' the sister said as she led James into the ward. It was filled after the air raid of the previous night.

'Is he conscious?'

'Comes and goes. He's sedated rather heavily, but from time to time he wakes up,' she said briskly. 'Ah, Mr Milne, you've a visitor.'

Crosby-Milne's eyes swivelled slowly and James thought he caught the flicker of recognition.

'Hullo, old boy. How are you?' He eased himself gingerly down on the edge of the bed. He felt a surge of affection for the broken man who lay beneath the spotless cleanliness of the bed linen. It was far too immaculate to conceal the ruins of his gut. Crosby-Milne moved his lips and James bent to catch his words.

'Damn country's been no good since the abdication crisis,' Crosby-Milne whispered, the words perfectly clear, though slowly and carefully enunciated as though it was important to the dying man that he communicated them. 'Forgotten how to do its bloody duty. Comes from the very top.' His eyes closed and James thought he had fallen asleep; then Crosby-Milne stirred and his eyes flickered open again. 'Going to be damn difficult to pull through this show. Did my best . . . not good enough.'

He subsided into silence, the effort clearly too much for him.

'You did your best, Number One. I've recommended you for a gong. Do you understand?'

There was the merest indication of comprehension and then his breathing became regular. For a few moments longer James sat on the bed, then he got slowly to his feet. The air in the ward was thick with the smell of carbolic and he walked with increasing speed, as though pursued by demons, until the sharp, acrid stink of what passed on bombed Tyneside for fresh air filled his nostrils.

'*Pro patria mori*,' he muttered to himself, 'a great and glorious thing.'

Like his ship's company, James had received a new appointment and he viewed it with mixed feelings. The order to report to the Admiralty for 'staff duties' filled him with dismay but he obediently entrained for London, hoping for a few days' leave to slip home to Dovercourt. He had heard nothing from Sonia for some time, though their sudden orders to leave Scapa Flow and proceed to the Tyne probably accounted for the disruption of his mail.

The overnight journey seemed interminable, the train waiting for hours, first at York and then at Peterborough, a circumstance that made him think of Geoffrey and John, both somewhere in the North Atlantic, before his thoughts came full circle back to Sonia. He wanted her, ached for her with the intense urgency of the seaman suddenly relieved of his responsibilities. His desire was fuelled by the cheeky repartee of the gallant NAAFI girls who wheeled the trolley of unpalatable but welcome tea the length of the train during their enforced halts. His companions in the compartment, two introspective army officers and a civilian whose defiant air advertised the fact that he was in a reserved occupation, passed the time with the perfunctory taciturnity of middle-class English travellers. To them the government's slogan, 'careless talk cost lives', was a fundamental tenet of life.

Somewhere on the outskirts of London the train stopped yet again and they woke from their dozing, cold and gritty-eyed. One of the army officers went into the corridor, opened a window and leaned out. Resuming his seat he said, 'Looks like a big raid. We could be some time.'

Ahead of them the darkness was pierced by the occasional flicker of fire and, as a yellow dawn broke, the columns of smoke rising from the results of an incendiary air raid added to the bleak desolation of the scene. The train moved jerkily forward, finally landing them on King's Cross station amid the confusion of rescue work and fire-fighting nearby. James deposited his luggage, found a mobile canteen and breakfasted sparsely. He managed to locate an open barber's shop and after a shave and change of shirt collar he felt better. He hated eau de Cologne, but the cheap, watery scent freshened his skin and he felt able to cross the threshold of the Admiralty with a fair degree of self-possession. He was not interviewed by Wyatt; instead a grey-haired and harassed RNR commander named Parkes informed him he was to join the team in the Trade Convoy Plotting Room.

'We need chaps like you, Martin; good sound naval background with bags of experience in merchant ships. I'll show you round now, then I'll get a Wren driver to take you up to your quarters. We've requisitioned a house in Kensington.'

James followed Commander Parkes into the unfinished concrete citadel which formed a grim annexe to the old Admiralty building. Here, in the Trade Convoy Plot and its ancillary Submarine Tracking Room, what would one day be known as the Battle of the Atlantic was being coordinated and monitored. Here the movements of convoys and their escorts were plotted. The positions of the heavy units of the British Home Fleet, of fast merchant ships sailing independently and the egregious collection of large and small ships that made up the northern patrol, the east coast and Channel convoys, were set against the intelligence reports that came in telling of U-boat sightings and the sinister, threatening lying-in-wait, of the big German capital ships. It was strategy on the grand scale, complemented by the tactical plot at Derby House in Liverpool where the Commander-in-Chief, Western Approaches, had his own headquarters. It occurred to James, in a distracted moment as his tired mind tried to hoist in the information Parkes was

271

feeding him, that one of the flags on the vast map might be John's corvette.

'And most of these fellows,' Parkes was saying in a hushed and almost reverential voice, indicating elderly civilian staff, 'are former merchant ship masters. Particularly useful chaps when it comes to the coordinating of convoy assembly, arranging departure and undocking times, giving us specific information about ship types, repairs and so on and so forth. Your job is to take a watch. Each watch is composed of three or four of these chaps, a couple of the ladies and a duty telephonist. We'll give you a day or two to settle in. You'll report back tonight at midnight. I'll stand your watch with you until you feel competent to take over. These fellows know the ropes, you're really the naval liaison.'

James nodded and smiled at one of the elderly masters. 'This is Captain Johnson,' Parkes said.

'Old Bibby man, Commander,' Johnson said, shaking his hand and looking askance at James's wavy braid.

'I'm one of you too. China Independent, though I started in the grey funnel line.'

'Good to have you aboard.'

James had not expected the car. 'I've left my kit at King's Cross,' he said as the Wren driver settled herself behind the wheel.

'That's all right, sir.'

'I'm not being a nuisance?'

'No, sir. I get to drive all sorts.'

He stared gloomily at the dull streets as the Wren drove back to the terminus. The bomb damage was terrible, piles of rubble littered the streets and barriers and shores held rows of buildings from collapsing into the gaps left by incendiary bombs and high explosive.

'It's pretty awful,' he said.

'You should see the East End, sir, and the docks.'

He watched the population going doggedly about their business, a certain grim determination on their faces.

'It's been going on since the end of August,' the Wren said, and James saw her eyes in the mirror, cool grey eyes, appraising him. He grunted and looked out of the car window again. A feeling of concupiscence stole over him, attributable perhaps to the soft luxury of the Humber's seats, his lassitude after a disturbed night, and the odd disembodiment of the girl's eyes. Without the rest of her face to look at, a man might imagine they signalled anything.

He began studying the back of her neck. Her hair was untidily thrust up into the ugly cap. It was auburn and mutinous wisps of it lay down her neck and across the shoulder of her blue serge jacket.

'How old are you?' he asked.

'Nineteen, sir. I volunteered the week war broke out. My father's in the Navy . . . destroyer.'

Mention of her father reined in James's idle thoughts. It might have been deliberate. She doubtless had to contend with all sorts of innuendoes. He felt rather ashamed of his inner self.

They swung into the forecourt of King's Cross and James rescued his gear from the left-luggage office. He made no attempt to revive the conversation as they made their way west along the Euston Road. She was nineteen, a child; he wanted Sonia with a fierce ache. Perhaps he could get her up to London and they could luxuriate in an hotel. A pink vision of Sonia waiting for him as he emerged from the citadel after a night's duty, of Sonia coaxing him into life again and their spending days in dissolute lovemaking filled his tired imagination.

'Here you are, sir. Your digs.'

He had been attached to the Admiralty a week before he saw Wyatt. Afterwards he knew the meeting was contrived, but at the time it seemed quite fortuitous.

'Heard you were here, Martin. Good to see you again.' They shook hands like old friends and James thought time, and perhaps the war, had mellowed Wyatt's chronically old-world attitude. Wyatt smiled and turned away, and then, as though struck by an idea, spun round on his heel, the silk handkerchief flying from his wrist. 'I say, Martin, are you free this evening?'

'Yes, until midnight.'

'Capital! Come and have dinner with me. I know a quiet little place.'

Wyatt's affability mollified James. He was not one to bear a grudge, nor to think the worst of anyone. He saw Wyatt's invitation as a genuine burying of the hatchet, and was glad. They had enjoyed the intimacy of common purpose on the *Celandine*, so perhaps Wyatt wished to make amends. Certainly his invitation lightened James's spirits. He had done little else since he arrived in London except attend to his new duties. Attempts to telephone Dovercourt had either been thwarted by the blitz or the unsociable nature of his free time. Nor had his letters done any better, for they had failed to elicit a response. He consoled himself with the reflection that a week was not long and, having expended his passion in his outpourings to Sonia, waited for her to join him. The diversion Wyatt offered him was therefore very welcome.

Wyatt's 'quiet little place' proved to be small, dark and intimate, apparently contemptuous of the blitz, judging by the crowd. It was also obviously exclusive, the uniformed officers wearing braid that made James's two and a half gold rings insignificant. However, here his RNVR status was no disadvantage for the Volunteer Reserve drew its officers from some high strata of society. It was clear, too, that Wyatt moved easily among this urbane set, and the civilian males were not the shufflingly apologetic worker bees in reserved occupations but the very directors of those in uniform and out, the mandarins of the War and Foreign Offices, the Intelligence Services and the Admiralty.

As for the women, a few were in uniform but most wore evening gowns, apparently unaware of shortages in a war-ravaged country.

'After Scapa I thought you'd like to see that life goes on, despite the worst efforts of the bloody Hun.'

'So I see,' remarked James as they sat at a table next to the bijou dance floor, 'though I have to confess "life" was never quite like this for me.'

'Oh, well, eat drink and be merry, for tomorrow . . . but you know the end of the quotation and it's bad *juju* to say such things. I suggest the duck *à l'orange*, it's usually pretty good.'

James choked down a protest that the normal rules of rationing appeared to be waived here. Wyatt's ease made him painfully aware how out of practice he was at this sort of thing. He had never been much good at social chit-chat, but Sonia had coached him well on the *Shantung* and he had attained an easy facility in small talk. But Sonia was not here and the *Shantung* seemed like something on another planet.

Wyatt ordered two bottles of Chambertin. 'My favourite tipple. See what you think of it.'

James tasted the wine. 'Yes, very pleasant,' he agreed.

'My dear fellow, it's more than "pleasant," it is superb. Napoleon used to drink the stuff, you know.'

There was something waspishly purposeful about Wyatt's bonhomie that suddenly sparked a reaction in James. He abruptly revolted against his own craven diffidence, recalling the dead body of Able-Seaman Renshaw and the dying Crosby-Milne.

'I'm a gin man myself; never could remember the names and dates of this stuff.' He held up the glass and peered through the Burgundy as though the muted light allowed him to appreciate its subtleties. 'Do you get much interruption from the Luftwaffe here?' he asked. 'Or do they only concentrate on the working half of London? They regularly disturbed our dinner at Scapa. Oh, and we got our machine guns. My First Lieutenant commandeered them from a destroyer that was badly shot up in the God-damned mess you chaps got us into at Narvik.'

'I say, there's no need for that.' Wyatt cast a quick look about them.

'He did a good job with them too,' James went on. 'Managed to shoot up a Heinkel that had it in for us. Not quite what you intended, was it, *sir*?'

'What the devil d'you mean?'

'I was rather hoping you'd tell me yourself.'

'Just remember where and who you are,' Wyatt hissed, and tapped the four gold bars on his right sleeve.

'I'm fairly certain you scuppered my chances during the Geddes business, Captain Wyatt, and I'd hate you to think I was too stupid to know. I don't know why, but I suppose it was something to do with my shooting those poor bloody Germans before they turned the tables on us.'

Wyatt's face was flushed with indignation. 'You were a bloody disgrace,' he began, but stopped, appearing to master himself with an effort that perplexed James. Then he expelled his breath.

'Well, Martin, that's cleared the air between us, let's enjoy the duck.'

The arrival of the waiter seemed a reasonable explanation for Wyatt's abrupt abstraction, and they ate in silence for a few moments. The band struck up, killing even the pretence at conversation, then Wyatt topped up their glasses, catching James's eye.

'Lovely women here, Martin,' he remarked casually, his glance swinging from James to the dancers filling the tiny dance floor. 'Look at that absolute peach in the emerald green dress.'

James followed Wyatt's gaze. The woman's back was towards them, the tight sheath dress swelling over her buttocks, catching the light as she and her partner gyrated slowly. Her partner's hands caressed the woman's rump possessively. As the dancers moved in a languid circuit, James watched the woman slowly turn towards him.

At the instant of recognition James knew he had been brought here deliberately. Furious, he turned to the smiling Wyatt, keeping his temper despite the promptings of his thumping heart. 'You bastard,' he said in a low voice, and saw, just for a fraction of a second, uncertainty in Wyatt's gaze. 'Who is the man?'

'Someone rather *potent* at the FO,' Wyatt drawled with affected theatricality. 'I wouldn't get involved if I were you.'

But James was no longer listening. He stood up.

'Sonia,' he called.

CHAPTER TWENTY-ONE

Manhood Held Cheap

'James?'

Even in the half-light he could see the colour drain from her face as she recognised him. The dancers halted. Lejeune detached himself and, with a small ironic bow, stepped back. The act was one of consummate finality, and left Sonia trembling. A moment later Lejeune withdrew. Husband and wife wordlessly faced each other, and although he never took his eyes off Sonia, James was aware of Wyatt's smug amusement.

Sonia's right hand, so lately clasped fervently by her lover, made a pathetically inadequate gesture after the departing Lejeune and then fell to her side.

Wyatt leaned forward on his elbows, asserting himself as architect of the scene.

' "Give me that man that is not passion's slave, and I will wear him in my heart's core, ay, in my heart of heart," ' he quoted. But his triumph was snatched from him. Hardly were Hamlet's appropriated words out of Wyatt's supercilious mouth than a diversion occurred from a totally unexpected quarter.

'Jim? Say, Jimmy, Jimmy Martin, is this really you?'

A tall, dark civilian loomed out of the throng of dancers, appearing where Lejeune had vanished, holding out a huge paw and grinning with boyish good humour. 'You don't recognise me, do you?'

James stared at the American, bewildered, his mind clouded by dark thoughts, unaware that his rising, Wyatt's lolling ease, Lejeune's retreat and Sonia's outstretched hand, looked to an outsider like nothing more than an exchange of dance partners.

'I don't think –' Wyatt began as the fruit of revenge withered on the bough of expectation.

'Juan Garcia,' the large American introduced himself, adding with a drop in his voice, 'Captain US Navy. Do you remember? The old *Schuyler*?'

With difficulty James recalled the friendly lieutenant aboard the American cruiser during his liaison duties at the German Fleet's surrender. 'Yes, yes, of course. Please sit down.'

'Don't let me interrupt.' Garcia cast an appreciative eye over Sonia who continued to stand, watching James uncertainly.

'That's quite all right.' The fog of indecision cleared from James's brain. He turned on Wyatt, depriving him of rank. 'Wyatt was just leaving.'

Wyatt stared at James for a moment, like a fencer measuring his blade, then he rose with affected insouciance and stepped away from his chair.

'*Au revoir, mes enfants,*' he drawled mockingly.

'Well,' said Garcia, 'ain't you gonna introduce me? I've just arrived in London, part of a mission. Well, I expect you know about it.'

James knew nothing of the military and naval mission from the United States. He was looking at Sonia as they sat round the table. She was, as she had always been, most attractive when vulnerable. At that moment, as his heart ached with more pain than pity, he felt the pricking urge to wound her. In the circumstances he could not acknowledge to Garcia that she was his wife, though it was clear they were acquainted. Nor did he want, at that moment, to signal forgiveness or even understanding to her.

'This is Miss Sonia Starlenka,' he said, and watched, quite detached, as Sonia automatically extended her hand and Garcia bent over it.

'You are an American?' she asked, in her breathlessly husky voice.

'Sure, honey,' answered the sleekly handsome Garcia.

For a prescient second, James wondered if pride had committed him to a great folly, but the air-raid sirens wailed their announcement of imminent attack and, without confronting his faithless wife, James, Sonia and Juan Garcia

278

made for the door and the nearest shelter.

Afterwards, James was never quite certain whether it was German bombs or his own lack of resolution that postponed his confrontation with Sonia. Not being a coward, he was, with hindsight and in view of the physical sequel, apt to blame himself. In fact his thinking dodged most of the real issues until he found himself defending Sonia against Vee some weeks later.

At the time the air raid and his resumption of duty deferred a showdown. He (and Garcia) discovered her lodging, a rookery for translators in St John's Wood where accommodation was held for her when she was not spending time with Lejeune. When James did call she was absent.

'Went to dinner with a Yank,' he was told. All was, he recalled, fair in love and war; Wyatt had had his revenge.

James returned to his own cheerless room and the smell of damp cement and plaster that still pervaded the recently built annex to the Admiralty in which the monitoring of the naval war progressed day and night. A sense of duty, and guilt at having neglected it in his fretting over Sonia, drew him back and kept him at his desk hours beyond his rightful stint. Rumours of his victimisation were whispered along the cream and green painted corridors, titillating glee in some and pity in others, for there were more than front-line casualties in the war and fifth columns other than the political at work.

He longed now for a sea-going appointment and petitioned his masters, aware that Wyatt would block anything that reduced James's discomfiture. In the meantime he buried himself in work, an opiate that satisfied the desolation of his life.

In truth, his troubles seemed small. London suffered nightly from the Luftwaffe's blitz and heavy raids had been made on other British cities. In the Admiralty Plotting Room they had marked the huge chart with the position of the Ellerman liner *City of Benares* which had been torpedoed by *U 48* as she evacuated children to Canada; and they had stood in mute tribute to the gallantry of His Majesty's Armed Cruiser *Jervis Bay*, an inadequately armed passenger ship that had sacrificed herself to the guns of the

279

Admiral Scheer in order for the units of Convoy HX 84 to scatter.

Despite Royal Air Force raids on Germany, the power of the Axis grew, subsuming Japan and giving James the cold comfort of foreknowledge.

'It was inevitable,' he told his worried colleagues.

Success in North Africa turned into disaster in Greece. Then, striking at the very heart of British pride, the escaped *Bismarck* sank the *Hood* and seemed to threaten every convoy on the North Atlantic. The Home Fleet, reinforced by units from Gibraltar, cracked every sinew to relocate the rogue enemy.

'We've got her, sir, we've got her!' James, slumped asleep over his desk, felt his shoulder gently shaken. He struggled awake, aware that his small office was filled with the faint aroma of eau de Cologne, an increasing rarity, and that a cheering echoed down the corridors from the direction of the Plotting Room.

'The *Bismarck*?' he asked, grasping the significance of the noise.

'*Dorsetshire* finally gave her the *coup de grâce*, after the *King George V* and the *Rodney*. Well, isn't it great news?'

'Is it?' He looked up, recognising the girl as the Wren driver who had met him on his arrival months earlier. The same grey eyes and rebellious auburn hair were given a wildness by the excited tone and high colour of the girl's expression. She stood over him, her blouse loose but lifting over her breasts. 'D'you know what it's like to be flung into the water when a ship like the *Bismarck* blows up?' he said with sudden intensity.

'But the *Hood*, sir . . .'

'Poor bastards,' he said quietly, ignoring her vengeful justification.

The Wren stepped back and then paused, apparently remembering something she had heard about Lieutenant Commander Martin. He was one of the most handsome officers in the building and his introspection conferred on him a potent beauty.

'I'm sorry, sir,' she began, but he butted in.

'Oh, it's not your fault.' He shot her a disarmingly charming smile, recalling the brief flight of fancy she had stimulated in that car ride. 'It's the bloody war.'

'I didn't mean about the *Bismarck*, sir,' she said, emboldened and closing the distance between her and the desk. 'I meant about your . . . your personal trouble.'

The last fog of his sleep dispelled in anger. 'I suppose the whole bloody Admiralty knows,' he said, then broke off. The rise and fall of her blouse, the sorrow – or what passed for sorrow in her imagination and pouted her red lips – drew him to his feet. Across the back of his mind flashed the arrogant signal, as ancient as mankind, that here stood the docile cow ready for the bull's pizzle; their eyes had met for too long for any other interpretation to be put upon her immobility.

Other messages flashed before him, messages of warning, of being no better than his estranged and lost wife, but they were messages to be ignored. Even the curious question of why this young and lovely woman wanted him, James Martin, beached and lonely failure, as her lover sank under the rampantly urgent tumescence in his loins.

As his lips found hers, his right hand sought and located the light switch, then the soft, scented roundness of her breasts. He was overwhelmingly rough with her, pulling her round, lifting her onto the desk, then reaching down for the hem of her skirt. His hands tore over the precious fabric of her stockings and he gasped as he found the silkier flesh of her thighs and parted her for his own entry.

Papers relating to four convoys fluttered to the floor as he bore down on her and was gratified by the upthrust of her own mounting climax. Not since his boyhood initiation with Emily had so sweet, so intense and so sudden a sensation of release flooded his being, so that they hung suspended together, amid the dust and papers, until his shrivelling withdrew him amid the unlovely tag-ends of shirt-tails and underpants, and he staggered backwards, heart thumping, breathless and ashamed.

He saw Sonia twice before he left the Admiralty. Once, by arrangement, in the neutral territory of the Café Royale.

'I'm to be posted to convoy duties,' he explained, 'and I wanted to speak with you before I left.'

'Yes,' she said. 'I am glad of that.'

281

'I'm going on leave,' he went on bleakly, 'to Dovercourt, just for a few days. I don't think there's any point in . . . in us any more, is there? If there's anything you want from The Lees I'll bring it up to London.'

'No, nothing.'

'I hope,' he said, standing up, 'you'll be happy.'

'I'm sorry, James.'

He could not look at her. Her eyes were full of tears, but they were not remorseful, nor supplicating. She did not ask to be forgiven, to be taken back. She seemed to accept the immense sadness of the inevitable. Neither words nor deeds could heal the breach between them.

He nodded at her and walked out.

'She was no good, James,' said Vee, as they sat in the chill parlour of The Lees, a pot of tea between them. 'I knew it as soon as I saw her.'

'She isn't like us, Vee. Her life had made her different. She is a person who lives for the moment; she could invest the present with an intensity of experience I cannot expect you to understand. You see, most of her past was painful and her future will always be uncertain. The man she was with will not be the last. Yuri, her Russian boyfriend, gave her refuge in Shanghai, I got her out. But then I abandoned her.'

'There are thousands of women who have been "abandoned," as you call it.'

'You see it as a weakness, Vee, because you see our lives as part of a continuum. We, as a family, have our traditions. We have a past with its own triumphs and tragedies and we both look to the future, using the excuse of our *duty* as a vehicle of progress. We hardly ever think of enjoying *now*, though God knows my mother told me to. We're so bloody English, steeped in our history and ridiculously proud of our roots. Why, look at you! You've immolated yourself for John in Tom's name.'

'James! That's not fair!'

'It's true, Vee. And you know it. Poor Sonia cannot understand any of this. She said to me once, for no particular reason that I could see at the time, "Oh James, I'm so happy!" She was emphatically sincere and was quite put out when I had to pause and think about whether I was too.'

Vera softened. 'Is it really better to have loved and lost than never loved at all?' she asked, the whole meaning of her barren life hanging on the question.

'Oh yes,' said James, touching her hand, his voice quiet as he thought of a lashed bundle of life-preservers and a thin canopy of dispersing smoke.

On the train to Liverpool James wondered why he could not have extended such rational justification of her motives to Sonia herself, but he knew the thing to have been beyond him. Wyatt had had his revenge and perhaps he himself had been proved of the same flesh when he ravished the compliant Wren in his office. She had not made an official complaint, but word had got out and his posting had come quickly thereafter.

He had seen Sonia, quite by chance, once more. She had not noticed him, for she had eyes only for the handsome American naval Captain on her arm. Garcia wore uniform now, for the Japanese had bombed Pearl Harbor. Sadly James reflected that he could not bear the thought of Sonia being left lonely and was glad his prediction to Vera had come true. He was pleased, too, Garcia was an American for he recalled Sonia's youthful enthusiasm for all things Yankee in those long-ago years on the China coast. Perhaps her last ambition was now fulfilled; perhaps now she would be content.

As the train jerked northwards James thought of his mother's words on the eve of the Great War. Maybe he had had the fullest measure of happiness life could give him, and only now perceived it. Whatever his personal misfortunes there were others with greater loads of grief, for the Japanese had not only sunk American ships at Pearl Harbor, but had bombed to destruction His Majesty's ships *Repulse* and *Prince of Wales* off the coast of Malaya.

James dozed over his newspaper, dreamed fitfully of the humiliation of bare-kneed discovery and woke in fear of strangulation by a ganglion of ugly, discarded clothing.

CHAPTER TWENTY-TWO

Ships That Pass . . .

Lieutenant John Martin, 'Pincher' to his crew, drooped wearily over the starboard bridge rail and stared down at the rainbowed surface of the sea where fuel oil slicked the gently heaving ocean. Further aft, beyond the break of *Nemesia*'s long forecastle, scrambling nets were draped over the corvette's rusty side and members of her crew, muffled against the cold, were assisting oil-blackened men out of the water. It had become too familiar a sight even to warrant much attention, and John stared instead at a foul object immediately below him, swilling among dark globules of heavy crude and the lighter mess of fuel oil. It was a torn pillow, the once white slip filthy, the blue and white striped ticking now grubby and torn. Feathers leaked from its innards, foul with oil, disgusting things that clung to the polluted surface of the sea with obscene tenacity.

He had been half dreaming of such a pillow, soft and white and inviting, for most of that murderous night as ship after ship of the east-bound convoy had exploded and sunk. It was nearly noon now, and he had been on the bridge continuously since four the previous afternoon. The first torpedo had struck at five twenty-three, according to *Nemesia*'s meticulously maintained deck log, kept in action by the navigator's yeoman, a doctor of philosophy in peace time. From that moment, *Nemesia* had manoeuvred in and out of the nervous columns of merchant ships in her attempts to counterattack.

They had had three positive contacts during the following hours but no success they could positively claim, though *Havildar* and their sister *Nettlewort* jointly claimed a kill.

284

Now they were recovering the last of the survivors, frightened young men from the United States, among the first to qualify from the Mercantile Marine Academy which was turning out sailors by the score to man the hastily constructed 'Liberty' ships Uncle Sam was producing. These were from the *Samtropic* which lay, broken-backed, with her cargo of tanks, aircraft, spares, drums of lubricating oil and essential chemicals, two miles below their keel. She had been built in two weeks, loaded in one and floated for little more than that before a German torpedo lodged in her engine room and blew her frail, poorly welded hull apart.

But John was considering none of these facts. Subconsciously his brain made its cold, mechanical estimate that, judging from their oil-saturated appearance and the hours they must have been in the water, the crew of the *Samtropic* had little chance of survival. His conscious mind simply longed for the support of a soft, down pillow.

Behind him a seaman was cleaning his Oerlikon anti-aircraft gun. It had been fitted during extensive modifications carried out at Birkenhead some months earlier, modifications designed to make *Nemesia* a more effective ocean convoy escort, supplementing the rather inadequate AA machine gun in its bandstand abaft the funnel. John had ordered a practice as they cleared the Mersey on their way back to join Ennis's escort group. The Oerlikons had shot both barrels over the wings of the bridge.

'Now they *are* fucking useful,' was the acid comment of one of the sailors.

The same man now cleaned his gun, a particularly tuneless whistle accompanying his actions, a noise that indicated not contentment but taut-strung nerves at *Nemesia*'s motionless state as she wallowed in the low swell, visible, it seemed, to any inquisitive U-boat for miles around.

'They're all aboard, sir.' Hindmarsh was beside him. 'I waved from the deck.'

'Must have dropped off. Sorry,' John mumbled. He stared down at the pillow. It was still there, though the feathers had spread out a little. He nodded at it. 'Why is it that war perverts everything?' he asked, then squaring his shoulders he turned inboard. 'Very well, ring on full speed, course zero seven two.'

He looked astern as Hindmarsh bent to the voice-pipes. A faint trembling ran through *Nemsia* and the gunner stopped whistling, quite unaware he had even started. Slowly the little battered ship, with her dazzle camouflage and rust-streaked plating, began to move to a different motion, her bow lifting to the sea as she drove forward. Astern, John caught a glimpse of the pillow churned to muck in the propeller race. He could get his head down now, but the idea seemed strangely repugnant to him.

The piercing whistle came to him as if from far off, penetrating his sleep. He reached for the voice-pipe.

'Captain, sir, U-boat surfaced astern of the convoy, five miles away . . . Captain, sir?'

'I heard. Action stations. I'll be up.'

He did not leap from his bunk, but lay until the alarm bells jangled and jangled and he could put off the moment no longer. The climb to the bridge seemed an endless ascent of ladders and only the bite of a rising wind finally cleared the sleep from his exhausted brain.

'I see her.' He followed Sublieutenant Kirk's extended arm, training his binoculars on a grey smudge that formed the centre of a feather of white.

'Starboard five, steer zero seven eight.' John looked over the sloping top of the asdic hut. Behind the four-inch gun shield the new Sub was pulling his steel helmet over his white anti-flash hood. He caught his Captain's eye and gave the thumbs up. John nodded and raised his binoculars again. 'Mr Kirk, see if the Chief can squeeze a few more revs out of her.'

'Aye, aye, sir.'

'Number One.'

Hindmarsh emerged from the asdic compartment. 'Sir?'

'He's going to dive the moment he's aware of our presence.'

John's words were drowned as the four-inch opened fire. *Nemesia* shuddered as the hot fumes rolled aft.

'I'll be ready,' Hindmarsh reassured him.

'Short!' snapped John, observing the fall of shot.

'She's diving, sir!'

Impotent, John watched the grey shape submerge and the

white feather disappear. He transferred his attention from the horizon to the open door of the asdic hut.

The questing sound reached eerily out, dispersing into the ocean unimpeded. John gritted his teeth. Surely to God almighty . . .

'Got him!' They all heard the faint response from the distant U-boat.

'Moving right, sir. Right, and fast.' Hindmarsh's voice was tense with concentration. John bent over the azimuth ring and ordered starboard helm put on the ship. The corvette leaned to the turn.

'Stand by the Hedgehog.'

They had newer toys than the Oerlikons. On the deck immediately below the starboard bridge wing a dozen mortar bombs waited to be lobbed *ahead* of the attacking corvette while she still held the enemy in the conical beam of her asdic and removing those last uncertain yards that had hitherto cheated them of success. No longer did the U-boat possess the advantage of sudden manoeuvre in those precious moments, nor did the Hedgehog bombs require setting, but detonated on contact. Provided they hit the enemy, they could wound and sometimes kill.

Provided they hit the enemy.

John and Hindmarsh and the whole tense group of men who were the brains and nerves of *Nemesia* were growing old at this task. The ugly corvette ducked and bucked, rolled and heeled in the ever-roughening sea as she ran down the pinging asdic beam arcing left and right across her dripping bow, catching first a northward evasion by the U-boat and then an attempt to break to the south. Both manoeuvres cost the U-boat commander speed and range. Patiently John dropped *Nemesia*'s speed, knowing from bitter experience that too-zealous attacks could lose him his quarry. It was frustratingly easy to overshoot. *Nemesia* slowed, the high bow wave fell from beneath the flare of her bow and the roaring of her screw race, heard by the hunted Germans, lowered its pitch to a hissing susurration of deadly intent.

'Tally-ho, tally-ho.' Hindmarsh's comment, though uttered in an intensely low tone, echoed out of the asdic compartment as the low boom of a wave breaking in a cave. The range diminished, called through from the operator bent over the asdic control, heard on the bridge as a sharp abbreviation of the machine's expanding ping, an ugly termination of its musical quality as it echoed into the vastness of the sea.

Ping . . . ing . . . ing, uh! Ping . . . ing, uh!

The echoing attenuation grew inexorably shorter until . . .

'Fire!'

With a not-quite-simultaneous thump the twelve Hedgehog bombs leapt from their bed, curved upwards and outwards in their predetermined pattern, then down in graceful curves; satisfying, mathematical curves that planted them in neat, white splashes, diamond-wise ahead of the corvette. They closed, and passed through the widening rings.

Ping, uh!

'Instantaneous echo, sir!'

Hindmarsh's voice, at the pitch of the kill, sparked the thump-thump of the depth-charge mortars aft and the jangling bell galvanised Leading Torpedoman Potterton to release the rail-held charges that rolled innocently enough through the ports in *Nemesia*'s stern bulwark. Preset to John's orders, the grey cans of amatol dropped silently through the deep and darkening water.

'Lost contact!'

'Starboard twenty!'

Nemesia heeled again and John found himself twisting the binnacle ridiculously in his eagerness for his ship to complete her oh-so-bloody-slow turn.

Out on the starboard quarter, as the corvette's stern flew round, heaping the seas on her weather quarter and cutting a smooth green slick under the lee, the whole surface of the ocean heaved.

John hung over the rail, and suddenly, insubordinately, Hindmarsh was beside him. He found he did not care. The whole confounded crew could hang over the rail and see the massive white, leaping columns that emerged as the sea released the energy of the explosions.

'Midships, five zero revolutions.'

Nemesia crept back over the spot where the violence of the eruptions had killed the wind effect and robbed it for a moment of its mastery over the surface of the ocean. The huge welling circle was sleek with uprising columns of bubbles, dead fish, and . . .

'*Oil!*'

'Any contact, for Chrissake?'

Hindmarsh ducked back into the asdic compartment as though whipped. John stared after him, hardly daring to hope in the tense seconds while he waited for the First Lieutenant's report. Around them the thin swirl of oil had thickened and the air was filling with the horribly familiar stink of it. Only this time it was not their own, not the lifeblood or the garnered cargo of one of the ships they were supposed to be protecting, but blood from the ruptured arteries of the enemy, the hated enemy.

'No contact, sir.'

The flat, noncommittal report was anticlimactic. Had the enemy below employed the ruse of discharging oil to fool them? John increased his ship's speed and made a wide circle. Hindmarsh instructed his operators to sweep round through 360 degrees.

'No contact, sir.'

Had they gone deep? There were rumours that the welded German submarines could dive deeper than their British counterparts, deeper even than the deepest settings on the British depth-charges. Had this bastard gone deep, taken his creaking steel command into the Kingdom of the Kraken?

'*Look, sir!*'

'Stop engines! Slow astern.'

John stared at the water. It was no longer smooth. Already the wind was reasserting itself, stirring up wavelets that would rapidly multiply into what land folk called waves and seamen called 'seas'. Only where the oil spread its foul coat over the water was this agitation of the wind resisted, and in the centre of the obscene placidity a grubby pillow slowly rotated, its centre stained red.

'They could have released it through a torpedo tube, smeared it with meat juices,' said Hindmarsh, voicing his own thoughts.

And then a gout of oil and air came up in a huge bubble from far below, a massive eructation that released for a second a foul stench of stale air, fumes, chlorine and the stink of human fear that stung their nostrils until the merciful wind carried it away.

'D'you want us to fish for that pillow, sir?'

'*No*! Full ahead, steer zero eight zero, secure from action stations. I'll be below!'

And Lieutenant John Martin, Royal Navy, stumbled to his cabin, while his crew cheered his success.

'Tell the Chief we've finished with engines.' John turned from the rail and his contemplation of the filthy and littered quayside of the shipyard. Never had debris, junk and the assorted accumulation of hundreds of dry-dockings, boiler cleans and refits looked so welcome. There were few feelings, he mused, lingering for a last moment, compared with those of a ship's commander as he lashed his vessel alongside a stone quay. The ebbing of tension, the shedding of responsibility, the opportunity to sleep uninterrupted seemed pleasures of the utmost luxury. It was the turn of others now; the sublieutenants could worry about moorings, the Chief Engine Room Artificer could fret over his boilers and cross-head couplings while the First Lieutenant could cope with the inevitable drunks, leave-breakers and human problems that were an inescapable part of contact with the shore.

Was it the Psalmist or some more secular poet who wrote of 'port after stormy seas'? He was too tired to bother finding out. He would have to report to Derby House later, but that could wait an hour or two. First he wanted a bath, and then a sleep.

'Wren messenger on the quay, sir. Cracking looker.'

John gave his Sublieutenant, Mr Foxe, a baleful glare. 'You'd better see what she wants.'

He went below and was waylaid by the ship manager from the yard. 'Dry-dock you day after tomorrow, Captain.'

'That's fine, if you'd like to find the First Lieutenant . . .' He fobbed off the yard man and then found Foxe confronting him.

'She wanted the First Lieutenant, sir,' he said eagerly. 'I've invited her to the party.'

'What party?'

'Why the party to celebrate our U-boat, sir.' Anxiety was

plain on Foxe's face. The sudden whim of a grumpy skipper might blight his chances with the Wren.

'You're not supposed to pick up uncommissioned Wrens, Sub,' he said.

'I'm not fussy, sir. Beg pardon, sir.'

'Buzz off. See if you can keep the moorings tight and the ship quiet while I have a kip. We'll see about a party later.'

He woke in mid-afternoon feeling like death. The ship was a bedlam of noise and he knew only the worst of his exhaustion had been slept off. In the alleyway outside his cabin he bumped into Hindmarsh.

'Bloody lot of noise. Any chance of a cup of tea?'

'I'll see you get one, sir. Actually it's quieter now. They've just finished blowing down the boilers.'

'Oh.' The loud hiss of venting steam had presumably drowned out the other myriad noises that were partly generated by the activities of the shipyard and partly by the ship's company itself. Now the steady, soothing roar had ceased – a noise one could sleep through after the broken nights of incessant convoy duty – the true cacophony penetrated even John's fatigue.

'They'll be starting on the boilers when we're in dock tomorrow.'

'Yes, I know. You've arranged the leave rosters?'

They fell to a discussion of watch details and domestic arrangements, and Hindmarsh joined John to enjoy a pot of tea when the steward arrived.

'I heard something about a party,' John prompted.

'Ah, yes, sir. A bit of a celebration.'

'Waiting until I'd buggered off for my leave, were you?'

'Well no, actually, sir, if we do that half the mess will be away. We thought tonight, before the dockyard mateys get their fangs into the old girl.'

John nodded over his tea. 'All right. That girl from Derby House anything to do with it?'

Hindmarsh frowned. 'Oh, you mean the floosie Foxe is lusting after? No. Well, only indirectly. We sent a message back that *Nemesia*'s wardroom was open house this evening. They've got Coastal Command WAAFs up there now. The boys call it Max's knocking shop.'

'Is that really how you should refer to the C-in-C Western

Approaches, Number One?' John asked with mock gravity.

'Probably not, sir.' Hindmarsh grinned, aware that the disgustingly sweet tea was improving his commander's humour. 'By the way, you will come yourself, won't you?'

'I thought you'd never ask.' The two exchanged smiles.

'And would you give permission for my sister to come aboard? She's up from London. I don't know why or how she got wind of our arrival, but she made her number with a friend in the WAAF at Derby House. That's what the Wren wanted.'

'I see,' replied John, rather confused. 'Yes, that's fine. I'd better get up there myself or Father Horton will want my skin.'

The party was in full swing when he returned. *Nemesia*'s gangway was dark and slippery in a slanting rain that matched his depressed mood. How the revellers had transited the heaps of shores, coils of rusting wire, odds and ends of discarded steel-work and piles of old rags that congested the shipyard without sustaining injury was to be wondered at, but more marvellous was the transition effected to the corvette once the blackout curtains were passed.

The wardroom's guests spilled out into the alleyways, the air was thick with tobacco smoke and the reedily jerking noise of a recorded dance band. The babel of laughter and conversation almost drowned out the desperately jolly music as unfamiliar faces smiled and nodded at each other. John recognised the ship manager and uniformed officers from *Nemesia*'s 'chummy ship' *Nettlewort*, not herself due for a boiler clean like her sister, but suffering from a lubricating problem in her main engines and moored ahead of them for a couple of days. It was the numbers of women that made the biggest impression on John. He had no idea where they all came from and said so to Hindmarsh as the First Lieutenant brought him a drink.

'We've been trawling, sir. Lot of mermaids caught in the net. Cheers.'

'Cheers.'

'I think we deserve it, sir. Earned it with that U-boat.'

'Ah . . . I hope you haven't made too much out of that,

Number One,' John said. 'The thing is they're not going to credit it to us.'

'Why in God's name not?' Hindmarsh asked angrily.

'Lack of evidence,' John replied.

'What the hell do they want? We know we got the bastards.'

'Yes, but apparently the Admiralty want concrete proof.'

Hindmarsh calmed down and met John's eyes. 'You mean they want –'

'Human remains, Audley. Bits and pieces. You'll need more than a few mermaids in your trawl net in future.'

'Christ!'

'Hullo.'

John turned as a young woman in a print dress and with a diffident air joined them.

'Oh, sorry Irene . . . Irene, this is the skipper, John Martin. My sister Irene, sir.'

She had short, wavy brown hair and level grey eyes. A faint dusting of freckles over the bridge of her nose gave her a girlishness absent from most of the other women who were habituées at such gatherings.

'Look,' Hindmarsh said, 'can I leave you two for a moment? I'd better spread the bad news discreetly among our fellows before they shoot their mouths off and end up with egg on their faces.'

John nodded. 'Your brother mixes his metaphors in a particularly disgusting manner,' he said to the girl, aware it was a ridiculously pretentious thing to say.

'Is it very bad news?' she asked, sipping her drink. He told her, as delicately as he could. 'That's awful,' she said, then an awkward silence fell between them though they smiled at each other as they tried to think of something to say amid the noise.

'Did you just come up from London to see your brother?' he asked at last, recalling Hindmarsh's earlier explanation.

'No, there's been some family trouble, a tragedy really.'

'Oh.' They fell silent again and he groped for an appropriately consoling remark but his wit appeared to have deserted him. 'I'm sorry, I'm not very good company tonight.'

'You look terribly tired.'

'We're all a bit done in, I'm afraid. Most of the raucous bonhomie is a reaction. They'll feel awful tomorrow, but much of the tension will have gone.'

'Was it a bad trip then?'

'One of the worst.'

'I'm sorry.'

'There's no need for you to apologise,' he said, rousing himself to a brittle gallantry. '*C'est la guerre.*'

'Yes, it's terrible. The bombing has been awful too, both here and in London.' She seemed close to tears and her plight suddenly made his own fatigue seem like self-indulgence. 'So many houses, little houses with their contents strewn about the street. You keep finding small, insignificant things, things that belong on a kitchen shelf or in a drawing room, things like a family photograph or a doll just lying in the street amid brick dust and rubbish and broken glass.'

He was telling her about the pillows when the air-raid sirens wailed and the party broke up, the last guest hurriedly crossing the brow as it was lit by the first tracer shells from *Nemesia*'s AA guns.

Lime Street station seethed with people as the train from London finally debouched its exhausted passengers. The arrival of a troop convoy had caused much of the confusion, James deduced, but it was clear that Liverpool had suffered a heavy air raid during the night which seemed to add to the heaving mass of people in the concourse. He found an elderly porter and collected his luggage. As he fought his way through the barrier he thought he saw a familiar face.

'John? Johnnie!'

He saw the young officer clearly and for a moment wondered if he had made a mistake. It occurred to him he did not know his own son well enough to be certain and the idea shamed him.

'John!' he called. The officer turned away and seemed to be talking to a young woman with children. 'Johnnie!'

He began to shove through the intervening throng, a nightmarish constriction of the throat urging him to greater effort.

' 'Ey dere, go easy, willya?'

James mumbled apologies and looked back over his shoulder to see if the porter was following. The peak of the man's hat was just visible behind him. He thrust forward again.

'Johnnie!'

But the tired young naval officer had gone and there was no sign of the woman with the children. James stood stock still, his heart hammering in his chest, an unaccountable sensation of panic welling up within him. He fought it back and was left with a feeling of overwhelming desolation. He found himself quite alone and felt his loneliness with an acute, poignant fear while all around him a tide of humanity ebbed and flowed.

'If you're trying to get a cab, sorr,' the panting porter said in his ear, 'you're going the wrong way.'

The train drew out of Lime Street station with a funereal slowness. Smoke still hung over the city in a dark pall. It was as though nothing could exist amid the ruin.

'I'm so very glad you were able to accompany us,' Irene said over the children's heads.

'Audley told me you were leaving today. And that you might need a hand.' He tried to smile reassuringly. She had a lovely face, he thought, watching Irene as she regarded the two saucer-eyed girls who seemed to have exhausted their capacity to cry.

'They're my cousin's daughters,' Irene said, gazing out of the grimy window.

'Yes, Audley explained about the bombing.'

It was a compassionate face, the kind one would love to see beside one on a pillow.

CHAPTER TWENTY-THREE

An Absolute Beauty

'So, you're a goddamn artist, eh?'

James looked up at the young man lounging in the cabin doorway, hands in pockets and the ubiquitous gum giving him the look of a direct descendant of a ruminant ape. It was odd: the Americans he had known on the China coast had hardly ever chewed gum, but the youthful crew of the SS *Samnova* seemed constantly occupied with the task.

'Come in, Captain, sit down. Keep the cold out with a nip of decent whisky.' James indicated the remains of a bottle of Johnny Walker lying on the bunk. 'And don't give me any bullshit about it not being as good as corn-pone or rye.'

Captain Daniel W. Richter, aged twenty-six, looked suspiciously at his guest. Old World facetiousness was a weapon he found hard to parry. He sat and picked up the bottle, unscrewed and swigged at it.

'Not bad,' he settled on, wary of the older, self-confident Briton. The watercolour painting showed small, grey ships anchored in irregular lines beneath the beetling mountains and glaciers of a wide fjord. Richter stared out of the porthole. Five miles away such a bleak slope, of talus and scree, rock outcrops and ledges streaked with snow, confronted him.

'It passes the time,' James said, rinsing his brush.

'Could you paint me a picture of the *Samnova*? Against this Goddamn rock and ice shit?'

'Sure. For half a dozen bottles of decent Scotch.'

'Done.' Richter scratched his head. 'You got any idea how much longer we've got to sit on our butts here?'

'Not much, I'd think. The White Sea must be clear of ice

by now. I imagine it's just a question of gathering the escorts and the covering force.'

'It's gonna be a pretty big show, I guess,' Richter said, draining the bottle. 'Cruisers from the British navy and the good old US.'

'Yes,' James said, 'and all under a British admiral,' he added drily.

Richter made a moue with his lips and stood up. He obstructed the porthole so the tiny, utilitarian cabin was thrown into an umbral gloom. 'Reckon we should be all right.'

'Was that a statement or a question?'

'Uh?' The young man turned.

'Clausewitz said in war nothing was certain, Captain, and the simple automatically became complicated.'

'He sounds like a clever Kraut bastard,' Richter said.

'A very clever Kraut bastard. And if he'd lived a few years later he'd probably have emigrated to the States.'

Richter relaxed when he saw James's smile. 'You Limeys,' he said, shaking his head and extruding a bubble of gum until, with a tiny pop, it subsided on his lower lip to be sucked in with what James supposed was an acquired expertise.

'I heard you got kicked out of the British Admiralty for screwing.'

'Did you now? I wonder who told you that?'

Richter shrugged. Ducking any kind of responsibility seemed as religious an attitude as chewing gum. James rummaged in his holdall and held out a small photograph frame.

'My wife ran off with a Yank. I took a rather mean revenge on a girl in London.'

Richter looked at the photograph, gave a low whistle and handed it back. 'I'm sorry.'

James smiled grimly; so the young man had a heart. 'Good of you to say so.'

'You gonna divorce her?' Richter asked.

'No; it hasn't caught on in Britain, not like the States.'

'It will,' prophesied Richter and, blowing a valedictory bubble, he stepped out on deck. James watched him go, aware that his own mood was brittle and Richter, in the intimacy the American and his British Liaison Officer were forced to endure, was capable of breaking it.

James had fought hard to stave off the depression that had caught up with him in Liverpool. The failure to speak to John (for he was convicted it had been his son) had precipitated a gloom peopled by regrets and ghosts. He had neglected his son and fate had deprived him of even a brief reunion. A few days later, while he still hurt from the desertion of Sonia, he learned of the fall of Singapore. The shock of such an imperial disaster hit him with the full force of personal tragedy: Emily was in Singapore and James was in no doubts as to the likely outcome of occupation.

It had been made much worse by the interminable waiting. He had been briefed at Derby House and even met Admiral Horton who spoke in complimentary terms of HMS *Nemesia*. James had visited the empty ship and found a lieutenant named Hindmarsh in charge. The young man had been cautiously friendly when James revealed his identity.

'We make quite a good team, sir,' Hindmarsh said as they shook hands on the brow. James asked to be remembered to his son.

'Tell him I'm going to Iceland, would you?' he said.

'Good luck, sir,' responded Hindmarsh.

'And to you.' He paused and looked back at the grimy corvette. 'Ugly little duckling, isn't she?'

Hindmarsh grinned. 'Don't despise ducks, sir.'

Despite the joke the experience further depressed him, but the waiting had ended at last and he had been ordered aboard a destroyer on passage to Iceland and the allied base at Hvalfjordur.

Here, in the weeks that followed, as the convoy of munitions and matériel assembled, he took up his appointment as Liaison Officer to the American merchant ships that were joining the Battle of the Atlantic in ever increasing numbers. Touring the functional Liberty ships, James found himself briefing their young crews on the forthcoming Russian convoy.

Richter was typical of his type. A native of Chicago he had been a seaman on Great Lakes steamers before volunteering for the Marine Academy which had, in a short time, passed him out as a mate. So fast were the shipyards of America turning out the standard Liberty ships that promotion to master had come rapidly. Richter, self-confident and able, was a 'veteran' of three transatlantic crossings, though this was his first in command.

But there was a darker side to the participation of such ships and men. Rumours of Yankee perfidy were current among the proud British who, alone in the war for so long, received assistance from their mighty ally with a relief that was tempered by a degree of hauteur. It lent currency to the stories told of Americans deserting damaged but seaworthy merchant ships, of whispers of Yankee cowardice and failure to stop and assist torpedoed sailors from British and European ships. Part of James's role was to gauge the resolve of these Americans, to stiffen it if necessary, and to report on it in due course. In their xenophobia, the British were even suspicious of men like Richter himself, who were of German extraction, mindful of early American reaction to the possibility of a British defeat.

Richter knew this, and it strained the relationship between the two men. James did what he could to hide the somewhat shameful motives of his mission behind a bluster of signals standardisation, convoy discipline and standing orders, and he gave out, on a more serious note, that the British were concerned at the losses of a number of Liberty ships due to weld failure.

'You gonna write a report if we sink?' asked Richter, a smile of amused derision competing with the mastication of gum for the domination of his mouth.

'I've been sunk twice before,' said James coolly, 'and they say things happen in threes.'

Richter had stopped chewing for just long enough to reveal he was impressed before he shrugged laconically and shambled off.

The convoy left Hvalfjordur on midsummer's day, heading north into the Denmark Strait, an impressive mass of allied shipping, nearly half of it American, sailing in four regular columns with an escorting force of British destroyers, corvettes and two asdic trawlers forming the outer screen. Within the convoy two converted fruit carriers bristled with ack-ack armament and flew the white ensign. Grandly designated 'anti-aircraft cruisers', their formidable array lent a grim purposefulness to the ships as they took station and settled in conformity with the Commodore's streaming flag signals. At the rear of this vast concourse of some fifty deeply laden merchantmen two small, tall-funnelled and elderly passenger ships tailed along. With their boats swung permanently outboard at the end of their luffing davits and with scrambling nets rolled at their rails they were the rescue ships, ordered to pick up the survivors from what the grand strategists called 'acceptable losses'.

'Daylight all the way,' mused Richter, looking round the crowded horizon and revealing his first indications of professional anxiety. Beside him on the *Samnova*'s bridge James nodded.

'I can tell you, now we're underway, that our Admiralty only wanted to run these Russian jobs in the winter. Roosevelt and Stalin insisted we keep the Red Army supplied all year.' Then, thinking Richter might resent the implication, he added reassuringly, 'Don't worry, there's the combined cruiser squadron to the east of us and we've units of our Home Fleet including your battleship *Washington* and our aircraft carrier *Victorious* at sea.'

'Yeah.'

Richter wandered into the wheelhouse and left James to himself on the bridge-wing. From beneath his duffle coat James drew out the sketching block and the 4B pencil. Two cables to the west of them in the adjacent column the low grey hull of a tanker, the *Empire Gladstone*, kept her station. Over her forecastle the steel latticework of an aircraft catapult supported an elderly Hurricane fighter. She was a CAM-ship, designed to give the convoy some minimal air cover, while in her tanks fuel for the ever-thirsty escorts slopped back and forth against the longitudinal bulkheads as the ships rolled easily in the long ocean swell.

Below their own hatches ten thousand tons of war matériel was packed. Tanks, aircraft, fuel, ammunition, guns, rations and all the sinews of war filled the wallowing merchant ships, ships from Great Britain, the United States and Canada. There was also a tanker flying the hammer and sickle while the ensigns of free governments in exile flew proudly over the sterns of Norwegian and Polish ships, the

300

flags the only spots of colour above the grey and drab of camouflage paint. As his pencil skimmed over the paper James reflected on the sheer allied effort contained within that visible horizon of placid, ice-blue sea.

But what was beyond the horizon? The Home Fleet and the covering cruiser force, certainly. That much had been made clear to all the masters at the convoy briefing; but beyond them, in the Leads of Norway, the inlets and fjords north of Narvik, behind the Lofoten Islands, hidden in the deep, narrow channels that ran north below the great mountainous spine of the occupied country lay a thousand secret anchorages. The *Lützow, Hipper* and *Admiral Scheer* were there, he knew, and so was the formidable *Tirpitz*, poised to outwit the Home Fleet, brush aside the weaker cruisers and pounce on the convoy. Such a sortie, supported by U-boat and air attack, could destroy the convoy and starve the Red Army of desperately needed munitions.

James closed his sketchbook. At the Admiralty in the now completed Citadel, the symbols of the latest PQ convoy to Northern Russia would have been moved onto the Trade Plot. Similar symbols would show the convergence of the covering cruisers, while off the Orkneys the *Victorious, Washington* and *Duke of York* would be leaving Scapa Flow. But what of *Tirpitz* and her deadly sisters? Would the Norwegian resistance have tracked and reported them moving north? Would a certain Wren driver with rebellious auburn hair see the plot? And if she did, would it cross her mind that Lieutenant Commander James Martin, RNVR, was involved?

He moved into the wheelhouse. Richter was standing beside the helmsman. 'I'll be below if you want me,' James said.

'Okay.'

James grinned to himself. Richter was too proud a man to call him and it was the privilege of a liaison officer, barring alarums, to spend all night in his bunk.

'She looks a pretty neat ship.'

Four days after leaving Hvalfjordur the escort Commander was refuelling the escorts in relays from the *Empire Gladstone*. Richter's grudging approval was for the

301

destroyer *Lancelot* which was greedily swallowing oil from the tanker.

'Yes,' agreed James, his pencil flying over the pad.

'Don't you get fed up with that?' asked Richter, replenishing his supply of gum with a fold of revolting pink.

'This?' James pointed his pencil at the drawing. 'No, it's the only thing that has given me consistent pleasure throughout my life, Captain Richter. I commend it to you.' James paused, then changed the subject. 'We should rendezvous with the cruisers tonight.'

' "Tonight" doesn't seem to have much meaning,' Richter said, 'it's just endless "today".'

'Yes,' James agreed. The constant daylight of midsummer in the high latitudes of the Arctic was disconcerting.

'From up there,' – Richter jerked his head at a cloudless blue sky – 'they'll be able to see us from one hell of a distance.'

The alarm bells went shortly before noon next day. A light breeze had sprung up from the west and puffballs of fair-weather cumulus dotted the sky, but the horizon was sharp as a knife edge.

'Aircraft, starboard quarter!' Richter shouted to James in answer to his unspoken question. James whipped his glasses up. They were coming in low, five, six, seven of them . . .

'Torpedo bombers!'

'Heinkel one fifteens. Give 'em hell, Frankie!'

Ensign Francis B. Howard of the *Samnova*'s naval guard waved his arm as his guns opened up along with many others in the convoy. On the flanks the heavier crump, crump of the destroyers' high angle armament tracked the attacking planes and the shell bursts gathered round the *Kamfgruppe*. One by one the dots dropped from the bellies of the Heinkels and they peeled away, roaring over the tail of the convoy and climbing as they headed back for the airfields of Norway.

'Watch for torpedo tracks!' yelled Richter and astern of them the columns of merchant ships were thrown into confusion as full helm was applied, but no explosions occurred and, to cheers from every ship in that huge convoy, a thin trail of smoke was seen to stream away from the last attacker, a stream that thickened to a dense blackness, a

302

filthy slur across the perfection of the day. As though its blackness added weight to the retreating Heinkel, the aircraft lost height, struck the sea and cartwheeled, breaking up instantly. The trail of smoke thinned slowly and then dispersed.

Around James on the *Samnova*'s bridge the helmsman, mate and Richter were laughing and grinning. Howard came up and had his back slapped as though he had been personally responsible for downing the Heinkel.

'That'll show the bastards!' Richter said, popping fresh gum into his dry mouth.

Two days later they ran into fog. Patches of pearly vapour clung to the surface of the sea, rolling down northward and betraying the not-too-distant presence of ice. Towing their fog-markers, the convoy ploughed doggedly on at eight knots, each ship watching the plume of spray thrown up by the fog-marker of the ship ahead. From time to time they saw their neighbours, ghostly shapes, grey and insubstantial.

Richter seemed more relaxed in the fog, concentrating on the straightforward if wearing task of maintaining station on the flurry of water under *Samnova*'s bow. James felt the nervous prickling of a sixth sense. He could not be certain, but it seemed likely that the mastheads of the ships protruded through the fog. The ships were like great ostriches, their heads buried in the vapour.

Suddenly the grey mistiness was pierced by an exploding flower of orange and red that metamorphosed instantly into a climbing column of dense black. Simultaneously the roar of a lone aircraft engine passed overhead, the Doppler shift of its progress making them duck involuntarily. It revealed itself for an instant, a hideous black crucifix gone as soon as glimpsed. The solitary plane had succeeded in torpedoing a Liberty ship loaded with ammunition on the extremity of the convoy. The rolling concussion of the explosion bounced back and forth, echoed by the slab sides of the ships as they maintained their course, held in a terrible hiatus of shock.

A few hours later the fog began to clear. For a while they traversed a smooth sea, but then a chilling breeze got up, freshening rapidly into a near gale that set the ships lifting and rolling. Again the lookouts shouted and the alarm bells rang. On the convoy's flanks the escorts' wakes fanned out as they spread their fields of fire. In the centre of the convoy the anti-aircraft cruisers began pumping tracer-led flak into the air as, from astern, the Junkers 88 bombers approached and the Hurricane was launched from the *Empire Gladstone*.

It was a futile gesture; once out of fuel the Hurricane had to ditch and the unfortunate pilot rely on a rescue ship or an escort to pick him out of the sea. Even in high summer the chill of the water could kill in minutes.

Around James the *Samnova* burst into angry, petulant and, James suspected, largely impotent life. Her bridge-wing machine guns spewed their streams of shells aloft, filling the ears with their painful chatter while their crews yelled and hallooed like demented English huntsmen. James tracked the Hurricane as it rapidly gained height, watched in spellbound admiration as it tailed onto a Junkers and followed the diving bomber, harrying it with a flood of fire from the inadequately light guns of its early marque.

But the pilot's persistence was rewarded, the Junkers burst into flames, slewed and crashed into the sea. The Hurricane flattened out, overtaking a second Junkers, unable to attack it, but funking the pilot so it too became a victim, though this time of an anti-aircraft cruiser. The Hurricane came on, parallel with the convoy, keeping below the umbrella of flak the merchant ships were throwing up. Then it began to climb, banking sharply to gain height and select another victim. As it passed the head of the left-hand column it passed over an American ship. Even as James watched, the aircraft burst asunder, shattered by shellfire from its ally.

'Oh my God,' he muttered, strangely moved in the middle of the surrounding cacophony, and watching the dissolution of the Hurricane and its pilot in the isolated field of vision of his glasses.

'Jee-sus!' Richter's blasphemy ended in a whoop. 'Will ya just look at this!'

James spun round. The attack by the Junkers had been no more than a feint, drawing the defences of the convoy upwards. Now, like a long, black skein of geese, an untidy echelon of Heinkel IIIs came out of the north their formation troubled by the wind.

'Aircraft to starboard!'

They whirled about. Much closer, a second wave swept in from the east. For the first time the *Samnova* came under direct fire. Splinters leapt from her bridge front and the whine of ricochets screamed left and right. In the starboard gun-pit a man was killed, his braced body, concentrating on his own gunsight, suddenly jerked like a thing shaken by madness and subsided into bloody inertia.

Ahead of them the boom of an exploding torpedo added to the gunfire and the shouting and the engine noise of the Heinkels. The columns opened up and passed the stricken ship as her crew busied themselves at the boat davits, leaving them to the rescue ships which, with cool and intrepid courage, stopped and scooped their crews from the inhospitable ocean.

Watching what he could see of the little drama far astern as the attack ended James was moved to remark, 'I believe more nerve is required in that task than any other in this bloody war,' but no one heard him, for the euphoria of survival had seized *Samnova*'s crew in the aftermath of battle, and he could not spoil their relief.

In the succeeding hours wave after wave of the Luftwaffe's aircraft attacked the convoy from their bases in northern Norway, at Banak and Bardufoss. Three more ships were sunk and a fourth, a tanker, was abandoned on fire and sunk by a shadowing U-boat before an escort could dispatch her. Terrible though the attacks were, they had shot down six aircraft and gained confidence. The losses were, as the strategists would say, 'within acceptable limits', and the escort Commander continually signalled his satisfaction as each attack was beaten off, the lamps blinking hearteningly between the ships, reminding them all, as they emerged from the lonely trauma of battle, of their collective strength.

Morale was high, James noted in his war diary, and the *Samnova* was accredited with the destruction of a Heinkel III, a fact that gave immense satisfaction to Ensign Francis B. Howard and Captain Richter.

But then the uncertainty of a distant and doleful influence was felt, an influence that, like the gravity of the moon, warped the reason of those far-off strategists. London had received unconfirmed reports that the *Tirpitz* had moved

305

north. Where were *Lützow, Admiral Scheer* and *Hipper*? Increased interceptions of German naval signals indicated activity in the Leads, but it was uncertain, imprecise.

Unknown to the merchant seamen of the allied nations who slept, smoked or ate sandwiches in the freezing wind of the high Arctic Ocean, the covering cruiser force was discreetly withdrawn to support the heavy units of the British Home Fleet, being no match for the German capital ships. A little later the escort Commander was ordered to disperse the convoy, a signal afterwards considered not to have adequately conveyed the urgency of the situation. It was followed by the more explicit order to scatter immediately. To the puzzled receiver the sequence of messages conveyed the utmost alarm. He passed the signal to the convoy Commodore and then, in conformity with naval strategy, gathered his destroyers and turned away to join the main British force concentrating on the Home Fleet which would be interposing itself between the convoy and the enemy debouching from the fjords of Norway. The convoy was left with its extempore anti-aircraft 'cruisers', three corvettes and a couple of elderly trawlers whose coal-fired boilers sent a column of smoke high into the clear Arctic air.

'What the fucking hell does this mean?' Richter waved the signal under James's nose with one hand and with the other gestured to the lean shapes of the British destroyers racing south-westward. James fastened his duffle coat and took the signal. 'Those Limey bastards are *deserting* us!'

James frowned, aware that Richter's anger was drawing his crew's hostility upon himself. 'The German battle group must be at sea,' he said, handing the flapping pink signal back to Richter. 'It's the only possible explanation. They' – he indicated the retiring destroyers – 'will be going off to join the cruisers, to bring the enemy to battle.'

'*Bring the enemy to battle*,' mimicked Richter with all the insolence he could command. 'What kind of crap British bullshit is that? They've fucked off, Commander.'

'That's impossible,' snapped James, growing angry himself. 'Our intelligence is pretty good.' It was a poor choice of words.

'Intelligence. Jee-sus!'

306

Richter ran a desperate hand over his cropped hair and replaced his cap, glaring at the horizon. The rigid conformity of the convoy was breaking up as ships swung out of column. Sirens and whistles whooped and boomed as the sudden dissolution of discipline became a matter of each master for himself. James, in an intuitive moment, realised Richter's dilemma. He had been trained to command, certainly, but prematurely promoted to do so only in convoy. Now the survivors would be those who could call on long years of experience; the grizzled Norwegian skipper of the freighter *Frederic Larsen*, the captain of the Russian tanker and the two score elderly British masters whose service under the grimy and undervalued red ensign had fitted them better for this moment than the young Richter.

'Go north, Captain, find the ice edge and use it for cover. It's the furthest you can get from the Norwegian coast and we may get Russian air cover to the east. At any rate the Admiralty are bound to send the fleet minesweepers out from Kola to replace our lost escort if this thing goes on. Don't forget,' he added as persuasively as he could, 'we ran convoys without escort in the early months of the war.'

'And look what happened to them,' put in Howard. James ignored the interruption.

'Go north, Captain.'

Richter nodded. 'Okay, north it is.'

Around them the ships of the convoy were scattering wildly.

They saw the first bergs a few hours later. Fantastic shapes, pinnacled and buttressed, they reminded James of fairy palaces drawn by an immaculate hand. He found them irresistible to his pencil.

Bergs possess, he noted beside his drawing in an inspired moment, *an absolute beauty*. He stared at them in wonder as the *Samnova*'s blunt bow thrust northward across the lead-coloured sea. The gale had abated but the temperature was falling rapidly as they approached the ice edge. This was betrayed by a faint smell borne on the wind and the 'ice blink' on the horizon ahead.

'Crazy,' remarked Richter beside him, though whether the American referred to James, his art or the iceberg was not clear. Nor did James particularly care. He was recalling once again to his comfort the truth of his mother's assertion that long-ago evening on Coniston Water, that happiness is a thing discovered not a thing achieved.

'We'll be on the edge of the pack soon,' he said, his tone of voice oddly unconcerned in the circumstances.

'Yeah,' agreed Richter, blowing a preoccupied pink bubble at the sky.

'And if you'll take a Limey's advice, you'll turn your crew to painting the ship white.'

The pink bubble burst with a soft pop audible above the passing hiss of the sea, and was retracted into Richter's mouth. 'Huh,' he said, 'play possum, eh?'

'Exactly.'

They were unlucky not to make it. They heard the first explosions to the southward where distant smoke smudges marked other ships of the scattered convoy. Then nemesis found them and overtook them with a sharp cry of alarm from a lookout: 'Torpedo track port beam!' Richter's instant 'Left full rudder!' was too late. The last James saw of Richter was the young man's face, white and terrified at the realisation of untimely death in a rictus of fear, his mouth agape. It was an instant image that marked the passing of an acquaintanceship, the last impression on his intelligence made by the experience of life.

As the *Samnova*'s cargo of ammunition reacted to the torpedo's exploding charge and blew up in a violent coda of destruction, James was flung into the sea. The succession of shock waves pulverised his body so that his bruised mind saw only visions. They were not visions of his past life, of gentle moments with Stella in the garden of The Reddings, nor of afternoons with Sonia in the little borrowed yacht on the River Orwell. Instead they were vivid images of the wheeling mass of a doomed battle cruiser's gun house, of the impact of heavy shells on a small destroyer's insubstantial bridge and the flowering eruptions of the chrysanthemum warriors.

As the chain of explosions subsided and the shattered *Samnova* sank, broken-backed, into the Arctic Ocean, he heard shouts and cries, strangely loud to one weighed down with heavy clothing sodden in the ice-cold sea. They came not from the dying crew of the Liberty ship, but from indistinguishable grey shapes, ghosts splashing towards him. He felt strangely glad to see them, as though he had waited a long, long time to explain something.

After a little while he no longer saw the visions, nor felt the cold or the constricting pain in his lungs. In the end there was only the absolute beauty of the last enemy.

CHAPTER TWENTY-FOUR

Fire

'Let go!'

Lieutenant Commander John Martin DSC watched the jackstay slipped from the supply ship *Glenartney*. Bending to the wheelhouse voice-pipe he passed an order that swung His Majesty's Destroyer *Talavera* at increasing speed in a slightly diverging course from that of the fast cargo liner and gave her master a wave. He had become a welcome and familiar figure in his white, tropical uniform, symbolic of butcher, baker, postman and general storeman to the ships of the British Pacific Fleet.

John looked astern; beyond the long-tailed bosun bird that quartered their wake their sister ship, HMS *Busaco*, took station on the *Glenartney*'s quarter, moving in to receive her own quota of food, ammunition and stores. John eased *Talavera*'s whining turbines and the bow dropped in the water as they settled to the thirteen knots of *Glenartney*'s replenishment speed and waited for *Busaco* to complete her own storing.

'Went very well, Number One,' John said as Lieutenant Taylor clambered wearily up to the bridge after supervising the operation.

'Thank you, sir. I never want to see another sack of spuds or can of corned dog as long as I live,' Taylor said. He was tall and spare, fair-haired with a pointed nose, undershot chin and an altogether unprepossessing appearance in his voluminous white shorts. One of *Talavera*'s Hostilities Only ratings, a former undergraduate with a burning enthusiasm for Egyptology, had christened him 'Anubis'.

'They certainly hove the stuff over at a fair old lick,' said

John, grinning, as Taylor draped himself over the rail in a pose of exaggerated exhaustion. 'She's the most efficient of all the ships in the Fleet Train, I think.'

'I wish she wasn't,' grumbled Taylor. They stared at *Busaco*, taking in her own stores at the same formidable rate. Oilers and store ships like the Glen liner had been formed into the Fleet Train to keep the ships of the British Pacific Fleet at sea far from any bases and in close support of the American Fleet as the Allies tightened the noose round Japan. Island after island was falling to the American marines as they stormed ashore under the cover of strikes from British and American carrier-borne aircraft.

Their present rendezvous with the *Glenartney* was to reammunition themselves, pick up mail for the BPF and accompany the escort carrier HMS *Gnasher* with her replacement aircraft that had come up with the supply ship from Manus.

'I thought you'd like your mail up here, sir, while we wait.'

'Thanks, Snotty.' John accepted the three letters from the midshipman. Leaning on the forward rail he turned them over, soaking up the sunshine. One was from Aunt Vera, the other two from Irene. With slightly shaking hands he opened Aunt Vera's, reading it quickly and imparting to the others of *Talavera*'s bridge the welcome and uncensored news that the allied armies had crossed the Rhine. Then, after deciphering postmarks to establish chronological order, he tore open Irene's mail, read the first with a beating heart and turned his attention to the second. It was brief: he was a father and she and the baby were in good health.

'Good news, sir?'

Anubis Taylor's *retroussé* nose scented an event. 'Yes. Boy, name of Robert.'

'Congratulations, sir.'

John nodded, oddly reticent and shy; he turned away and studied the horizon, then reread Irene's letters, aware that his eyes misted periodically and his legs felt unsteady. *If only Audley had been here*, his wife wrote.

John thought of Audley, dying like thousands of poor seamen, dying like John's own father, in the freezing waters of the Arctic. Audley had got his corvette when John handed *Nemesia* over to a newcomer and Hindmarsh had taken command of *Nettlewort* with the coveted half-stripe of Lieutenant Commander on his cuff. John himself had briefly replaced Ennis aboard *Havildar* when a preoccupied Admiralty awoke to the fact that they had a regular officer in charge of what was properly thought to be a reservist's command. John suspected Ennis of having engineered the whole thing, of handing over his escort group, on his own promotion to captain, to someone who would hold his team together as they began to get the upper hand in the long, bitter and almost personal struggle the Atlantic convoys had become.

John had earned his Distinguished Service Cross in *Havildar* and Hindmarsh a mention in his despatches after a night in which they had conclusively destroyed two U-boats and forced a third to surface where a long-range Liberator of Coastal Command had bombed her next day. A grateful Admiralty had earmarked Hindmarsh for one of the new Castle-class corvettes, but *Nettlewort*, diverted to North Russia, had not returned.

John had been in London prior to taking command of *Talavera* when he learned of *Nettlewort*'s loss. He had telephoned Irene to express his sympathy. He might have put the phone down on her grieving silence, but he had held on, remembering the girl in the train from Liverpool. He did not know then that with her brother dead she was alone, that her widowed mother and the two children rescued from the Liverpool blitz had been killed by a doodlebug. The flying bomb had dropped from a blue summer sky three weeks after the allied landings on the Normandy coast.

'Are you still there?' he had asked uncertainly.

'Yes.' Her voice seemed small and distant.

'Can we meet again? I'd like to . . . I don't have long.' He had thought of his orders, the long passage to the Pacific and the chances of war against the Japanese. Was it fair to burden her further? Perhaps she would refuse.

'I'd like that.'

They had met in Trafalgar Square and crossed to the National Gallery to listen to Dame Myra Hess play a Beethoven piano sonata. By the end of the performance they were holding hands and afterwards had eaten at Lyons

Corner House in the Strand. Watching her toy with the limp slice of 'beef' swimming in thickened gravy, he had asked, 'Will you marry me?'

Without looking up she nodded and murmured her acceptance. The world had little substance beyond the present, and what happiness there was available seemed only attainable together. Married by special licence, John had the tact to invite Vera to London. She brought Ruth and Joachim and expressed her approval of the match by insisting on paying for a tea by way of a wedding breakfast.

Vera looked older, John thought sadly, a foster mother to the two Jewish children who seemed haunted now that news of their people's fate was seeping out of Hitler's Europe.

'I hope you'll be happier than your father, Johnnie,' she said, kissing him as they parted. 'She's a nice girl, not like that Russian trollop.'

'What happened to her? Father wrote to say they were no longer together.'

'She ran off with an American. It's happening every-where. You're lucky.' Vera had nodded at Irene, squeezed his arm then fled, her eyes filled with tears. Ruth had pecked his cheek and hugged Irene; Joachim solemnly shook his hand.

Almost sexually innocent, the newlyweds had found in tenderness a form of love more acceptable than naked awkwardness. Perhaps because of this Irene had fallen pregnant on the eve of John's departure to his new destroyer.

'*Busaco* signalling, sir: "Lead on Macduff." '

John was jerked back to the present. Anubis Taylor stood expectantly by the battery of voice-pipes. 'Carry on, Number One.'

At twenty-two knots the two destroyers set course in line ahead to catch up with *Gnasher* and her replacement aircraft. As they overhauled the flat-topped 'Woolworth' carrier an hour before sunset, a shaded signalling lamp blinked at them.

' "Any news?" That's interrogative and personal, sir.'

'Yes Chief, thank you. Make: "New boy in need of Godfather," if you would.'

'My pleasure, sir.' The aldis clattered and a brief burst of

313

light came back from the austere silhouette of the ungainly ship.

'Reply, sir: "Delighted to oblige." '

John smiled in the gathering darkness as the tropical night closed swiftly in. Geoffrey Ennis, Captain Ennis DSO and bar, commanding officer of HMS *Gnasher*, was continuing his personal interest in the Martin family. Aunt Vee would approve of that, John thought, touching her crushed aerogramme in the pocket of his shorts.

'Excuse me, sir.' The Chief Yeoman of Signals was shuffling awkwardly beside him.

'Yes, Chief?'

'On behalf of the ship's company, sir, I've been asked to give you and your wife our 'eartiest best wishes, sir.'

'That's very kind of you. I appreciate it very much.'

What had his father said, that night before the war when *Shrike* had been moored in the River Stour? 'One never finds exactly the right moment, or exactly the right words to express oneself.' How true. John stared at the phosphorescence streaming down *Talavera*'s hurrying flanks as she drove steadily northward into the Pacific night.

'Morning, sir.' Anubis Taylor moved from the binnacle, levering his angular frame into a more deferential stance as Lieutenant Commander Martin raised his binoculars and swept the horizon. It was shortly after four a.m. and still dark. *Talavera*'s crew were standing to action stations. The bridge was crowded: Captain, First Lieutenant and Navigator, the duty Sublieutenant and Midshipman; the signals staff and messengers stared about them, awaiting the Pacific dawn and another day of attrition aimed at the empire of the Rising Sun.

To starboard the twin funnels and three forward gun turrets of the cruiser *Argonaut* could just be made out against the lighter horizon as the dark, unseen swells lifted the two ships. *Argonaut* and her destroyer escort, HMS *Talavera*, acted as advanced radar pickets for the British Pacific Fleet thirty miles away. Beyond the BPF lay the might of the United States' own Pacific squadrons.

For the Americans the Pacific war was an act of personal vengeance for the disgrace of Pearl Harbor, an act in which the participation of the Royal Navy of Great Britain, the historic enemy of the Union, was not entirely welcome. But Task Force 57, as the Americans called the BPF, had adopted American procedures and copied American methods of long-distance supply with a suprising willingness. And if its component parts were apt to regard themselves as genteel if poor relations of their ally, arriving bloodied but unbowed from the Atlantic, they felt they had earned their laurels in bearing much of the brunt of the Battle of the Atlantic.

'How's the world's second largest Navy?' one senior American officer had been moved to signal when British ships began arriving in the Pacific.

'Fine thanks,' had been the cool reply. 'How's the world's second best?'

It is, John wrote to Aunt Vee with a sententiousness that betrayed his youth and would defy the censor, *a fleet the efficiency of which rivalled the old squadrons of Jervis and Cornwallis as they blockaded Napoleonic France; those 'storm battered ships upon which the enemy never looked', to use the phrase coined admiringly by Captain Alfred Thayer Mahan, of the United States Navy itself.* And certainly something of this *esprit* existed in the two fleets which became, for a few months at the end of the cataclysm, perhaps more than the sum of their separate parts.

Thirty miles astern of the radar picket, the marine buglers on the flagship and carriers were summoning their flight deck and air crews to flying stations. Exhausted air engineers and ordnance parties staggered below after their night's work of repair and rearmament.

As John aboard *Talavera* studied the horizon and received the 'no contact' report from the questing asdic, aboard the fleet flagship HMS *King George V*, Vice Admiral Rawlings would be studying the plot in his fighter direction room, and aboard the *Indomitable* Vice Admiral Sir Philip Vian, commanding the First Aircraft Carrier Squadron, prepared to launch the initial air strike of the day. The action was replicated on every ship of those two fleets. Linked by TBS radio the distant pickets watched and waited. John passed the 'no contact' report to *Argonaut* at roughly the same time as the *Indomitable* flew off her aircraft. They too carried out an anti-submarine sweep.

'Aircraft green one six five!'

The lookout's report swung them all round, binoculars elevated to catch, high on the starboard quarter, the rays of the rising sun flashing briefly on the cockpits of the early Combat Air Patrol.

'Hellcats,' said someone.

They trailed the aircraft as they flew a wide, reconnoitring circle round the outer tactical perimeter of the fleet, disappearing periodically into banks of fluffy cumulus. Then they could see each other's faces and the sun itself broke brilliantly over the rim of the world.

'Ah-ha, the current bun,' quipped Anubis Taylor, 'and what will this day bring us? The Chief tells me we're running a bit low on Texas tea.'

'I sent in our fuel state yesterday. We'll be recalled today or tomorrow.' John saw the approaching messenger. 'I wouldn't be surprised . . .' He took the signal, unfolded and read it. 'Yes. On being relieved by *Busaco* we're to fuel from *Indomitable* then play KK ship to her.'

'Oh terrific,' said Taylor without enthusiasm.

'There they go, sir!' squeaked the Midshipman excitedly, and they watched the waves of strike bombers and their covering fighters, the 'Ramrods', heading north-east for the enemy targets on Miyako Shima.

'Bloody fly-boys have all the fun, don't they?'

It could be a monotonous war. The protection of the carriers was a vital but dull task and even the historical moments seemed to catch them at a disadvantage, for the fleet was fuelling on 3 May 1945 when they heard the news of Hitler's death. Perhaps as a reaction to this the decision was made to bombard the airfield of Miyako Shima with the big guns of the fleet. The following day the battleships *King George V* and *Howe*, escorted by five cruisers and the 25th Destroyer Flotilla, left to shell the island, keen to employ their large-calibre weapons. Admiral Vian's carriers remained on station, screened by a handful of destroyers, *Talavera* among them, to provide anti-aircraft protection.

The grey ships pitched easily on the slate-grey ocean, head to wind to enhance the wind speed over the carriers' decks. Hellcats, Avengers and Corsairs of the Ramrod sorties took

316

off after refuelling and rearming aboard *Indomitable* and *Formidable* whose decks were a scene of ceaseless activity. Overhead the Combat Air Patrols circled the ships, while astern of the carriers a lone destroyer was stationed.

At her own 'KK station', HMS *Talavera* wallowed in the wake of the *Indomitable*, covering the favoured approach path of the *kamikaze* pilots. In the sunshine her crew lounged at general quarters, listening idly to the distant boom of bombs and heavy guns beyond the horizon to the west.

'Shagbag taking off,' someone remarked on *Talavara*'s bridge, and a few glasses were raised to watch the ungainly amphibious Walrus lift from *Formidable*'s deck and rumble off over the sea in a westerly direction.

'Some poor bugger splashed,' remarked Anubis Taylor laconically.

'Radar's reporting unidentified targets!'

'Is that from the outer pickets?' John asked, lowering his binoculars.

'Not sure, sir.'

'Captain, sir!'

'Very well, wake 'em up!' John swung his glasses upwards, where the lookout was pointing. Alarm bells jangled throughout the destroyer, transforming the appearance of the men at their quarters. He caught sight of tiny dots, high up in the blue sky.

'CAPs engaging!' Far above them the protecting Seafires were surrounded by tiny puffball explosions. Several of the enemy formation engaged the British fighters, but a nucleus flew steadily on.

'*Kamikazes*!' hissed Anubis Taylor.

'Pass the word!' John snapped, raking his ship from end to end with a quick, critical glance before raising his binoculars again.

The approaching aircraft were no longer dots, no longer objects of distant curiosity, but an imminent threat. The drone of their engines began to rise, drowning the noise of the distant dogfights, and implacably increasing towards a screaming crescendo.

Tin-hatted, John shouted orders, duty-bound to trail in the wake of *Indomitable*, throwing up a barrage of shells to

317

protect the carrier and her vulnerable deckload of fuelling aircraft. He was aware of a nervous voice on the TBS and the arrival of instructions from the Admiral, but beyond shouting the formal 'Acknowledge!' to the operator he took little notice, his attention riveted on the approaching Mitsubishi aircraft.

Trained round, the destroyer's two twin 4.5-inch forward turrets waited for targets to bear; by contrast the single open-breeched 4.5 and the twelve anti-aircraft Bofors guns abaft *Talavera*'s single funnel burst into life with a deafening noise. The Japanese suicide planes roared closer and closer, impervious to punishment, absorbing what seemed like hit after hit without deviating from their targets, the aircraft carriers.

'You bastards!' someone was yelling senselessly as the tracers played round the first Zeke until it was low over *Talavera*'s port quarter, no more than a ship's length away. John thought he could see the dot of the pilot's head beneath the perpex canopy as the plane flattened out, aiming for the *Indomitable*. And then the wall of lead finally shattered the enemy's mythical invulnerability. The divine wind of imperial wrath exploded in clear view. The wings tore away, their integral fuel tanks igniting like burning sword blades slashing at the air before falling into the sea and quenching in a mixture of smoke and steam. The fuselage, nose and spinning propeller held their course as though some diabolic will forced them through to the target until, less than half a second later, the explosive charge the aircraft bore blew it apart in an expanding ball of fire.

'Christ!' The pain of the concussion struck their ears and the stink of explosive gases rolled over the *Talavera* as the debris of the *kamikaze* and its incinerated pilot hit them.

'Check, check, check!' John screamed, his voice cracking and wheezing in the sudden, engulfing heat. Someone cried out with pain and the clatter and thump of parts of the Zeke hitting the destroyer coincided with a sudden rash of holes and tears in the splinter matting. But John hardly observed this, for his attention had focused on the opposite quarter. 'Shift target, starboard quarter!'

Taylor was shrieking his repetition of the order to the defence stations. *Talavera*'s gun barrels slewed round to catch the second *kamikaze* in their sights. *Busaco* was already concentrating on it, while a third and fourth were in close support to overwhelm the British defenders. They were too late. The Mitsubishi Zero, officially code-named 'Zeke', screamed past them, struck *Formidable* in a ball of flame which rolled forward along the flight deck into the aircraft park, igniting subsidiary explosions as fuelled and armed Hellcats and Corsairs blew up.

'Bloody hell!'

'Thank God for armoured flight decks!' shouted Taylor. 'That's one thing the Yanks didn't have to teach us . . . shift target, green one five five!'

The third *kamikaze* came at them from right astern, almost level with the horizon.

'Hard a starboard!' John yelled at the voice-pipe, aware that the enemy pilot's responses were far faster than those of his ship and with the thought came a great weariness, as though his spirit wilted under the ceaseless heat and deafening cacophony of the guns, the thump-thump of the Bofors and the deep, slower boom of the hand-served 4.5s. It seemed the din would never end, that the patient stalking of U-boats in the cold, grey waters of the North Atlantic was preferable to this insane battle with men who, almost alone, fought with a terrible, terrifying obedience.

The roar of the Mitsubishi's Kinsei engine gradually overcame the sound of the guns, as though the persistence of the pilot compelled a kind of comparative reverence, a tribute to blind, stupid courage. The conviction leapt unbidden across John's mind in a fleeting instant that the man approaching him had a son, a very young son who was no more than a babe in arms, perhaps fathered on the eve of some departure like his own.

And in the instant that seemed now inexplicably attenuated, something leapt between the two of them, something beyond reasonable explanation, but something sublime in its intensity and the indelible impression it left upon John's mind; a message clear in the purity and simplicity of its truth. Neither of the young men wanted to do to the other what each was now doing.

John saw the wings dip and caught a glimpse of the neatly stowed undercarriage. For a split second he thought the

Japanese pilot was turning away, and almost willed the tracking gunfire to go wide, but then the aircraft dipped towards him and he could suddenly see, below a brief flash of sunlight glancing off the perspex hood, the face of his enemy as the pilot aimed for the *Indomitable*.

And then a shell from the 4.5-inch gun abaft the funnel struck the screaming Kinsei engine, scattering its moving parts, while forty-millimetre shells from the after Bofors guns ripped into the alloy fuselage, hitting its deadly charge just as the plane drew level with them.

The Zero exploded in an incandescent fireball, temporarily blinding the men on *Talavera*'s bridge. The searing heat of the explosion was accompanied by a vicious hail of shrapnel, peppering the funnel and bridge, carrying away flag halliards, destroying the ship's whaler and ripping the heavy splinter matting.

The paintwork bubbled obscenely and ventilators were torn from their trunkings; the thin plating of the funnel buckled with the blast and men stationed on the upper deck suffered skin burns where their anti-flash gear had been drawn back by their exertions.

A flying shard of the Kinsei engine's block struck Lieutenant Commander John Martin's thigh, severing the femoral artery. He fell where he stood, beside the binnacle, a pool of blood spreading around him.

Part Three – Drifting Smoke
1950-1984

'Smoke comes aye down again, however high it flees.'

Scottish Proverb.

CHAPTER TWENTY-FIVE

A Postwar Childhood

The wooden bow of the toy destroyer thrust aside the long grass of the lawn, leaned a little as it turned, and loosed off a broadside from its nail-studded gun turrets at an imaginary bomber attacking from the direction of the house. The small, grubbily bare-kneed boy pushed the homemade ship further from him, closing one eye and lying down on the damp grass to enhance the perspective. His extended right hand rocked the wooden hull from side to side and he made 'whooshing' noises interspersed with the crackle of gunfire. Curling grass blades over-hung the little ship and he suddenly looked up.

'Daddy, what is the worstest storm you ever had?'

John lowered his newspaper. He was sitting on the sunlit terrace that ran across the rear of The Lees. 'Not "worstest," Bobby, "worst, worst storm," ' he said, taking the pipe from his mouth and watching his small son. He wished the boy did not so delight in playing at war. 'It was a hurricane,' he answered.

'Was that in the Pacific?'

'No,' John said, 'no, you don't get hurricanes in the Pacific. They're called typhoons.' He wished, too, the boy had never heard of the Pacific.

'Was it *very* bad? Like in *Gulliver's Travels*?' the boy persisted.

'Yes, pretty awful,' John replied abstractedly, returning to his paper.

'But what was it *like*?'

John collapsed the paper with an air of resigned exasperation, mastering a sudden flare of temper with

323

difficulty. Peering from the grass, the boy's inquisitive face tore at his heart strings, accusing him of parental inadequacy. Even the length of the grass itself chided him for his disability and, as always when he thought of it, the stump of his missing leg, strapped in its prosthetic substitute, itched abominably.

'Well, even in moderate weather a little corvette will roll and pitch. We used to say they would roll on a field of wet grass. You go up and down and every time you go up your stomach sinks, and then when you start to come down again you leave it behind. Just when it catches up with you as you get to the bottom of the wave, you meet the next and crash into it with a judder that shakes everything on the ship. Sometimes you scoop the sea up and over your deck in big lumps and it bends things and it's very dangerous to be outside. The wind screams and the air is filled with flying spray and you can't see and . . .'

'Oh, darling, please get up off that wet grass. John, *can't* you keep an eye on the boy?' Irene stepped out of the French windows into the sunshine.

'He's all right. Is that the post you have there?'

'Yes. I brought it out to you. There's one from the Admiralty. Aunt Vee's just making a pot of tea. She said that as it's a nice morning we should drink it out of doors. Bobby, please come here.' Robert unwillingly relinquished his game. She ran her hands over his damp clothing. 'He's soaked,' she said to her husband.

'It's just a bit of dew, Irene. Don't fuss.'

'My ship's been in a hurricane, mummy, that's why I'm all wet,' Robert explained reasonably.

Irene ignored the five-year-old precocity. 'He only has three pairs of knickerbockers, John, things are difficult enough.'

'We'll manage,' John said, cutting her off, his voice grim.

With a chink of crockery Vera stepped onto the terrace.

'Aunt Vee, I'm all wet from being in a hurricane.'

Vera smiled over her spectacles, said that that was 'very nice', and called back into the house: 'Ruth . . . Joe!'

Robert sat and accepted his glass of orange juice. In his other hand the toy destroyer continued to roll and pitch, pivoting on his grass-stained knee.

'News is bloody depressing,' his father said.

'Language, darling,' reproved Irene, glancing in Robert's direction. The boy bent over the ship.

Ruth and Joachim joined them. 'Any letters for us?' Ruth asked.

'Yes,' Irene held out an envelope she had been concealing. 'I think this is the one you have been waiting for.'

Robert watched Ruth's and Joachim's faces as they tore excitedly at the envelope with the tricoloured border. There followed a long, suspenseful moment as they read, Ruth holding the letter, her lips moving slightly as she did so, Joachim leaning over her shoulder. Their eyes were alight with expectation. Robert turned away.

'Aren't you going to read *your* letter, daddy?'

'In a minute.'

'Who's for a nice cup of tea?' asked Vera. Her question was drowned in whoops of triumph from Ruth and Joachim.

'It's all right! We can go!'

Later, drawn by the sound of the violin, Robert sought out Joachim and found him in his bedroom. Joachim put down the instrument as Robert entered.

'I didn't think you wanted to go to America,' said Robert as Joachim lay back on his bed. 'I thought you wanted to go to Palestine.'

'Israel,' said Joachim, propping himself up on his elbow and looking at the little English boy sitting on the end of his bed, 'don't call it Palestine.'

'Aunt Vera says it's Palestine.'

'Aunt Vee doesn't understand,' Joachim began, but broke off, unwilling to revive old arguments. Ruth had schooled him to silence, just as Vera had schooled young Robert to this superficial and precocious knowledge. 'You wouldn't understand either . . . you're English.'

'What's wrong with being English?'

'Nothing, if you remember it's Israel not Palestine.'

He could not explain to the boy how his gratitude to Aunt Vera was painfully mixed with his feelings for his people; nor how their fight for a homeland had brought them into direct conflict with the British.

Robert felt confused, as though his nationality was somehow suddenly a disadvantage. He ran downstairs, where he found Ruth talking excitedly to his mother. He stopped, listening from the doorway.

'It's so kind of Sonia,' she was saying. 'She always was kind, you know, despite what Aunt Vera says about her. Aunt Vera never liked her. But she's been in touch with all the refugee organisations and her new husband has been able to pull some strings and we shouldn't have any trouble with entry papers. She remembers what it was like to be a refugee, you see; she was one herself.'

'Yes. John told me about her,' Irene said as she darned a pair of Robert's socks. 'I think he rather liked her, though he doesn't say much for fear of upsetting Vera.'

'And we mustn't upset Vera now, must we?' said Ruth archly.

Irene laid aside one sock and picked up another. 'They are very close, Ruth,' she said with a hint of bitterness. 'She was almost a mother to him.'

'Yes,' said Ruth flatly, and Irene regretted her tactlessness in forgetting Ruth's own mother's fate. 'I'm sorry, dear.'

Ruth had no place in the little provincial seaside town. It was, like the whole of Britain, introverted and exhausted after the war and coming to terms with its cost and its long-term effects. The Labour government was gamely trying to establish a new, equitable social order, an ambition that was constantly disrupted by incongruous intrusions from an imperial past. These intrusions were eagerly seized upon by those who thought that by exploiting them Britain's decline from a world power could be arrested and reversed.

Aunt Vee personified this attitude. She had habitually hectored them at the dinner table as though they were personably responsible for, as she put it, 'giving away' India, or allowing the Chinese Communists to make trouble in Malaya. But it had been the imbroglio in Palestine which caused real dissension in The Lees. Vera was fiercely indignant that British police and soldiers operating under the mandate were being assassinated by Zionist extremists while they undertook the unsavoury duty of preventing the immigration of Jews and the dispossession of the Palestinian Arabs. Her very attitude had encouraged a passionate Zionism in the two young Jews and this in turn provoked more than one charge of ingratitude from Vera.

326

For Ruth and Joachim the revealed horrors of the Nazi extermination camps and the eventual confirmation of their parents' death in Auschwitz, swept aside all such pettifogging considerations. They were not ungrateful; but they could not understand the complexities and the delays, the broken or at least unfulfilled promises in the terrible aftermath of the Holocaust. For them only the future held any meaning; the past was a nightmare of death.

'Aunt Vee doesn't understand us, Irene,' Ruth said after a pause. 'She can't. I don't blame her. I think she's always lived in the past and that is very easy for you English,' Ruth went on intensely. 'Whatever happens in Israel is *our* business. Joachim and I want to be part of it. We cannot be passive . . . We're very grateful to you and your husband, and to Aunt Vee, more than we can ever say. I know she feels our decision is some sort of insult, but we must go.'

Robert watched from the door. Ruth fascinated him with her beauty, reminding him of a picture in his book of fairy tales. He had tried to copy the picture several times in secret, but his failure to do it justice frustrated him.

'I think I understand,' said Irene, smiling and patting Ruth's hand. 'I'm sure that if I was in your position, I would feel just the same.' She sighed. 'You cannot spend your whole life obliged to someone else.'

'That's why accepting Sonia's offer and going to the States is best for us. From there it will be much easier to get to Israel.'

'I'm sure you're right. And Sonia's done a lot for you.'

'Yes. Yes, she has.'

Robert sensed something passed wordlessly between the two women, something forbidden to his immature understanding. He retreated to the dark well of the stairs and made his way to his bedroom. In the twilight he undressed and climbed into bed. The world was a strange place. All about him he sensed danger. He had been told his father was a hero, that the War had been won; but the evidence did not square with this assertion. Only tonight Joachim had inferred there was something shameful about being English. There had nearly been more fighting over Berlin and British soldiers were being killed in Malaya, so the War could not be over.

He did not know these matters in detail, only that they were events he had heard discussed, events which became nameless terrors that stalked him and threw their shadows on the walls of the small room in which he tried to sleep.

Downstairs Vera switched off the radio. 'I've been trying to get you alone to ask you what was in your letter,' she said to John as the sounds of washing up came from the scullery.

'I'm not too difficult to find, Vee.'

'Don't let yourself be bitter, Johnnie. It's bad enough seeing you like that.'

'It's bad enough being like this without watching you cry, Vee . . . don't, please.'

They smiled at each other as Vee hurriedly wiped her eyes. John fished in his jacket pocket. 'Here, you can read it. They have at least gone to the trouble of replying. They won't listen to an invalided lieutenant commander, but I happen to know a lot of ex-BPF people have expressed their anger about it.'

' "It is the decision of their lordships that the cooperative practices adopted by the British Pacific Fleet when operating with the United States Navy be abandoned now that peace-time routines have been re-established," ' Vera read softly, ' "that they were only adopted temporarily and as a political expedient . . . knowing your father's enthusiasm for accepting innovation, I am writing personally to explain that it is not considered necessary for these practices to become permanent in place of the established routines of the Royal Navy." ' Vera stared at the signature. 'Rear Admiral Wyatt . . . Where have I heard that name before?'

'He was on the Second Sea Lord's staff dealing with appointments.'

'Yes, I remember now. I wrote to him. Geoffrey pulled some strings.'

'Have you ever heard anything so stupid? "Political expedient" indeed! It was sheer obvious pragmatism, and to abandon it is absolutely daft!'

'Well, I do see . . .'

'Vee, I know you're a traditionalist, bless you, and I know you care for the service more than half the people in it, but we simply must not pretend nothing has altered. We've been slow adapting before. Remember the submarine?' John puffed himself up and adopted a pompous voice: ' "A damned un-English weapon!" So we never took it seriously, even when we thought we had the answer to it. We became complacent because we simply didn't think the Germans could be better than us at sea. We weren't ready, we didn't foresee things as we should have done and *thousands*, Vee, *thousands* of poor bloody sailors died. They were mostly merchant navy men, not quite people like us, we were taught, good chaps and everything, but by God if we'd not had them, this little island of ours would have been beaten. It's funny how war changes one, but I was actually told they weren't as important as the fighting navy! Irene's brother was a merchant Jack. A terrific chap. I wish you'd met him.' He paused for a moment and then said, 'You know, this attitude of it being all right to put the clock back, to pretend the world hasn't changed and that Britain still rules the waves and the Americans can't teach us the odd lesson or two, or that we must snuff out any national aspirations that conflict with our own, is all quite contrary to the feelings of ordinary people. No, don't scoff, Vee, *We're* pretty ordinary really, and I think if this attitude persists, it'll do us more harm than if we'd lost the war.'

'That's an awful thing to say! Don't exaggerate!'

'It may be awful, Vee, but if we don't change our thinking the world will change around us and leave us behind: Darwin and evolution, and all that stuff. What about the influence of the A bomb?' He began to fill his pipe.

'I don't know anything about the atomic bomb.'

'Well,' he said, striking a match. 'It's changed everything.' He sucked on the pipe so that the flame danced up and down above the briar bowl, punctuating his phrases. 'Like the birth of Christ, or the invention of gunpowder or penicillin . . . though whether it's for good or for bad remains to be seen.' He extinguished the match with a flick of his wrist. 'If, as they claim, it means the end of war I've yet to be convinced. We're about to get involved in Korea by the look of things. In any event, it seems pathetic that mankind has to be compelled to become peaceful by the threat of a bloody great bomb.'

'I think you're being naive in expecting some sort of golden age without the threat of ultimate destruction to keep people in their places.'

'I think it's bloody dangerous to think of one *with* it. Besides, whose version of the golden age do we adopt? The Russians' or the Yanks'?'

'The British, of course.'

'Vee! You haven't listened to a damn word I've said!'

They fell silent, thinking of the past. Before the war when here, at The Lees, Vera had brought John up in preparation for his career in the Royal Navy they had often talked politics. It had become Vera's grand passion. Watching him quietly smoke his pipe as the coils of blue smoke rose lazily above his head, she felt she had failed. He was just over thirty and a pensioner; a man with a broken body and he spoke what sounded to her like heresy.

She had a mind to continue the argument but he caught her eye and she realised they had both become aware of the sound of Joachim's violin. He was playing something unfamiliar, an insubstantial air that floated down through the darkened house from the attic bedroom.

'It's odd that a boy who can play like that should want to be a Jewish soldier,' Vera said, staring abstractedly before her, 'but I suppose Jonathan played his harp.'

John looked at her in pity and, unobserved, shook his head. Bloody tragedy, he said to himself.

'Darling,' he said to Irene later that night as they lay side by side, 'I've been thinking. I don't want Bobby to join the Royal Navy. If he wants to go to sea let him join the merchant navy. It was good enough for both his grandfather and his uncle.'

'I don't think any mother really wants her son to follow the drum,' Irene said.

'No. Probably not. Vee won't agree, but then she never had any children.'

'It's none of her business anyway,' Irene added sleepily.

'No, of course not.' John listened as Irene's breathing became regular. His missing leg itched again and he fancied he could sense his toes; it was a bad sign and he knew he would not sleep until the dawn. He was right about the boy, though, and glad he had expressed his wishes to Irene and sounded her opinion. She accepted so much and, if anything happened to him, he did not want her to fall under Vera's influence. Somehow Vee seemed indestructible. More so than himself.

330

Much later he heard the noise. The drone became a roar as the black plane sped towards him. All the guns were firing with the desperate chatter that met every air attack now. The empty charges rattled on the deck, their brass shining in the brilliant sunshine. The jackal face of Anubis Taylor beside him grinned, then slowly peeled away to reveal the flawless white of exposed bone, and slowly transformed itself into the bound brow of the Japanese pilot.

'No!' he was screaming. 'No!'

And John fought the great weight that hung on him and forced himself to speak, to utter the words he knew he must say, though his very body seemed to impede him with its heaviness. Slowly, with infinite effort he began, supported by the shadowy figures of others. Taylor was there again, and so was Hindmarsh, and his father. And there was someone else, someone whom he did not know but whose presence seemed strangely comforting. They too were uttering the words, a slow, forbidden creed he knew belonged to the dead:

'We are one . . .'

'Ruth?'

'What d'you want?'

'Got something for you.' He stood on the landing outside her bedroom, his heart pounding with the impudence of what he had done.

'Come in.'

She was sitting at her dressing table and the triple reflection of her in the mirrors, of her back as well as her front, suggested an embarrassment of riches which rocked him with a sudden thrill he had never felt before. She wore nothing over her slip and its thin straps and those of the brassiere beneath cut across her shoulders, adding to the contours of her body. One hand held her hairbrush and her luxuriant dark hair cascaded down her back.

He would have fled at the slightest hint of annoyance on her part, but she held out her hand. He was aware of the inadequacy of what he had done and felt shame at his intrusion. She pulled him towards her.

'What have you got there?'

He drew the half-hidden sheet of paper from behind his

331

back. 'It's a picture of you,' he explained, knowing he had not done her justice.

She had expected a black crowned moon face, with the crescent mouth and button eyes of childhood perception, but the drawing was far better than that. 'You have real talent, Bobby. You're a prodigy, like Joachim was with his violin.' He did not understand what she meant, only that it was exciting to stand close to her and breathe the scent of her and feel her warmth.

'You are going away, aren't you?'

'Yes.'

'I don't want you to.'

'Will you write on the picture for me?' Ruth asked, and he bent over the paper, the tip of his tongue protruding from his mouth as he carefully formed the letters with far less facility than he drew.

Suddenly she lowered her head and kissed him. Her loose hair fell about his face and she remembered, with poignant intensity, her mother kissing her goodbye for the last time.

Three days later Irene took Robert for a hair cut. When they returned home Ruth and her brother had left for the United States of America.

Robert grew up in the long shadow of the war. Behind doors at The Lees there was always the awkward figure of his father, swinging his crutch, or clumping on the artificial leg he hated. There were occasional visits to the doctor, and Robert learned his father suffered from 'circulatory problems' as a result of his wound. Gradually, for reasons Robert could not grasp and which he felt were disloyal, his father seemed less of a hero. Short-tempered and peevish, John Martin became a moody husband and father. There were unsettling arguments about money which filled the house with an almost tangible gloom.

In the outside world, things seemed little better. Food rationing and queues, shortages and the make-do-and-mend philosophy which condemned Robert to wear shirts of a disgusting brown – and no assurance that the material was parachute silk would mollify him – seemed to dominate his entire childhood. There were children at school who were somehow 'different', who never spoke of their fathers and were often secretly referred to as 'Yank bastards'. There were others whose fathers had come home changed men after years in Japanese prison camps.

And beyond, the wider world of great events impinged on so politicised a household as The Lees, filling Robert's imagination with further portents. He knew there was fighting in Korea and learned the words *Mau-Mau* from newspapers, knowing nothing of the corruption of colonial life; he heard, too, of places called Dien Bien Phu, Quemoy and Panmunjon without really knowing where or what they were. They became incantations, invoking the dark shadows in his cold bedroom. His insecure heart strove to hold unsuccessfully to the invincible myth of a country capable of the achievements of the Festival of Britain, to which Aunt Vera insisted on taking him.

But sometimes the dark shadows became reality and invaded the daytime. He and his mother had been shopping on a dull Saturday in Colchester when they saw an infantry battalion returning from Korea. It snaked up North Hill from the station, towards the cantonments at Hyderabad Barracks, a long khaki column of tired men who had sent their rifles by lorry and marched with raincoats slung over their shoulders. The nails of their boots crunched on the road in exhausted unison, as though only their corporate movement, monotonously sustained, kept them together. People stopped to watch them swing past and a few clapped or cheered, but most stood in silence. There was no band; the only ceremony the twin cased colours borne at the slope. Robert felt a smarting behind the eyes in sympathy for the soldiers whom no one seemed to appreciate. When he looked at his mother it surprised him to see she was crying. With uncharacteristic abruptness, she jerked his arm. 'Come on,' she snapped, 'we can't stand here all day.'

He had been at the high school when Mr Eden sanctioned 'Operation Musketeer'. The Lees had had an almost personal interest in the war that had erupted between the new state of Israel and Colonel Nasser's Egypt. Three years earlier, as Britain celebrated the conquest of Mount Everest and the coronation of Queen Elizabeth II, Joachim had written to tell them he had become an Israeli citizen and a soldier. Much later they had received another letter to say he was a tank commander. They watched, first with interest and then with mixed feelings, as the confrontation between Jew and Arab became a war in which France and Great Britain were embroiled.

'The Americans will not support us in this crazy venture,' Robert's father said when the Suez crisis culminated in the invasion of Port Said.

'It's none of their business,' Aunt Vera said tartly. 'This man Nasser must be taught a lesson. You're old enough to remember the dangers of appeasement, for goodness sake!'

'Stop living in the past, Vee. Look at Hungary instead.'

But whatever his father meant was not clear, for Russian tanks were suppressing the Hungarian uprising. Robert felt only the shame of his own country when the Americans condemned the Anglo-French invasion of the Suez Canal Zone and Eden succumbed to pressure amid universal howls of anti-imperialism.

'We have to seek a new direction,' said his father at this moment of national humiliation, 'something that transcends the old, national barriers; a federated Europe to counter-balance this insane rivalry between Russia and the States.'

'I don't know how you can say that,' said Vera, her thin, ageing face haggard, as if she had taken the Suez debacle personally. 'What have we got in common with the French who hate us, or the Germans who have dragged us into two world wars in my lifetime?'

Robert watched his father pass a hand across his mouth, as though stopping angry words at their source. Intuitively Robert sensed a desolation, felt that his father knew the same nameless fears for the future that he himself experienced.

John looked at his son. The boy's eyes regarded him unblinkingly. It was useless to argue with Vee; it was the boy who was important now. The thought brought him no comfort. He experienced a terrible sense of despair. How could you explain to a boy that in the split second of a stranger's death you had glimpsed something inexplicable?

'There's always something for even a one-legged man to do on a boat,' John said, belaying the mainsheet of the old

334

gaff-rigged cutter, satisfied with the trim of the heavy brown flax mainsail.

'D'you want to take the tiller?' Robert asked.

'No, you've picked it up very well. It's good to see you enjoying yourself.' They smiled at each other. John had had a modest success with a book of war reminiscences and had bought the elderly yacht the previous year in the glorious summer of 1959. These new interests and activities had improved his health and this was their second season sailing together. 'I'm sorry I'm so bloody useless, Bob, and that you've had to live in a house full of women.'

'Most boys don't see as much of their fathers as I do,' Robert said loyally.

'True. But I'm not much of a father.'

'This's all right.' Robert gestured at the boat and the little waves dancing away on either bow. 'These have been the best two summers of my life.'

'Mine too.'

'I like the way this boat is called *Merlin*, dad,' Robert said, gazing up at the long pendant streaming from the masthead.

'Do you? Why?'

'Oh, you know, the mysterious old wizard, the spirit of Britain, that sort of thing . . .'

John looked at his son for a moment, watching the boy handle the boat and a quite unexpected feeling of contentment stole over him. He roused himself, ducked his head under the boom and studied the Suffolk shore.

'There's the buoy. Harden in the sheets. Here, let me . . . now, down helm. Lay a course for the buoy but make allowance for the tide.'

Robert pushed the iron tiller over and swung the *Merlin*'s long yellow spruce bowsprit towards the Martello tower at Felixstowe ferry. On their starboard bow the green copper spires of Bawdsey Manor rose among the trees.

'They did a lot of work on radar there in the war,' John said as the boat heeled and a roil of white water lapped along the toerail. 'Can you see the leading marks? Hold them in transit. That's it, well done.'

They thrashed past the Haven buoy and felt the inward surge of the rising tide. Suddenly the sea surrounding them lost its benign appearance and swirled wickedly with the dull

335

roar of moving shingle just below the surface.

'Here goes, 'twixt Scylla and Charybdis!' John shouted, exhilarated. 'One false move . . .'

The yacht drove in for the shore. The turrets of the manor were drawing abaft the beam, a wall of sand and shingle surmounted by the martello tower loomed ahead them. On either hand the yellow hummocks of shoals hemmed them in with the surge and suck of the rushing tide swirling about them.

'Stand by to veer the sheets and come hard a-starboard . . . now!'

The bowsprit seemed to Robert to be almost grazing the sand and he needed no second bidding as he jerked the tiller towards him while his father eased the sheets and paid out the main boom. Awkwardly, balancing on one leg, John leaned forward and eased jib and staysail.

'There! Success!'

Ahead of them, at right angles to their initial line of approach, the River Deben opened out. They waved to the ferryman, cleared the Horse shoal inside the bar and made their way upstream. A solitary seal lying on the bank raised its head and watched them scud past, while pterodactyl-like cormorants, drying their wings in the wind, stared at them with beady eyes. They found an anchorage two miles below Waldringfield under a crumbling cliff of red crag and bundled ashore in the tender to fry sausages over a fire of driftwood. Overhead, precariously perched pine trees swayed in the breeze and the pipe of oystercatchers and the lonely cry of the curlew pierced the evening as the chill of night closed in. Soon the only lights were from the leaping flames of the fire and the yacht's anchor lantern.

'Your mother didn't want me to buy *Merlin*,' John said. 'She thought it a terrible extravagance when I had already said we couldn't afford to send you to Holbrook.'

'I'm awfully glad you did buy her.'

'So am I. To be frank she wasn't expensive.'

'And I don't mind about Holbrook.'

'I never liked it much, but I had a rather lonely childhood with my father in the Far East and my mother dead. Aunt Vee, as you know, can be a bit wearing. That's why I wanted you and I to get to know each other. It seemed particularly

336

defeatist to let a missing leg prevent that, so the boat appeared to be the answer. Besides, the doctor was nagging me. I suppose I'll have to sell her when you go to sea.'

'D'you have to?'

'I can't sail her single-handed and your mother thinks I'm crackers.'

'She's worried about you, dad.' He sought to draw together the two people he most loved and who, he feared, were drifting apart.

'Well, the little *Merlin* there's given me a new lease of life.'

'Surely I can help keep her.'

'Do you know how little they pay merchant navy apprentices?' John laughed. 'No, she'll have to go.' He hesitated, then asked, 'I suppose you do want to go to sea? I wouldn't press you if you preferred to do something with your art.'

Robert shook his head. 'No, dad. I want to go to sea. I enjoy drawing and painting, but I do want to go to sea.'

'Your grandfather was quite proficient with a box of watercolours . . . Bob, did you ever want to try for the Royal Navy?'

He watched his son in the firelight for any sign of resentment at being denied a career in the Senior Service. But Robert smiled, and gave a snort of mild contempt. 'Aunt Vee used to nag me, try and win me round, but no, dad, never. The Navy will cease to exist in a few years. We've no use for it and it's shrunk so much it's virtually useless.'

'I'm rather glad you decided things that way.'

'I know you had to fight Hitler, but I hope there won't be another big war.'

'Amen to that,' replied his father, lighting a last cigarette from a burning twig. 'You know, you must never do something you think is wrong just because someone in authority tells you it's right.' He threw the twig back into the fire. ' "With what a genius for administration," ' he quoted, ' "we rearrange the rumbling universe – And map the course of man's regeneration – Over a pipe"!' He laughed awkwardly. 'Or in this case a cigarette.'

Across the fire his son lowered his eyes to stare into the glowing embers.

'I learned that from a *kamikaze* pilot,' John went on, 'just before his exploding Zeke cut off my leg.' He smiled ruefully.

337

'I have just imparted to you the entire wisdom culled in my lifetime. Help me up, will you?'

Robert hoisted his father onto his crutch, kicked out the fire and dragged the dinghy back into the water. 'You know,' said John wading out and clambering in, one hand supporting himself on Robert's shoulder, 'it never occurred to me that Long John Silver only ever got one foot wet.'

'That's what my friends call you.'

'What? Long John Silver?'

'Yes.'

'Bloody cheek! Apt, but still a bloody cheek!'

Later, in the darkness of *Merlin*'s saloon, John lay under his blankets and stared out through the small square of the hatch. A dark patch of sky was spangled with stars. He listened to Robert's even breathing and wondered if, unlike his own father, he had finally learnt to say the things he meant to his son.

CHAPTER TWENTY-SIX

Singapore

The black hull with its smart, white-painted superstructure, varnished teak bridge, brown masts and sampson-posts and buff funnel, drove through the blue sea with a feather of white at the bow, lifting and falling gently in the low Indian Ocean swell. The sea was glassy, its smooth surface disfigured only by an occasional pattern of ripples where a zephyr disturbed it. As the cargo liner *Loch Barcadale* ran eastward at a steady sixteen knots flying fish lifted from its path, dispersing on either side of the hurrying bow in long low glides. From time to time dolphins would streak in from the quarters to gambol and frolic in the ship's wake, or ride the submarine pressure wave under the bow that preceded the huge hull.

For Apprentice Martin, keeping his first watches on the bridge or turned to chipping and painting with the amicably rough-tongued seamen, such an ambience was touched with magic. Warm without being hot (a marvellous contrast after the northern winter they had left, or the ferocious heat of the bunkering station at Aden) the air possessed a quality of freshness that tingled in his nostrils.

The sense of freedom Robert experienced was overwhelming, marred only by a tinge of guilt at his disloyalty to his home. The Lees seemed now to have attracted by its sheer gravity, an excessive measure of gloom. His father's immobile frustration, his mother's disappointment and Aunt Vera's political obsession had, it seemed, rendered the very air of the place unbreathable in his last few weeks there. The only bright memories were those of sailing *Merlin* with his father, when he had seemed a different man from the morose invalid he became in the house.

'Do you *have* to sell her, dad?' he had said as they came ashore for the last time.

'Yes. Let's not be sentimental. Without you, I shan't do any sailing.'

'What about when I come home on leave?'

His father had laughed, a trace of bitterness in it. 'You won't want to hang around The Lees, my lad, or at least I hope you won't. No, it was good while it lasted . . .'

But his father's last letter, received at Aden, had said no more than the yacht was on the market and Robert, with the optimism of the young, thought he might yet save her and recapture those happy days again. Nursing such illusions, Apprentice Robert Martin walked up and down with no more clouds on his personal horizon than there were above the circle of sea visible from the bridge of the motor vessel *Loch Barcadale*.

Apart, that was, from the verrucas. His three fellow apprentices were decent enough young men, except one of them had infected the shower stall and Robert was suffering in consequence. He was beginning to limp rather conspicuously, and the ball of his right foot was an unpleasant sight.

'You should show it to a quack when we get to Singapore,' advised the Second Mate with whom he stood his watch. 'See the Mate about it.'

Robert bore the increasing discomfort stoically. Sympathy, he quickly discovered, was in short supply at sea. 'In my day,' said the First Mate drily when asked to make arrangements for Apprentice Martin to consult a doctor, 'we used to cut them out with our sheath knives.'

'I thought in *your* day you bit them out with your teeth,' said the Second Mate, overhearing Robert's request.

'We were not so clever at opening our mouths and putting our feet in it as you, Second.'

And Robert grinned, delighted to be among this light, amiable banter between easy-going, confident men. It augured well for the future and held a bright promise of adventure. He remembered two events in his childhood that had seemed to indicate such excitement existed outside The Lees, excitement divorced from the grim fear of war but which tested courage and endurance in the eternal struggle

340

of man against nature. The idea of such adventure had gripped Robert's imagination early.

The first of these was the loss of the American merchant ship *Flying Enterprise* which had occurred in the English Channel when her cargo of grain shifted. The ship listed and shipped water in appalling weather. The endeavours of the salvage tug *Turmoil* to tow the disabled ship into Falmouth and the determination of her master, Captain Carlsen, left on board alone after ordering his crew to abandon ship, seemed an epic from the pages of the *Boys' Own Paper*. It became national news and was followed for several days with avid interest until the ship sank and Carlsen came ashore to a hero's welcome.

The second such event had been the loss of the South Goodwin lightvessel, torn from her moorings during an exceptionally violent winter storm and dashed on the Goodwin Sands with the loss of her crew. Only one man had escaped, an observer from the Ministry of Agriculture, Fisheries and Food, whose poignant account of her last moments captured the sentimental imagination of a lonely boy.

The long, curving crescent of Keppel Harbour at Singapore was full of ships. The white liners of the Messageries Maritimes and the P and O were in sharp contrast with the black-hulled cargo liners and tramp ships. A few Danes, Swedes and Norwegians, a pair of German, three Japanese and two Russian cargo vessels discharged or loaded cargo. Others waited for berths, at anchor in the Eastern or Western Roads. Among the tramp ships the Panamanian and Liberian flags were prominent, but the majority wore the red merchant ensign of Great Britain. For whatever Aunt Vee's gloomy prognostications as to the fate of post-Imperial Britain, the great British shipping houses were adapting to a changed world and the trade that had in truth preceded the flag seemed set to outlast it.

Accorded the precedence of a scheduled run, the *Loch Barcadale* eased into her berth without the assistance of a tug. Robert was swept into the organised bedlam of cargo work in an oriental port. The immaculate, yacht-like appearance of the ship was transformed into an overcrowded, dusty hulk, the neatly stowed derricks were topped up and swung over hold and wharf, their wire runners snaking dangerously when slack and jerking tight as sling after sling of machine parts, drums of chemicals, reels of wire, vehicles, beer, spirits, processed food, light manufactured goods and all the necessities of twentieth-century modernity were lifted from her capacious holds. Gangs of dockers, Malays and Chinese, toiled in the heat, their bodies gleaming with sweat, the air raucous with their hawking and chatter. During their rest periods the ship's upper deck alleyways filled with their inert bodies, prone upon coconut matting. Robert found himself thrust out 'on deck' to assist the junior mates in the supervision of the discharge, somewhat disappointed he had not been the first to hobble down the gangway in search of treatment for his foot.

'Martin!' He was in the lower hold of number two hatch, searching for a lost item of cargo, when the Second Mate's bellow drew him to the hatch square and he screwed up his eyes against the glare of the sky above. 'Agent's here with his car. You can go to the doctor.'

Robert looked down at his soiled khaki denims, then began the long ascent up the vertical ladder. A gang of Chinese working in the tween-deck grinned at him. One made an obscene gesture. 'You fuckee dirty woman, eh Johnnie?' They burst into laughter. At the top of the ladder the Second Mate grinned. 'Go on, bugger off. But come straight back, you're not a bloody tourist.'

The hospital was crowded. Shuffling Chinese women in black *samfoo* pyjamas, Malays in *sarongs*, the men in T-shirts, cotton trousers and flip-flops, chattered and smoked. Children of all ages seemed to be everywhere, lolling on their mothers' backs, toddling uncertainly a few arm's lengths from the maternal reach, or running about madly. The air smelled of humanity and a heartless antiseptic reek that compounded to remind one of mortality. The agent's runner left him, conspicuously English, in a long queue.

'You'll be here a couple of hours. Can you find your own way back to the ship? You can always take a taxi.'

Robert checked on his small advance of Malay dollars. He had hoped to spend them on something more tangibly

342

exotic, but he said, 'Yes, I'm fine.'

He found the agent's runner had not exaggerated. The forenoon wore on and the squalling of babies became an integral part of his headache. From time to time a white-coated houseman breezed through the narrow corridor and Robert considered the novelty of consulting a Chinese or Indian doctor. He watched a gecko chase flies, and, when the nurses made their appearance to call in the next patient, he lusted mildly after them and thought idly of Ruth. He must have dozed, for one of them, a pretty, slightly pockmarked Chinese girl was bending over him. 'Mr Martin? Come this way, please.'

The curtained area was part of a larger space. The hum and noise of humanity seemed undiminished. With a rasp of curtain rings the nurse left him. He sat, took off his shoes and socks and waited. The curtain rasped again and a woman doctor appeared. Her face was averted as she continued to speak to someone out of Robert's sight. Then she swept the curtain behind her and turned to him. For a moment he thought it was she who was ill, for she was elderly, a fine-boned, handsome woman whose bronzed complexion suddenly became the colour of ivory.

She caught the frame of the consulting couch and steadied herself as Robert stood and put out a hand. He felt the intensity of her scrutiny with discomfort. 'Are you all right, ma'am?' he enquired, alarmed and embarrassed.

She waved him away, and recovered her composure. 'What's your name?' she asked abruptly, taking the offered letter headed with the agent's name that he held out. 'What ship?' She was fishing for spectacles which, when she found them, she did not put on, but held like a lorgnette. 'Martin!' she breathed, before Robert had had a chance to answer.

'Yes,' he said, 'from the *Loch Barcadale*.'

'Date of birth?' She was quizzing him, her blue eyes uncomfortably piercing.

'Nineteen forty five. These verrucas . . .'

'Your father,' she went on, speaking urgently. 'When was he born?'

'My father?' Robert frowned.

'When was he born? And did your grandfather ever live in Hong Kong?'

343

'Yes, he was master of the . . . er, the *Shantung*, I think.'
Comprehension dawned on Robert. 'Did you know him?' he
asked.

'Where does he live now? Is he still at sea?' she said, not
answering him.

'No, he's dead.'

Although she was standing stock still Robert thought
afterwards his words had stopped some forward movement
in her. Perhaps it was her eyes, for they were amazingly
bright, and it seemed to him that the light in them became
extinguished. 'When was this?' she asked, and her voice,
too, seemed diminished.

'He was killed in a convoy during the war. I never knew
him.'

'Do you know his wife?'

'The Russian lady? No, I believe they separated before I
was born.'

She sighed, recovering her composure. 'Sit down and let
me have a look.'

'She lives in America now,' he added, raising his infected
foot.

'She would.' She picked up a scalpel and probed the mass
of verrucas. 'You're infested. It's a viral infection, you
know. Eventually you'll acquire immunity.' She glanced up
at him. 'You're incredibly like your grandfather. I think
you'd better have dinner with me this evening, if they'll let
you off your ship. Now, these verrucas can be intrac-
table . . .'

'Yes, they're rather painful too. D'you mind if I ask your
name?'

'Plunkett,' she said, wielding the scalpel. 'Doctor Emily
Plunkett.'

The excoriations of the sulphuric acid on his foot combined
with a note to the Chief Officer of the *Loch Barcadale* to
ensure he was waiting for her at the foot of the gangway that
evening. He hobbled across the wharf to her car.

'What did you tell them?' she asked as she let in the clutch
and the aged little MG tourer accelerated in a swirl of dust.

'That you were an adopted aunt, an old friend of the
family.'

344

'I don't know that "friend" would be quite the right description for me,' she said. 'I was your grandfather's mistress.'

'Oh!' Robert looked at her with sudden prurient interest. Her grey hair was drawn back and rolled at the nape of her neck; in profile her fine drawn skull reminded him of an Italian renaissance portrait. She glanced at him briefly and smiled.

'Are you shocked?' she asked.

'Er, I don't know. I suppose I shouldn't be . . .'

She changed gear, her hand close to his knee. The dark blemishes on the delicately thin skin, the prominent blue of her blood vessels told of age, but the capability of the hand, the assurance in the movement of a long thigh double declutching beneath the elegant silk print dress were far from repulsive.

'No,' he said, suddenly emboldened, for he felt thrilled, liberated by this strange encounter, 'I'm not shocked at all.'

'Good,' she said. 'If you were I'm sure we wouldn't get along.'

They arrived at her bungalow, a modest, tree-shrouded building on the road to Seletar. As she prepared the meal, a *laksa* accompanied by a hot *sambal*, they chatted amicably.

'It should almost be ready,' she said. 'I think you'll find a Tiger beer in the fridge.' Then she added, 'You'd better call me Emily. It's the fad nowadays to use Christian names, isn't it? I certainly don't want you calling me "aunt".'

He stood in the kitchen doorway as she stirred the seafood balls and scalded the rice vermicelli. Once, needing something from the living room, she slipped gently past. As she returned she stopped in front of him and smiled, looking directly into his eyes, then abruptly leaning forward she pecked his cheek. 'You're so like him,' she said, before busying herself at the stove. 'Do you like oriental food?'

Over the meal he told her about his family, about his Jewish 'cousins' and his mutilated father.

'Ah, the Japanese,' she murmured, but it was her only interruption, for she listened intently. Robert felt flattered and wallowed in this accession to adulthood, talking confidently, telling her of the *Merlin* and his ambitions for the future.

345

'I recall your grandfather was from a Royal Naval family,' she said, and he told her of his unhappy childhood and the seeming threat of universal cataclysm.

'Of course, it was mostly imagined,' he concluded, 'but it exerted a strong influence on my thinking.'

She shrugged. 'Perhaps you are right. Sometimes children see things very clearly. The world can be a terrible place.'

Their eyes met over her glass and he felt a surge of desire. She was still attractive; the tropical sun had not desiccated her as it did some white women and she possessed a lithe grace even in her sixties. Watching, Emily knew it had not been difficult to prescribe the precise amount of beer to get Robert mildly drunk.

'I won't offer you brandy,' she said matter-of-factly. 'You'll only be sick. Sit on the settee and I'll get some coffee.'

He sat as he was bid, a delightful lassitude sweeping over him. Next to the settee on a small table beside the telephone lay a pad and a pencil. He picked them up and began to draw her profile as she had been in the car.

'I'm sorry,' she said, returning with the coffee, 'I probably sounded a bit auntish then, but I don't think brandy on top of beer is a terribly good idea for a young man.'

'It's okay,' said Robert, trying to conceal the drawing.

'Is that me?' she asked, with the devastating directness he found rather forbidding and definitely auntish. She was bent over the sandalwood coffee table and he could smell her perfume. He shed his reticence and showed her the sketch. 'It's from memory, so it's not very good.'

'*He* could draw,' she said, taking it from him.

'I'm sorry?'

'Your grandfather.' She returned the pad and handed him coffee, sitting at the other end of the settee and crossing her legs in a susurration of silk. 'He was a bastard, and I loved him passionately. We lived together in Hong Kong, then he fell in love with a Russian singer in a cabaret in Shanghai, so I walked out on him. Stupid thing to do; it was just what he wanted. I came to Singapore and began to train as a doctor before the war.'

Robert listened. Almost unconsciously he had begun drawing again, his eyes lifting to her abstracted face. He had

346

never thought of people having handsome skulls before, but Emily's jaw and the sweep of her brow owed little to the covering of flesh nature had left her.

'After the war and independence, I stayed on. I had nowhere else to go and there was plenty for me to do. There still is.' She paused. 'I'm sorry. I'm boring you.'

'No, no, I'm not bored. I just couldn't help myself.' He waved his pencil deprecatingly over the drawing.

'Let me see.' She extended an imperious hand. Reluctantly he gave her the drawing and she stared at it for a long time. When she passed it back her eyes had misted.

'I didn't mean to offend . . .'

'No. It's very good. I *am* an old woman.'

'How old are you,' he blurted out, adding 'Emily' in an attempt to mitigate his rudeness.

'Sixty-four.'

'I think you're attractive in a way.'

' "In a way." ' She laughed sadly. 'If I didn't know that was the beer speaking, Robert, I'd be flattered. My colleagues think of me as a dehydrated husk.'

'No, I meant it. Beauty is an odd thing. I don't really understand it.'

'You've been at sea a long time and you're – what, sixteen?'

'Almost seventeen.'

'Now you're being nephewish. I think I prefer you as a quiffy gallant.'

They fell silent. Robert finished his coffee. 'I suppose I'd better be going.'

'There's no need,' Emily said.

'It's quite late.'

'Are you a virgin?' she asked, rising and putting out the light. For a moment the darkness and the question bemused Robert's fuddled brain. From outside the open windows the sound of the cicadas seemed to surge into the room, filling it with danger and uncertainty.

'Are you a virgin?' Emily repeated, and the lower timbre of her voice sent a thrill of anticipation through him. He could see her again now as she stood just beyond the coffee table. She possessed a stillness at once threatening and inviting; it stimulated a response and drew him to the edge of the settee.

She was unbuttoning the silk print dress, peeling it back so

347

he could see in the dim light filtering in from the street her tall, lean body. She was naked except for her white knickers. The dark crescents of her limp breasts rose and fell. They were old, empty, yet for Robert, rising slowly to his feet, they held no quality that repelled him. She held out her hand and he felt her skin, dry and cool. He caught his shin on the corner of the coffee table as she drew him after her into the darkness of her bedroom. Here he knew nothing of her age, for the same cool touch guided him and he felt the soft, ageless enclosure of her and was enraptured.

After the first, hurried climax he explored the slenderness of her escarped hips and the long, fruitless expanse of her flat belly. He kissed the sculptured hollows of her throat and ran his fascinated fingers across the long arches of her collar bones. Then, deliciously, he felt her touch him to renewed vigour and kissed her paps as she bent over him and seemed, for a while, to possess the small, delicate breasts of a girl.

Only at dawn, when prompted by nature he sought the lavatory, did he experience a first touch of self-disgust. She slept, mouth half open, her grey hair spread untidily across the rumpled pillow. But she was awake when he returned, smiling ironically as though she guessed his inner thoughts. She patted the bed beside her and a little unwillingly he obeyed. She pulled the corner of the sheet off his loins where he held it.

'I'm a doctor,' she reminded him. 'I've seen an awful lot of them. Though yours' – and he felt her breath – 'is rather special.'

There was no diffidence or awkwardness in his last tumescence. He took her aggressively and she thrust back, her energy amazing him. It crossed his mind he might kill her, but beneath him her blue eyes blazed and he came with a shuddering gasp that had her on top of him, riding him until it hurt and he was limp. Then she raised herself, her head thrown back in a kind of triumph before collapsing beside him.

For a while they lay still as daylight seeped through the shutters. At last he rose, searching for his clothes while she lay still with her eyes closed.

'Don't run away, as though you are ashamed,' she said, startling him.

348

'I'm sorry, I thought you were asleep. I must go. I'll be in trouble.'

'You are the first man I've had since your grandfather.'

A feeling of revulsion rose like bile in Robert's throat. The second of flattery at being described a man withered on the mention of his grandfather. An old man, long dead.

'Except, that is, for Captain Tanaguchi and Lieutenant Nakamura of the *Kempei Tei*, not to mention Privates Ozuma, Genda and Takashita of the Imperial Japanese Army . . .'

Robert was looking at her with real horror in his eyes. 'It's how I spent the war, Robert, being raped and learning how to survive. All you've done is lost your innocence and joined the human race.'

But Robert was thinking of the jeering dock workers and their jibe of only yesterday: 'You fuckee dirty woman, Johnnie!'

Emily realised his anxiety and smiled grimly. 'You're all right, my boy. I'm quite safe. I made sure of that years ago. You were better doing it with me than many of the gonococcal girls in the clubs of Anson Road. I'll make you some breakfast and then take you back to the ship.

By the time the *Loch Barcadale* had completed her discharge in Yokohama and begun her homeward loading schedule, Robert had overcome such squeamishness as he had felt after his affair with Emily. His speech acquired a certain authority, his steps a certain swagger and his self-esteem a degree of superiority after their stop in Hong Kong when a fellow apprentice began worrying over a persistent and painful gleet. He enjoyed the company of the bar girls of Izezaki Street in Yokohama and the Motomachi in Kobe, but could refuse their blandishments without regret. He seemed, in the words of his mentor, the Second Mate, to have 'cut the apron strings', and to be 'shaping up nicely'.

He telephoned Emily when they arrived at Singapore and spent the night with her. 'Have you heard?' she asked as she drove him away from the ship, the beams of the car's leadlamps cutting through the soft, insect-infested tropical darkness. 'They've built a bloody great wall right across the centre of Berlin.'

349

'Yes, we heard.'

He knew she was thinking of the future, and was flattered she was thinking of it for him. Tentatively he reached out and laid his hand on her thigh.

'You'd better drive if you're going to do that.'

He crashed the gears abominably, and the little tourer kangaroo-jumped down the road until he got the hang of it and turned into the driveway of her bungalow with a degree of panache.

'Not bad.' She led him inside and they made love immediately, she with a frightening urgency, he with the thoughtless energy of the very young.

'You'd better not tell anyone at home that you met me,' she said as they lay together. He agreed; he had no intention of doing so. 'Come and see me again, when you're next in Singapore,' she added. He smiled and assented, seeing in her swimming eyes only regret at their parting, not the uncertainty of age.

He did not return for some time, his ship being diverted to the South African service. They were in the South Atlantic heading north when the radio officer came onto the bridge one night. He had sat up late, his headphones on, listening to what was happening in the world beyond their visible horizon.

'D'you know what? The Yanks have spotted Russian missile sites in Cuba,' he said.

'Cuba? Christ, that's right on Uncle Sam's doorstep!' exclaimed the Second Mate.

'They photographed them from satellites, apparently. Kennedy's told Khrushchev to shift them or else.' No one needed to ask 'Or else what?'

'D'you think Khrushchev will?' asked Robert, a sudden ancient fear displacing his new-found self-confidence. He recalled the horrors that had accompanied the lives of others: Aunt Vera's bereavement, his grandfather's death, his own father's wounding, Emily's rape at the hands of the Japanese; why should his generation escape unscathed? And the full import of what might happen haunted him as he paced the bridge; if Kennedy provoked a showdown could the unthinkable happen? Nuclear war made no sense, yet alone on the dark and desolate sea it seemed possible.

Occasionally they passed other ships, small microcosmic worlds lit by their regulation lamps that shone across the black water. Were their crews held in this awful suspense? They were anxious days that followed, days when the usually careless sailors sought news of what was happening, lest the world be blown apart and they knew only when the dust clouds filled the sky and it was already too late. The thought of being left behind, ignorant survivors, when the world had exploded was more terrifying than the fear of a sudden, searing death.

It seemed to Robert that the camaraderie of the ship was diminished in those anxious few days, yet that every act was invested with a new importance. Even dhobying his socks seemed a sacramental act; might this not be the last time . . .

A few stout souls cracked black jokes and laughed with brittle courage, but most heaved a sigh of heartfelt relief when they learned that Khrushchev had capitulated to Kennedy's threats and they cheered insanely when, a few days later, they passed a pair of Russian freighters bound northeast, their decks covered with canvas-shrouded deck cargo.

In accordance with the Loch Line's policy, Robert shifted from ship to ship, accruing the sea time and experience necessary to qualify as a candidate for examination and the first step in the ladder to command. In November 1963 he was serving on the *Loch Etive* and the ship lay at the piers in Manila when, as he was called to go on deck at midnight, he was told of the news of Kennedy's assassination. The event seemed monstrous, incomprehensible. Was it possible, he wondered, thinking of his father sitting beside the River Deben, 'to map the course of man's regeneration'? He felt the same disgust at the sex scandals that rocked the British government during those libidinous years, but most of the time he was preoccupied with his own lusts.

He saw Emily from time to time, but occasionally his ship would call at Singapore and he would not find time to contact her. Home again, Robert found himself in Liverpool, attending a training course and seeking excitement in the Cavern Club and the Mardi Gras dancehall. The rock music of Merseyside had acquired a world-wide reputation and

Liverpool was the only place to be. Amid the raw, assertive music Robert danced with the short-skirted madonnas whose straight hair and pouting lips drove all thoughts of his elderly mistress from his head. Pamela and Anne and Kirstie gave themselves with a willing eagerness that made his Singapore adventure seem to have occurred to someone else.

'God, you're fab, Bobby, I'm crazy about you,' gasped Pamela, her head jerking in response to his own frenzy.

Shore leave, when it came, was taken at the gallop because it was brief and infrequent. But these excesses were offset by weeks at sea and the tedious hours of cargo duty in port. They even palled when, during the long weeks of the seamen's strike in 1966, he was prevented from sitting the examination that would convert Apprentice Martin into a *pukkah* deck officer with the responsibility of his own watch. With the certificate of competency would come a proper salary and his release from the poverty of indentured status. But he was a few weeks short of the requisite sea time and consequently frustrated by the enforced idleness of ship keeping in Glasgow where his ship was stranded by the exodus of her crew.

There were good reasons for the strike, he knew; the country was enjoying a bonanza of high wages and full employment that the seamen felt they had a right to share, but coming as it did with frequent dock strikes it found little sympathy in Britain at large.

In the end he sat his examination and passed with ease, shipping out for the Far East in the late autumn as Third Officer of the *Loch Eriboll*.

He saw Emily for the last time that Christmas. He was shocked by her appearance. She seemed to have collapsed, to have lost her elegant poise and suddenly become an old woman. They dined at a small restaurant, their conversation horribly stilted. Robert took her back to her bungalow in a taxi, for she had sold the little MG, but he did not stay the night. He felt no desire for her and on the way back to the ship he wondered cruelly what he could ever have seen in her sexually. When his ship docked in Liverpool two months later he received a letter from her asking him not to call again; she had cancer.

352

Moved by pity and remorse he wrote back at once and telephoned her when he next berthed at Keppel Harbour. The number was unobtainable. At the hospital he learned from a Chinese colleague that Dr Plunkett had died three weeks earlier.

CHAPTER TWENTY-SEVEN
Business in Great Waters

'My God, they're incredibly beautiful!'

Second Officer Robert Martin's pencil raced with practised ease over the sketching block, capturing as best he could the rolling majesty of the school of whales to starboard. Apprentice Roland watched the cetaceans through binoculars, trying unsuccessfully to count them as they appeared and disappeared bewilderingly.

'Mr Martin! What the hell are you up to?' Captain Walker's heavy built figure loomed at the top of the bridge ladder. 'We're not a bloody art class. Can't you be satisfied with a photograph, like the rest of us?'

Apprentice Roland diplomatically retreated to the opposite wing of the bridge.

'All I'll get with a camera is a grey hole in the oggin which the whale has just vacated, sir,' replied Robert, his tone unrepentant and his pencil's progress uninhibited by the Captain's appearance. Walker's gin-tainted breath fumed across the paper as he looked over his Second Officer's shoulder.

'You're lucky I'm a tolerant bugger, Mr Martin.'

'I know, sir.' Robert grinned. His charmingly handsome features disarmed Captain Walker's protest.

'And don't patronise me. Go on, finish your sketch. What d'you do with 'em anyway?'

'I keep them, sir. Not for any reason, really.'

'I suppose you *do* 'em for a reason.'

'That's very perceptive of you, or was that a question, sir?'

'Eh? What d'you mean?'

Perceiving a minefield, Robert desperately changed the subject. 'Do you know what kind of whales they are, sir? I'm not very good at identification. I thought they were Blues.'

Walker raised a pair of binoculars and studied the creatures. 'No. The Blue spouts like that, but rarely lifts his jaw so far out of the water. See – there – that white flash of the chin and then the humped-up slow roll as they sound? They're Fin whales. You don't see their tails when they sound. You probably would if they were Blues.'

'Oh.' Robert scribbled *Fin whale school, Indian Ocean, April 1971*.

'I did a couple of voyages in Salvesen's whalers just after the war,' said Captain Walker, as if offering provenance for the accuracy of his identification. 'You won't see many Blue whales nowadays. They've been practically hunted to extinction. Pity.' The Captain took out his briar pipe. 'Perhaps *that*'s a good enough reason to draw 'em.'

'Yes. Yes, I think so.'

Walker stoked the coke-clogged pipe and Robert thought with a sudden pang of nostalgic pain of his father, dead before he was fifty, a belated casualty of war though his death certificate said the cause was renal failure.

'They're like us, the whales. Like you and me,' Walker said, emitting alternate words and puffs of smoke as the match flame rose and fell. 'On the way out.'

This was the last voyage of the *Loch Torridon*, a sister ship of the *Loch Barcadale* which she was now following to the breaker's yard in Kaioshung.

'The ships'll go, sir, that's inevitable, but there'll still be a need for men.'

'I disagree. I think we'll follow.' Walker looked at Robert's face. 'I'll be all right, but I don't think the future's looking too rosy for you.'

'But we're to take delivery of a new ship.'

'Aye, built in a Japanese yard, not Robb Caledon's of Leith, or Camell Laird's on the Mersey. Unfair competition in the ship-building industry (unfair because elsewhere it's supported by government subsidies and cheap labour) will soon become unfair competition on the high seas. You mark my words. You count the red dusters when we reach

Singapore and compare it with the number you saw on your first voyage to sea.'

Robert did as he was bid and found Walker was correct. There were more Japanese ships, more Russian ships and more under the flags of convenience of Panama and Liberia.

'I told you so, Mr Martin. Government subsidy for Japan, uneconomic freight rates for the Comecon ships and lower standards in the flags of convenience. It all adds up to curtains for us.'

Captain Walker's gloomy prognostications seemed invested with more substance when they arrived at Kaioshung. The place was a wasteland of broken ships, rusted hulks being cut down by the implacable flames of oxy-acetylene torches. The once cosseted liners of several British mail lines, whose teak decks had been daily swabbed to a pristine whiteness by the labours of fifty lascars, whose brass wheelhouse fittings had been brick dusted and polished by generations of grumbling apprentices and cadets, whose derricks and running gear had lifted billions of tons of exports out of Britain and imported billions of tons of raw materials and food, lamb carcases from New Zealand, beef from the Argentine and grain from the United States, submitted to the unremitting labour of swarms of Taiwanese scavengers.

'It's not their fault, they have to live, but they look like vultures, don't they?' said Captain Walker as he leaned for the last time on the rail of his ship, reluctant to leave, though he had already rung down 'finished with engines' on the big brass telegraph. 'Tomorrow they'll start on this one.' He straightened up and gave the teak toprail a last hearty pat with the flat of his hand. 'That's the *Glenartney* over there,' he said. 'She was one of the supply ships to the British Pacific Fleet. I remember seeing her in Manus at the end of the war, after they dropped the bomb on Nagasaki. She had the reputation of being capable of the fastest stores transfer in the Fleet Train. Oh well,' said Walker, turning from the rail, 'thank God I'm not young any more.'

The mood of depression hung over the whole of the ship's company until they left Taiwan and flew out to Japan and the Kawasaki Heavy Industries shipyard at Kobe. There

356

they joined the newly completed container ship *Loch Moidart*. With a gross registered tonnage of fifty-nine thousand tonnes she was a Panamax giant, capable of loading two thousand eight hundred standard container units and still able to use the Panama Canal, for she was intended for employment on the Loch Line's round-the-world joint service with a Swedish company.

After completing trials, the new *Loch Moidart* left Japan for Hong Kong to initiate the new service, and from the Crown Colony returned to Japan. On completion of loading at Yokohama, she sailed for Los Angeles.

The size of an aircraft carrier, the *Loch Moidart* was nudged gently alongside the wharf at San Pedro Port, Los Angeles. Captain Walker, intimidated by his new ship's size, nervously followed the insouciant Californian pilot as, baseball cap at a jaunty angle and beer gut hanging like a deformation over the belt of his slacks, he spoke the unfamiliar jargon of the Californian radio freak into his VHF handset.

'Okay, control, ten four, that's us all see-cu-er in number five. Come back.'

San Pedro port control squawked incomprehensibly in the hand set and the pilot turned to Walker. 'Okay, Cap, that just about wraps it up.'

Robert Martin came up from the afterdeck breathless from the long climb.

'Bloody accommodation block is like an Alp,' he complained, staring out over the white glare of the vast concrete apron with its cranes and stack after stack of containers in the artificially gay colours of company logos. Beyond, the glass and concrete jungle of the city of the angels baked under the sun, surrounded by distant hills and the villas of the rich. Over the city a sulphurous pall lay like a shroud.

'Changed a bit since George Vancouver's day,' Captain Walker said. 'Does the traffic cause that floating heap of shit?'

'Yes, the met books call it industrial haze, but I believe "pollution" is the in-thing to say these days,' said Robert.

'We used to have fogs like that in London from all the smokey chimneys.'

'I remember going Christmas shopping in one as a boy. It left your shirt collar covered with a yellow grime.'

'It stopped with the Clean Air Act from which ships were exempt when flashing up their boilers in the London Docks,' Walker reminisced didactically. Far below them on the white concrete an open-topped sedan, agleam with red cellulose and chrome, swung in a half circle at the foot of the gangway and stopped with a squeal. A seaman on the main deck below gave an appreciative whistle which echoed back against the wall of waiting containers as a tall, dark woman wearing sunglasses got out.

'That sure as hell ain't the Goddamn agent,' said Captain Walker in his best Yankee drawl. 'That sweater looks painted on her.'

From the height of the *Loch Moidart*'s bridge they watched the woman as she took off her sunglasses, shook a mane of blue-black hair free of a scarf and looked up at the ship. She saw them staring down at her and shaded her eyes. Then she waved.

'Robert? Bob Martin?'

Howls came from the main-deck where six able-seamen, their hard-hats pushed back on their heads and cans of lager in their hands, wolf whistled and made puns on the Second Mate's name which was synonymous with that of a patent dog medicine. The woman ignored the hoi polloi. 'Bob? Is that you?'

'Good God! Ruth!' Robert turned to the master. 'Sir, if you don't mind . . .'

'You've got 'til midnight. I'll explain to the Chief Officer. Don't pass up a lassie like that for a heap of bloody boxes!'

He ran for the ladder and scrambled down. Reaching the main-deck he grinned at the impudent and suggestive remarks made by the envious seamen.

'Ruth!' They hugged and he felt the soft, full warmth of her clasp him, oblivious to the yelling deck crowd above him. She was in her mid-forties, but wore skin-tight jeans, high-heeled shoes and a tight-fitting cashmere sweater. A heavy gold necklace graced her brown skin.

'My God, Ruth, you look fantastic!'

'You've just crossed the Pacific.'

'Yes, with only the Chief Engineer's wife to stare at, but

that doesn't stop me.' He grabbed her again, and she laughed and wriggled and pushed him away. He let her go. 'I thought you were in Israel.'

'I was, but I left soon after the Six Day War. I came back to California. Can you get away?' She pulled him towards the car.

'Yes, I'm free until midnight.'

They drove off in the direction of Beverley Hills. 'Joachim is still in Israel,' she said as he luxuriated on the spacious seat. 'He's a full colonel now.' She pronounced the rank with its full complement of vowels and not, as she might once have done, as the centre of a nut.

'What do you do? Where d'you live? How the dickens did you know I was coming?'

' "How the dickens," I haven't heard anyone speak like that for years. I knew you were coming because Irene wrote when your father died. I hadn't left Israel then and had sent her my address in Tel Aviv. When I left I stopped over in London. I had some business to attend to and Irene and I met at the Savoy. Of course I asked after you and Irene kept me up to date by mailing me a couple times a year. She wrote and said you were on this new ship and were coming to LA, so' – she shrugged – 'here I am.'

'And very glad I am to see you,' he said. "You really do look fantastic. Are you married? I suppose you have been three times and divorced three times.'

'Once.' Her face became serious.

'Oh, I'm sorry.'

She shrugged again. 'I met him on the kibbutz I worked on when I first went to Israel. He got a job as a journalist and we moved to Jerusalem where he worked for the *Jerusalem Times* and then to Tel Aviv. The marriage didn't last. What about you?'

'Me? Oh, marriage and seafaring don't mix, especially in today's free-for-all. But what do you do now?'

'I'm in TV. I started in Tel Aviv, then got involved with an American team filming in Israel. When my marriage fell apart, I kind of drifted back here. It's funny, but I realise now that I always thought of California as home. Tell me something about yourself.'

'Nothing much to tell. I'm a Second Officer and a qualified

master mariner.'

'That sounds very English. What does it mean?'

'It means if I live long enough and keep my nose clean I'm qualified to command any type of merchant ship.'

'Wow!'

'It's not as glamorous as being a steeplejack or an airline pilot,' Robert said drily. 'Joseph Conrad called it "a useful calling," but then so is being a rat-catcher.'

'Do I detect a note of disillusion?'

'You've seen that bloody thing I've just crossed the Pacific on. It's like working on top of a block of flats – somewhat divorced from reality. Even a good gale barely rocks the boat.'

'I think I'd appreciate that . . . Here we are.'

With a faint squeak of tyres they pulled into a driveway before a white-walled Spanish-style villa built on a wooded hillside and set into a small re-entrant valley. The semi-circular hollow now accommodated the villa and its swimming pool. They walked through the cool house and Robert was surprised to see a large oil painting of a sea battle and a grey model of a destroyer in a glass case. The shimmer of reflected light through the windows told of the presence of the pool before Ruth led him onto the sun-drenched patio behind the house.

'There's someone I want you to meet,' she said.

He was quite unprepared for the encounter. The nauticalia had led him to expect some handsome ex-naval hunk as Ruth's lover, but the woman lying on the sunbed seemed to have no connection with those masculine artefacts he had just seen. She too wore the obligatory sunglasses, but she removed them as she sat up and swung her long legs off the sunbed, clearly expecting his arrival. She seemed to Robert to typify California. The years of flower power and sexual licence, where the rich and elderly could buy back their youth in instalments, seemed personified in the creature that confronted him. She sat like a fantastic, ageless goddess, her refulgently voluptuous flesh preserved at the instant of its finest bloom. And yet it was an image, an attempt at perfection almost blasphemous in its appearance. Her oiled body was perfect in shape, though the skin betrayed her age. The skimpy white bikini with its

360

under-wired cups thrust her large breasts up and out with an arrogant assurance, and the taut facial skin, pertly pretty from a distance, seemed immobile on closer inspection. The dark hair rustled with a wiry unnaturalness as she stretched a formal smile. She was at the same instant lasciviously arousing and hideously repulsive. He thought suddenly, guiltily, of Emily.

As he drew closer the woman lost her smile. Robert realised she was short-sighted.

'Oh honey,' she gasped, putting one beringed hand to her striated throat and holding the other out to Ruth. 'Oh, honey,' she repeated, 'he's so like him!'

Her incongruous appearance had invited comparison with Emily, but her opening remark made Robert momentarily dizzy with *déjà vu*. He understood: the accent was not American but Russian. This was the woman his grandfather had preferred to Emily Plunkett.

'Sonia?' he said, as Ruth patted her hand reassuringly.

'Yes, honey, yes, I'm Sonia . . . Sonia Garcia, but once I was Sonia Martin . . . And you are Johnnie's son? I would recognise you for your grandpapa' . . . you are *so* like him . . . you'll have to forgive an old woman her stupidity . . . Let me look at you.'

He submitted to the scrutiny of the once beautiful green eyes. It seemed so incongruous, this mummified beauty claiming the weakness of age without any of its dignity. Ruth bent solicitously over Sonia and rubbed oil into the old lady's shoulders so Robert could see the skin dragged obscenely across the tired muscle beneath. The bizarre tableau was shattered by a bellow from the house and he was dimly aware he had heard a car draw up outside.

'Hey Bob! How ya doing? By God it's damned good to see ya!' A huge brown paw wrenched his fist as a giant of a man, well built, tanned and fit, with a mane of iron-grey hair smoothed back over his skull, literally burst upon them. Before waiting for a reply he bent over Sonia and kissed her wetly on the mouth. 'Hi, honey,' he said, 'hi, Ruthie . . . Hey, haven't you fixed his guy a drink yet? He's a Goddamn sailor, not one of your TV faggots. Scotch okay? On the rocks? I got gin or martini, you name it we can supply it. I knew your grand-paw. Met him first at the end of World

361

War One when you British still ruled the waves. Next time I'd gone over to London in the bad days of the blitz. Jeez, I took my hat off to your people. I was part of a military mission, being an engineer specialist.'

Garcia handed him the glass of whisky in which ice-cubes tinkled. Ruth whispered, 'For God's sake don't mention Vietnam.'

'Hey, what d' ya say to a swim, Bob?' Garcia said. 'No shorts? Jeez, don't worry, this is California. Just jump in!'

The hospitality was overwhelming. At first its very excess seemed to mark it as false, but Captain Juan Garcia, USN (Ret'd) radiated a seamless bonhomie and the two women seemed to accept it with indulgence. It seemed uncharacteristic for Ruth to be an obviously familiar part of the odd *ménage*, but as the afternoon wore on Robert detected that under Garcia's noisy, good-natured bluster there was evidence of something else.

'I've had a fantastic time,' he said to Ruth as she drove him back to the ship aware for the first time that day he had employed the adjective properly. 'They're an incredible couple. She's just amazing.'

'She was incredibly beautiful when I first knew her,' said Ruth, and there was something in her tone that attracted his attention. She turned for an instant and looked at him. 'I knew her when I first escaped from Germany. I was very young.'

It sounded like a confession. Robert said, 'You were lovers?'

She nodded. 'We still are.'

He visited the *ménage à trois* occasionally when the *Loch Moidart* called at Los Angeles and he was free of duty. He was a casual visitor, a friend, conscious of his inbred English reticence in a way that surprised himself. He had no wish to become involved, though an invitation was implied. In due course he was promoted Chief Officer, and kept preoccupied with the ship's cargo work. Captain Walker had long since retired and the ship's new master was himself approaching the age for superannuation. Robert's only goal now was his own command. It began to concern him he had no stable home life beyond infrequent visits to his mother and Aunt Vera at The Lees. The house was looking shabby, and though he did what he could when on leave he never stayed long.

He was aware he had become a lonely solitary and took to spending his free time driving aimlessly about the country with his box of watercolours. The *Loch Moidart* had, perforce, become his wife.

One bright, sunny spring afternoon, when the ship was off Alderney and bound up-Channel he had gone to the bridge. Walking up and down in black trousers and pullover, Apprentice Anne Bagshot kept the lookout. She had proved an able cadet, and won over most of the traditionalists on board. The Second Officer was calling in to Jobourg, the western end of the Channel routeing control.

'Good afternoon, Jobourg, this is British ship *Loch Moidart*, New York to Rotterdam. Over.'

'Sheep calling Jobourg Traffique, good afternoon, sir, pleez spell your name. Over,' came the French operator's reply.

The Second Officer raised his eyebrows to a grinning Robert. 'Yes Jobourg, my ship's name Lima Oscar Charlie Hotel . . .'

Robert stared at the red hull of the Channel lightvessel three miles to the northward as it tugged at its mooring in the low westerly swell. A large white gannet half folded its wings and plunged into the sea, emerging a moment later with a silver fish in its predatory bill.

The Second Mate clipped the VHF handset back in place on the wide instrument console. 'Bloody froggies,' he said without rancour, crossing to where Robert stared out of the window at the foredeck full of containers. 'I'm sick of that view.' Robert nodded silent agreement.

'Oh!'

Both men looked round at the exclamation. Anne Bagshot had her glasses to her eyes, focused on something close to the ship. 'What is it?' snapped the Second Officer.

'It's a guillemot. It's covered in oil.'

'Is that all? It's nothing new,' began the Second Officer, cocking a chauvinistically intolerant eye at the girl's outrage and pointing at half-a-dozen soiled gulls ridge-soaring above their stern.

'It's awful, sir,' the girl said.

The dying bird vanished swiftly astern as the huge ship rushed eastwards at twenty-seven knots into the English Channel.

'Don't be sentimental,' said the Second Mate and the girl glanced despairingly at his superior, the Chief Officer. The Second Mate's cavalier attitude annoyed him, both on the girl's behalf and on that of the helpless guillemot. He scanned the sea ahead, aware something was wrong with its appearance.

'There's a slick there, see?' His arm swept across the bow from the starboard to port. 'You can smell it now. Hell, it runs for miles and it's medium to heavy grade oil.'

'There are more birds covered in it, sir,' reported Anne Bagshot, pointing as they carved through a foul welter of oil and dying razorbills who struggled vainly to get clear of the ship's bow.

'Oh, this is awful,' the girl said again, and Robert found himself wishing she would swear.

'This is a major oil-spill,' said the Second Mate. He was suddenly repentant, realising he had made something of a fool of himself. 'I'd better report it to Jobourg.'

'It's awful,' repeated the girl yet again as the liveliness of the sea was suddenly quelled by the thin blanket of oil and their nostrils stung with the stench of it.

'It's bloody appalling,' said Robert with sudden vehemence. He turned for the stairwell, seeing again dark, menacing shadows leaping unbidden on a bedroom wall. Did all his generation suffer from this sense of foreboding? Was it a consequence of living under the nuclear shadow and why they grabbed avidly at every passing pleasure?

The stink of the oil followed him as the *Loch Moidart*'s air-conditioning plant sucked it into the accommodation. He stood stockstill in the centre of his cabin. It was laid out like a penthouse suite, a huge void space in which he rattled his life away for the profit of a ship-owner. He felt unreasonably angry, an anger spurred by a deep-seated, childish fear. He remembered feeling this sensation of foreboding in Manila the night Kennedy was shot: the act was so outrageous that nothing could ever be the same afterwards. He knew of people who felt the same way about the explosion of the

364

atomic bomb, despite the fact that more people had been killed in the saturation bombing of Tokyo. He remembered, too, meeting young Roland, with whom he had once sailed, by the boat landing at Collyer's Quay in Singapore.

'Let me buy you a drink,' Roland had said, dragging him across the road and into an air-conditioned bar.

'Where are you now? I heard you had left the Lochs.'

'Tankers,' said Roland abruptly, taking deep draughts of his Tiger beer. 'Third Mate. We're loading Avgas, among other things, at Pulo Bukum.'

'Vietnam?' Robert had asked.

Roland nodded. 'Sodding Saigon River. Fucking terrible.'

'Good money,' Robert had said, guessing why Roland had transferred to an oil company.

'Bugger the money. It's why I went into tankers, I know, but this . . . Jesus, this is something else.'

'Well I suppose you don't get a war bonus without earning it.'

'Oh, it's not the danger. You get used to thinking the VC are going to pot you from every tree. We got hit twice. They hit the sandbags on the bridge and the only casualty was an apprentice. Fucking sandbags fell on his legs and broke one of them! No, it's the whole thing: the corruption, the way the Yanks are kidding themselves they're going to win, the way they bomb the shit out of everything . . . napalm, high explosive, even defoliant, for God's sake! Christ, there's little kids and women. The women were poxed deliberately, I tell you,' Roland had said, speaking with vehement intensity, 'it's like the end of the whole fucking world.'

The oil slick might have been a portent, for when they arrived at Rotterdam they received news of an infinitely more shocking kind. The company's chief personnel officer boarded the ship and handed each of them an envelope.

'Oh, bloody hell, no!'

Robert read the notice of redundancy with disbelief. *In-house reassessment has resulted in . . . the cost-effectiveness of flagging out . . . economies forced upon us by rising oil prices . . . resulting in reassessment of manpower resources . . . increased crew costs . . . in cognisance of your loyal service . . .*

'Bullshit!' he muttered contemptuously.

The argot of management in the monetarist age bore down upon his life with its ruthless, inhuman logic. At the end came the sop, the price at which every man might be purchased – the payoff.

'What price a sailor's soul?' he murmured to himself, the words echoing in the large, empty cabin. 'The bastards have just fucked up my life.'

CHAPTER TWENTY-EIGHT
Drifting Smoke

'What are you going to do?

Aunt Vera's question hung in the air as she peered at Robert over the rim of her spectacles, an old woman, eighty that year, with eyes that were as undimmed as the brain that lay behind them. He thought, inconsequentially, of Emily and Sonia, the other two women he had known from his grandfather's generation. Of Emily, courageous and energetic to the last, bowed only by death but never by misfortune; of Sonia, the voluptuary, seduced by a culture that had made of her beauty nothing but a sham; and of Vera, 'Aunt' Vera, unfucked, an old maid of uncompromising faith and undiminished determination. Unliberated souls, the three of them, though Robert remained in awe of the last who quizzed him on that April morning.

'Do?' he temporised, irritably defensive. 'What can I do? I've been made redundant, Aunt Vee; redundant.' He looked at his mother. She poured tea, avoiding conflict by useful self-effacement. She seemed tired and ill. He sighed, annoyed with Vera for bringing this up again. 'Redundant,' he repeated, 'it means "unwanted" . . . "surplus to requirements." '

'Don't be ridiculous!' she snapped back, tapping her newspaper. It was as though the present circumstances justified everything she had believed in, as though the more things changed the more they stayed the same.

A photograph showed the old liner *Uganda* undergoing conversion to a hospital ship in Gibraltar and another of a County-class destroyer leaving Plymouth, surrounded by the small craft of well-wishers.

The papers, the television, the radio, had been choked with the images and names of ships these last few days in the wake of the Argentinian seizure of the Falkland Islands. It was as though the British had suddenly rediscovered their maritime heritage. Even the gulf between the Royal and the merchant navies had become blurred. Columnists and commentators had awoken to the fact that, although the former had been preserved despite the rising costs to the defence budget, the latter had almost vanished. Almost, but not quite; enough ships remained to convey the impression of continuing maritime might.

Some of the papers had been predictably inaccurate. He recalled the specious and misleading description of the requisitioned *Queen Elizabeth II* as 'the flagship of the British Merchant Navy'. Such erroneous statements convinced the uninformed that nothing had changed and he half wished the decline in merchant shipping had been a little faster, that the reporters had been unable to chortle about the 'ships taken up from trade', unable to relish the acronym STUFT as if it reflected the blunt, uncompromising earthiness of the bulldog breed. But there was an underlying unfamiliarity with matters nautical which betrayed a national ignorance. Robert winced at the 'remarkable efforts of the dockyards in preparing the armada'.

God! What an inapt and inappropriate collective noun! 'Taskforce' was preferable, it smacked at least of ancient doggedness.

Oh, yes, it was very comforting in its way, especially for Aunt Vee.

'They're going to need merchant ships to support the fleet,' she said sharply, as though he was still a boy and needed teaching.

'The fleet can look after itself,' he said with a vehemence that made his mother glance up reproachfully. 'It ought to be able to,' he added defiantly, 'the amount of tax-payers' money that's been lavished on it.'

'But the merchant navy's the fourth arm of defence!' Vera replied.

'Tell that to the ship-owners,' Robert snapped. 'The merchant navy hardly exists.'

'I don't know what's the matter with you, Robert. Here's

368

a heaven-sent opportunity to do something useful, to get a new job . . .'

'For God's sake, Aunt Vee, I'm not getting involved with an anachronistic colonial mess!'

'I'm glad your father isn't here.' Vera glared at him, shocked and frail, as though this was the final shot she could fire, almost an imputation of cowardice.

'My father would have understood,' roared Robert, standing up and banging the table so that the teacups leapt on their saucers. 'The government can get its own servants to do the government's own work. I'm thrown on the scrapheap.'

He left them both open-mouthed and stalked from the room. He felt a degree of guilt, a sense that perhaps he too should be playing his part in the best traditions of his family. He stood indecisively in the hall, stung by the verbal assault from Aunt Vera. He was acutely aware he had reached a crossroads in his life and this Falklands trouble offered him a possible way out, but as he inclined to this pragmatic approach he felt a surge of resentment. He remembered what he had just said about his father understanding his true state of mind. Whatever his fate, it was not to be rescued by war! Nor were his personal circumstances so reduced that he must become a mercenary. He still had most of his redundancy pay and had visited his bank, seeking investment advice. The 'personal banker' who had sat and patronised him with a charmingly insincere smile only confused him. She spoke in an unfamiliar jargon and the encounter reminded him that he had not only been bought off by the capitalist system, but was now being persuaded to reinvest in the very thing that had dispossessed him of his way of life.

He left the house and drifted disconsolately off on an ancient bicycle, watercolours and paper on his back, cycling round the backwaters south of Harwich. It was a grey, breezy day, in tune with his bleak mood. He wanted to lose himself in the wilderness, to watch the waders scavenging the tideline for food, as he had done when a boy, but he found his way barred by a concealed chemical works. Its presence only fuelled his ill humour and he strode on by road, only stopping when he reached the Red Lion at Kirby-le-Soken.

The beer, beef and pickles made him feel better. Leaving his bicycle propped against the pub wall he wandered down

369

Quay Lane. New houses had been built where he remembered only trees and undergrowth, but the southernmost extension of the marsh still reached, at high water, to the old quay. He was laying on the first washes when it began to rain, a driving squall that slashed ruinously across his paper.

'Bugger it!'

About fifty yards away, just above the high-watermark stood an ancient clapboard cottage. It had probably once housed an eel fisherman, and was surrounded by bushes and stumpy apple trees. He gathered up his gear and ran towards the shelter of its overgrown hedge. Out of the wind he squatted on the rim of the reed bed, where the land slipped imperceptibly into the sea in a muddy morass marked by sticks, wisps of straw, dried bladder wrack, plastic bottles and a Coke can.

The high spring tide was near the turn and lapped almost to his feet. Beside him an old stake protruded from the ground. A frayed rope was tied to it and led into the reed bed. The final inflow of the tide was stirring something hidden in the reeds and gently tugging at the rope. Curious, he stood up as the squall passed. He could see the curve of a counter stern covered with peeling paint. He took an impetuous step into oozing mud. It dragged at his impatient feet as he waded in, knee deep. He thrust the reeds apart scarcely daring to hope, then let out a mad whoop of joy. There, across the stern of the neglected and mastless yacht, he read her name: *Merlin*.

He knew now what he was going to do. At least, for the foreseeable future.

It took him a week to find the owner and another to negotiate a price. Even when he had acquired her he had to wait for the next spring tide to float her out of the hole she had made for herself among the reeds. A boat yard at Walton-on-the-Naze proved friendly and provided both a motor boat to tow the old yacht into Foundry Creek, and a berth for her where he could work.

'That old *Merlin* used to belong to a one-legged bloke,' drawled the boatyard owner. 'Navy man, he were. Lived over by Dovercourt.'

'I know,' Robert said, 'he was my father.'

There followed one of the busiest periods of his life.

Returning to The Lees exhausted with the labours of the day, he suffered the lugubrious televised bulletins that charted the progress of the Falklands campaign. He was embarrassed at Aunt Vee's satisfaction when the *General Belgrano* was sunk. He thought of his grandfather drowning in the Arctic Ocean as he stared at the poor quality picture of bobbing heads and liferafts with the crippled cruiser in the background. But he was as shocked as she and Irene were when the *Sheffield* was lost, and then the catalogue mounted: the *Ardent* and *Antelope*, the *Coventry*, the *Sir Galahad* and *Sir Tristram*. When the merchantman *Atlantic Conveyor* was hit it seemed the blood of both navies had once again reached its historic comingling, and he felt a genuine regret that he had not been there to participate in some small way.

He must have shown it in his face, for he caught Aunt Vee watching him, and he knew she was in some way mollified by this regret, satisfied to know it would eat into him with its lasting imputation of pusillanimity.

'What are you going to do with this boat?' Aunt Vera asked. She seemed unimpressed with the fact that it had once been John's.

'I'm going to bum around for a bit,' said Robert.

'You're too old to behave like a . . . like a beatnik.'

Robert smiled. 'I think you mean hippie, Vee,' said his mother patiently.

Most mornings he cycled off to Walton, rain or shine, to renovate *Merlin* and restore her to her former glory. By a small miracle he discovered her mast, boom, bowsprit and gaff stored in one of the boatyard sheds. Even in the matter of sails he struck lucky, finding, through the local bush telegraph, a set in nearby Brightlingsea. He had them recut by a local sail maker.

As he worked he brooded on the war in the South Atlantic. Opinion among fellow merchant seamen was divided; quite apart from the moral issues, many felt that volunteering to serve in the support ships of the Task Force would focus government attention on the vital need to maintain a merchant fleet, even at the cost of a subsidy. Many young men from Harwich, faced with the alternative of the dole queue, had gone off on a requisitioned North Sea ferry with that reasoning in mind.

Embittered with the trauma of dismissal, Robert felt that, though the Argentinian occupation was indefensible, the losses being incurred were inexcusable. Freedom had its price and the wrong people were paying it. If war was but an extension of diplomacy, then the blame lay, he believed, with the inertia of politicians whose cynical game of endless negotiation in place of realistic settlement had done much to provoke the Argentinian invasion.

'I'm damn near forty,' he told himself as he worked on *Merlin*, 'but I'm my own man. They paid me off to prove it.'

But he overheard the well-heeled yachtsmen in the clubhouse pontificating on the situation in the South Atlantic, talking about 'nuking the Argies', and he watched them sail off on their cruises like the lords of creation while real seamen were dying for them and their notions in the inhospitable waters round the Falkland Islands.

'Accountants,' he muttered bitterly, 'and loss adjusters and finance advisers and company directors; superior beings who have inherited the earth . . . What the hell do they know about an isolated fleet operating without adequate air cover or airborne early-warning radar?'

By midsummer the Argentinians had surrendered the Falklands and a wave of patriotic euphoria swept the country. In Dovercourt the seamen came back to heroes' welcomes, their houses festooned with banners, their bonuses in their pockets. But their ships continued to be sold.

That winter brought news of the death of Geoffrey Ennis. Vera, Irene and Robert attended the funeral in Somerset. The ancient church was filled with the black and gold of naval uniforms. Robert was glad to get away; even the solemnity of the occasion could not mute an atmosphere of triumph after the South Atlantic victory. Aunt Vera's dry-eyed grief was full of obscure accusation and he returned to resume work on *Merlin* with the single-mindedness of the unhappy. His only future lay with the yacht, and though he felt sorry for his mother, compelled to live with the increasingly difficult Vera, he was determined to get away, to escape the claustrophobic atmosphere that must have weighed so heavily upon his father.

'But how are you going to support yourself?' his mother asked anxiously.

'I'll manage, mother, don't worry. I thought of selling paintings.'

'What paintings?' His mother's tone was incredulous.

'Or I can teach the over-loaded yuppies to sail . . .'

He doubled *Merlin*'s frames and replaced planks sustained by such ideas through the following summer. He had finished work at the end of March 1984 and by early April the repaired yacht lay in Brighton marina among the motorised gin palaces and slick offshore cruiser-racers, a genteel dowager among parvenue princesses. It was midweek, and the place was almost uninhabited.

He first caught sight of the woman on another boat, a big ketch moored to an adjacent pontoon. She was lifting plastic bags of shopping aboard and her straw blonde hair caught his eye as he idly buffed up the brass binnacle in *Merlin*'s cockpit. She bent to the doghouse door and flicked a wave of hair over her ear. It reminded Robert of the sixties' style in its long, straight simplicity. He watched as she passed the bags to someone below and then followed them inside. He thought no more about her until he was in the marina office, making arrangements to keep his visitor's berth for a further two days. The weather forecast was poor and he did not relish a rough-weather passage single-handed. She was walking along the catwalk carrying a coil of rope and he paused to let her pass.

She smiled her thanks. He put her at thirty-two or three, and well-shaped beneath the androgynous sailing smock and jeans. Her hair was tied back with a twist of silk scarf and her face had a pleasant, open look, with fine grey eyes. He felt a twinge of desire and stared after her. It was a very long time since he had slept with a woman.

As he resumed his walk back to *Merlin* he studied the ketch. A man of about his own age appeared from below. Robert smiled, said 'good-morning,' and he was rewarded with a monosyllabic grunt. The gale struck in midafternoon and the rat-tat of halliards on alloy masts became a maddening tattoo until one got used to it. Robert tucked himself away in the cabin and reread Conrad's *Nostromo*. He became aware of people arguing somewhere nearby, but at first took no notice; it was none of his business. But the row continued unabated, disturbing his enjoyment of

373

Conrad, and he realised it came from the ketch. He put the book down, stood up in the hatch and cautiously looked in its direction. The woman was again bent at the entrance to the doghouse, but her outstretched arm no longer passed provisions below, for it was being pulled hard and her other hand was braced against the doghouse side in strenuous resistance.

'Let me go! You *can't* and you bloody well *won't*, damn you!' She struggled again and he saw her head strike the door jamb. 'You bastard!'

Robert stepped out into *Merlin*'s cockpit.

'No, I won't be quiet! Oh, shit!' Her voice rose desperately as her assailant appeared and got his arms round her. He tugged violently at her and as he did so she turned and caught sight of Robert. 'Help me!' she shouted, but an instant later she disappeared, an arm shut the doghouse door with a slam and she had vanished.

Robert leapt onto the pontoon and ran to the neighbouring berth. He could hear muffled cries and the man shouting: 'Shut up, you bitch! You know that's what you fucking came for!'

Robert jumped aboard and tried the door. It opened noiselessly and he stepped quickly inside. An opened holdall, its contents spilling half out of it, lay beside the top of a short ladder that descended from the doghouse into a luxurious saloon. Robet ducked into the saloon. The woman was lying on the carpeted deck her back against the squabbed settee. Her head was pinned by the man's right hand. He was kneeling between her spread legs, his left hand fumbling awkwardly with her belt. Without thinking Robert thrust his right forearm round the man's throat and locked it in the crook of his left, the hand of which he slapped across the base of the man's skull, then he jerked backwards.

The man's hands left the girl and scrabbled at his unseen attacker.

'Get out!' Robert yelled at the girl and, rubbing her throat, she scrambled to her feet and pushed past the struggling men. Robert twisted sideways with all his strength and flung his victim from him. The man recovered and turned. Robert kicked him in the crutch and as he doubled

374

up, beat a hasty retreat. On deck he drew the doghouse door after him and caught a turn of the neatly coiled mainsheet round its handle. Gasping he looked about him.

'Don't wait for the bastard! Come on!'

She was standing on *Merlin*'s deck carrying the holdall, and beckoning him frantically.

'He's drunk!' she called. 'He'll kill you when he gets out.' It occurred to him that he had never acted violently before; he had done so instinctively and after the heat of the moment he would be inadequate to the task of defending himself. The woman might be exaggerating, but it seemed foolish to wait and see. Behind him the door rattled and the man's furious face was at the glass. Robert ran to *Merlin*. The woman had cast off the moorings and held the yacht alongside by a short bight of rope which she threw off the mooring cleat the moment Robert jumped aboard. The wind caught the boat and widened the gap between it and the pontoon. *Merlin* began to drift to leeward where a high, opulent motor cruiser lay.

'What are you doing?'

'Start the engine,' she said desperately, glancing round at the elderly boat. 'You have got an engine, haven't you?'

'Jesus Christ!' He dived below, glad he had lavished money on the diesel engine and not thrown it out as he had considered at one time in order to return to reliance on natural forces. It coughed into life and he leapt back to the cockpit. The woman was forward, setting a handfender over the side as they blew down onto the motor cruiser. A bellow astern told the man aboard the ketch had got free. Robert pulled the gear lever into reverse and increased the throttle. *Merlin* backed into the swinging area and he reversed thrust, kicked over the iron tiller and spun his little ship hard aport to point her long bowsprit towards the marina entrance.

On the pontoon the man was screaming abuse at them. Someone had come out onto the observation platform by the marina office.

'Have you got a VHF radio?' the woman asked, dropping nimbly into the cabin hatch.

'No, sorry.'

'Shit!'

'I assume you want me to put to sea?' he said, as he swung

375

Merlin round the inner breakwater and she began to feel the surge and scend of open water beyond. He looked at her properly for the first time. She still stood in the hatch, but she held a sheath knife and it was pointed at him.

'Now listen. Thank you for what you did, but if you've got any ideas about doing the same, forget it. I'll kill you if you try.'

Robert sighed and averted his eyes, watching the waves curl round the outer breakwater with the full force of the gale behind them, their tops whipping off and driving to leeward.

'You seem very handy on a boat. The stays'l's rolled up forrard. There are lifejackets under the bunks. Put one on and go and set it, will you? Second halliard on the pin-rail to starboard of the mast.'

He watched her work on the pitching foredeck. *Merlin* rolled violently as a sea smashed against them. The bowsprit stabbed at the sky, the stern sank and the water lapped aboard under the toe-rail. The woman was surefooted as a cat, whipping the sail tie off, and subduing the flogging canvas with a foot as she reached for the halliard on the pin-rail. Robert swung the yacht into the wind. The bowsprit dipped and the stern rose, throwing the propeller into less dense water where it raced alarmingly. Robert realised he had had no experience of rough weather in a yacht since he was a boy, and *Merlin* had been an elderly boat then. It was too late to worry now.

The staysail rose with a rasp of hanks on the steel forestay and flogged and boomed as the woman bent to swig up and belay the halliard. Then she came aft and Robert let *Merlin* pay off the wind, the sail filled and began to draw. The woman trimmed the staysail sheets and Robert killed the engine. *Merlin* scudded to the eastward, running before the wind with the grey seas foaming up under her counter, their breaking crests shredding into streaks of spume which raced past them.

'Will he follow us?' he asked, as she stood in the cockpit beside him. She shook her head.

'In this weather? No, I was the sailing expert. He's got money and thinks it can buy him anything.' She averted her face. Robert left her to herself for a while; then he said:

376

'I could murder a cup of tea. If you take her for a bit I'll make a pot.'

From the shadowed obscurity of the cabin he watched her as he waited for the kettle to boil. She sniffed a couple of times and was clearly composing herself, though she was not forgetful of the boat and managed the tiller beautifully as the old yacht scended down the advancing waves. Despite a swelling eye she was pretty. He suppressed any prurient thoughts with the consideration that she was scarcely likely to favour his advances after the experience she had just been through. When the two mugs of tea were made he grabbed a bar of chocolate and passed it all up into the cockpit.

'Here, you'll feel better after this.'

'Thanks. D'you want to take her?'

'No, you're doing fine.'

'She's a lovely boat.'

'Yes, she is . . . and I could see from the way you belayed the stays'l' halliard that you're familiar with a bit more than the usual plastic rubbish. All that stainless steel wire and chromed winches.'

'Where are we going?' she asked, heading off his clumsy attempt to become personal.

'Where d'you want to go?' She shrugged and shot him a suspicious glance. 'I live on the boat,' he said as reasonably as he could, 'and I've cleared outwards with the customs people, so the world's your oyster.'

He wanted to remind her that he had not abducted her and that it was she who had cast the boat off. She continued to eye him warily for a moment then seemed to make up her mind.

'A boat of this vintage wasn't designed to beat to windward. Let's go where the wind blows – east.'

'Okay. Suits me.'

'My name's Sandy. It's short for Alexandra.'

'Alexandra's a good name.'

'I prefer Sandy,' she said sharply, and Robert regretted his over-familiarity.

'Sorry. I'm Robert, or Bob if you like, but as my surname is Martin and I object to being reminded of a dog medicine, I prefer Robert. More tea?'

'How long have you had her?' she asked, looking up at the

masthead as it gyrated giddily against the low fractus cloud. He found himself telling her about the *Merlin* and how she had once belonged to his one-legged father. And while she tended the tiller and the Seven Sisters passed in the spume to port and then the red and white tower of the lighthouse loomed at the foot of Beachy Head, he told her, too, of the loss of his job and with it his self-esteem. It was getting dark when he finished. The Royal Sovereign winked on the starboard bow and the wind blew with unabated fury, howling in the rigging and driving the yacht before it.

'Tide'll be against us soon,' he said. 'We're in for a wild night. I'll put the nav. lights on and rustle up something hot to eat. Are you all right here for a bit longer?'

'As long as you like.'

'There'll be a lot of shipping in the Dover Strait.'

'I can manage,' she replied.

As he struggled in the small galley space, glancing out at her so that once their eyes met and he smiled at her, he could not escape the conviction that she was his kind of girl.

They did not stop at either Boulogne or Calais. Sandy vetoed it and Robert realised that while they were at sea they occupied the cabin at different times and there was no awkwardness about the sleeping arrangements. They pressed on under the staysail alone while the gale blew so as not to strain the boat, but the recaulking proved itself and his confidence in *Merlin* increased by the hour.

The gale finally blew itself out during his watch below and he found she had let him sleep in. Puzzled, he went up to relieve her, pausing to look at the last fix on the chart. They were well off the coast, thirty miles to the north of Ostend. It did not really matter to him. Brighton or . . . he ran his finger along the Dutch coast. Or Breskens, it did not matter a damn! He clambered into the cockpit.

'Morning. Thanks for the lie in.'

'You were tired,' she said.

'Are we off to Breskens?' he asked, relieving her at the helm.

'If you like.'

'It's a Dutch fishing port, I believe.'

'I know,' Sandy said.

'Are you worried that he's following us?' he asked. 'You said the weather —'

'No, it's not that,' she said vaguely.

She lingered on deck, apparently unwilling to go below. Robert scanned the horizon for the featureless Dutch coast and became aware of a low cloud lying over the eastern horizon.

'What's that?' he said, frowning. 'It can't be pollution off the shore. Or can it? Whatever it is it's held down by a temperature inversion.'

They watched as the filthy, rust-coloured smudge stained the sky.

'It's the *Phoenix*, a ship that loads industrial waste and burns it in international waters. The cloud is full of toxic gases,' Sandy said in a tone of quiet confidence.

'You mean she just swans around offshore spewing out that crap?' he asked incredulously.

'Yes.'

'It's outrageous, unbelievable! How can reasonable people do such a stupid, irresponsible thing, let alone build a ship specially for it?'

'They'll go on doing it somewhere until we stop relying on what produces the waste, but you can advance reasons for doing the most appalling things. There's always the lesser of two evils.'

'Yes, but that's a specious logic. It's irresponsibility on a massive scale.'

'And invites retribution, do you think?' she said, tilting her head at him.

'Yes, I think so,' he said, gaining conviction as he spoke. 'If we don't stop doing it, it will do for us. Of course, the vast majority of people don't want to give any of their comforts up so they won't take the initiative. Lots of people care in a vague, helpless sort of way.' He stopped, then added disconsolately, 'so these things are always left to a few cranks to blaze the trail.' And quite unaccountably Robert recalled Sonia Garcia trying to live forever and the hurt look in young Anne Bagshot's eyes as her ship sliced through the dying razorbills and Nick Roland sitting in the Singapore bar saying, 'It's like the end of the whole fucking world.'

'I'm glad you think that way,' Sandy said. 'I'll get

something to eat.' She disappeared below and Robert checked the sails. Both main and jib were now set as they ran down towards the coast. There were ships all about them, heading in for the Maas and the vast port of Rotterdam where he had unhappily left the *Loch Moidart*. But he had eyes only for the rust-red cloud that rose from the waist of the inaptly named *Phoenix* as it coiled upwards and spread in a sinister pall.

She passed coffee and sandwiches up and followed them into the cockpit with a camera.

'You should get some sleep,' Robert advised.

'I'm all right . . . Christ, what a smell!' She stared up at the ruddy sky, clasping the mug of coffee and wrinkling her nostrils as they were assailed by faint whiffs of chemicals. ' " 'In the last days, saith God, I will display signs' ",' she murmured, draining the coffee and picking up the camera, ' " 'on the earth below – blood and fire and drifting smoke.' " '

Robert did not catch the quotation properly, for the words were lost in the click and whirr of the Nikon's motor drive and he was watching the noisome pall of hanging smoke as it drew overhead.

'Robert,' she suddenly said, turning to him and speaking with a warmth she had not used before, 'could you ever be a trail-blazing crank?'

CHAPTER TWENTY-NINE
Acts of Apostles

'You didn't do an extra stint at the helm for my benefit, did you?' Robert asked. 'You steered *Merlin* well off the coast quite deliberately to intercept that ship.' He pointed astern to where the ugly, fuming outline of the *Phoenix* broke the line of the horizon.

'That's clever of you. Did the camera give it away?'

'That and your conversation. You obviously care. But what I don't understand is if I hadn't been handy in Brighton, were you and your supposed friend on the way to do this? To photograph the *Phoenix*?'

'Yes, we were. I suppose I owe you a proper explanation —'

'Wait a minute,' Robert broke in, his tone irritable. 'Before you suborn me with a frank explanation, do you mind telling me if you expect me to break the law on behalf of you, or whatever organisation you represent? Is that why you asked me if I was prepared to become a crank?'

'Yes,' she said quietly, 'I suppose it was. It was a crazy plan, I know, but that bastard back there . . .' She ran a hand through her hair with an air of desperation. 'Have you got anything to drink?'

'There's a whisky bottle in the port locker under my bunk.'

'Do you want one?' she asked, returning with two tumblers and the bottle.

'Why not?'

She poured the measures and he sat at the tiller. She swallowed the fierce spirit with a supressed shudder. He knew she would talk if he was patient and he did not misjudge her. The *Merlin* ran south-east, her mainsail boomed out on the port quarter on a broad reach, scending gracefully down the swell left by the gale, a light breeze cutting a fine chop over the sun-dappled sea.

'I'm a freelance journalist,' she began, 'television, magazines and newspapers, you know the kind of thing. I specialise in wildlife and the environment. That bastard Brian is a lawyer. He's very successful and like a lot of people spawned by the enterprise culture, he's ready to jump on any bloody bandwagon if there's dosh to be made out of it. To be fair to him, and setting aside his idea that a BMW, a sodding great yacht and a gold credit card give him vaginal access when and where he feels like it, he was doing us at Eco-watch a lot of good. The project we were working on was to chart the actual movements of the *Phoenix*. She's supposed to incinerate further offshore and we felt if we could get her on a technicality we'd have a rather better chance of exposing these people for what they are: irresponsible profiteers who don't even obey the pathetically inadequate laws they are supposed to. It was his boat; he usually potters round the Solent and he wanted me along for the navigation and the watch-keeping as much as my journalistic involvement.

'You were quite right,' she went on. 'I've done a lot of sailing, including an *Observer* transatlantic, and I was a boat nigger in the West Indies when I was in my teens. I've got a bit of paper, like you, to say I'm a proper sailor. We needed someone with credentials to establish the position of the *Phoenix* when we located her, and Brian's legal mind (assuming he could get it off the subject of sex long enough) to do the necessary ship-to-ship on the VHF radio.' She sighed. 'You don't have a radio, so the plot's gone off at half cock.'

'Well, I'm sorry about that,' he said, 'but you can't now be serious about sabotaging that thing? I mean even if your holdall's stuffed with army surplus limpet mines and we succeed in sticking them to the hull of the *Phoenix*, all we'll do is dump that load of toxic shit in the North Sea.'

She managed a tired laugh. 'I knew you were a bloody romantic the moment you came to my rescue. No, but if you want to help there is something you can do. I'm shattered.

The Scotch has made me drowsy. D'you mind if we talk about it in Breskens?'

'No. I'll give you a shout when I need you. Sleep well.'

He was surprised how much he meant that last remark, and as he trimmed the sheets and handled the tiller he realised that he was supremely happy.

How long, he wondered in the weeks following that evening in Breskens, does it take one person to come to know and love another? He had sailed with men for months and known them no better at the end of the time than at the beginning. He had known women for years (even intimately, like Mitsouko in the Yokohama bar whom he had liked and loved in the technical sense) without ever loving them. What was it about Sandy that made the difference? He could scarcely have started a relationship in a more bizarre way, for she was at least temporarily hostile to men generally in the aftermath of the attempted rape.

But under that apocalyptic cloud they discovered they were of one mind. When they berthed *Merlin* in Breskens and found the deck and sails covered with a fine red dust, they had not wanted to wander ashore like wide-eyed tourists, but continued the discussion begun earlier in the day. They sat in *Merlin*'s saloon while the rapacious screech of the gulls wheeling excitedly about the incoming fishing boats filled the air outside.

'So you're completely free?' Sandy asked, as they sat on opposite sides of the extended mahogany table.

'Absolutely. Yours to command, in fact, up to a point.'

'The point of legality?'

'Yes. Romantic I may be, but I've an ingrained respect for order. Sorry, it's genetic and induced. Too many years of professional service. Besides, I'll support eccentric cranki-ness but not piracy, which is what some environmental bodies have been pretty close to attempting.'

'So,' she said, choosing her words carefully, 'you're opposed to the philosophy of coopting the lesser of two evils.'

'I'd rather not employ evil at all. It weakens the case.'

'So you wouldn't fight fire with fire?'

He thought for a moment and then shrugged. 'It would be

foolish to be categorical, wouldn't it? Foolish to be expected to obey a hypothetically arrived at promise. I might, but I might not. It would depend on circumstances.'

She seemed to accept this half-hearted commitment but he thought by her silence that she had written him off. He found the notion hurt him; he did not want rejection.

'Let me explain,' he went on with a faint air of desperation. 'I've been at sea since I was a boy. My father died as an indirect result of a war wound; my grandfather died at sea during the last war after having a lucky escape at Jutland in the first when his ship blew up; the explosion killed his cousin and I've an ancient "aunt" still living who has burnt a candle all these years in his memory. Somewhere in the family's cupboard there's the skeleton of an admiral who shot himself for losing a battleship or something, and any number of sailor boys who left their bones to bleach, in the line of duty, on foreign shores.

'Now people who cite their antecedents as evidence of their own worth are generally deeply boring, but bear with me . . . have another Scotch.'

'Thanks. I'm listening. Go on.'

'The aunt isn't the only female casualty. My grandfather became a widower in the 'flu pandemic after the First War and married again. His wife's still alive, I think, a weird and once very beautiful woman whom I met a few times in the States. She's a casualty not because she's odd, but because she was a victim of the Russian Revolution. We also took in two Jewish children, refugees who arrived before I was born from Germany. One's a lesbian, which I can't think is what Jehovah intended her to be, the other is a major general, or somesuch, and continues the military traditions of Gideon by knocking walls down with tanks.

'Somewhere in all this is a potty woman, the wife of the Admiral, who went mad. Then there's my own mother, a disappointed soul, who tended my father until his early death and now, poor dear, has the unenviable task of looking after the aforementioned aunt Vera.

'Then there was the other woman in my grandfather's life, his mistress who was captured when Singapore fell. She had a terrible time at the hands of the Japanese. I met her too, and I may as well tell you now that when I was sixteen and

384

she was in her sixties I had an affair with her. She was the first woman I ever slept with.

'All in all, one way or another, contentment or happiness or whatever our strivings are supposed to earn us, has been in somewhat short supply. I don't suppose for a moment we're unique as a family, but I grew up with a burden of historical obligation on my shoulders. I hated it and hated everything to do with war. My father didn't seem like a hero to me, particularly as he made my mother's life difficult. He looked more like a piece of wreckage.

'When I went to sea I decided I was not going to marry. Then the bastard ship-owners sold the entire shipping company, lock, stock and barrel. Of course I can still go to sea on a substandard rust-bucket with a crew of underpaid Filipinos, no financial security and not much prospect of leave, but when I see the likes of your Brian riding the hog's back, I ask why should I?

'And when I'm expected to volunteer to serve Queen and country in the Falklands, do you blame me if I cavil a bit, and ask cynically what for?

'Oh, sure, the owners of the once-great Loch Line gave me a redundancy payment and, thank God, I bought *Merlin* with some of it and spent the rest on this Scotch, but I'm a bit short on the patriotic enthusiasm for the new Britain. Besides, as a merchant seafarer, I regard myself as an internationalist, if that doesn't sound absurdly pretentious. Didn't someone wise say the day of the nation state is over?'

She nodded. 'Teilhard de Chardin, a French Jesuit and palaeontologist.'

'That's the fellow. Anyway, here endeth the lesson and thanks for listening'

She twisted the glass in her strong brown fingers. 'With those admirals and things, I'm not surprised you rebelled.'

'It's a funny thing. My father was in the Andrew, and he had some sort of mystical experience in the war with Japan. He asked me to break the family tradition and never to serve in the Royal Navy. I think he foresaw something of the mess the world's in. Anyway, I agreed, not entirely for the highly charged moral reasons he intended, but because it seemed the Royal Navy had little future and the merchant service offered a better career.' He smiled bitterly. 'Ironically, the reverse has proved true. The Falklands gave the Royal Navy a new lease of life and the merch. won't survive.'

He drained his glass and stood up, fishing for a box of matches on the stove to light the oil lamps. The rosy glow reflected off the varnished woodwork and gleamed on the brass porthole fittings, giving the saloon a cosy, intimate air.

'Why did you say "I may as well tell you now" about your affair with the elderly lady?'

He shrugged. 'I don't know.'

'Were you . . . *are* you ashamed of it?'

He shook his head and looked directly at her. 'No. I just wanted to tell you. It seemed important.'

'It sounded like a confession.'

'Maybe it was. Maybe it was all a confession. What about you?'

'Me? I'm not going to confess!'

'I don't expect that, but are you married?'

'There's your bunk, Robert.'

'That's not what I mean, for God's sake. I just want to know.'

'Yes.' She sighed. 'Yes, I am. Sorry.'

'What are you apologising for? I'm hungry. Shall we eat ashore?'

She made a face. 'Can't we have something on board? I don't want to turn into a tourist.'

'Or our partnership into boy-meets-girl?'

'You're too perceptive for your own good,' she said.

Robert opened a locker. 'There's some pasta and a tin of Bolognaise sauce. I think there's even some parmesan cheese somewhere . . . yes, here.'

'That'll do fine.'

'Tuck this away in the big drawer underneath you.' He passed her the folded chart to make some room. She did as she was bid while he busied himself with a tin-opener and a saucepan of water.

'Did you do these?' She had taken an untidy folio of sketches and watercolours from the chart drawer.

'Yes. I had some notion of making a few bob by selling them. Enough to get by with for myself and keep *Merlin* in varnish and anti-fouling.'

She was leafing through the stiff sheets and he found it

gave him great pleasure to let her see them.

'They're very good, epecially this one.' She held up a watercolour of a breaching humpback.

'The whale has become a sort of totemic symbol, hasn't it?' he said. 'Nice, middle-class, liberal, ecology-minded people have stickers in their environmentally destructive estate cars saying "Stop the Bloody Whaling!" and "Save the Whales!" Very English to mobilise an animal to rally a cause.'

'You're getting cynical again,' she cautioned.

'Sorry.' He tipped the pasta into the boiling water and poured them each another whisky. 'They, the whales that is, are a bit like British seamen.'

'You mean ugly and misunderstood?' He laughed at this manifestation of a sense of humour.

'No, I mean we will only value them when there aren't any left.' He began to lay the cabin table. 'What was it you were saying when you were photographing that toxic cloud?'

She put the folio aside. 'Oh, that. It's the only bit of the Bible I can quote. It's from the Acts of the Apostles. " 'In the last days,' saith God, 'I will display signs . . . on the earth below . . . blood and fire and drifting smoke.' " I remember it because it was used in one of those dreadful religious education lessons at school where an agnostic mathematician was obliged to teach thirty alleged Christian girls, one Hindu, one Confucian and a Muslim, about,' – she held up two fingers of each hand and wiggled them as quotes – ' "religion". This poor woman had decided to address the problem of our generation growing up under the threat of nuclear war, though she used the euphemistic term "umbrella". She told us we were privileged to live in the last epoch (quite why I can't remember now, though I think it had something to do with man dispensing with the superstitions of religion and embracing a scientific philosophy). Anyway, according to our mentor, the reference to "blood" alluded to the holocaust of the First World War, and "fire" the explosion of the atomic bomb. "Drifting smoke", she thought, meant the danger signs of letting science fall into the wrong hands, signified by the genocide of the Jews. You know how these things grip your imagination when you're a teen-ager. I've never forgotten that lesson. I suppose in a way it

387

influenced my life. I don't believe in prophecies, but it never occurred to me until this morning that the sequence of disastrous "signs" our poor RE mistress revealed to us was better explained if "drifting smoke" referred to pollution and the death of the planet. First we kill each other. Then we kill whole nations. Finally we murder the planet.' She gave a short laugh and added self-deprecatingly, 'It's very silly really. It's what journalists call "looking for an angle", some line to hand an article on.'

He placed two plates on the table. 'So what are we going to do about it?'

She thought for a while, tucking into the meal appreciatively. 'Tell me how far afield you would take *Merlin*?'

He shrugged. 'Anywhere within reason. It's supposed to be spring. I've nothing else on the agenda.'

'Okay. Tomorrow I will make a telephone call, then I'm going to buy you a VHF radio. We'll also have to lay in a fair stock of food and water.'

'I accept the radio with thanks and the food will come in handy. But what's the significance of the phone call and where are we going?'

'The phone call's to my husband.'

'Ah. What does that mean?'

'Several things. It means I'm married and I'm letting him know where I'm off to with you.'

'Oh, I see,' he said, confused.

'Does that mollify your inordinate male pride?' she said, eyebrows raised. 'Though don't let it raise expectations in other directions.'

'Of course not. Anyway, where *are* we going?'

She turned to the settee where she had laid the folio of watercolour paintings. 'How well do you really like whales?'

CHAPTER THIRTY
The Last Battle

'*Gaia, Gaia, Gaia*, this is the yacht *Merlin* calling, over.'

Sandy waited, listening for a reply on channel sixteen. She had been calling at hourly intervals since dawn without a response. She put her head through the hatch. 'Nothing,' she reported.

From the tiller Robert thought she looked exhausted. Under a hard reefed mainsail and spitfire jib, *Merlin* drove to windward as best she could. The wind was strong, near gale force and cutting up a rough sea that, superimposed on a heavy swell, made life on board uncomfortable. A lowering overcast promised more of the same, if not worse, and the appearance of petrels dabbling in their wake only emphasised the likelihood of a full gale by the evening.

'Let's tack and make for the Shetlands. We can be tucked under the lee of Unst by nightfall and get a good night's sleep.'

'All right.' She nodded almost listlessly and dropped out of sight, pulling the hatch closed.

Robert checked the mainsheet, took the coil of the lee jib sheet off its belaying pin and saw the lazy weather sheet was free.

'I'm going about,' he called, warning Sandy of *Merlin*'s imminent manoeuvre. He waited a moment, struggling to adjust the running backstays, then gently pushed the tiller away from him. *Merlin* turned into the wind, no longer heeling and surging steadily forward but leaping up and down, her bowsprit alternately stabbing sea and sky. Beyond the stem, halfway along the bowsprit and tugging at its steel traveller, the flapping spitfire jib flogged its two sheets. The heavy flax mainsail thundered as the wind played on both sides of it and the vibration, transmitted via the mast to the heavy elm step on the keelson, shook the whole boat. The big yellow spruce boom swung back and forth above Robert's head, the bights of the lazy jacks whipping like crazy lassos. He ducked with the ease of practice, held the tiller over with his hip and cast the starboard jib sheet off its cleat, holding a last turn in his hand until *Merlin* paid off onto the port tack. Behind him the main sheet ceased to thud back and forth across the horse as the great brown sail filled with wind and the backed jib suddenly increased the yacht's swing.

Satisfied, he let fly the jib sheet he was holding and trimmed the sail to the new tack. Playing for a moment with sheets and tiller, he balanced *Merlin* satisfactorily, took a turn with the tiller rope to hold her steady and leapt from the cockpit.

Throwing back the hatch, he dived below in search of a chart and a new course. Sandy was standing half naked in the saloon, trying to wash from an inadequate amount of water slopping in a plastic bowl on the cabin sole.

Sorry,' he muttered, bending over the chart to cover their mutual embarrassment, 'I need a new course.'

They had gone to some pains to avoid any such intimacy before, a tacit agreement existing between them that physical contact was not, as it were, on the agenda. The affair at Brighton and the existence of a husband laid an embargo on all reference to it after the night in Breskens. In port or at anchor Robert simply went on deck while Sandy undressed or changed, slipping into his own bunk in his underpants and a T-shirt afterwards. At sea the routine of watch-keeping, until that moment of altered plans, had kept them automatically apart.

Robert quickly manipulated the Decca navigator and laid the new course off the chart. He had only a few moments in which to work before *Merlin* demanded his presence on the helm again. When he had finished he turned quickly aft, repeated his apologies and put out his hands to climb on deck.

'Robert!'

He turned. She stood braced against the table one arm

holding the hand rail that ran below the starboard portholes. She was naked from the waist upwards. Full-breasted, she had a lasciviously small waist, a waist that reminded him of the Sri Lankan nautch girls he had once seen performing erotic wonders in the cave paintings of Sigiriya.

Merlin lost her heel and began to tremble. Robert hesitated for a moment longer, then he leapt for the tiller. As the yacht heeled again and steadied on her new course, Sandy smiled to herself and reached for her sleeping bag.

Robert came aft from the foredeck where the anchor bit into the clean sand bottom of Haroldswick Bay. A mile away the houses of the village huddled beyond a crescent of sand at the head of the bay. Beyond lay a background of rock outcrops and bare, windswept moorland.

Robert made fast the mainsail ties and killed the idling engine. In the sudden silence the piping of the oyster-catchers seemed unnaturally loud and filled with a poignant sadness. He recalled the same birdcall on the banks of the River Deben years earlier, when he and his father had righted the world's wrongs over a fire of driftwood and a cigarette.

'Aren't you hungry?' Sandy called from the cabin.

'Coming.' He went below and swung aside to the chart table. 'Good of you to cook,' he said abstractedly as he wrote up the log book.

'Least I could do after the lie-in.'

'You looked exhausted, and I can manage to anchor the old lady on my own. Pity we can't locate *Gaia*.' He put down the pencil and turned to her; his mouth fell open in astonishment.

He could not deny he had spent many of the past hours thinking about her, wondering why she had behaved as she had. He uncharitably concluded that she had teased him deliberately, even, perhaps, perversely. It was a disappointing thought.

Seeing her now his uncertainty was undiminished.

'Well?' she said, half smiling. 'What d' you think?'

All he had ever seen her wearing were oilskins, sweaters and jeans, a sailing smock or a jogging suit. Now she wore a pair of ski pants and a white silk blouse, cinched in to that slender waist with a wide belt. An amber necklace lodged a huge golden pendant between her breasts.

'I, er . . .'

'A bit tartish, I'm afraid. My bimbo look for Brian, but wasted on the bastard. It has the virtue of folding up small. Let's eat before it gets cold.'

'Yes. Sorry. I'm a bit surprised.' He remained confused rather than surprised, but was guarding his tongue. In any case he was ravenous.

'No,' she said, 'it's me who should apologise. I don't know why I behaved like that earlier. It was unfair. But it was also unpremeditated.'

'I had you marked down as a prick teaser,' he said frankly. 'I'd even begun to make excuses for our friend Brian.'

'Did I? Tease it, I mean.'

'It's insufferably arrogant of beautiful women to assume every man wants to fuck them.'

'Well that's a conversation stopper.'

And so it proved until the plates were empty.

'Do you want to take a stroll ashore?' Robert asked.

'No.' She stood to clear the plates, moving with a deliberate grace. He lit the oil lamps and sat back on the settee as she bent to let down the table leaves, her strong brown wrists within reach. He put out his hand and touched her.

'You're quite free to sit opposite and talk ecology until we fall asleep, you know.'

She straightened up, grasping his hand and pulling him to his feet beside her. The amber necklace, articulated by short lengths of gold chain, moved with her breathing, catching the gentle glow of the oil lamps and a star of refracted pale gold light spilled enchantingly across her breasts. He drew her towards him, though he hesitated, thinking of Brian and Brighton.

'For God's sake, Robert, kiss me.'

He drew her onto the bunk, undressing her tenderly. He felt the desiccation of her tension and soothed her until she relaxed and signalled her readiness.

They did not pull apart afterwards, but lay wordlessly together, as only people in their situation can, until nature withdrew him and they were again separate beings.

'Do you believe in fate?' she asked, when her heartbeat had subsided. 'Do you believe we were somehow meant to meet?'

'No.' He laughed quietly. 'But once we had met I rather hoped we were fated to do that.'

'You're no better than Brian,' she said without rancour.

'I thought I was a lot better than Brian.'

'Yes,' she whispered, 'you were.'

He lay still, aware their thoughts were drifting apart on the different tracks that made nonsense of notions of fate. The reflection filled him with an almost unbearable sadness.

'The Brians of this world have got a lot to answer for,' he murmured, attempting to arrest the distancing. She propped herself onto one elbow and gazed down at him. The amber necklace continued to shed its golden rays across her voluptuous body.

'I've told you before, you're too bloody perceptive,' she said, bending and kissing him. 'Don't ask too much of me, will you?'

'I don't ask anything of you.'

'I've been hurt before . . . and I've hurt other people. I just don't want to be unfair.'

'Of course not,' he said, and the kiss tasted bitter on his lips. 'Of course not.'

The late twilight of the high latitude settled over the bay and the wind went down with the sun. After a while he asked, 'What about your husband?'

She sat and drew up her knees, regarding him from troubled eyes. He wanted to reach for his pencil and capture the pathos of her.

'I've been a bastard to you, Robert, I'm sorry. We've been separated for three years.'

'But you've never divorced?'

'No.'

'I think you should revise your lack of belief in fate, Robert,' Sandy said, flinging back the hatch to let in a brilliant shaft of sunshine. 'Look!'

He struggled out of his sleeping bag and stood beside her, his arm about her waist. In the bay, three quarters of a mile away, lay the *Gaia*.

'There she is, the flagship of Eco-watch, a perfect rendezvous.'

Robert studied the former North Sea oil-rig supply ship. Painted a livid orange, with the well-known logo of Eco-watch conspicuous on her sides, her jagged silhouette looked incongruous in the lonely bay.

'Come on,' said Sandy with sudden proprietorial pride, kissing his unshaven cheek, 'I'll introduce you to Mark.'

'Who's Mark?'

'The project director,' she said. 'He's a biologist.' She was laughing at him.

'What's so funny?' he said.

'He's also my husband.'

The *Gaia* wallowed at slow speed, her wheelhouse crowded with a motley collection of scientists, seafarers and seasick volunteers who manned her. They wore brightly coloured anoraks and parkas against the cold of the high Arctic, their hands in mittens. *Gaia*'s captain, a bearded master mariner known to all as Adrian, stood beside Sandy's husband, Mark. The two men were studying a ship on the horizon across a gently heaving waste of grey-green sea under a cloudy sky. There was an air of expectancy about the little crowd.

Robert leaned on the chart table alongside Sandy as she chatted quietly to a Japanese micro-biologist, a beautiful young woman with long, straight, black hair who reminded him of Mitsouko. They were rediscovering a lapsed friendship while he was staring at the chart and the outline of Jan Mayen island in the wild desolation of the Greenland Sea. To the north of their pencilled position the pecked lines of the pack ice limit wandered sinisterly across the mathematical precision of the meridians and parallels. He thought briefly of *Merlin* far to the southward, lying to head and stern anchors in Haroldswick Bay. He hoped she was safe.

She would be all right. It *was* all fated anyway. He glanced at Sandy and felt the quickening in the pit of his stomach that was the body's first response to the prickling of intense desire. He loved her helplessly and felt a strong, foolish urge to secure her love by the ancient rite of marriage. He knew

394

she could divorce Mark, but some link clearly remained between them. Perhaps it was just professional, for she had made her attachment to himself obvious when they boarded *Gaia* and signed on as supernumary volunteers. Mark seemed to have accepted the fact with an easy tolerance, yet there still remained those doubts planted by Sandy herself.

'It's the factory ship, all right,' said Adrian authoritatively, and a *frisson* of excitement went through the waiting group.

'I've got two . . . three, no four echoes to the north and west of her.' The voice came from the visor of the Racal-Decca radar set where the hidden features of the *Gaia*'s Second Mate sought out their real quarry just over the horizon.

'They'll be the catchers,' Adrian said as he entered the wheelhouse.

Automatically Robert drew back from the chart table allowing Adrian and Mark to study the chart. There was a mumbled conversation and then Adrian thrust the engine controllers hard against the stops and began to turn the control knob of the automatic pilot. With a trembling lurch that set a trio of female students squealing, the *Gaia* swung to port and increased speed. She began to vibrate as the big diesel engines wound up to their maximum speed and her ugly, bluff bow smashed aggressively through the Arctic seas, sending icy spray over the wheelhouse windows where the wipers scraped incessantly.

The Second Mate had finished plotting the positions of the catchers and Adrian was stepping off distances with a pair of dividers. He pointed to one of them and Mark nodded his approval. Adrian picked up the PA hand-mike from the control consol.

'Do you hear there?' he said in a commanding voice and the giggling in the wheelhouse subsided. 'Targets are in sight. There'll be a briefing in the mess in one hour. Target time, about four this afternoon.'

'Well,' Mark said to Sandy, 'you and Robert seem to have brought us some luck at last. Let's go below.'

The *Gaia* dipped below the factory ship's horizon and began to stalk her prey.

*

'You all know what to do. We harass without breaking the law. We want hard evidence of them acting illegally, particularly in respect of young, undersized whales or gravid females. Any questions?' Mark dealt with a few queries and then looked at his watch. 'Right, once we go in it's a war of attrition. We keep at them until they stop, so you've time for three hours' sleep.'

It seemed to Robert an impossibly tall order.

Down in the tiny cabin Robert made love to Sandy. Afterwards they both dozed until the *Gaia*'s klaxon woke them and Adrian's voice came over the PA system.

'Stand by. We've half an hour to launch time. Stand by.'

They separated with a kiss and helped each other clamber into their orange survival suits.

'I think they're quite glad we came,' Sandy said. 'Extra inflatable crews mean they can sustain the harassment for much longer. Just remember, keep away from the catchers' sides. The bastards like nothing better than to chuck a load of shite over us.'

'You can drive if you like.'

'We'll make a good team, whatever we do,' she said smiling at him.

On *Gaia*'s bridge Robert watched through binoculars with mounting indignation and anger. He was indignant on behalf of the whales, knowing how low their numbers had dwindled, for the remorseless action of the catcher struck him as stupid, but he felt angry because of their impotence to effectively stop the Russian whaler.

She had been caught in the act of harpooning a Right whale as the *Gaia* had arrived on the scene and launched her three fast inflatable Seariders. The big boats bounced across the heaving sea that surged between the two ships, the thick eutrophic soup the docile Right whales strained for krill between their baleen plates.

'They'll go on and on and on like this until they've simply wiped out the cetacean population,' Mark said, a note of despair in his voice. 'Even governments who oppose whaling in principle lubricate certain parts of their guided missiles with sperm oil.'

And Robert felt again the old hatred of war which

seemed, in the charged moment, to insinuate its insidious influence into every action of mankind.

'Well we can't save *that* poor bugger,' said Adrian, slowing *Gaia* and taking her in a slow circle round the Russian catcher as it drew its prize alongside and secured it. A flock of predatory seabirds screeched and wheeled, dipping down towards the dead whale in a frenzy while the swirling red stain of the cetacean's blood rusted the sea.

The low monotone of someone dictating into a small tape recorder and the click and whirr of cameras accompanied their scrutiny. The Russian sailors working on deck ignored their presence, but on the catcher's bridge they were being studied through huge binoculars.

'She's reporting our presence to the factory ship, Adrian,' the radio operator reported, 'and calling up the nearest of her sister ships.'

'How far away is she now, Jim?' Adrian asked his Second Mate.

'She's been closing for the last half hour at speed,' said the headless voice from the radar. 'I think she's pursuing a pod. Eight and a half miles, bearing two nine three.'

Adrian picked up his glasses. 'There she is and you're right! There are spouts ahead of her, some way yet. Mark! Let's recall the Seariders and try to head off this other pig.'

'Okay, let's go!'

They saw the whales clearly forty minutes later with the second catcher close behind them. The high, flared bow with its heavy harpoon gun bore down on the frightened beasts whose fine double spout and heavy jet-black bodies identified them.

'Bowheads!' said Mark excitedly, lowering his glasses and making a note. 'There are estimated to be less than two and a half thousand of them left anywhere now, and hardly any have been reported here in the Greenland Sea.'

'And once,' said Rudolf, a German cetologist who had been dictating into his portable tape recorder, 'they were so numerous you could anchor your ship at Spitzbergen and simply row about in your whale boat catching as many as you wanted.'

Robert watched the Seariders despatched again, watched them daringly drive in close under the catcher's bow and interpose themselves between the lethal harpoon gun and the helpless whales. The bowheads swam obligingly in a tight-knit pod and a straight line, perfect targets for the whalers.

'They're enjoying it,' Robert muttered, 'they're actually *enjoying* it, those bastards. It's a real war to them, with our people dashing in and out and making them prove their tenacity and skill and all the old supposed virtues of the huntsman.'

'They get fed up in the end, though,' said Mark. 'It depends on whose nerve lasts longest, then they make mistakes.'

'You mean they miss?'

'Yes.'

'They're talking to the factory ship again,' reported the radio operator.

'Okay. Let's start relieving the boats' crews. Sandy? Robert? You two ready?'

'Yes, sure.'

'I think the factory ship's launching a chopper,' said the radio operator.

Adrian slowed the ship and they began effecting the transfers. The first Searider to be relieved bounced alongside the low afterdeck of the *Gaia*. Fuel tanks were exchanged and fuel pipes connected. Sandy took the bowman's place and relieved the young student at the controls of the big twin fifty-horsepower Mercury outboard engines. Then Robert lowered himself after her and the grinning young student scrambled out stiffly. Robert took hold of the painter, Sandy gave a thumbs up. He cast off, nearly fell as she gunned the engines and put the helm over. The Searider leapt forward, crossed the smooth fan of water behind *Gaia*'s bow wave then leapt clear of the sea with a roar of cavitating screws as they crossed it. Then they were alone, the *Gaia* with her large Eco-watch logo on hull and funnels dwindled rapidly in size, a skua swept low over them and they were flung roughly about as the speeding Searider smashed from wave top to wave top under full throttle.

The Russian catcher loomed close as Sandy found its outer wash and, just behind the advancing crest, used the smooth water thus created to overtake and sweep in under the catcher's port bow.

Robert could smell the stale stink of the catcher and the

sour whiffs of the whale's exhalation as they decelerated. Abaft the forecastle of the catcher a group of Russian seamen in blue coats and fur hats were gathered.

'Watch those bastards,' yelled Sandy, 'brace yourself!'

'I've been doing that anyway.'

The jet of ice-cold water from the hose struck them and almost overturned the boat, but Sandy pushed the throttles hard down and they were right under the catcher's bow, her anchor dipping and rising dangerously close above their heads.

Ahead of them the other two boats, one waiting for them to relieve her, bobbed astern of the whales. A bucket of excrement was sluiced down the hawse pipe and cascaded over the Searider.

'Bastards!' roared Robert, joining the general shouting marking the exchange of views between ecologists and whaler. With thumbs-up the relieved boat accelerated and pulled away. Sandy drove the Searider close astern of the second inflatable. Then it too side-slipped as they took over the main task, closed right up in the very wake of the panting whales. The plumes of their spouts rose into the crystal clear air drenching them with a fine warm spray, and the great jet-black humps of their bodies rose and fell as they strained to escape. Just below the surface of the sea and disturbing it far less than the thrashing Seariders or the hissing bow of the catcher, Robert could see the powerful stroking of the bowhead's huge flukes.

He looked astern. The rusty arch of the catcher's bow loomed above them, rising and falling in the swell. The abrupt flare of her plating exposed the gun platform and the cruel barbs of the harpoon in its brutish muzzle. Two booted men, muffled in heavy coats and with fur caps pulled down over their eyes, stood on either side of the gun. One was shouting and waving his arms. The other watched them coldly. He carried a hunting rifle.

Robert bent to Sandy's ear and shouted to her above the roar of the engines. 'One of those bastards has got a rifle.'

'They'll try and puncture the inflatable chambers. It doesn't matter too much.' She pointed at patches on the grey neoprene tubes that gave the glass reinforced plastic V of the lower hull its buoyancy. 'But we might have to retire.'

The air, already filled with the roar of the Mercurys, the hiss of the blowing whales, the splash and thump of the Seariders and the thunder and thrash of the pursuing catcher, was suddenly split by the sharp crack of the rifle. The boat astern began to lose air, its coxswain making frantic signals that he was pulling away as a second then a third shot pierced the fragile neoprene fabric.

Once their Searider was alone under that predatory bow, Robert realised they were engaged on a forlorn hope. Their efforts could not be crowned with success, for the resources of the hunters would outlast their own. He suddenly felt too old, too disillusioned for the cause. Was he a coward, as Aunt Vee had once implied, or did he in truth lack the commitment Sandy expected? He could not tell, except that his experiences had made him cynical and a man, after all, was but the sum of his experiences.

He glanced back over his shoulder. The Russian with the gun was drawing a bead on them. For a moment the man's head lifted above his gun sight and he stared at Robert, the ghost of a smile playing about his thin mouth. Robert recognised the hated ancient eyes of the warrior, the disturber of peace.

'It's our turn now!' he yelled to Sandy.

'Move about in the boat! Confuse him!' she shouted over her shoulder.

He did as she said, leaping about like a mad sprite so the Russian marksman's rifle wavered uncertainly. How long could he keep it up, clinging to handholds as he tried to confuse the angering man above him? He felt his breath coming in gasps, he slipped and missed his footing, jumped up again and raged inwardly at the futility of what he was doing. Taunting the Russian only made more certain the end of the chase.

To port of them Indian war whoops came from the remanned Searider they had first relieved. Her helmsman, less skilful than Sandy, came rocketing in from the beam. It struck Robert that the contrast between themselves and the Russian was incomprehensible to these well-motivated youngsters. The Eco-watch volunteers came bouncing alongside cheering and yelling abuse with something Robert could only feel was an arrogance inappropriate to the struggle.

400

Something more effective had to be done, and he had little time to think for to the wild noises about him there was now added the approaching drone of a helicopter.

And in the instant these thoughts flashed across his mind, the Russian had acted. The rifle slug tore through their own Searider. He could hear the insistent hiss of escaping air.

'Shit!' Sandy swore. Her eyes met his and in that split second he made up his mind.

He reached out across the punctured chamber, his body restricting the leak, stretching across to grab the life line running round the outside of the neighbouring Searider. The coxswain understood and the boats came together.

'Swap boats!' Robert roared. *'Now!'* Generations of petty authority came to his assistance. Sandy obeyed for reasons she could never understand in the rational light of hindsight, beyond acknowledging the ferocity of his expression and shocked by the closeness of the Russian shots to herself.

A second slug passed through the buoyancy chamber on the far side of the Searider and the bow wave of the catcher foamed up and over them, flinging them aside, clear of her bow. Sandy tumbled into the other boat.

'What are you going to do?' someone shouted.

'Keep out of my way!' Robert yelled back, letting go of the grab line.

'Robert?' There was sudden anxiety in Sandy's voice, but Robert had seized the deflating Searider's controls. The other boat, with Sandy aboard, fell back. Two of its inflation chambers were already sagging emptily.

The catcher's bow had overtaken Robert. The Russians had run back and were now busy round the breech of the harpoon gun, clearly thinking they had thrown off their tormentors. The loaded barrel depressed towards the whales.

He forced the Searider's throttles to full speed.

'Robert!' He heard Sandy's cry and from the corner of his eye saw the other Searider accelerating again in a crazy attempt to support him by regaining station and preventing the kill. He waved his arm.

'Keep back!' he shouted. 'Keep back!'

'No, Robert! *No!*'

'Look after *Merlin*,' he roared, howling the yacht's name

401

as a battle-cry to sustain his courage as he bent low over the Searider's steering wheel. He throttled back alongside the largest Bowhead, a female with two calves on her flanks, then he put the helm over.

The Searider's solid V-shaped lower hull struck the whale and its whirring propellers wounded the ligamentous fibres of its blubber. But the harpoon struck Robert, struck him between the shoulders and its charged head exploded below his heart.

'Please sit down, my dear,' said the younger of the two elderly ladies.

Sandy shook her head and remained standing in the drawing room of The Lees. To sit would mean a capitulation, an acknowledgement that she too had joined the long list of mutilated women Robert had catalogued that night in Breskens.

'It was kind of you to come,' went on Robert's mother.

'I felt partly responsible,' Sandy said, aware of the lifting of a burden as Irene shook her head.

'It was his life. He wasn't a child,' she replied, 'but it was kind of you to tell us how it happened.'

'But *why* . . . why did it happen?' the older woman's voice quavered and Sandy saw that she was very old and enfeebled, though her eyes still possessed a gleam of undiminished fire and the newspaper that lay in her lap rustled with a querulous movement of her arthritic hands as she leaned forward.

'Vee!' Robert's mother was distressed that the old woman should want to pick over further what Sandy had already told them.

'Because,' she began, driven by the conviction that it *was* important to explain exactly why Robert had died, 'he believed in what he was doing, that it was the only way. Because he loved the sea for itself.'

'You see,' Robert's mother said, turning to the old woman with an air of triumph, as if Sandy's words provided proof to end a longstanding debate between them. 'I knew it.'

The expression in the old lady's face softened. She nodded and sat back in her chair. 'He was the last,' she murmured, 'wasn't he, Irene?'

'Yes,' Irene said, her voice trembling and her hand at her throat. 'Yes,' she whispered, 'and perhaps the best . . . '

They fell silent and the air in the room felt to Sandy overwhelmingly oppressive.

'Perhaps, after all . . . may I sit?' She sank gratefully into an old-fashioned winged armchair.

'Oh, my dear,' Irene said, rising.

'Please, I'm all right,' Sandy said. She laid the fingers of her right hand gently on her stomach. 'There's something else I have to tell you.'